She didn't have to read his mind to know his wish.

"Yes," she whispered. "I would very much like it if you would kiss me."

His thumb and forefinger at her chin tipped her head just so a second before his lips brushed hers.

"You kiss so divinely."

"This isn't kissing. This is merely a rehearsal, a prelude." Then he claimed her mouth again. "I want you. So much that I ache. *I ache.* I want you body and soul, Lily Jane Meeker. Oh, what a preposterous name for such a woman as you. You're not Lily the Meek. You, my fiery-headed witch, are Lily the Bold, Lily the Lionhearted."

She smiled at his foolishness. "Shall I roar now?"

"Just kiss me again."

FIRE LILY

DEBORAH CAMP

AVON BOOKS ◆ NEW YORK

FIRE LILY is an original publication of Avon Books. This work has never before appeared in book form. This work is a novel. Any similarity to actual persons or events is purely coincidental.

AVON BOOKS
A division of
The Hearst Corporation
1350 Avenue of the Americas
New York, New York 10019

Copyright © 1991 by Deborah E. Camp
Inside cover author photograph by Robert Eilers
Published by arrangement with the author
Library of Congress Catalog Card Number: 91-91782
ISBN: 0-380-76394-X

First Avon Books Printing: August 1991

AVON TRADEMARK REG. U.S. PAT. OFF. AND IN OTHER COUNTRIES, MARCA REGISTRADA, HECHO EN U.S.A.

Printed in the U. S. A.

RA   10   9   8   7   6   5   4   3   2   1

For Bonnie Jeanne Perry.
More than a good friend. More than a good writer.
She's the best of both. A friend who writes. Who
could ask for anything more? Thanks, dearest B.J.

Now folds the lily all her sweetness up,
And slips into the bosom of the lake:
So fold thyself, my dearest thou, and slip
Into my bosom and be lost in me.
                    —Alfred Lord Tennyson

Chapter 1

The storm descended on Fort Smith, Arkansas, with all the fury of Armageddon. Hours earlier it had been distant rumblings, but now the thunderheads hovered over the house to rattle windowpanes, blow damp breath down the chimneys, and fling bright lightning bolts.

Another booming fist slammed overhead, and Lily Meeker glanced apprehensively at the beamed ceiling of her aunt and uncle's front parlor. She halfway expected to see telltale cracks. The fire in the hearth hissed and sputtered, scattering ashes and embers. Lily swept back her long skirt, afraid the hem might tempt the flames. She gathered her wool shawl closer around her shoulders and retreated from the small inferno. Her gaze moved haltingly from her Uncle Howard to her Aunt Nan. Both wore tired expressions, placed there by unrelenting worry. The skin on their faces was no longer taut and rosy. Time and circumstance had created lines, loose folds, and paleness.

The past two months had been nightmarish for the entire Meeker clan. So much for a happy, prosperous 1889, Lily thought, recalling how she'd received the news of her cousin Cecille's disappearance on New Year's Day. Never had a year dawned so dismally. Next month spring would arrive and still no word of Cecille. The growing fear that Cecille might never be found had driven them to grab at straws and believe in things they would have scoffed at before. Desperation had led them to this tense vigil.

1

"Thought we could all do with some hot tea," Orrie Dickens announced, entering the parlor with tray in hand. Black and gray corkscrew curls bounced on her head. Her white apron seemed blinding in the dimly lit room. She set the tray on the low table near Nan and poured the steaming tea into the cups. "He probably won't come. The storm'll waylay him."

"Perhaps," Howard said, stroking his curly brown beard. Pellets clattered against the house. "Is that hail? If I were on the road tonight, I'd be finding shelter."

"He'll be here," Lily said with characteristic certainty. She'd never been one with a mouthful of maybes. "Neither rain nor hail nor the hounds of hell could keep him away tonight." She realized her melodramatic flair had done nothing to reassure the others and she laughed lightly to dispel the tingling apprehension. "Good heavens! You should see yourselves," she chided. "All round eyes and slack jaws. Be calm, will you? We're not receiving the devil himself."

"And why shouldn't we be as jumpy as bullfrogs on a full-mooned night?" Orrie asked, handing a cup of tea to Lily. "He's not the devil, true, but he's a man of mighty powers."

"*Alleged* powers," Lily corrected the family servant, then shook her head in amusement. "I can understand why you're beside yourself, Orrie. You always were a glutton for such things. You dragged poor Cecille and me to every circus, carnival, or Gypsy caravan that came anywhere near Fort Smith. We were fed a steady diet of freak shows, fortune-tellers, and magicians."

"And who was it who used to beg me to tell her a scary tale before she went abed?" Orrie challenged. "Why, I never saw a child more in love with frightful things than you."

Lily shrugged. "Yes, as long as they were *stories*. But I have no use for those who try to make people think they're magicians or sorcerers. What nonsense. We

shouldn't have listened to Father.'' She released a long
sigh of disgust. ''Father doesn't believe in this so-called
psychic, but he managed to palm him off on us.''

''We can't turn our back on any offer of help,'' Nan
said, laying aside her knitting to accept the cup and saucer
Orrie offered her. ''If there's the slightest chance this man
can locate Cecille . . .'' Her voice trailed off and she took
a tentative sip of the tea. ''His room is ready, Orrie?''

''Has been since morning,'' Orrie said, serving Howard. ''Why don't you sit, Mr. Meeker? You and Lily are
wearing holes in the rug with your restless pacing.''

''I am a bit high-strung tonight.'' Howard sat stiffly on
the camelbacked sofa. Thunder rent the air and he glanced
up. ''It's this storm that's put my nerves on edge.''

The storm and this waiting, Lily thought. Usually Aunt
Nan was the flighty one, always bustling and worrying
about imagined slights, silly details, and every other thing
her pessimistic mind could grasp. But tonight she was one
of several nervous Nellies, Lily acknowledged, looking
from one anxious expression to the next. This waiting . . .
this hated waiting for the infamous Griffon Goforth had
everyone leaping at every sound, every shifting of light.
Lily went to the bay window and drew back the heavy
draperies. The night was so black that she could see only
her own reflection staring back at her.

Cecille, where are you? she wondered, not for the first
time since New Year's Day, when she'd received the telegram that had alerted her to her cousin's disappearance.
She'd been visiting her father and stepmother in Cambridge, Massachusetts, and the disturbing news had made
her hurry back to Arkansas.

Lily squinted to see the rain, but couldn't until flashes
of lightning illuminated the moonless night. She caught a
glimpse of white and glanced over her shoulder to address
the others.

''It *is* hailing. I can see the small balls bouncing on the
street.''

"Thought so," her uncle murmured.

"Hope this terrible weather doesn't keep him from us," Orrie said. "I've been so anxious to meet him. I don't think I can wait 'til the 'morrow."

"Really, Orrie," Lily gently scolded as she faced the window again. "The moment you heard that Griffon Goforth was a Gypsy, you fell under his spell."

"Did no such thing," Orrie denied hotly, then added, "but everybody knows Gypsies make the best fortune-tellers. They all got gifts in that way."

Lily made a face, then smiled at her image in the glass pane. She loved Orrie, who'd practically raised her and Cecille with Aunt Nan's fussy supervision, but the family retainer was a hive of superstitions. Well, the others might be taken in by Goforth's reputation, but she wouldn't be. Lily fixed a serene expression on her triangularly shaped face. Icy skepticism shone in her gingersnap eyes. She raised a hand to tuck wisps of her dark red hair back into her topknot and wondered what Cecille was doing on this storm-tossed night. Was she safe and warm? Did she long for her family as desperately as they longed for her?

"I pray this gentleman has some kind of gift, since the law officers around here are completely powerless when it comes to finding lost lambs," Nan said.

"Yes," Howard agreed. "If I hear them say once more that Cecille might have run off with a man without a word to us, I'll . . . I'll . . ."

Lily turned from the window in time to see her uncle ram one fist into the palm of his other hand, making a loud smack.

"Cecille wouldn't have done such a thing," Lily said. "And even if she had, she would have contacted us so that we wouldn't worry needlessly. She'd never allow our suffering."

Thunder and lightning chased each other and everyone fell silent to listen. Lily drank some of the tea to warm her insides.

"Listen to that wind howling," Orrie whispered. "Mercy me, it's an hellacious storm. Won't it ever let up?"

Suddenly, a pounding rattled the door and Orrie and Nan smothered shrieks. Howard soared to his feet as if he'd been goosed by the sofa cushion. Lily felt her heart leap with a stab of fear before she forced laughter past her constricted throat.

"What a flock of scared chickens we are," she said, still laughing. "Which of us will be brave enough to unlatch the door? It seems our visitor has arrived."

Nan managed a twittering laugh. "I suppose a part of me didn't think this man actually existed."

"Well, he does." Howard slipped into his suit jacket and went to throw the bolt and open the door. He staggered backward and lifted one arm to shield his face from the buffeting sheets of rain.

The sound and the fury of the storm entered, sweeping leaves and other debris across the entry's tiled floor. A mossy, dank smell filled the area and drifted into the parlor where Lily craned her neck to see the caller. The arched doorway obstructed her view. The fire in the hearth fought the current of air and danced wildly, throwing shadows hither and yon. A stranger stepped into the center of the foyer and Lily caught her breath in expectation.

Dressed in a black cloak that swung in deep folds from his wide shoulders, the man seemed larger than life. He was the same height as Howard, but twice as wide. He stomped his booted feet and pushed back the hood of his cape with a decidedly theatrical air, then turned his round, bearded face toward the parlor.

He certainly doesn't look like a Gypsy, Lily thought, noting the man's pale complexion and light-colored eyes. He was older than she'd imagined. Father had said he was a ward of a Harvard College colleague, so she'd assumed the colleague was her father's age and that his ward would be years younger. But this man was certainly in his forties, as old as Father and Uncle Howard. He'd trimmed his brown beard to a point and he'd waxed his mustache. His eyes flashed with vivacity and his teeth glistened when he smiled.

"Good evening," he said in his actor's voice. "This is the Meeker residence, is it not?"

"It is, sir," Howard answered, leaning sideways to see past him. The door closed, shutting out the storm and its roar.

But what had closed it? Lily wondered.

A black glove shot out from the folds of the man's voluminous cloak. "Howard Meeker, is it?" He carried two travel satchels in his other hand.

"Y-yes." Howard shook hands with him. "Welcome to Fort Smith and our home."

"You've been expecting us," the stranger said, and it was a flat statement, not an inquiry. He looked all around, eyes devouring the entryway, the parlor, the staircase. "And a fine house it is. A rich man's house."

Lily stiffened at that. The charlatan was already weighing Uncle Howard's purse! Wait . . . had he said . . . ? She stepped forward, drawn by the "us" reference. She peeked around the archway and caught sight of another figure, also wearing a hooded cloak. What's this? she wondered. An assistant, manservant . . . perhaps Father's colleague.

"May I take your cloak, Mr. Goforth?" Howard asked, reaching out an unsteady hand to the large, bearded stranger.

The man's laughter boomed more loudly than the galloping thunder. "I am not Goforth," he said with merriment, then swung off his cloak dramatically. It swirled from his shoulders like a dark cloud.

"Then who, pray, are you?" Lily demanded, thinking they were mad to admit two strangers on such a loathsome night.

The big man peered at her as if *she* were the oddity. "I

am Balthazar, young miss," he said, pronouncing his name with theatrical gusto. "Balthazar, faithful and grateful aide to the great and gifted Griffon Goforth." He stepped back and flung out an arm to indicate his companion.

Lily's attention shifted, her interest piqued as the other man lifted one hand to wipe the hood from his dark head. The dim light caught at a heavy gold ring on his middle finger. And was that . . . ? Lily stifled a gasp. Yes! A tiny, thin circlet of gold glinted in his left earlobe.

"Thank you for welcoming us into your home," Griffon Goforth said, his voice gentle and musical in contrast to his aide's booming intonation. "I'm sorry to be dripping on your rug, but I'm afraid we're soaked to the skin."

He was an inch or two taller than Balthazar, but half as wide. Rain had plastered his dark hair to his head and drops glittered through it. As he glanced toward the parlor, Lily saw that he had beautiful eyes—silvery blue and deeply set, framed by plentiful, inky lashes.

"Orrie, take those wet cloaks and hang them near the kitchen hearth to dry," Nan said, breaking through the trancelike silence. "I'm Mrs. Nan Meeker, gentlemen, and this is my niece, Miss Lily Meeker, and our housekeeper, Orrie."

"Pleased to meet you, ladies," Griffon said, inclining his head, then he removed his cloak and gave it to the domestic.

He was dressed all in black, making Lily think of him as a dark knight. While his aide cultivated charisma through his flamboyant mannerisms, Griffon Goforth wore it as naturally as a leopard wears spots. Lily was hard-pressed to understand why; she only knew that she had difficulty averting her gaze from him.

"We got to thinkin' the storm would force y'all off the road and you might not show up 'til mornin'," Orrie said, edging closer to peek at Griffon. "I sure am glad you're here. I was beginnin' to fret you wouldn't come a'tall."

"But I gave my word," Griffon said, smiling faintly at Orrie. "Although it is a devil of a night out there."

"We met the train this afternoon, thinking you'd be on it," Howard said.

"We took the train most of the way, but I was feeling cramped and I forsook it for a pair of fast steeds."

Balthazar issued a groan. "Yes, and where he goes go I. The ride upon that nag almost killed me." He rested his hands on an ample belly that stretched his plaid waistcoat and challenged its gold buttons. "But we are here at last and ever so grateful to be in out of that cold, drenching rain."

"Care for a cup of tea?" Orrie offered.

"Kind woman, I would give all my worldly goods for one," Balthazar enthused, garnering a twittering laugh from Orrie.

"Please, won't both of you join us in the parlor?" Nan suggested, indicating the tea tray. "Sit near the fire and warm yourselves."

Balthazar motioned for Griffon to precede him. Lily stood beside the hearth while the two guests settled on either end of the sofa and waited for Orrie to serve them.

"I could scare up some sweet biscuits, if you want them," Orrie said, getting another smile from Balthazar.

"Anything would be most appreciated," the big man said. "I am, as you can see, a man of appetites."

Orrie giggled as she hurried from the parlor to fetch the biscuits.

Nan perched on the edge of the rocking chair opposite her guests, hands clasped tightly in her lap. "We've prepared a room for you, Mr. Goforth, but we didn't expect your assistant, so we'll—"

"Zar can bunk with me," Griffon said, referring to his aide. "We won't take advantage of your hospitality for any longer than is necessary."

"You are welcome to stay as long as needed," Nan said. "We're grateful for any help you can offer. It's been about two months since we last saw our daughter and . . . we're . . . well, we're . . .''

"Desperate," Lily supplied with a touch of malice. "Desperation is what drove us to employ your . . . services." She spoke the last word grudgingly.

"Ah-ha!" Balthazar held up one finger, poking at the air, eyes alight. "We have among us a true skeptic." He smacked his lips. "Goody. I love to watch Griffon bring unbelievers to their knees."

Lily arched a brow and stared down the bridge of her nose at the paunchy daredevil. "I have never, nor shall I ever, bend my knees to any mortal man." She shifted her gaze to Griffon. "You *do* claim to be mortal, don't you?"

"Decidedly," he answered, completely unruffled. "And you *do* claim to be a skeptic?"

"Proudly," she rejoined with a lift of her chin.

His smile sent a tingle down her spine. "May I say that narrow-mindedness is most often an ugly thing to behold, but it becomes you. It lights in your eyes a most attractive fire."

The others shared a spate of laughter, but Lily stared daggers at Griffon Goforth. Curls of steam rose off his damp clothing, making Lily imagine that he smoldered, coughed up fresh from hell.

Arrogant Gypsy goat! she seethed inwardly. The object of her ire suddenly jerked back as if she'd struck him. His eyes narrowed. Danger emanated from him, landing her a blunt blow, then dissipated as he swung his gaze away from her. Lily released her pent-up breath, chiding herself for feeling a moment of panic. But the sensation persisted, and she couldn't shake the notion that Griffon Goforth had heard her scathing epithet, although she'd not uttered a word of it aloud.

"If our manners are wanting, please excuse us," Uncle Howard said, breaking through the uneasiness. He stood on the other side of the hearth, and the look he sent Lily was more searing than the heat from the fire. "Lily is headstrong, but bears no ill will. In our home, guests are welcome, especially those who have traveled on such a dreadful night to offer their help in our time of distress.''

''Oh, yes,'' Nan enthused, her bright eyes shimmering with tears. ''Any help would be a godsend. It's been months since our daughter was last seen.''

''By you?'' Balthazar asked. ''She was last seen by you?''

''No, by the dressmaker, I suppose. I saw Cecille that morning before she went out. She looked so lovely. . . . '' Nan's eyes filled with tears as she turned to her husband, beseeching him to continue for her.

''The last time we saw our daughter was on the thirtieth of December,'' Howard said. ''She left the house around ten that morning to go to her dressmaker's for a fitting.''

''The gown is a lovely thing, meant for a New Year's Eve ball. It's upstairs in Cecille's room,'' Nan said, then swallowed a sob.

''The dressmaker said Cecille kept her appointment and left the shop at a few minutes before noon,'' Howard continued. ''Cecille had made plans to join two of her lady friends for tea in one of their homes.''

''The Spencers,'' Nan supplied. ''Mr. James Spencer is an architect of some note, and his wife is president of the Fort Smith Literary Guild.''

Howard smiled indulgently at his wife's intrusion. ''Yes, well, Cecille never arrived for the appointed tea. Janelle Spencer, Cecille's friend and hostess, sent one of their domestics around later that afternoon to inquire about Cecille's absence. It wasn't like her not to send regrets.''

''Oh, no,'' Nan agreed, her blue eyes wide with alarm. ''Cecille would never be so rude. She'd sent word three days before that she would be most happy to attend the tea. If she'd changed her mind, she would have sent Orrie or Ginger—the girl who works for us three days a week— around with a note excusing herself.''

Lily closed her hands into fists of irritation as her Aunt

Nan's inconsequential digressions stretched her tolerance. She means well, Lily reminded herself. Aunt Nan couldn't help being a scatterbrain any more than Lily could help being impatient. Griffon Goforth and the gregarious Balthazar didn't seem the least bit perturbed. On the contrary, they listened to her aunt as intently as they did Uncle Howard.

"Of course, we began an immediate search," Howard said, picking up the events they'd all gone over countless times. "When the marshals turned up nothing, I contacted a private investigator."

Lily made a disparaging sound that brought all eyes to her. She shrugged, feeling she should make some response.

"You find this hired man incompetent?" Griffon asked.

"He turned up precious little and took quite a tidy sum for his uselessness," Lily said, staring pointedly at Griffon. "It's distressing to see that the world contains a variety of human leeches."

"Now, Lily," her uncle said in a tone he used to sooth tempers and reinstate calmness. "I'm sure the man did his best. After all, he traced Cecille to Van Buren before he lost her trail."

"Why would Cecille go to Van Buren?" Lily asked, not for the first time. "She doesn't know a soul there."

"Perhaps she was taken there by someone who does," Griffon suggested. "Does she have a beau?"

"Cecille has many suitors," Lily answered, although Griffon had addressed the inquiry to Howard. "And all of them are respectable and wouldn't take a lady out of the city unchaperoned."

"She isn't in love, then?" Griffon asked.

"What does that have to do with anything?" Lily demanded, exasperated.

"Love makes us do uncharacteristic things. If Cecille is in love with someone, she might follow him to the ends of the earth if he asked."

"You know nothing of Cecille," Lily charged.

"Ah, but I know about love and the toll it often charges."

"I resent your suggestion that she'd traipse off with some man and leave her family in agony. We've heard such hare-brained theories from the local authorities. We needn't hear them repeated by you."

"Lily, dear, your manners," Aunt Nan reminded. "The gentleman didn't mean to cast aspersions on Cecille's name."

"Quite," Griffon agreed. "I can see that Cecille was raised in a most respectable household. I only meant to discern her state of mind and heart on the day she vanished."

"We understand," Howard said, jerking at the hem of his waistcoat and sending Lily a warning glare. "It's true that others have suggested that Cecille might have been blinded by love, but she would have come to her senses by now. She would have contacted us . . . sent word somehow that she's safe."

"Yes, I'm sure you're right," Griffon said.

Lily turned her back to the room, pretending to warm her hands at the fire. She winced, knowing she had sounded like a shrew. The fact that she had run dry of patience, and didn't think for a moment this soothsayer could return Cecille to them, didn't give her license to be rude and overbearing. She closed her eyes for a few moments, dipped into her reserve of tolerance, then faced the visitors and her family again. The Gypsy, she noted, had been staring at her. He finished his tea and set the cup and saucer on the tray. When Orrie made a move to refill it, he nodded.

"Yes, please, and I believe I'll have a biscuit before Zar gobbles up the last."

"I'll leave that one for you," Balthazar assured him.

"Orrie could prepare a late supper, if you gentlemen wished it," Nan said.

"How delight—"

"No, thank you, madam," Griffon said, interrupting Balthazar's jubilant acceptance. "We'll be turning in soon. It would be rude of us to keep our gracious hosts from their rest." He patted his aide's knee. "Zar, be a good chap and take our baggage upstairs. I'll be along in a minute."

"Orrie, show Mr. Balthazar to the guest room," Howard said.

"Balthazar," the jovial man insisted. "That will suffice, kind sir." He turned merry eyes on Orrie. "After you, dear lady."

Orrie swished toward the staircase with Balthazar ambling behind her.

"The marshals turned up nothing? No trace of Cecille?" Griffon asked, settling back on the sofa to relish his cup of tea and sugared biscuit.

"Nothing," Howard answered, pulling fretfully at his curly beard. "It's as if she vanished into thin air. I, of course, hope she's still in the city, but where, I can't imagine."

"I regret to inform you, sir, that she's not in Fort Smith."

"Oh?" Howard leaned toward his guest in anticipation. "And why do you say that?"

"I get no sense of her presence in this place." Griffon took a big bite of the biscuit.

Lily exchanged a cynical smirk with her uncle. "Then by all means, let's mark this area off our lists." She dipped her head in a mock bow. "The Great Goforth hath spoken."

Nan made a clucking noise of distress and glanced nervously at her guest, but Griffon seemed to take no affront from Lily's scorn.

"You don't sense her presence," Howard repeated. "I'm afraid we're going to have trouble trusting your . . . your hunches."

"Why should my hunches be any less trustworthy than those of the private detective you hired?" Griffon swept crumbs from his dark trousers.

"The detective at least made inquiries and followed clues," Lily said. "Or so he reported."

"I'm following clues as well," Griffon said. "I understand your inability to grasp the way I work; it's only natural that you are skeptical of something you don't fully understand. My feeling that Cecille is no longer in this city is quite strong, and I learned long ago not to question my sixth sense, but to follow it. I'm sure Edward Meeker told you of my modest success at finding missing articles, as well as missing persons."

"Yes. Very impressive," Howard allowed.

"Your success *in England,*" Lily amended. "It's rather difficult to verify actions that occurred overseas. But, then, you must be aware of that."

"Not so difficult," Griffon said, rising slowly to his feet. "I have newspaper clippings detailing my work. Luckily, I brought a few. I'd be more than happy to show them to you tomorrow, Miss Meeker."

"And I should be most interested in seeing them," Lily rejoined, not entirely convinced he had such proof.

"So be it." He plucked at his damp shirt and made a face of disgust. "I think I'll retire, if you don't mind. These clothes are beginning to stick like cooling wax to my skin."

"Where's Orrie gone off to?" Nan asked, rising from the rocker. "Orrie!"

"Yes'm," Orrie called, then bustled into the parlor, breathless and pink-faced. "Ready to join your assistant, sir?" she asked Griffon.

"Yes, please."

"Good night, Mr. Goforth," Nan said, extending her hand, which Griffon kissed politely.

"Thank you for your hospitality, madam." Griffon turned and shook hands with Howard. "And thank you, sir.'' His gaze drifted lazily to Lily. When she didn't offer her hand, he nodded his dark head in a salute. ''Good evening, Miss Lily.''

Lily managed a weak smile. ''Rest well, Mr. Goforth.''

''I shall,'' he assured her, then followed Orrie upstairs. He made not a sound, his tread light, his movements limned with grace.

''Doesn't he take the prize?'' Nan asked when he was well out of earshot.

''He seems capable, I suppose. Doesn't have much of an English accent.'' Howard dropped onto the sofa as if he were exhausted.

''Yes,'' Nan agreed. ''Not like Elizabeth Battenburg's cousin from London. Remember meeting him last year at the cotillion?''

Howard nodded. ''Could hardly understand a word the man said. I just nodded and smiled when he talked to me. If he was speaking English, it was a form of it I was never taught.''

''Wondering about Mr. Goforth? He's a Scot,'' Orrie whispered, rejoining them in the parlor. ''I asked Baltha-zar. Mr. Goforth was raised in Scotland and went to England in his early teens. Balthazar's from Belgium.'' Orrie's eyes widened as if Belgium wasn't part of this world. ''Imagine that! Why, I never heard of anybody bein' from that place.''

''I'm not sure where that is located,'' Nan said, worry lining her brow. ''Belgium. Is it part of Europe?''

''Yes, dear,'' Howard said with a labored sigh. ''It's quite the civilized country, I assure you.''

''I'm sure our guests are civilized,'' Lily said. ''But I'm also sure they're both as worthless as Confederate currency.''

Howard delivered a weary glance. ''What say we give them the benefit of the doubt? Is that too much to ask, Lily?''

Sensing his fatigue, Lily softened and patted his shoulder. "No, Uncle Howard." She went toward the window to view the abating storm. Doubt is all I'll give them, she thought. That inept detective had lightened her poor uncle's purse while giving little in return. She wouldn't let Goforth and his bulky associate steal her uncle blind. No. She'd watch the two opportunistic vultures like a hawk.

"I think I'll go to bed myself," Lily said, moving from the window as she lifted a hand to cover a yawn. "It's been a long day and an even longer evening."

"Good night, dear," her aunt said, angling her head so that Lily could drop a kiss on her cheek.

Lily gave Orrie's arm an affectionate squeeze as she passed her on the way to the staircase. "You're the only one of us who doesn't look completely wrung out," she noted. "You thrive on mystery." Laughing lightly, Lily climbed the stairs and tiptoed past the guest room to reach her own room on the second level.

This was her home, although she was quite welcome in her father's house near Harvard College. But she never felt comfortable in Cambridge. She always felt like a guest of her father and stepmother, Angela. Fort Smith was home. She'd been born here and would be happy to die here, just like her mother, who had died from a snake bite when Lily was seven. They'd all been on a picnic near the Arkansas River when her mother had stumbled into a nest of water moccasins. Lily recalled little of the ensuing tragedy, other than that her mother's had been a painful death. Afterward, her father had handed her over to his brother and sister-in-law to raise. She'd felt deserted for a while, but had adjusted because her uncle, aunt, and cousin loved her, and had made a special place for her in their family.

Once in her room, Lily sat on the window seat and stared at the glistening night. The steady beat of the rain lulled her. The house was so quiet without Cecille. And so lonely.

Her thoughts meandered to the midnight guests. They exuded mystery, and Orrie had lapped them up like a kitten going after cream. She smiled at that, then likened the psychic to a big cat. He moved like one, quiet and with a graceful stealth. Maybe he's part griffon, she fancied, hence his name.

Father had offered scant information about Griffon Goforth. He had been a ward of one of her father's Harvard colleagues and he'd left England for America to oversee the newly established American Society of Psychic Research, having been on the English branch's board of directors.

High-sounding, Lily thought with a sniff of contempt. The ignorant might believe in psychics and fortune-tellers, but she'd never been weak-brained. She'd only agreed to Goforth's visit because of her father's recommendation. Besides, all conventional methods to locate Cecille had been exhausted. But she questioned the wisdom of accepting Goforth's help now that she'd seen him and his flamboyant companion. Balthazar. What a showman! The man belonged in a circus! How could anyone take him or Goforth seriously?

To convince her aunt and uncle to discharge the two charlatans was another matter and one Lily didn't think she could accomplish. They were desperate to find Cecille . . . to learn anything they could of what had become of their only child.

What if Cecille's dead? Lily wondered, wincing at the stab of pain that caused. Yet, she had a strong sense that Cecille was alive. In danger, perhaps, and possibly ill, but alive.

Good heavens! She sounded just like Goforth! She pressed her forehead to the cool windowpane and closed her eyes. Hunches couldn't be counted on. False hopes shouldn't be thrown out to the desperate. It was wrong to prey on people's weaknesses. That's what made Griffon Goforth so appalling. A good-looking, bright man like him resorting to such sordid business was unforgivable!

Her uncle had been so polite, ever the genteel businessman, that he hadn't discussed fees with that private detective at the outset. The man had presented them with an outrageous bill, which her uncle had grudgingly paid. How much would Goforth demand? Knowing her uncle, he'd be loath to pin Goforth down about his fee. It would be left to Lily to breach business etiquette and make it clear that the Meeker family would not be fleeced again.

He'll not get one penny until he proves he's worth it, Lily promised herself. If she was branded rude and obnoxious, so be it. This was not a time for the fainthearted. This was a time for the lionhearted.

She smiled, tickled at the image. Griffon Goforth's not the only sleek cat in this jungle, she thought. Then, giving in to a streak of frivolity, she purred.

Chapter 2

Seated at the dining room table, Griffon admired the delicate pattern of pink and yellow blooms on the china cup and saucer. A part of his mind kept pace with the conversation flowing around him, but he didn't bother to add anything to it. Between Balthazar and Nan Meeker, one could hardly get a word in edgewise anyway.

His gaze strayed, taking in the highly polished serving table with its turned-out legs, the stocked china cabinet and silver keeper, the velvet draperies of golden bronze pulled back to let in sunlight.

In his former life he would have made a quick inventory of the things he would steal from the house and how much they might bring on the black market. Now he only admired the craftsmanship of the furniture and the artistry woven into the crocheted tablecloth. Funny how he couldn't completely shake the dirty, thieving, foul-mouthed Gypsy vagabond he'd once been. Thurman Unger had educated him in the ways of civilized men, but it seemed his tutoring hadn't been entirely successful. Guess the raggedy lad will always live within me, he thought, then brought his gaze to bear on Lily. She would agree with that, he knew. She thought of him as a Gypsy goat with a penchant for hoodwinking innocent souls.

When Lily refused to meet his gaze, he shrugged as if it meant nothing, although he would have enjoyed a glimpse of the topaz fire in her eyes. He flexed his shoulders and rocked his head to relieve the tight muscles in his neck. He hadn't rested well. His mind had been invaded by dream images that made no sense. Dolls with golden hair. One with ink stains on its face. A window with a padded bench below it. A swing suspended from a tree branch. Girlish laughter.

He'd tossed and twisted, bedeviling poor Balthazar throughout the night, finally leaving the unfamiliar bed to sit in a chair near the window to wait for the dawn. It had not come quickly enough for him. He'd tried to discover the meaning of his dreams as his grandmother, Queen Sofie, had taught him. However, he'd made no sense of them and that disturbed him. Usually, his dreams held the future or at least pointed the way, but what could dolls and swings have to do with his life?

His head felt full as if stuffed with cotton, and he realized he was eating the breakfast Orrie had prepared but tasting none of it.

"Mr. Goforth? . . . Mr. Goforth?"

Griffon forced his attention to his hostess. "Yes, Mrs. Meeker?"

"You've hardly touched your food. Is there something wrong?"

"No, not at all," he assured her. "I'm a man governed by moods, and my behavior leans toward the obsessive. I either eat little or gorge myself. I sleep like the dead or hardly at all."

" 'Tis true," Balthazar attested, sopping up the last of the milk gravy in his plate with his fifth biscuit. "He's a restless soul, that one."

"Dearie me," Orrie scolded gently as she moved around the table, filling coffee cups and juice glasses. "That can't be good for a body."

"I seem to be faring well enough," Griffon said.

"Tell us about your magic powers and how you're going to use them to find Cecille," Nan urged.

He quirked one brow. "I don't think of myself as having magic powers."

"What do you have, then?" Nan persisted, and the others around the table waited for his answer—even Balthazar, who surely knew it by heart.

"A keen sense of perception," Griffon said by rote. Having been asked this question countless times, he'd fashioned a pat answer that seemed to satisfy the unenlightened curious. "Everyone has five senses—sight, touch, taste, smell, and hearing. I have honed mine. I take more in than the average person, and therefore I'm able to perceive things others might miss."

The answer seemed to work nicely, although Griffon knew he'd barely skimmed the surface. What he'd been born with was a conundrum to him and to those who had studied him. Some people were blessed with musical talent, others with the ability to write, or to solve complex mathematical problems. He'd been given the ability to hear thoughts, to sense feelings, to trespass on a person's mind. His was a gift that could be considered both a blessing and a curse.

"Isn't that interesting?" Nan said after a pregnant silence. Then she began buttering a steaming blueberry muffin. "How clever of you to sharpen your basic skills. We should all be so astute, so industrious."

"Which sense will you use to find Cecille?" Lily asked, joining in the conversation for the first time since she'd come downstairs, dressed in white eyelet and beribboned in pink. "Will you sniff her out or develop a craving for a bite of her?"

Nan Meeker laughed uneasily. "Don't be a goose, Lily."

"*I'm* being a goose?" Lily countered. "This man hands out a lame story about sharpening his senses and we let him think he's appeased our disbelief? I shan't sit here and say nothing. Cecille is like a sister to me and I want

to find her as much as any of you, but at what price this
time?''

Her eyes dared Griffon to spar with her, and he felt a
quickening, an eagerness to match wits with the chestnut-
haired beauty. Last night he'd sensed in her a mixture of
fascination and condemnation, but this morning the mix
was different: more fascination, less condemnation, and a
new ingredient—attraction. Just a hint of it, but there. Def-
initely there. No doubt she'd sooner cut out her tongue
than admit it. A smile bubbled up from his heart and he
couldn't keep it from his lips. She was talking tough, but
she wasn't as sure of herself as she had been last night.
Perhaps he wasn't the monster she'd pictured, he thought,
and she'd hit a snag in her plan to unmask him as a two-
bit soothsayer.

"Lily, mind your tongue," Howard said, his brows
lowered over thunderous eyes. "If memory serves me cor-
rectly, we *all* agreed to give Mr. Goforth a chance to find
Cecille. If you had any misgivings, a week ago was when
you should have voiced them. Not now when he's traveled
all this way to help us."

"I *did* voice my concerns, but the rest of you ignored
me," Lily protested. "I thought that once you saw him
you'd realize he wasn't a haloed champion but only another man looking for big purses and small minds."

"That will suffice, Lily," Howard said, his voice breaking, then climbing toward a shouting match level.

"Please, Mr. Meeker," Griffon said, verbally stepping
between the two. "She has every right to question my
methods." He swung his gaze to Lily. "I hope to locate
clues to your cousin's whereabouts that others have missed.
I can tell when someone is lying or trying to hide information. Often, I can learn the truth when others are sty-
mied." He forsook the refulgence in Lily's eyes to confront
the sadness in Nan Meeker's. Although the woman tried
valiantly to be a pleasant and charming hostess, the burden
of her worries defeated her. A wave of sympathy made

him yearn to lighten her load. "I wish I could promise that I will return your daughter here to you before the sun sets on another day, but I can't. I can only swear to you that I'll do my level best."

"How much will you charge, Mr. Goforth?"

Nan gasped at Lily's bold question, and Balthazar shook his head in sad reproach. Howard cleared his throat and blustered for a few moments before he managed some intelligible words.

"Lily Jane, I believe you are poking your nose into *my* business!" Howard warned. "I will be the one to pay Mr. Goforth, not you. Ladies shouldn't be speaking of money!"

Nan nodded so vigorously she shook loose a lock of pale hair from its chignon. "That's right! That's right! Especially at the breakfast table. It's not ladylike behavior at all, Lily, dear."

"*Somebody* in this family should be asking how much he intends to charge," Lily insisted. "That last thief gave us a two-page report and a bill for sixty-two dollars."

Howard looked as if he were ready to blow like a whale. "Lily, I must insist that you retire to your room and stay there until—"

"It's all right, Mr. Meeker," Griffon said, giving a careless flick of his hand to extract the fangs from Lily's skepticism. Then he faced Lily squarely, amusement tickling his throat. He knew she strove to anger him, but he found her brash behavior delightfully different. Certainly not conduct befitting a lady, he allowed, but ladies tended to bore the stuffing out of him. He noted that her spirit was flying high, aided by gusts of righteous anger, and he knew his answer would snip her wings and send her tumbling down. "I'll ask for nothing unless I produce results, Miss Meeker."

Lily sucked in a noisy breath. Howard and Nan exchanged startled glances. Balthazar looked at him as if he'd lost his mind. Then Lily pulled herself up sharply and glared at him.

"What sort of results?" she demanded. "If you trace Cecille to some other town that leads us to another blank wall, will you claim that as a result?"

"Lily, please, it's not your place to question our guests," Nan said, fretfully. "Mr. Goforth will think you uncouth."

"I don't care what he thinks of me," Lily said, never letting her gaze waver from his. "Will you kindly answer my question, sir?"

"With pleasure. If I don't locate Cecille, then I'll charge your family not one shilling . . . rather, cent." He paused to witness the defeat darkening her eyes to umber. She had nearly perfect features, he decided, but he particularly liked her retroussé nose. He had the oddest desire to press his lips to the tip of it and then work his way down to her full, shell-pink lips. He made himself recall the conversation and forgo his fantasies for the moment. "If your aunt and uncle are pleased with my services, then I shall leave it to them to decide what amount they'll donate to the Society."

"Th-the Society?"

He nodded and offered up a smug grin that made her frown even more mightily at him. "The American Society of Psychic Research," he defined more clearly. "It is through the Society that I'm here." He glanced around the table at the others. "As you must know, Edward Meeker—your father," he threw out at Lily.

"I *know* that, Mr. Goforth," she said, nearly spitting the words at him.

He grinned, thoroughly enjoying her feistiness. "Edward Meeker agreed to allow my mentor, Thurman Unger, to see if Cecille can be found using psychic powers. I've been very busy at the Society, but I can't refuse Thurman anything. He's like a father to me. So here I am. But any money earned should be sent to the Society, since I'm actually on loan, so speak, from it. If I find Cecille, I'll hope that you'll speak well of me to others so that I might build on my reputation and cast a pleasing light on the Society.''

Balthazar made a choking sound and held a napkin to his lips. His nut brown eyes bulged at Griffon, and Griffon knew that Balthazar was having difficulty keeping his mouth shut and his protests to himself. Griffon cast a warning by lowering his brows, and Balthazar gave an almost imperceptible nod of reluctance.

''More than fair, young man,'' Howard said, then glared pointedly at his niece. ''Wouldn't you agree, Lily?''

''Yes.'' She swept the linen napkin from her lap, dabbed at the corners of her mouth, then dropped the napkin neatly beside her plate. ''I'm sorry if I hurt your feelings, Mr. Goforth.''

''I appreciate your honesty, Miss Meeker, and as for my feelings, you needn't worry. I'm made of tough material.''

Lily pressed her lips together, and Griffon enjoyed witnessing the flags of color rise in her cheeks.

''I should be leaving for the bank.'' Howard scooted back his chair. ''Linger over your breakfast,'' he urged his guests. ''But if I don't open the bank right on time, I'll have some disgruntled people on my hands.''

''We understand,'' Griffon answered him.

''I believe I'll take a stroll,'' Balthazar announced. ''I've never been to this fair city and I enjoy exploring new places. Won't you come with me, Griffon?''

''Orrie is going to the market,'' Griffon said. ''Perhaps she'll let you escort her there. You could help carry her purchases home.''

Balthazar's glance toward Griffon bode ill will, but then he fashioned a smile for the bright-eyed maid. ''Might I tag along?''

''Don't mind a'tall.'' Orrie furrowed her brow. ''How'd

you know I was goin' to market right after breakfast, Mr. Goforth?''

Griffon tried to look perplexed, unwilling to reveal the depth of his abilities just yet. He'd found that the less people knew, the easier it was for them to accept him and his abnormalities. ''You mentioned it, didn't you?''

''No, I don't think so.''

''I don't remember her saying anything about it,'' Nan said. ''But it *is* Friday, and Orrie always goes to the marketplace on Fridays.'' Nan reached out to pat her husband's coat sleeve. ''I'll see you to the door, dear.''

Howard offered Nan his arm and the two left the dining room. Orrie gathered a stack of dishes and beamed at Balthazar.

It was obvious to Griffon that she had romantic intentions toward Zar and could hardly wait to get him alone. Judging from the gleam in Balthazar's eyes, the feeling was mutual.

''I'll be heading for market in a few minutes, sir,'' Orrie told Balthazar.

''Then I'll fetch my overcoat and meet you at the street door,'' the portly man said, rising to his feet, then smoothing a hand along the side of his oiled hair that was thinning on top.

''That'll be fine.'' Orrie shoved a shoulder against the swinging door that separated the kitchen from the dining room and hurried through, letting it flap in her wake.

Too late, Lily realized she'd been left alone at the table with Griffon Goforth. She started to leap up and make a clean getaway.

''You weren't here when Cecille turned up missing?'' Griffon asked.

Affording him only the swiftest glance, Lily entertained the notion of simply leaving the room without answering him, but then she thought of Cecille. If there was a chance this man could find her cousin, then the least she could do was answer his questions. After all, he'd promised in front of the entire family not to take a cent unless he could produce Cecille Meeker. Giving a mental shrug, she resigned herself to her immediate fate.

"I was visiting my father and stepmother in Cambridge. Cecille had written me Christmas Day. That was the last time I heard from her."

"Her letter reflected nothing unsettling? She appeared in good spirits?"

"Yes." Lily sat back and folded her arms at her waist, relaxing as much as she dared.

Griffon drummed his fingers against the tablecloth and tried not to dwell on the outline of her breasts. "Miss Meeker . . . may I call you Lily?"

"No." The word was brittle, chilling; chipped from a block of ice.

"Why not?" he asked, gouged by her unwillingness to pay him the smallest gesture of familiarity.

"Because it isn't proper for you to use my Christian name."

"A few minutes ago you weren't being proper at all."

"Sometimes it's necessary to forsake manners," she said, almost snapping at him. She owed him no explanations!

He shrugged. "Lily, why are you being so obstinate? I've made it clear that I'm not out to steal money from your relatives."

"Mr. Goforth, please restrict your questions to Cecille and her disappearance or I shall leave the room." She fiddled with the tablecloth while the voice of reason chastised her. *Be civil,* it urged. *He makes you nervous, but that's not his fault.* Lily glanced at him. He was smiling, his silvery blue eyes as inviting as a spring-fed pond. "Mr. Goforth," she began, but he made a scoffing sound.

"Griffon," he said slowly. "Can you manage that? Come now. Try. Grif-fon. You can do it."

Lily tightened her hands until her knuckles looked as if they might split the skin. "I'm not an imbecile."

"That's right. You're an intelligent young woman, so behave yourself." He'd made his voice crack like a whip, and she responded as he'd hoped. Her eyes flashed with fire and blood pooled in her cheeks.

"You ill-mannered misogynist! How dare you speak to me in that way!"

A smile tweaked the corners of his mouth. "Misogynist, am I? Far from it, Lily. I happen to adore women. I find them utterly fascinating, confounding, and tantalizing. I even find you attractive, although you conduct yourself as if you're queen of the shrews."

Hot anger pumped through her. "I hate you."

"I'm heartbroken," he said, unfeelingly. "Truly." Then he stood and strolled to the six narrow windows set in the east wall of the dining room. He could feel the heat of her anger directed at his back.

Irish temper, he thought, seeing the dark red color of her hair in his mind's eye. She was probably an inferno in bed. "You mentioned a report from the private investigator." It amazed him he could ask intelligent questions while a corner of his mind dwelled on matters of lust. She stared holes through his back, so he finally turned sideways to look at her. God, she was a beauty! Why hadn't some lucky chap grabbed her and swept her to the altar? he wondered, then thought she might intimidate men of social standing. She wasn't one to follow behind or demur.

"What about the report?" she asked, wondering why he was looking at her as if she were a riddle.

He blinked, bringing his thoughts into focus. "Mightn't I see it?"

"Ask Uncle Howard for it. Better yet, conjure it up for yourself."

"Why are you blocking my efforts to find your cousin?"

"Simple. I don't like you and I don't trust you."

He sent her a look that called her a fool. "The report; can you lay your hands on it?"

Seeing that he was determined to make her fetch for him, she marched from the dining room and into her uncle's small study off the front parlor. Finding the detective's report was an easy task, and she returned to Griffon within minutes. Lily thrust the parchment at him as if it were a dirk. He took it and slanted it toward the light streaming in from the bank of windows. She could see the ring on his middle finger clearly. A gold griffon, she noted, surreptitiously examining the bas-relief of the leonine creature. Her gaze lifted, almost against her will, to the mark of a rebel—the gold earring. Something about it appealed to her, and she found that agonizing.

It's all that rubbish Orrie fed me as a child about wandering Gypsies and romantic nomads, she thought. Then she noticed the scar—a faint, pinkish curving at the outer corner of his left eye—another sign of a pirate dressed as a banker, she fancied, taking in his proper gray suit, shirt, and striped silk jabot. A wolf in sheep's clothing?

Under other circumstances, she would have found him darkly, dangerously handsome. But she reminded herself again that, even though he'd sworn his honesty to her family, he *still* claimed to possess magic. A man of true character wouldn't cling to such buffoonery. He *had* to be up to something. He simply wouldn't work for free. One didn't perfect a trick only to tell everyone how it was done!

Lily whirled, intent on leaving him to his reading.

"Wait, Lily," he said. "This report says . . ." He frowned, looking up from the paper. "It's incomplete. The detective writes that Cecille was seen in Van Buren, but he doesn't tell how he knew to look for her there."

"Perhaps he's psychic," she rejoined with a stinging smile that only received a chiding from Griffon. Sighing, she moved closer to him, lured by his detection of what had angered her about the sketchy report. He smelled better than any man she'd encountered in Fort Smith. His scent was musky—a combination of wood smoke and fresh lemon. Clean, bracing. She caught his sideways regard of her and hurried to speak to cover her girlish attack of nerves.

"Don't you find it atrocious that he asked Uncle Howard to pay for that pitiful pile of non sequiturs?"

"Yes." He smiled at her use of language and was glad for his Oxford education. "Why didn't you demand a better report?"

"Because I'm a laaady," she said, drawing out the last word to give it a lick of disrespect. "It's Uncle Howard's place to ask, but he never does. He believes business should be courteous. Such questions would be the same as calling the investigator's work inadequate, and Uncle Howard is too much the gentleman for that."

"Being a lady is rather inhibiting, isn't it?"

"Most certainly," she said, amazed that a man would be sympathetic to a woman's social boundaries. "I know women are second-class and expected to remain in the background, but I don't *feel* inferior and I find living in shadows unbearable."

"And so you should," he said, thinking that the sunlight made her eyes sparkle like jewels. "Nothing can grow to its fullest potential in the shade, Lily."

Lily studied his serious expression, and something wonderful fluttered near her heart. For a moment, she yearned to fling her arms about his neck and deliver a smacking kiss of gratitude to his lean cheek. At last! A man who understood the chains attached to women! Caution, however, prevailed, and she inched away from him, but that spark of wonder remained in her.

Griffon cleared his throat, undone for a few moments by the animation in her face. Her face! It would feed his sexual fantasies for weeks—months!

"So you don't know what led the investigator to Van Buren?" he asked, desperate to return to his purpose.

"Uncle Howard wouldn't ask, although I begged it of him." She glanced at Griffon, wondering if she owed him an apology. The gentleness in his eyes swayed her. "That's why I was blunt this morning. I think questions should be asked and answers should be forthright.''

"I couldn't agree more. May I keep this?" he asked. Getting her nod of approval, he folded the report into threes and tucked it into his inside jacket pocket. "My first order of business will be to speak to this detective.''

She poked at the rug's fringed edge with the toe of her shoe. "I'm returning books to the library today, and his office is across the street from it. I could . . . that is, we—''

"Are you suggesting that you and I . . .'' He feigned a shocked gasp. "To be seen on a public street in my company! What of your reputation, Lily?'' He laughed at her furious scowl, then looked out the window to admire the glistening, rain-splashed lawn. "It's a lovely day for a . . .'' His breath stopped in his throat as his gaze collided with the swing.

"What is it?" Lily asked, stepping beside him to see what had drained the color from his face.

"That swing," he said, giving a sharp nod to indicate it, suspended from a thick oak limb.

Lily looked from it to him. "It's been there since I was a girl," she said, trying to discern the significance.

"You and Cecille played on it?"

"Yes, as children we did.''

"Your room . . .'' He glanced up. "It's the one directly above us, isn't it? It affords the same view.''

"Yes, but I don't—''

"You have a window seat in your room?"

"Yes," she answered, growing irritated. "But what has that got to do with anything?''

"Did you and Cecille play with dolls, too?" he asked, relieved to find a key to his disturbing dreams. They hadn't been his thoughts, his impressions. They'd been *hers*.

"Don't all little girls play with dolls?" She laughed softly and stepped closer to the sunlit windows. "I dreamed last night of Cecille and about a doll I had.''

"You *dreamed*?" he repeated. How was that possible? He'd never received another person's dream before.

"Yes . . . a dream about a doll," she continued. "A blond doll. Cecille had one just like mine. We were given them for Christmas. But I was tired of having the same everything as Cecille. I wanted something different, so I—" She laughed again, recalling her rash solution.

"What?" Griffon asked, leaning so close that his chest pressed against her shoulder. He was hardly aware of the contact, dumbstruck by the power of her mind to have sent him dreaming images that had kept him awake. "Tell me."

"I decided my doll should have black hair, so I poured a bottle of ink over her pretty golden tresses. It was a terrible mess. Orrie and Aunt Nan were beside themselves because I'd ruined not only my doll but also my dress and the rug in my room. I managed to splatter ink everywhere." As she related the prank, she took note of his rapid breathing and the excitement building in his cornflower-blue eyes. "What's wrong? Why are you so interested in this?"

He turned away from her, shuttering his feelings. "I'm trying to get to know Cecille. Is she older or younger than you?"

"Younger by one year. She's eighteen. How old are you?" she asked, then wished she hadn't when he glanced slyly at her. Drat! Now he'd think she was actually interested in him.

"I believe I'm twenty-five."

"You *believe*?" she asked, intrigued despite herself. "Don't you know?"

"Not for certain. Gypsies don't pay much attention to the calendar. It's just not important to them, so they make no effort to record the exact time, day, or year of birth."

"What about your birth certificate? Surely it lists that information."

"My mother delivered me in the back of a Gypsy wagon near the shores of the North Sea. No doctor, no birth certificate. Just Mother and me and my maternal grandmother, so I was told. I have no memory of it. My memory begins at age two, or thereabouts.''

''You recall something when you were but a babe?'' Lily asked, already counting this as a tall tale.

''I remember holding my mother's crystal ball,'' he said, the memory releasing the pristine innocence of his youth. ''She snatched it from me, upset that I'd touched it. Later, I was taught that males aren't supposed to handle things to do with the *boojo* magic. Anything mystical is strictly *marimay* to Gypsy men.''

''Marimay?'' Lily asked, hanging on his words.

''Unclean . . . forbidden,'' he translated. ''It is my *boojo* powers that made me an outcast with the Rom.''

''I know what that is,'' Lily said. '' 'Rom' is Gypsy.''

''Yes, that's right.'' He regarded her for a few moments, sensing a bubbling excitement. ''How did you know that?''

''Orrie used to take us to the Gypsy circus when it came to town, and I heard them call themselves that. Orrie says you're a Scot.''

''Scot, Irish, English, Russian, maybe even Egyptian. Gypsy blood is a hodgepodge.'' His gaze moved over her chestnut hair and he had to remind himself again of his mission. ''How did you hear of Cecille's disappearance?''

''Uncle Howard sent us a telegram.'' Her thoughts circled back to that day. ''Father wasn't alarmed. He thought Cecille would turn up. He said she was pulling a stupid prank.'' She crossed her arms and ran her hands up and down them as a remembered chill overtook her. ''But I felt cold.''

''Cold? Numb, you mean?''

''No, chilled. To the bone.'' She swallowed the stickiness in her mouth. ''Cecille is a lively sort, granted, and not above trickery, but I felt certain she was in trouble when I read the telegram. I can't explain it. . . .'' She shook her head, trying to dislodge the clamminess clinging to her like a wet shawl. ''I had an immediate sense of foreboding. I . . . I started crying. Father became quite concerned and made travel arrangements for me immediately.''

"Concerned" wasn't accurate, she thought. Father had been frightened of her—not *for* her, but *of* her. And not for the first time.

"I was shivering," she continued, "and I . . . well, I felt positively ill until I arrived back home. Once I stepped into this house, the chill vanished." It dawned on her that she had revealed something to Griffon that she'd kept to herself, not even sharing with her family. "It's silly, I know," she murmured. "Foolish of me to tell you about it."

"Don't dismiss your feelings so quickly," he cautioned. "They are never counterfeit, Lily." He looked past her as if someone had entered the room, but when Lily glanced over her shoulder, no one was there. "You wouldn't mind if I walked with you to the library?"

"No, of course not."

"I believe your aunt has an errand for you to run while you're out."

"Lily?" Aunt Nan called as she came into the dining room. "Here you are. When you go to the library today, will you stop in at the printer's on the way home? Your uncle's business cards are ready."

Lily felt her mouth drop open. "Y-yes, Aunt Nan." She drew in a shuddering breath and tried to see through Griffon's ruse. When her aunt had left them alone again, Lily confronted him. "How did you know that? And don't tell me you read her mind."

He shrugged. "In that case, it was a lucky guess."

"I don't believe that."

"Naturally. It's a lie."

"I want the truth.'

"No, you don't." He shook his head sadly. "You want me to say what you're ready to hear."

"Aunt Nan must have mentioned the errand before I came down to breakfast."

He lowered one eyelid in a knowing wink. "That must be it."

"I'm not as soft in the head as you seem to think." Lily nodded, proud of herself for seeing through him. "Surprised that a feebleminded female could unravel your mystery? You'll have to do better than that to impress me."

He angled closer to her. The scent of lilac lifted from her creamy skin. "Begging your pardon, Lily, but I'm not here to impress you. I'm here to find your cousin." He straightened and strode past her. "Just give me a few minutes to polish my crystal ball and I'll meet you in the foyer."

She glared at his imposing back and wished for something solid she could throw against it. *Impudent bastard.*

He checked his stride and turned slowly to face her again. Lily felt blood rise up to scald her cheeks, although she told herself she had no reason to be embarrassed.

"Do you think you're the first unbeliever I've come across, Lily?" he asked, mildly irritated that she could hurt him, if only for a moment. Her opinion shouldn't matter, he knew, so why was he trying to convince her of his integrity? He regarded her, feeling her confusion. But it was the degree of fear in her that gave him pause. Most people were uneasy when confronted with his inexplicable oddities, but she gave out sheets of hard fear, as if believing him, only a little, would be a catastrophe. "Why are you afraid of me?"

"Afraid?" She managed a harsh laugh, although her heart felt as if it belonged in the body of a rabbit being chased by a hound. "I am hardly that. I simply don't believe in you or your alleged powers."

He shook his head, still perplexed by the strength of her mind, countered by the trembling in her soul. "Given time, I'll discover the why of you. I'm a prospector of feelings, Lily, and you can't bury them deep enough that I can't find them.''

Lily stared after him, feeling exposed, like a rabbit flushed from its hiding place with nothing ahead of it but an open field and the glaring eye of the sun.

Chapter 3

Tucking two volumes of poetry high up under her arm, Lily stood in the printer's office and waited impatiently for Mr. Bingham to fetch her Uncle Howard's business cards. She peered through the dusty window to the turreted brick building across the street where George Vick, private detective, kept his office. Having returned her library books and checked out more, she'd dashed next door to the printer's. Now she willed Mr. Bingham to shake a leg so she'd be in time to join Griffon Goforth when he questioned Vick about the report. Her nose itched, anxious to be placed in the middle of whatever was transpiring between the Gypsy soothsayer and the thieving detective.

"Here we are," Mr. Bingham said, emerging from the ink-smelling press room. He held a small package wrapped in brown paper and tied with a stained length of cord. "Let me yank off this wrapping so you can check them. I want you to be satisfied."

"Don't bother, Mr. Bingham. My uncle will be in touch if he isn't pleased. Send the bill around to him at the bank, won't you?"

"Will do." He screwed up his eyes behind his thick glasses. "Sure you don't want to look at them yourself?"

"No, really. I don't even know what Uncle Howard wanted printed on them."

"You heard anything from Miss Cecille?" he asked, his

gray-tinted fingers still plucking at the cord around the package. "I'm not asking as the newspaper printer, you understand. I'm asking as one caring Christian to another."

"I understand." Lily held out her hand for the package. "We've heard nothing, Mr. Bingham."

"Terrible thing." His eyes widened behind his glasses. "Speaking of terrible . . . they hung that train robber yesterday. Judge Parker says two more will swing tomorrow morning. Did you read about it this morning in the newspaper?"

"I haven't had a chance to look at the paper." And I don't wish to stomach a description of the latest hanging, she added mentally. She nearly tore the package from his hands, then she dropped it into her velvet drawstring purse. "Good morning, sir." She was out the door and crossing the street before Mr. Bingham could respond in kind.

Vick's building was buff-colored and two-storied, and after checking the directory, Lily learned that his office was on the top floor. Lifting her skirts ankle-high, she mounted the narrow staircase, which sent out creaks and groans that echoed in the dark corridor, lit only by a skylight set in the roof's apex. The strip of rug running the length of the second-floor hallway was threadbare and a dusty shade of green. Vick's office was the third one on her right. His name was printed in chipped black paint upon a frosted pane set in the door.

Lily knocked, heard nothing, and let herself in. A sour-faced woman with frizzled brown hair sat behind a squat desk.

"You lost?" she asked around a throat full of gravel.

"No, I'm not." Lily looked from the frowning woman to the interior door. "Is Mr. Goforth still in there?"

The woman nodded. "Want me to holler for him?"

"No, thank you." Lily moved as confidently as she could toward Vick's office. "I'll just join him, if you don't mind."

"Him and my boy are talking business, lady."

Lily paused, looking curiously at the woman. George Vick's mother? She wondered if Mama worked for George or if George worked for Mama. "I'm aware of that. If you'll excuse me . . ." She rapped smartly on the door and swung it open without waiting for a response. Her entrance came in time for her to see George Vick half rise from his desk to shout at Griffon.

"You calling me a liar, boy?" Vick had a bulldog's face, all loose folds of skin and sagging pockets of flesh under piggish eyes that now focused on Lily. "You'll have to wait outside, Miss Meeker. Me and your man here are still talking shop."

"I'd like to join in." She advanced with purpose. "After all, it's *my* cousin you're discussing."

"Yes, but this here is man talk."

She smiled tightly. "I promise not to faint if you let slip a discouraging word." Her gaze skittered to Griffon. He'd stood at her entrance and now waved her toward the other ladder-backed chair in front of Vick's desk. "Thank you," she murmured, sitting in the chair. "I seem to have interrupted an argument. Is there a problem?"

"No problem, 'cepting I don't got a hankering to be called a liar by somebody who don't know an ox yoke from an egg yolk," Vick said, sitting heavily in his desk chair.

Griffon crossed one leg over the other, his demeanor unruffled, uncaring even. "I've been trying to help Mr. Vick retrace his steps. He's forgotten how he knew to follow Cecille's trail to Van Buren."

"How could you have forgotten something like that?" Lily asked. "I've wondered time and again why you thought to look for Cecille there. She doesn't know anyone from that area that I know of."

"You don't know everything there is to know about your cuz," Vick said, smiling unpleasantly. "You only think you do. Everybody's got secrets, Miss Meeker."

"Perhaps you can enlighten us on Cecille Meeker's,"
Griffon suggested, a hard edge to his voice. "You seem
to know something we are ignorant of, Mr. Vick."

"Why would I keep something from y'all?" Vick
charged. "I'm working for the Meekers."

"Then why not tell Miss Meeker here what led you to
Van Buren? Surely you recall something. It must have been
a most important clue. *The* most important, if you ask
me."

"Nobody's asking," Vick snarled.

"I am," Lily piped up, clutching her purse, her nerves
stretched and quivering. "Who told you that Cecille had
traveled to Van Buren?" She noticed that Vick was staring
at Griffon, and she glanced at the man beside her. His
eyes were fixed straight ahead in the general direction of
George Vick, but Griffon didn't seem to be looking at
anything. He never blinked. Finally, he heaved a quick,
noisy sigh and closed his blue eyes. Lily held her breath
as apprehension scraped along her spine. She knew he was
going to say something she'd have a hard time explaining
away.

"Jeff . . . David," Griffon said, making Lily, then
George Vick, flinch with surprise. "Why wasn't he in your
report?"

"Who's that?" Vick asked, laughing hollowly. "You
know what he's jabbering about, Miss Meeker?"

"No, I . . ." Lily knitted her brows as she worried with
that name. Could he mean the dressmaker's son? She
looked at the detective again. "Did you speak to David
Jefferson about Cecille?" She knew she was right when
strawberry spots broke out on Vick's baggy cheeks. "Why
didn't you tell us about this before? Does David know
what happened to Cecille?" She turned toward Griffon.
"David is the dressmaker's son and a family friend."

"Him and his mama don't know nothing," Vick said,
disgustedly. "I didn't say nothing to you 'cause there's

nothing to say. End of the trail.'' He made a chopping motion with his hand.

''Perhaps we should pay a call on the dressmaker ourselves,'' Griffon said, already easing himself from the chair.

''Now just hold on.'' Vick patted the air. ''No need to bother her or her son. I've done told you they don't know a blamed thing.''

''Then they shouldn't mind telling us that themselves,'' Griffon said.

''I told them they wouldn't be bothered with this no more.''

''*Bothered* by it?'' Lily broke in. ''Why should it be a bother to them? Cecille is one of Bea Jefferson's best customers, and Bea and David are our friends—or so I always thought.''

''That's right,'' Vick said. ''And they're sick at heart over this whole mess, but they can't help you none in finding Miss Cecille. Take my word for it.''

Lily sniffed with disdain. ''Why should your word satisfy me, Mr. Vick, when you've just admitted to keeping information from me and my family?''

''I did no such thing, ma'am.'' He shook his bullish head adamantly. ''That's why I didn't want you poking around in this business. Women get all emotional and can't deal with cold, hard facts.''

''I haven't fainted yet,'' Lily said. ''Is there anything else you've withheld? If so, out with it, please, before Mr. Goforth and I leave to speak with Mrs. Jefferson and David.''

''Now I told you there's no need for you to pester them about this. They're good folk. That boy of Bea's is as bright as a new coin. Got quite a future ahead of him.''

At the familiar use of Mrs. Jefferson's Christian name, Lily exchanged a speaking glance with Griffon, then rose to her feet, prompting the two men to do the same.

"I'll be back if I need any gaps filled," Griffon assured George Vick.

"I don't work for free," Vick said, his upper lip lifting in a snarl. "You want information, next time you pay for it, boy."

"We *have* paid for it," Lily reminded him. "My uncle paid you well for only half of what you know, so it seems. We owe you nothing, Mr. Vick."

"I wasn't speaking of your people," Vick said. "I'm talking about this foreigner here. I don't have to give him—"

"He is my family's representative in this matter," Lily interrupted, gaining a startled look from Griffon and a malevolent one from Vick. "If you have any information about my cousin, I'll thank you to share it with Mr. Goforth." She squeezed the library books between her arm and her side, then tugged smartly on her open-weave gloves. "I intend to inform my uncle of your failure to impart all you know about my cousin's disappearance."

"Hey, lady, I told y'all what was important."

"All that *you* deemed important," Griffon corrected.

"*I'll* talk to Bea Jefferson. I don't want you going near her," Vick said, grabbing hold of Griffon's coat sleeve.

Griffon lowered his gaze to the man's hand, then lifted it slowly to Vick's face. Not a word was spoken, but Vick must have seen something in Griffon's expression, for he removed his hand as if he'd placed it in a pot of hot grease.

"Shall we go, Mr. Goforth?" Lily asked, interrupting the tense standoff between the two men. She pivoted sharply, her skirt and stiff petticoats twisting around her legs before falling into place to allow her to make her way to the door.

Griffon was there before her to hold it open, then ahead of her again at the corridor door. He retrieved his hat from the tree and directed a polite nod toward Vick's mother, who gave him an impolite snort in return. Once they were downstairs, Lily turned to him.

"And what are you smiling about?" she asked.

"Did you think that Vick and I would join forces to milk your poor uncle of more funds?"

"I'll show you to Bea Jefferson's shop."

"That's why you barged in on my meeting with him, wasn't it?" he persisted.

Lily stepped onto the wooden sidewalk, glad to be out of the musty-smelling building. "I wanted to confront George Vick myself," she said, hoping to appease him.

"You didn't trust me to handle him."

"It's not . . ." She clamped her teeth down on the lie. It was true; she didn't trust him. But there was more to it. "I'm tired of standing back and doing nothing while the weeks slip by with no word from Cecille."

He fit his dark gray hat carefully upon his head, then angled the curved brim to shadow his face. "I suppose you fully intend to question the dressmaker as well?"

"Of course. I've known Mrs. Jefferson for years. She'll be most happy to speak with me."

"Then you don't need me." He started to turn away, but Lily reached out and grabbed the tail of his coat.

"No, please!" The two books she clutched under her arm slipped and fell to the sidewalk.

"Allow me." He stooped and retrieved them, examining each before handing them over. "Romantic poetry. Are you in love with someone, Lily?"

"That's none of your business." She refused to acknowledge that she was blushing, although her face felt as hot as a stove lid. Then he did the most outrageous thing! He placed the tip of his forefinger against her nose and gave it three taps before she could retreat. "What do you think you're doing?" she asked, breathless, anxiously glancing around to see if they'd been noticed. The street was busy, but no one seemed interested in Lily or her tall, dark escort.

"I love your nose," he said, grinning. "The way it tilts up just so." He laughed under his breath. "Charming. It says so much about your character."

"Behave yourself or I won't be seen with you again," she whispered, incensed that he didn't seem to take her warning seriously. "I mean every word of that, sir."

He placed a hand over his heart and pretended to be on the verge of a swoon.

Lily looked pointedly along the street in the direction of the dressmaker's. "Bea Jefferson's business is two blocks from here." She saw wariness enter his silvery blue eyes and knew she'd have to allow him his responsibilities. "She'll probably be much more cooperative if I come along, don't you think? I'm a friend and you're someone she's never laid eyes on before. I'll introduce you and then leave the questions to you."

He cocked his arm, beckoning her. "Off we go then, partner."

"We aren't partners," she said, slipping her hand in the proffered nook. The material under her fingers was of the finest, and she angled back a little to scrutinize him from stylish hat to polished boots. He's a fine-looking man, she thought, but his air of unpredictability put her on guard. He wasn't a man to be trifled with. George Vick would attest to that. One look from Griffon had singed the man.

"I appreciate your willingness to help me in my investigation," he said, checking his stride when she had to trot to keep up with him. "However, if this is part of your plan to expose me as a—" He stopped and peered ahead. "Is Mrs. Jefferson's shop the one with the pink sign swinging above the door?"

"Yes." Lily looked from Griffon's chiseled profile to the shop ahead of them.

"I believe I saw George Vick dart inside just now."

"I didn't see anything."

"That's because you were too busy ogling me, while I was looking where I was going."

"I was *not* ogling," she said, fuming—and mortified that he'd noticed. "But how could it have been Vick? He didn't pass us."

"The back way, I suppose." They'd reached the end of one block, separated from the next by gaps in the sidewalk. Pedestrians were forced to descend three steps, cross the mouth of an alley, then ascend three steps to the next block of sidewalks fronting buildings. Griffon looked down the alleyway. "He must have raced along the back of these buildings. He wants to warn her of our visit."

"Let him. She'll talk to me, nonetheless. I can't imagine what she's been hiding all this time. She knows my family. Why wouldn't she help us if she could?"

"She's protecting her own."

"Why do you say that?" Lily asked. He had that keen look in his eyes that she was beginning to recognize as a sign that his mind was leaping nimbly to places she couldn't go.

"Just a feeling," he said nonchalantly, then glanced at her. Imps cavorted in his eyes. "It's something I read in my crystal ball this morning."

"I'm not amused by your attempt at humor," she informed him haughtily, then swept into Bea Jefferson's quaint shop in time to see George Vick pushing a confused Mrs. Jefferson toward the curtained-off part of the shop where the fitting rooms were located. Bea Jefferson was a small woman, dressed today in a cream frock of her own design. She looked like a lamb being herded by a bulldog.

"Mrs. Jefferson," Lily called. "Might we have a word with you before Mr. Vick spirits you away?" She smiled, hearing Griffon's low chuckle slightly behind her.

"I . . . Lily, how nice to see . . . George, please!" Mrs. Jefferson jerked her arm from Vick's clutching fingers, her voice dipping to a whispery hiss. "It's too late for this now." She smoothed curls of her ash-colored hair from her forehead and moved with hesitant, mincing steps down the aisle to Lily. When she spotted Griffon, she stopped, tipping her head at a curious angle. "Lily, what can I do for you and this gentleman?"

"Mrs. Jefferson, this is Griffon Goforth. My family has retained him to find Cecille."

Griffon, hat in hand, bobbed his head politely, and Mrs. Jefferson responded in kind.

"He'd like to ask you a few questions, Mrs. Jefferson."

"Me?" The seamstress glanced over her shoulder at George Vick, who had been a moment too late in rescuing her. "I can't imagine why. I told Mr. Vick here that I don't know what happened to Cecille after she left my shop that day."

"Is your son here?" Griffon asked.

"Yes, he's upstairs, but he doesn't have anything to do with this." Her glance landed like a dollop of displeasure on Griffon. "Lily, I thought your family hired Mr. Vick to investigate."

"We did, but we weren't pleased with his work." Lily sent Vick a scolding look. "My father suggested that we give Mr. Goforth a try. He's had some success at locating people. So . . . David's upstairs?"

"Yes, he's studying for his exam."

"The one that will license him as an attorney?"

Mrs. Jefferson nodded. "I don't want him disturbed."

"Mr. Goforth might have a few questions for David, and I must insist—" Lily chopped off the rest when Griffon cupped her elbow in one hand.

"He's coming downstairs," Griffon said, so softly she was the only one who caught his words.

David parted the curtains and stepped into the room. "Mama?" Vertical lines appeared between his dark green eyes. He finished slipping into his suit jacket, then adjusted his tie nervously. "What's all this about? Hello, Mr. Vick, Lily." He cocked an eyebrow at Griffon. "I don't know you, do I?"

"Griffon Goforth," Griffon supplied, moving forward, past Lily and Bea Jefferson, hand extended. "You must be David Jefferson."

"I was telling your mother that we've hired Mr. Goforth

to find Cecille,'' Lily explained. "He seems to think you might know something—something you told Mr. Vick about, but which he failed to include in his report to us.''

David's eyes widened and he and his mother traded uneasy glances. "I don't know what you're talking about, Lily.''

"David, I thought we were friends.''

"We are.'' He brushed past Griffon to take Lily's hands in his. "You know how much you mean to me.''

"Then why are you lying? Mr. Vick has as much as admitted that you and your mother know something about what happened to Cecille.''

"I said no such thing,'' Vick said, his voice rising to a roar.

"George, please,'' Bea Jefferson said, placing a hand on Vick's coat sleeve. "Let's keep this civil.''

"We don't know anything,'' David told Lily. "Not about that. We don't know where she is or what happened to her. Honestly.''

"Why did you tell Vick to look for Cecille in Van Buren?'' Griffon asked as he examined a summery yellow frock draped on a cotton-stuffed form. His question was answered by a telling silence while Vick and the Jeffersons tried to talk to each other with guilt-ridden eyes.

"For pity's sake,'' Lily declared, snatching her gloved hands from David's. She filled her hands with the two library books so that David wouldn't be tempted again to grasp them. "I can't believe that you would conspire to keep information about Cecille from me and my family. I thought Griffon was mad to suggest such a thing, but here it is staring me in the face and . . . well, I'm heartbroken.''

"Dearest Lily,'' Mrs. Jefferson said, rushing toward her. "We aren't keeping secrets. That is . . . we mean no harm. What we know didn't amount to anything. George checked it out himself and it came to nothing, so there wasn't any need for us to involve ourselves any further. It's a terrible business, is it not? And with David on the brink of his law profession, we felt it best if we stayed well out of it.''

A woman entered the shop and extended them a curious stare. "Good morning, Mrs. Jefferson. I'm here to look at the fabric you ordered for me.''

"Yes, Mrs. Spencer." Bea Jefferson rushed forward, all quick movement and nervous gestures. "It's over here. I think it will be perfect for that gown you're planning. The shade of pink is all the rage in Paris and should enhance your coloring.'' Mrs. Jefferson guided her customer to a corner of the shop where bolts of fabric were shelved, all the while casting worried glances over her shoulder at the others.

"Perhaps we could conduct our business elsewhere," Griffon said, looking meaningfully at the curtains toward the back of the shop. "Is there a private office?''

"Follow me," David said tersely, leading the way through the curtain, past the fitting rooms to a cluttered area with a secretary desk shoved against one wall. A few tattered chairs, stuffing leaking from corners, rimmed the desk. David lifted a stack of fashion books out of one. "Please, Lily, won't you make yourself comfortable?''

Lily sat down and fluffed her skirts around her slim legs. It occurred to her that Mrs. Jefferson had sewed this dress for her last spring. She glanced apprehensively at Griffon when he stationed himself beside her chair, standing over her like a castle guard. David glowered at him, then leaned against the edge of the desk. George Vick slumped into one of the other lumpy chairs, his face drooping into deeper folds of jiggly skin.

"Might as well tell them, David," Vick grumbled. "They won't be leaving you or Bea in peace until you do.''

"If you've nothing to hide, then whatever you tell us can't hurt you," Griffon said. "If you are a friend of the Meekers, you should be willing to cooperate.''

"I am most certainly a friend of theirs," David said,

then looked beseechingly at Lily. "I'd never hurt you Lily. You . . . you're special to me."

Lily clasped her hands on top of the books in her lap and stared at them, unwilling to accept David's earnest assurance. Betrayal ate away at the edges of her faith in him and his mother. Curiously, she felt closer to Griffon Goforth at that moment than to anyone else in the tiny, musty room.

"Do you recall that family from the Ozarks who performed during the spring cotillion?" David asked Lily.

She had to sift through the memories of that day and night of whirlwind activity. David had been her escort. Cecille had been on Scott Hamilton's arm. Scott had left a month later to enter an Illinois college.

"They call themselves the Jeffers Gypsy Band," David said.

"Gypsy?" Griffon repeated. "Gypsies in the Ozarks? Whereabouts?"

"They aren't real Gypsies," David said. "But they travel all over Arkansas, Kansas, and Missouri, so they call themselves that to make themselves sound more exciting."

"What about them?" Griffon asked.

David fixed his hope-filled eyes on Lily. "Do you recall how Cecille was simply mesmerized by them, Lily? She thought the one who danced and played those spoons like castanets was wonderful. She went on so about him that she made Scott Hamilton jealous. The dancer had long, dark hair and black eyes. Tall, lithe, but hard, muscled." David swept Griffon from head to toe. "Not unlike this man you've hired."

Lily's gaze followed David's over Griffon's body. "I remember vaguely, but Cecille was forever getting wobbly-kneed over dark, mysterious men. Especially Gypsies."

"Is that so?" Griffon asked, eyes suddenly alight. "You never mentioned that."

"I haven't mentioned much to you at all," Lily reminded him. "We only met late last night." She didn't like the way he was smiling at her, as if she'd revealed some bald fact about herself. "Orrie put all that in Cecille's head. She used to read us stories about Gypsies and fairies and other such nonsense. What is so amusing, Mr. Goforth?" she demanded when he released a short bark of laughter.

"Placing Gypsies in with fairies," he explained. "As if the two are somehow connected."

"In Orrie's mind they are. Anyway, Orrie's stories fed Cecille's wild streak, and she thought Gypsies and circus people were the most exciting in the whole world." She returned her attention to David. "But what has this to do with Cecille?"

"She . . . she . . ." David sighed and looked distressed.

"She took up with the dancing one." George Vick spoke up. "The two of them snuck around and saw each other from time to time, and he and his people make their homes out Van Buren way."

"Took up with him?" Lily asked, her spine solid as iron. "What are you saying?" She looked to David for help, but his head was bowed. "Cecille is decent. She wouldn't do such a thing as slip off and sport with a total stranger."

"They weren't strangers after a spell," Vick said with a snicker. "I told you that you didn't know your cuz as well as you thought. When you get right down to it, nobody knows nobody at all."

"If this is true, you had no right to keep it from us," Lily charged. "We've spent week upon week searching for Cecille, and all the while you knew what happened to her."

"No, no, Lily," David said, frantic. "Mr. Vick went to Van Buren. Cecille isn't there. The Jefferses didn't even know she was missing."

"And you believed them," Lily said, folding her arms

against her laboring heart. The news of Cecille's sporting with someone behind her back had shaken her firm belief in her cousin's good sense. "Complete strangers. You took their word just like that?"

"They aren't complete strangers." Bea Jefferson entered the corner office, and her face was pinched with anguish. ·

"But like we've been telling you," George Vick broke in, "this has got nothing to do with your cousin. She left here to talk to that backwoods fella, but got lost somewhere between here and there."

"She was to meet him that day?" Griffon asked, abruptly. "She left your shop to meet with this man?"

"Yes, but it was to be the last time. I didn't know she'd been meeting him," Bea Jefferson said, the words tumbling out in a rush. "David kept the secret. Cecille didn't want anyone to know. I found out that day. Naturally, I put my foot down on the whole business. Cecille thought the man was dashing and exciting. She wasn't thinking clearly about him, so I told her the truth." Bea drew in a deep breath. "He was a married man."

"Oh, heavens." Lily dropped her head in her hands as her heart caved in on itself.

"Cecille was livid," Bea went on. "She has quite a temper, as you know. She said she was going to meet him and tell him what was what. She just had to give him a piece of her mind before she broke it off with him. But she never made it to the meeting. Something happened to her along the way. When he got to the place, she wasn't there. He was a few minutes late, he told George, so maybe someone else . . . oh, I don't know. All I know is that he didn't know Cecille was missing. George asked him. Didn't you, George?"

Vick nodded and picked his teeth. "They don't know snuff."

"How are you so familiar with these people?" Griffon

asked Bea. "Just how did you know they live in Van Buren?"

Bea sighed and exchanged a tortured look with her son. "They're family."

"Family?" Lily asked, gasping.

"My husband was a Jeffers. I lengthened the name after he died, and brought David here for a better life." Bea's eyes filled with tears. "They're hill people, you see. Common."

"Dirt poor," George Vick offered. "Not an educated one amongst 'em. Bea was right to take David away from there. He's smart. Got a good future."

"This man Cecille was seeing," Griffon said. "Is he directly related to you, Mrs. Jefferson?"

Bea nodded, tears slipping down her cheeks. "He's my nephew. David's cousin."

"You lied to us," Lily said, her voice coming out hoarse. "You said she came here for a dress fitting."

"Don't blame Mama," David said. "I kept Cecille's secret."

"Why?" Lily asked.

"Because . . . oh, it's stupid." He shoved his hands deep into his pockets. "My cousin and Cecille said they'd tell everybody in town that me and Mama were cut from coarse cloth." His gaze wandered to his mother. "Mama has tried so hard to separate us from the Jeffers clan, to gain the respect of people here, and I didn't want her upset over this, so I kept quiet."

"Where did Cecille rendezvous with this man?" Griffon asked.

"In a shed behind the livery," Vick answered. "Then he'd take her to the old Sutton place. There's a barn out there."

Lily covered her face with her hands. "This is too much! What would possess Cecille . . ."

"That's it," David said. "When it came to Anson, Cecille *was* possessed. I tried to talk her out of seeing him, but she wouldn't hear of it. She said he was the most exciting man she'd ever met. She said he was out of a storybook.''

Lily groaned and cursed Orrie Dickens and her fanciful tales of Gypsy fortune-tellers and sorcerers with magic wands. Griffon's hands curved around her shoulders, and his breath tickled the side of her face as he leaned down to whisper in her ear.

"Lily, are you all right? Would you like to go home and leave this to me?''

"Get your hands off me! Don't touch me,'' she ordered, shaking her shoulders to dislodge his hands.

For a few moments of confusion, she saw in Griffon all that was wrong with her world. He embodied the evil and the deception that had spirited Cecille to some nether-world, and she cringed from him, her face twisting with disgust.

Griffon stepped away from her, his mouth thinning into a taut line. In the next moment, Lily regretted her scathing words, but it was too late. His eyes, steely blue, told her that she'd wounded him. She winced, feeling his pain as if it were her own.

"Forgive me,'' she begged, looking into his eyes for a glimmer of understanding.

"Don't apologize,'' he said, his voice as sharp as a knife blade. "You were only reminding this arrogant Gypsy goat of his place.''

Lily recognized those hate-filled words. Arrogant. Gypsy goat. She'd called him that. No, no. She gasped and her lungs bellowed painfully in her chest. She hadn't *called* him that. Oh, God in heaven! She'd *thought* it.

Chapter 4

"**H**ave you taken leave of your senses?" Balthazar fumed, pacing the length of the bedroom he and Griffon shared. "Generosity is a virtue, but you've taken it too far by asking not a penny for your services here. What if it gets around and people start expecting your help out of the goodness of your heart? How will you make a living? How will *we* make a living?"

"Calm yourself, Zar." Griffon lay on the bed, hands stacked under his head, eyes trained on the ceiling. He knew he was sulking and despised himself for it. Stinging from careless remarks made by a snippity young woman was the stuff of adolescence, he told himself firmly, but his pride still throbbed from being trounced on by Miss Lily Meeker's high-button shoes.

"Will we pay for our expenses from our own purses?"

"We're far from destitute."

"Howard Meeker is far from destitute as well. Much farther from it than us."

"Zar, have you forgotten that we're unknown on this continent? We've made our reputations in England and Europe, not here. Thurman persuaded me to take on this case personally because the Meeker family is a respected one. If we find Cecille Meeker, then we'll take a giant step in becoming credible in this country. Money is secondary at this juncture."

"Money is never secondary," Balthazar grumbled,

standing at the foot of the bed, his brows knit in worry. "Did you make any headway this morning? I was pleased to see no knife hilt emerging from the middle of your back." He smiled unpleasantly at Griffon's confusion. "Miss Lily. I half expected her to try and do away with you if given the chance."

Griffon shifted irritably. "As Lily suspected, the detective wasn't telling all he knew."

"Lily, is it? Played out *Lily*'s hunch, did you?" Balthazar chuckled when Griffon scowled at his teasing. "You found out where Miss Cecille is?"

"Not exactly, but I've caught the scent of the chase." He twisted onto his side and propped his head in one hand. "Zar, do you think I'm overtly odd? I mean, if you saw me on the street and didn't know me, would you be frightened? Would you cross to the other side?"

"Don't be preposterous. Of course I wouldn't. On the outside, you're perfectly normal. Why do you ask? Does Doubting Lily treat you as if you're tainted?"

"Yes, she does."

"She's the odd one, if you ask me. The others here are quite sociable, but her corset's too tight."

Griffon laughed. "And my asking you to point out an oddity is like asking Siamese twins if the bearded lady is peculiar." A tentative knock sounded at the door, and Griffon swung his legs around and placed his feet on the floor. "Yes, who's there?"

"Miss Meeker. May I have a word with you, Mr. Goforth?"

Balthazar arched a brow as Griffon tugged on his boots. He started to grab his jacket, then batted aside the notion.

"Aw, to bloody hell with it. Why should I be presentable around a girl who calls me a goat? I'll tell you all the rest after I see what she wants," he told Balthazar. He finger-combed his hair before opening the door and stepping out into the hall. "Yes, Lily?" He heard the crackle in his voice, but didn't give a damn. It was one thing for her to be suspect of his psychic power, but quite another for her to view him as beneath her.

"I was wondering what you planned to do now." She retreated, creating a discrete distance between them.

"Actually, I was discussing what I've learned with Balthazar. I believe I'll go to the place where Cecille met her secret admirer and see if I can turn up anything useful."

"The Sutton place, you mean? May I go with you? I can show you where it is."

He hooked a finger over his shirt collar and tugged. "I'm not used to wearing a leash. Can't say that I like it," he said, nearly growling at her.

To her credit, she didn't retreat, but a contrite smile curved her mouth. "You have every reason to be angry at me, but I was hoping you'd understand why I was abrupt with you at the dress shop. Hearing about Cecille jolted me. I wasn't myself and—" She pressed her lips together to vanquish the smile. "No excuses. My snapping at you like that was rude. Please accept my apology, Mr. Goforth."

"Griffon." He held her gaze, eyes hooded, until she bobbed her head in agreement. "Apology accepted, but you needn't accompany me to the Sutton property. I have a lick of sense and can find the way." He started to turn aside, but she snagged his sleeve.

"Please, let me come with you."

"Still don't trust me? What kind of mischief do you think I can do out there?"

"It's not that. I'm desperate to find my cousin, and I'm tired of sitting around and waiting for reports. I won't get in your way."

He knew he could wound her by telling her he needed no woman hanging on him while he worked, but retaliation seemed petty when faced with her lustrous eyes and clutching fingers. He wanted her company. She intrigued him, titillated him. She was difficult to puzzle out, and life held too few curiosities for him. Her grip tightened on his sleeve and her brown eyes implored him. She wouldn't have believed how easily she could sway him, Griffon thought. He could hardly believe it himself!

"Can you be ready to leave within the hour?" he asked.

"I'm ready to leave right now." Her hand fell away. Excitement sparkled in her eyes.

"I'll rent a carriage—"

"No, we can take ours. It's at the livery."

"Very well. I'll join you out front in a few minutes." He let himself back into the bedroom to find Balthazar pacing again. "I'm going for a ride with Lily."

Balthazar cut his shrewd eyes in Griffon's direction. "Is she to be your assistant on this case, Griffon?"

"No, of course not." He laid a hand on Balthazar's shoulder. "Don't take this personally." He winked and gave the man a jocular hug. "I merely want time alone with the russet-haired lass."

Balthazar gasped audibly. "You're not attracted to that brazen-tongued girl, are you? Why, she . . . she thinks you're loathsome, or hadn't you noticed?"

"Methinks she protests too much," Griffon loosely quoted from Shakespeare. "You know how I love to convert skeptics."

"If you prefer her company to mine . . ." Balthazar shrugged.

"Come, come. Don't take offense. Why not chase Orrie's skirts while I'm chasing Lily's? That maid fancies you something fierce."

"That she does." Balthazar looked pleased. "And she's not a bad sort. She has an open mind and a game spirit."

"And a fair figure," Griffon added. "Plump, but pleasingly so. I'll be back before nightfall and we'll speak at length," Griffon promised, fitting his hat on his head. "I'll want your counsel."

"On the missing person case or the protesting woman?"

Griffon grinned. "Both, quite possibly."

* * *

The buggy rattled over the cattle guard and onto property formerly owned by the old Sutton family. Deserted now, the acres of farmland were overgrown. The farmhouse had burned a year ago, leaving only a rocky foundation and a tilting chimney to mark its passing. In the distance stood the humpbacked barn, unpainted but surrounded by early wildflowers. Spring was hard on the heels of winter, chasing the blustery old man out of Arkansas earlier than usual.

During the journey Lily had answered Griffon's questions about Cecille, which were numerous, but she welcomed them. She'd hoped to gain a new perspective on her cousin, since the Jeffersons had revealed that she didn't know Cecille as well as she'd thought.

"It appears your cousin is quite popular," he commented as he handled the reins with authority, guiding the bay horse and buggy across the open field to the barn.

Lily tightened her bonnet's bow under her chin and gripped the handhold as the buggy jostled over the soggy ground. "She's lively company. Cecille loves to laugh and she's always ready for an adventure."

"And you have your share of beaus, as well." At her sharp look, he added, "The dressmaker's son is quite taken with you."

She felt her face flame, not wholly from embarrassment. David Jefferson was a touchy subject, especially since she'd learned he'd kept secrets with Cecille. "Not really. Oh, David likes me," she allowed with a flip of her hand, "but he's one of Cecille's castoffs."

Griffon angled a sideways glance at her. "Castoffs? He was rejected by Cecille?"

"After a time. He was her escort for a month or so, but Cecille grew tired of him, so she tossed him my way. She does that, despite my objections. I like David and he likes me, but I'm fairly sure he only escorted me to be near Cecille. Especially after what we heard today."

"Not necessarily." He reined in the horse. "You still

don't entirely believe that your cousin could take part in a secret affair, do you?"

"It's not something I particularly want to believe." Lily stared at the abandoned barn, trying to picture it as a trysting place. She imagined Cecille slipping into the barn with a dark stranger; kissing, fondling, caressing. The image wavered and broke up as her heart rejected it. "Why wouldn't she tell me about this man? Cecille and I talked about *everything.*"

"Would you have approved?" Griffon asked, tying off the reins and setting the brake. "Would you have encouraged her to keep seeing the man?"

"Heavens, no!"

He delivered a sage look before jumping nimbly from the buggy. He came around to her side and offered his hand. "Cecille probably decided she didn't want a naysayer casting a pall on her latest adventure."

Lily considered this and agreed. If Cecille was anything, it was headstrong. Lily slipped her gloved hand into Griffon's and let him help her to the ground. He wore knee-high boots, and the choice was a smart one since mud and puddles dotted the area around the barn. Keeping her hand in his, Lily hip-hopped over the ground, trying not to soil her skirt hem.

Sunlight slanted through cracks in the walls and ceiling, illuminating the inside of the barn.

"I do believe they were here," Griffon murmured, hands propped at his waist, head thrown back, eyes closed. "Something secretive went on here. I still feel it. A kind of thrill in the air. Cecille liked coming here."

Lily observed him for a few moments, battling against a desire to believe him. Her rational self prevailed, but just barely. Something—probably a rat—scurried to a corner of the barn, ruffling through the hay strewn over the dirt floor. Drawn to the loft, she started to ascend the wobbly ladder.

"Be careful." Griffon's hands circled her waist to steady her. "Perhaps I should go up first."

She stepped away, tingling from their brief physical contact, and he climbed with the agility of a cat. Lily moved more slowly, hindered by her petticoats and slick-soled shoes. Aside from smelling dank from the recent rain, the barn held a bird cage odor. Their intrusion set off a flurry of wings. Lily glanced up at swooping owls, startled sparrows, and even a couple of pigeons.

"Quite a roost up here," Griffon said, gripping her elbows to help her to stand beside him. "I'm wondering if Cecille would climb up here. It doesn't appear too inviting."

Lily straightened, acutely aware of the warmth of his hands on her arms, got her bearings, and glanced around the mote-filled area. The loft door was open, letting in sunlight. Reaching out, she laid her hand against a smooth cypress post that supported the roof. A sudden chill passed over her and her vision dimmed. The world compressed around her, and her sight narrowed to pinpoint a scene. She felt detached from her body.

She saw a man, and while she didn't know him, the eyes she now used were familiar with his dark hair and swarthy complexion. Tall and sinewy, he leaned against another support beam, a cocky grin riding his thin lips, his black eyes dancing. He waited for her to approach him. She felt herself moving, although a part of her knew she remained immobile. It was her mind that moved to him. He uncrossed his arms to embrace her. Anger pulsed through her and at him. The man stopped smiling, caught the anger, and flung it back tenfold. Hands gripped her forearms, and her vision blurred as the man shook her. She wobbled like a rag doll. Anger dissolved into fear. A voice, thick with fury, bludgeoned her.

"You think I'll letcha go just like that?" The hurtful voice enveloped her, and then she saw that it was the stranger talking. She saw his lips moving . . . like a dream, like in a nightmare. "You're my everythin'. I'm not lettin' you go. You hear me? I'll do what I have to. You're mine, Goldilocks. Mine . . . forever an' ever an' ever. Jes' like in them storybooks."

Her mind struggled violently, shaking the keyhole world apart. Light flooded into her eyes again. She blinked, felt warmth seep under her skin and dispel the chill that gripped her. Her muscles felt stiff as if they'd been frozen. A face swam before her. Fingers bit into her upper arms. She winced, cried out in fear. Was it the stranger? Was he here with her?

"Lily! It's Griffon, Lily!"

The world she knew engulfed her again. Griffon stood before her, concern etched on his face. She began to shake, afraid of what had happened to her. It had occurred before—this slipping into another world and seeing with someone else's eyes—but long ago. She'd thought that it wouldn't ever happen again. But it was upon her once more, this helpless, irrational journey to somewhere else in time.

"What did you see, Lily?" Griffon asked. "Did you see Cecille?"

She stared at him in amazement. He knew what had happened to her! Lily clung to him, grateful for a strong shoulder and an understanding heart. But then denial topped her inner horizon, riding to her rescue, and she shook her head violently. *No!* her mind screamed. *You're normal. You're not a freak. Nothing happened. You imagined it.*

"Lily, talk to me. Tell me what you saw while it's still fresh in your mind."

"N-nothing. I saw nothing. I was . . . was daydreaming."

"Daydreaming?" he repeated, incredulous. "Quit this silly game and tell me what you saw."

"Nothing. I told you." She struggled, trying to escape him, but he held fast. "I was only imagining things."

"Like hell."

"Don't speak to me that way!"

"You're lying. Don't you want to find Cecille?"

"Of course I do."

"Then why are you blocking my way to her?"

"I'm doing nothing of the kind. You're the one who's supposed to *see* things." This time she was successful at jerking from his grasp. "You're the strange one, not me."

He delivered a speculative glare. "Strange? You find me strange, do you? I'm not the one who went into a trance a moment ago."

"I wasn't in a trance. But, of course, that's what you would call it." She tried to laugh it off. "I was imagining what it might have been like for Cecille here, something quite common for *normal* people to do."

He crossed his arms against his chest. "All right. If this is how you want to play the game, what did you imagine?"

Resentment stirred in her at his condescending tone. "It's not important."

"It's important to me." His voice rapped like hard knuckles.

"Very well." She sighed, surrendering to his obstinate manner. "I imagined her with a dark man—the Gypsy dancer."

"He's not a Gypsy."

"Well, whatever he is," she said, waving aside his point. "He was angry."

"About what?"

"About Cecille not wanting to see him again, I suppose. He said he wouldn't let her go. She belonged to him, he said."

"Was she frightened?"

"Oh, yes. She felt panicked. She knew she'd made a mistake by expecting him to be civilized. He's not civilized. He's wild and exotic. That's why she likes him . . . liked him." Lily realized she'd slipped backward into her waking dream, finding feelings she'd overlooked before. She blocked out the rest and glanced nervously at Griffon. He smiled arrogantly.

"Quite an imagination you have there, Lily."

"At least I call it by its rightful name and don't try to dress it up as something it isn't." She looked around at the roomy loft. Bird nests took up every corner and spilled over cross beams.

Griffon removed his hat and twirled it on one finger. "You're telling me that you think all I possess is an active imagination? That's what you really think about me, Lily?"

She didn't answer, but pretended to examine the rusted pulley suspended outside the loft opening. She wished he'd concentrate on Cecille and not on her.

"I'll be glad to concentrate on Cecille, if you'll only quit this stupid game of pretending I'm a lying thief who has come to lift your uncle's purse."

Almost against her will, her gaze shifted slowly to him as an ice-cold drop of alarm rolled down her spine. Her exact mental words, she thought. He'd spoken them back to her.

"I can't read your mind entirely or constantly," he said, still twirling his hat, his light-colored eyes bound to her. "But I can pick out bits and pieces. Enough to know that your refusal to believe me or in me has very little to do with me. What happened, Lily, to make you so afraid of the sixth sense?"

"There's no such thing."

"You don't believe that."

"I just said it, didn't I?"

"Yes, like a recital, like something you've been told to say. But you don't believe it."

Lily kicked irritably at the hay. "What has this to do with Cecille?"

"At least tell me this—do you feel she was taken away against her will by this dark stranger?"

"How should I know? I wasn't there!" She heard the edge of hysteria in her voice and strove to erase it. What was it about Griffon Goforth that put her on edge, made her want to scream and cry and run away? He was always pushing her into corners, that's what.

"Very well, do you *imagine* this man might have kidnapped Cecille, or did she go willingly? Do you *imagine* she's still alive?"

"I don't know," she said, frostily. "But I *imagine* if we don't leave this silly talk behind I shall be forced to slap your arrogant face!"

He paced briefly, hat in hand, eyeing her as if she were a puzzle he had to solve. "Stand near that post again."

She looked at the spot. "Why?"

"Just do it," he bit out.

With an exaggerated roll of her eyes, she obeyed and then fixed a bored expression on her face. "What, pray tell, does this prove?"

"That's where you were standing when you went into your trance."

"I wasn't having a trance," she objected, but not heatedly. Arguing with him, she found, drained her. She leaned a shoulder against the post to show her weariness.

A chilly breath blew over her and the world dimmed again. She felt smothered. She tried to make a sound, but couldn't. Something was over her mouth, cutting off her wind. Terror blossomed in her. Pain, sharp and piercing, exploded in her skull. Lily grabbed her head in both hands and squeezed her eyes shut.

As quickly as the events had galloped over her, they were gone. She opened her eyes. Griffon stood in front of her, his knowing eyes seeing everything, understanding what confused her, embracing what frightened her.

"What do you feel, Lily?" he asked, hands framing her face with a gentleness that found its way to her heart.

"He took her away," she whispered, slowly gathering her senses again. "I think he hit her on the head. She

blacked out. He took her with him. The pain . . .'' Lily
blinked as tears stung her eyes. "The pain in my head.
Something hit me—her.''

Griffon nodded. "Okay then." He pulled Lily into his
arms and held her against him. He pushed her bonnet off.
It fell, unheeded, to the loft floor. "Now we have a direction. I'll go to Van Buren. That's where he took her, don't
you think?''

She nodded, rubbing her cheek against his lapel. He
smelled of masculine things, and she purred with contentment. Curiously, she had no wish to leave his shelter-
ing embrace. She liked the security of his arms around her
waist and back, the solid strength of him.

"I'm certain I'll find something in Van Buren. Vick
didn't even try that hard. He asked, got an answer, didn't
question it, and left. I won't be so easily pacified.''

"She's still alive," Lily whispered. "I know it.''

"So do I, but time is precious.'' Treasured seconds
ticked by before he spoke again. "Lily, are you all right?
You're not trembling anymore. Feel chipper, do you?''

"Yes.'' She hadn't been aware of trembling until he
mentioned it. She eased back to look into his face. The
understanding she saw in his eyes was comforting. "I think
if anyone can find Cecille, you can.''

"I appreciate that, especially coming from you.''

Lily sensed he wanted to kiss her. She knew she could
simply step out of his arms to elude the kiss, but her heart
held her in place. It beat wildly, pumped longing in her
veins. Her hands inched up under his collar to his shoulders as he bent over her. A thrill arrowed through her
when his lips touched hers. She rose on tiptoe and pressed
her mouth more firmly to his. Her response started a fire
in him that blazed out of control in a split second.

He caught her against him and his tongue probed the
seam of her lips. A relative novice at deep kisses, Lily
resisted the urge to part her lips, partly in fear of what
such an action might trigger in him. She turned her head,

and his mouth left a moist trail across her cheek. He buried his face in the side of her neck.

"Lily, kiss me again," he said, his voice hoarse, his breath like the lick of a flame.

"We shouldn't . . ." She managed to squirm from his embrace. Her heart fluttered like the startled birds overhead.

This is lust, she thought, somewhat dazed. This is what Cecille had described; overwhelming warmth that steals the breath and sets the heart to beating like a drum. Lily had never felt it . . . until this moment. It stunned her that she should feel passion for Griffon Goforth, but a wiser side of her made her see how true to character it was for her to want this dark, mysterious Gypsy. Like Cecille, she had been raised on Orrie's romantic stories. But unlike Cecille, Lily thought, she wouldn't succumb to such nonsense.

Lily fit her bonnet onto her head again and tightened the bow under her chin. "We won't speak of this again."

"Speak of what again?"

"Of what just happened between us," she said, glancing over her shoulder to find him looking perplexed. "It was a . . . a momentary lapse. A mistake."

"Speak for yourself."

She touched her lips, remembering that flash of pure pleasure. "I think we should go now."

"Yes, I have to make travel plans."

"So do I." She started for the ladder, but he hooked her elbow.

"What do you mean by that?"

"I'm going with you to Van Buren."

"Oh, no you're not. Zar and I will handle this from here on."

"I'm going with you," she repeated, snatching her elbow from his hand.

"We'll see about that." He went to the ladder and

started down first. "I don't believe your aunt and uncle will allow it."

"And why not?"

"A young woman running off with two bachelors?" He clucked his tongue, chiding her. "I think not, Miss Lily. You'll just have to trust me."

Mischief sparkled in his blue eyes, so she didn't bother to argue. She'd save her arguments for when she spoke to her aunt and uncle. She'd need her full arsenal then.

Chapter 5

Seated under a grape arbor in the backyard, Griffon and Balthazar listened to the angry voices drifting from the Meeker house.

"Absolutely not!" Howard Meeker boomed. "What would your father say if he heard that I'd allowed his only child to travel with two unmarried men?"

"I doubt if Father would care all that much," Lily answered, her voice calmer but nonetheless agitated.

Griffon looked across at Balthazar and arched a brow. "Sounds like there's trouble between Lily and her father."

"I asked Orrie about that earlier. I thought it odd that Miss Lily lived here instead of with him." Balthazar slouched lower in the cane chair. "She said Lily preferred living in Fort Smith, and she said several times that Professor John Meeker is quite a busy man. Must not have had time to raise a child by himself, so he let his brother and sister-in-law do it for him."

"I wonder how Lily feels about that," Griffon mused.

"She surely resents it. Who wouldn't? Show me an abandoned child and I'll show you an adult with a grudge."

Griffon chuckled. "True. So true. Heaven knows, I've nursed my own share of them." He lifted a finger to his lips as the voices rose again.

". . . tired of playing by rules I had no part in making!" It was Lily. "If I wanted to sport with either of those men or both of them I could do it right in my own backyard. I surely don't have to travel to Van Buren for such behavior.''

"Oh, dear. Oh, dear. Such talk. . . . I feel faint," Nan Meeker wailed. "Orrie, the smelling salts. Quick!"

Balthazar started laughing, and Griffon shushed him, although he, too, was amused by Nan Meeker's theatrics.

"Look what you've done," Howard Meeker said. "Hasn't your poor aunt had enough woe without this?"

"Orrie can go with me," Lily said, her voice rising with hope. "Orrie will be my chaperone. That'll make everything proper, won't it?"

"Why do you want to go in the first place? Mr. Goforth and his assistant will only be hindered by you," Howard said.

Balthazar grunted. "I hope she listens to him. One thing we don't need is two nosy women dogging our footsteps."

"Oh, I don't know about that." Griffon stretched out his legs and crossed his ankles. "Might make the trip that much more interesting."

"I do believe that redheaded witch has cast a spell over you."

"Zar, I told you about the trance. She's psychic. I swear she is."

Balthazar shrugged. "And so? You can find Miss Cecille without Miss Lily's help. This might be dangerous business, Griffon. We shouldn't involve the weaker sex. They should remain here, safe and sound."

"She might be useful, Zar. Lily seems to have a connection with her cousin, even though she doesn't realize it. Also, I'm intrigued by why she's so afraid of her gifts. I'd like to find out—" He chopped off the rest, sensing someone's approach.

"Mr. Goforth?" Howard Meeker ducked under the arbor.

"Yes, Mr. Meeker." Griffon stood up from the chair.

"Zar and I are taking advantage of this lovely evening. Is something wrong?"

"My headstrong niece is trying our patience. She wishes to go with you to Van Buren."

"Yes, she mentioned that to me."

Howard tugged at his beard. "Would you strongly object? I know it's unorthodox, but she seems to think she might be able to help find Cecille. Orrie has agreed to chaperone her on the trip. I'll quite understand if you'd prefer to go alone with Balthazar. The important thing is that Cecille is found. If you think Lily and Orrie will hinder you in that, then I'll demand that this whole idea of theirs be dropped."

"Hinder, yes," Balthazar said, lurching to his feet. "Griffon, you must concentrate *solely* on locating Miss Cecille. Having others along will distract you."

"Then it's settled," Howard said, starting to turn back to the house. "I'll tell Lily that you've—"

"No, wait." Griffon faced Howard Meeker. "I have no objection to Miss Lily and Orrie coming along with us to Van Buren."

"Griffon, don't be a fool," Balthazar said. "You're not thinking with your head, but with your—"

"Your opinion is noted, Zar." Griffon glanced at his friend, and Balthazar backed off. "Now, as I was saying, Mr. Meeker, if Miss Lily wishes to travel with us, she's welcome. She won't be a burden."

"Well, if you're sure . . ." Howard ran a hand through his beard. "I admit I'm baffled. I thought you'd be adamant that she not be allowed to go along with you."

Griffon smiled. "If by accompanying us she'll receive some peace of mind, then I'm happy to let her come along."

Howard studied Griffon for a few moments, then nodded. "Of course, you're right. Lily has little patience. She's been chomping at the bit ever since I hired Mr. Vick. Perhaps this trip will calm her." He chuckled under his breath. "Making her stay here certainly won't make our lives any easier. When she doesn't get her way, Lily can be quite cross and unpleasant."

Griffon laughed with him, knowing this to be true, if not an understatement.

"However, I will require your word as a gentleman that Lily won't be compromised in any way. This trip is unorthodox, and I allow it only because Orrie swears she won't let Lily out of her sight. I must have your solemn promise that you'll not take advantage of my niece or of this situation, sir."

Griffon nodded. "A gentlemen's agreement. You have it."

Howard looked pleased. "I'll inform Lily of your graciousness." He pumped Griffon's hand. "Thank you, sir."

"You're welcome. It's nothing, really," Griffon assured him, and the man took his leave.

"A gentlemen's agreement? How magnanimous," Balthazar said sarcastically when Howard had returned to the house. "Since when have you ever taken such an agreement seriously? What has gotten into you, Griffon? Has this girl gone to your head like cheap wine?"

"Zar, I'm a man who lives by his instincts. Do you want me to go against them this time?"

"You mean, your *instincts* tell you to let Lily Meeker have her way with you?"

Griffon smiled, liking the sound of that, although he knew Balthazar had meant it to rile him. "I mean that there's more to Lily Meeker than meets the eye. If you'd seen what happened in that barn loft earlier today, you'd understand. She could find Cecille by herself, probably, if she believed in her own mind power."

Balthazar shrugged. "You're the boss. I am merely the lowly assistant to the great and glorious Griffon Goforth."

Griffon shook his head. "Zar, our carnival days are over. We are trying to be taken seriously these days, remember?"

The larger man fashioned a pitiful expression. "I miss the good old days. There was more drama back then . . . more excitement!"

"More money," Griffon added, drolly.

"Exactly!" Balthazar rubbed his hands together and his eyes glinted with greed.

"And most of that loot was ill-gotten," Griffon reminded him. "It's a wonder we weren't caught and thrown into prison."

"We were too good to be caught. Not feeling guilty, are you? Where's your Gypsy morality?"

Griffon smirked. "You mean that it's not wrong unless you're caught?"

"You remember," Balthazar said, glowingly.

"Of course. All of those conveniently self-saving rules were drummed into me from the time I drank my mother's milk." A thrill erupted in the pit of Griffon's stomach, but before he could identify its cause, Lily spoke up and did it for him.

"Excuse me."

Both men whirled in the direction of the soft voice. Lily moved beneath the arbor toward them.

"Yes, Lily?" Griffon greeted her. "I hear you and Orrie might be going with us to Van Buren after all."

"That's right." She sent him a sidelong glance. "I'm surprised you gave your permission."

Griffon motioned to one of the chairs. "Won't you join us?"

"Well, I . . ." She glanced at Balthazar. "I don't want to intrude."

"You aren't," Balthazar said. "I was just going inside. Thought I might read some before turning in." He offered his hand to her. "Good night, Miss Lily."

She slipped her hand in his, and Balthazar touched his lips to the back of it before leaving her and Griffon alone under the grape arbor. She sat in one of the chairs, stiff-backed, a wariness hovering around her that intensified when he took the chair across from her.

"Does Balthazar like me?"

"Of course."

She bobbed one shoulder, then fixed him with unflinching eyes. "Why did you tell Uncle Howard it was all right if Orrie and I went along to Van Buren with you and Balthazar?"

"Because I knew it was important to you."

Her smile mocked him. "And you live to make me happy. Is that what you'd have me believe?"

He laughed lightly, amused by her saucy tongue. "We're leaving quite early tomorrow. I'd like to catch the first ferry across the river."

"We can take the carriage."

"You and Orrie can. Zar and I will ride horseback."

"How long do you think we'll be gone?"

"It's difficult to say. A few days . . . perhaps as long as a week or two."

"I'm trying to figure out what to pack."

"Sensible clothes," he suggested. "We won't be making social calls. At least, I won't be."

Crickets began making music around them. Lily crossed her ankles and slanted her legs to one side. She arranged her skirts carefully, fluffing and smoothing the white eyelet material that draped in front to make a fetching apron. Her gaze bounced nervously to him, but Griffon waited, forcing her to speak her mind. He sensed her curiosity about him and wondered just how long she'd be able to hold out against it. He felt it grow, felt her struggle against the questions crowding her mind, then knew she'd reached her threshold.

"So, you can read my mind. Is that it?" She twisted her hands in her lap and frowned peevishly at him. "That's your gift?"

"Part of it, yes."

"And how long have you been able to poke around in people's heads?"

"Since as far back as I can remember." He tented his fingers in front of his mouth, camouflaging his pleased smile. Finally, he thought with relief. She's finally breaking out of her shell of bigotry.

"Were you made to feel that it was normal?"

"By whom?"

"By your parents—or whoever raised you."

"Not by them, no. My people believe that such powers are given to females. When it became obvious that I had certain abilities, I was cast out."

"When was that?"

"When I was just a lad. Nine or ten years old."

"Where were you sent?"

He shook his head, not understanding her question. "Sent?"

"You said your parents sent you away. To where? Other relatives?"

"Out into the streets. I was on my own."

Her hands stilled in her lap. "A boy of nine on the streets? How could your parents do that to you?"

"Like you, they were afraid of my abilities."

"I'm not afraid. I just find them hard to swallow."

"I sense fear in you."

"And you're never wrong? If you sense it, then it's there?"

He shrugged nonchalantly. "I'm wrong sometimes, but not about this."

She looked away from him. "It's because of what happened in the barn . . . that's why you're letting me go with you to Van Buren, isn't it?"

"One little kiss would hardly sway me to—"

"No, not that," she said, disdainfully. "The . . . episodes when I saw Cecille in my mind's eye." Shadows drifted across her face, hiding most of it from him. "You . . . you think I'm like you."

Her rejection of that was so blatant it slammed into him like a fist. "And you can't think of anything more despicable than that, can you? To be linked in any way to a Gypsy goat! Horror of horrors!" He faked a shudder.

"I was wrong to call you that," she said, then clamped her lips together in a mutinous expression. "As a matter of fact, I *didn't* call you that."

"Not out loud," he pointed out, grinning.

"That's another thing," she said, rising to her feet. When he stood, too, she tipped up her chin to stare at him. "I don't want you in my head. Stay out of it!"

"Watch out, Lily. You've just admitted that I *can* slip into your mind. Next, you'll say that you're curious about me, that you even find me attractive."

"You . . . that I find you attractive?" she sputtered. "Just because I allowed one indiscretion in the loft doesn't mean that I find you attractive."

"But you and your cousin Cecille have always had a soft spot for dark, dancing Gypsy men, isn't that right? Can't say that I'm much of a dancer, but I am dark-complected and I most certainly am Gypsy."

"Cecille is the enamored one. Not me."

He trailed a fingertip down her cheek and was pleased when she didn't flinch or pull away. "Not even a little bit?" he whispered. "Is that my heart or yours beating so loudly?"

"Yours." Her eyes sparkled in the semidarkness of the grape arbor. A smile colored her voice. "Mine's fine, thank you."

"Wonder what I'd find among your thoughts right now?"

"Please, don't pry."

"Then tell me. Tell me true, Lily." He leaned closer still, drawn by her beauty, her spirit. "Wouldn't you like a good-night kiss from me?"

Expectation sizzled between them. Lily's lustrous eyes

grew heavy-lidded as Griffon cradled her chin in his hand, tipping her parted lips up to him.

"Lily? What's going on here?"

They broke apart guiltily to stare at the intruder. David Jefferson planted himself at Lily's side and glared at Griffon as if he were a monster and David had come to slay him.

"David, thank heavens it's you. I thought it was Uncle Howard, and if he'd seen us like this—" She placed a hand to her forehead. "Well, he'd never let me out of Fort Smith." She drew in a calming breath and released it slowly. "What are you doing here?"

David fixed cold eyes on the other man. "Goforth, what was going on here just now? Were you trying to take advantage of this young lady?"

"No, she was trying to take advantage of me," Griffon rejoined, having no use for theatrics after a lifetime of it.

"Stop it, please." Lily stood between them and rested a hand on each man's chest. "Spare me the absurdity of a duel." She gave her attention to David. "Whatever was going on is none of your business."

"Lily!" David's mouth dropped open. "I have a mind to consult with your uncle over this matter."

"Haven't you damaged me enough?" she bit out, and David's self-righteous manner dissolved under the heat of her temper. She turned to Griffon. "Would you mind? I'd like to talk with David privately."

Griffon found that he did mind, but he acquiesced and moved from beneath the arbor.

Lily waited for the shadows to swallow Griffon before she whirled to face David again.

"Lily, what I just saw . . . you weren't going to let that man kiss you, were you?"

She owed him no explanation and refused to offer one. David had deceived her. He'd withheld information from her and her family. *Crucial* information.

"I won't discuss that with you."

"Please, Lily, don't be a fool. Look what happened to Cecille when she got involved with a Gypsy."

"From what you've told me, your cousin isn't a Gypsy."

"That's beside the point. Goforth isn't the kind of man a lady should be consorting with. I spoke to Mr. Vick about him and was told that Goforth purports to have magical powers. He's a charlatan, Lily, and you shouldn't—"

"David, have you anything else to tell me about Cecille?" Lily cut in, resenting his preachy attitude. "Did you remember any other secrets you two kept?"

"Lily, it wasn't like that," David said on a long sigh. "You know how devious Cecille can be."

" 'Devious' is a word I associate more with you than with Cecille."

"Lily, don't let this come between us." He reached out to her and Lily retreated. "I never meant to hurt you."

"Then why did you lie?"

"I was protecting Mother. We did what we could without being roped into this thing. We sent Mr. Vick, didn't we? He checked everything out for us."

"Mr. Vick was supposed to be working for Uncle Howard," Lily whispered fiercely, trying to keep her voice down. "My family hired him, not yours. If you'd told us about your connection with those people, we would have understood. You didn't have to lie to us, David."

"I didn't want to. I didn't want to keep secrets with Cecille, either."

"Then why did you?"

"Cecille was serious about telling everyone that we were related to those hill people." He shoved his hands into his pockets and kicked at a tuft of dry grass with the toe of his boot. "You know how persuasive she can be."

"Yes, especially with men who are in love with her. Men like you."

"No, Lily." David shook his head vehemently. "It's not like that."

"Please, David. Be honest. The only reason you escorted me was because you couldn't be with Cecille. You've been hoping that Cecille would change her mind and want to see you again. I was a substitute." She looked squarely in David's eyes to prove to him she wasn't destroyed, that she'd survive. "You're a nice man, David, but you've done me and my family a disservice."

"Won't you accept my apology?"

"It seems insignificant at this juncture." She shrugged, but his crestfallen expression stirred her compassion. "Very well. I accept your apology, but by doing so I do not condone your actions."

He released his breath and offered a smile of relief. "Thank you, Lily. I *do* care for you, and I want to find Cecille as much as you."

She sent him a dubious glance. "I'm going to Van Buren tomorrow with Griffon Goforth. I have a feeling she's there, no matter what your friend Mr. Vick says."

"You're going to Van Buren with that . . . that Gypsy soothsayer? Surely your uncle won't allow this."

"Orrie's going as my chaperone."

"This could start tongues wagging."

"Oh, I don't care what gossips say. Cecille is missing and I'll do whatever I can to find her."

"You'll be wasting your time in Van Buren."

"Why?"

"Those people know nothing. Anson thought he'd been stood up by Cecille that day. He had no idea she was missing."

"Anson. That's his name.?"

"Yes, Anson Jeffers."

"All you have is his word. That's not enough, David. I'm certain Cecille and he met and went out to the Sutton place. They argued there. I think he took her with him by force."

"Why do you think that?"

She shrugged, unwilling to explain the strange mental

pictures she'd received. "Griffon and I went out there to-day." From David's expression, Lily knew he wanted something definitive, but she was unwilling to give it. "Let me ask *you* something for a change. Do you think Cecille was in love with your cousin, or was it just another of her flings?"

"She was serious about him, but she admitted that she couldn't imagine bringing him home to meet her folks. She knew it was an impossible union."

"What about him? Did he love her?"

David shook his head. "I didn't have anything to do with him."

"Nevertheless, you took Anson's word that he didn't know where to find Cecille."

"Anson wouldn't be stupid enough to kidnap her. He knows it would bring all kinds of trouble on his head."

"If he were caught," Lily noted.

"I'll be worried about you while you're gone. That Goforth fellow isn't a gentleman. I hope Orrie keeps a close eye on you." David took her hands in his. "I wish you wouldn't go. It's foolhardy."

"I'll be fine." Lily pulled her hands from his. "You must go. It's getting late."

David nodded. "I am sorry for all this, Lily. I do care a great deal for you."

"Good-bye, David." She watched him leave through the back gate. As far as she was concerned, David Jefferson had shown his allegiance and she wasn't interested in continuing any kind of relationship with him. He and his mother were on the run from themselves and they'd step over anyone who got in their way.

Leaves rustled nearby and Lily glanced in that direction. Griffon stepped into the light cast by a bright moon.

"Have you been eavesdropping?" she demanded, propping her hands on her hips.

"Me?" He fashioned a shocked expression. "No, not me."

Lily whirled in a circle. "I'm surrounded by liars."

"I remained at a respectful distance," he said, laughing a little. "I couldn't hear what was said. Did David shed any light on his cousin's shenanigans with Cecille?"

"Not really." She looked at the house and spotted Balthazar spying on them through one of the windows. "Where did you meet Balthazar?"

"In the circus. He was a carnival barker and I worked a game where I guessed names and ages. Zar took me under his wing. He watched out for me."

"How did you meet Thurman Unger?"

"He heard about my carnival act while he was on sabbatical in England. He came to see me and was convinced I was a true psychic. He sent me to the best schools and helped me get into Oxford. He's like a father to me."

"And Zar?"

"He's my best friend."

"He's watching us," she said, nodding toward the house. "He's probably hoping you'll talk me out of going to Van Buren."

"He thinks you'll be a distraction."

She started to laugh, then a thought struck her. "You didn't tell him about kissing me out at the Sutton place, did you?"

"I didn't have to. Zar knows me inside and out."

"I wish you'd forget about that incident."

"You're the one who keeps bringing it up."

She opened her mouth to deny this, but couldn't. Clamping her lips together, she weathered the incongruity.

"I can understand how it would haunt you," he said, his voice dipping to a purr. "The memory of it certainly haunts me."

"I won't speak of it again. It's forgotten."

"Can you forget it so easily? I find myself wanting an encore. If David hadn't interrupted us, we might have—"

"Excuse me. I must go inside now to pack. Good night."

"Run, Lily," he taunted, laughing as she scurried to the house. "You can run, but you can't hide. Not from me, and certainly not from yourself."

Chapter 6

D uring the journey to Van Buren Lily often worried that she'd made a mistake in coming along. Her first qualms occurred when a wave of fascination washed over her when Griffon came downstairs that morning, dashingly attractive in black, his mood matching it. Gone were the civilized suit and tie. She decided the closely tailored trousers and loose, collarless shirt were more his style. The thin gold earring didn't seem out of place. The knee-high boots made his legs seem all the longer. She fancied him as a Gypsy king. That's when she wondered if she wasn't being foolish to embark on a journey with him.

He'd seemed driven, dogged by a need to get on the road. Instead of being miffed by his curt orders, Lily found his mood attractive. It added to his overall mystery. Again, she worried. More and more, she was acutely aware of the mighty pull she felt around him. She was a serene sea except when he was there, and then he acted like a full moon upon her calm surface, tugging at her, sending her into a frenzy of crashing ideals and raging emotions. Around him, she didn't know what to expect of herself. While she was skeptical about his unearthly powers, she had no doubt of his power over her.

On the first leg of the trip to the Arkansas River, Orrie kept up a breathless monologue. It was her first time across the river to Van Buren, and from the way she chattered like a magpie, one would think they were about to cross the Nile and explore ancient Egyptian tombs instead of the muddy Arkansas en route to a sleepy town. The ferry ride almost sent Orrie onto a swoon, and Lily had to laugh at the woman's childlike enthusiasm. Even Griffon had chuckled at Orrie's squeals of delight as the ferry bobbed across the river like a giant cork.

Then they'd eaten the meal Orrie had packed, whiling away more than an hour on the riverbank, before hitting the trail again. By late afternoon Lily spotted clusters of farmhouses and knew Van Buren must be near. Farmers worked in their fields. Jersey cows mooed to them as they passed by. Roosters crowed in the distance. Somewhere a school bell rang, signaling the end of the day and sending children home. Lily watched a woman hang clothes on a line: a man's shirts and work pants, a child's nappies and baby blankets, aprons and day dresses. She knew a pang of longing for a home of her own, children of her own, a man of her own. Her gaze swept to Griffon ahead of the buggy. She realized she was looking at him as a possible husband and jerked her gaze away, startled by such a wild fantasy.

Lily took the reins from Orrie, giving the woman a rest and giving herself something more to do than dwell on ridiculous dreams. The buggy jostled over an uneven but well-traveled road. Ahead, Griffon and Balthazar rode side by side.

"Look at the way Mr. Griffon sits that horse," Orrie whispered. "Don't he look regal?"

Lily examined Griffon's straight back, loose wrists and hands, relaxed shoulders. The black stallion he rode had started off prancing but had settled into a more sedate stride as the day wore on. Balthazar's chestnut plodded, its anvil-shaped head moving up and down with each step. Lily glanced at Orrie, noting that the woman was waiting for an answer.

"He rides well," she conceded.

"How come you've set your mind against him?"

"When have I said that?"

"You don't have to say it. The thing is, I think you *try* to hate him, but it's a real chore for you."

"I'm not trying to hate him," Lily objected. "I hope he's what he says he is and that this trip won't be wasted. Just think, Orrie, we could have Cecille seated between us on the journey back. Wouldn't that be wonderful?"

"Sure would." Orrie clasped her hands in her lap and a wistful expression bathed her face. "That would be a prayer answered, it would. I do believe if anybody can find Cecille, it'll be Mr. Griffon. That man is no fake, Lily. That man has been blessed with a seeing eye." She pulled down the lower part of her left eye to illustrate a phenomenon that Lily found hard to embrace. Sounded like more of Balthazar's carnival talk to Lily. "Zar says he's had it since birth," Orrie explained. "Says that when Mr. Griffon was just a sprout he and his grandmama could talk to each other by just using their minds. His grandmama was a Gypsy queen and she had the seeing eye, too. That's probably where he got it. Inherited it through her blood."

"You'd be wise to believe only half of what Zar tells you. He strikes me as a man who stretches the truth."

"Oh, he's a bit of a braggart, it's true, but he believes in Mr. Griffon's powers. He says he's seen him find everything from lost letters to lost children. In England he was famous. Headed up that psychic society that's spread over here now."

"What are they supposed to do at that society?"

"From what Zar told me, they study all kinds of mysterious goings on. Ghosts, haunted houses, psychics, all those spooky things."

"Right down your alley, Orrie."

"Not only me. You listened to your share of scary stories. You used to beg me to tell you the headless horseman story."

Lily experienced a lovely chill. "Oh, yes. My favorite,'' she admitted with a giggle. "How I love to be frightened.''

"He frightens you some, don't he?'' Orrie nodded at Griffon.

"No,'' Lily said, attempting a laugh. "Why would he?''

" 'Cause he has the power and that scares you.''

"You're mistaken, Orrie. I'm leery of him, but not frightened.''

"If you'd get to know him, you might find that you two are a lot alike.''

"We're nothing alike.'' She regretted the sharpness in her voice and laid a hand on Orrie's arm to show it. "That's an odd thing for you to say. What on earth could I have in common with a Gypsy?''

"You both live by your senses,'' Orrie said, her voice gentle, her gaze lingering on Lily's face. "Now don't go getting upset, but you know as well as me that you got good instincts. Didn't you tell me just the other day that you was sure Cecille was still alive because you felt it deep in your bones?''

"Orrie, dear, everyone has such feelings about loved ones. It's a hunch, not a mystic power.''

"Call it what you will, but yours can be counted on. I've never known you to be wrong about whether a baby's going to be a boy or a girl. You touch the mother-to-be's stomach and you can tell, just like that. And you're always right. Always. That's not guessing. You know somehow.''

Lily faced front, letting the statements hang between them. She couldn't deny that what Orrie had said was true. But it wasn't sensory perception. Just luck.

"You and Zar seem to have had quite a few heart-to-heart conversations.''

Orrie blushed and grinned broadly. "I admit he makes my body twitch.''

Lily glanced at her, shocked. "Why, Orrie. What a thing to say!''

"Oh, you're growed. You know about such things. No

need in me treating you like I used to when you was a child. You surely can see that me and Zar are sweet on each other.''

''I . . . I knew you were friendly, but I wouldn't presume—''

''Well, go ahead and presume.'' Orrie pushed some escaped corkscrew curls back underneath her bonnet. ''I don't care who knows that I like Balthazar. And he likes me.'' She grinned suddenly. ''Feels good to have a man sparking with me again. It's been a while.''

Lily laughed to hide her embarrassment. ''We've never talked like this before.''

''It's time we did.''

''Yes, I suppose so. We're both grown women.''

''That's right.''

''To be honest, I never thought about you having gentlemen callers,'' Lily admitted.

''Haven't had too many. I was married once.''

''Married? You?''

Orrie nodded. ''Married when I was but sixteen. He was twenty. Got kicked in the head by a mule two years later and that killed him. That's when I started hiring out as a maid, then later as a nanny. A few years later I got on with the Meekers and I stuck with them. Guess I just fell in love with you and Cecille. You was the babies I never had. I almost married again a few years back, but he was too nice.''

''Too nice?'' Lily repeated. ''That's why you didn't want him as a husband?''

''I want a man I can't read like some book. Elmer—that was his name—was as sure as summer drought and just about as much fun.'' Her eyes moved to find the two men ahead. ''But Balthazar . . . now he's one big, old surprise.''

Lily smiled. ''He certainly is that.''

Orrie blinked as if coming out of a dream. She straightened and looked around at some children walking along the side of the road. A wagon, heavy with hay, rumbled past. Ahead of them another wagon, this one full of dusty men and tired-looking women, rocked from side to side.

"Traffic's picked up," Orrie said. "Is that Van Buren ahead?"

Lily nodded. "That's it. Don't expect too much, Orrie. It's smaller than Fort Smith."

"Oh, I do so love to travel. Isn't this excitin'? New places, new faces. Makes the blood run freer."

Lily laughed lightly, caught up in Orrie's delirium. Griffon turned in the saddle and pointed ahead. Orrie waved at him, almost jumping up and down.

"We'll go straight to the hotel," he called, and Lily nodded to let him know she'd heard.

Orrie pointed out every building they passed—bank, mercantile store, post office, saloon, an impressive train depot. The hotel was a two-story affair on a corner of the busiest intersection. Balthazar tied off the horses while Griffon helped both Lily and Orrie to alight from the buggy. Twilight gathered quickly, and a few windows showed yellow lantern light already.

Lily noticed that the wagonload of people had stopped in front of the bank. Several men jumped over the sides and went inside the institution. Payday, Lily thought, and felt sorry for them for having to work so hard for so little. She'd never had to labor in the fields, had never picked cotton or vegetables or fruit. If nothing else, her father had given her a life of leisure.

The hotel clerk had Griffon sign the registry and then he and his son carried the luggage upstairs. Lily and Orrie were shown to one room, Griffon and Balthazar to another right across the hall.

"Is there a place to eat around here?" Griffon asked the clerk.

"Let's see . . . it's getting late. Our dining room has closed down for the night." The clerk screwed up his mouth in consideration, then nodded. "The Lucky Spoon is still open for business, but you'd better hurry. If Gladys don't have any customers, she'll close 'er up by seven. It's across the street, halfway down the next block.''

"Thanks." Griffon pressed a coin in the man's palm. "What's the sheriff's name here?"

The man regarded him for a few moments. "Macinaw. Delbert Macinaw, but we all call him Sheriff Mac. Got yourself a problem?"

"We're looking for someone."

"Do you happen to know the Jeffers family?" Lily asked, drawing a scowl from Griffon for barging in. "I believe they live outside of town."

"Sure, I heard of them. I think they live out in Devil's Den country."

"Devil's Den?" Orrie repeated, eyes wide. "What's out there?"

"Just woods," the clerk said, tugging at his bow tie. "Hills and trees. Lots of them hill people live out yonder. Them Jeffers come into town every so often for supplies. They got themselves a family band and they travel some. Play at barn dances and the like." He made a scoffing sound. "I heard 'em once and they sure weren't nothing special. Just made a bunch of noise with spoons and washboards. Sure weren't pretty soundin'."

"Is Devil's Den far from here?" Griffon asked.

"Not too. Take you a day's ride to get there." He pocketed the coin. "Fresh linens on the beds and that room at the end of this hallway is the water closet. Bath'll cost you ten cents extry, but you can fill your washbasins for free. Chamber pots under the beds, and we've got an outhouse 'round back." He grinned at the women, tugged at his bow tie, and turned to leave. "If'n you need anything and I'm not around, ring the bell on the desk."

"Why don't you ladies freshen up and meet us downstairs in, say, ten minutes? Will that give you enough time?" Griffon asked.

"Long enough for me. I'm mainly interested in getting some food in me," Orrie said.

"Ten minutes," Lily agreed, then stepped into the room ahead of Orrie. It had one bed covered with a pink chenille spread. Lily tested the springs while Orrie opened the luggage and removed their toiletries, placing them on top of the bureau. "It's been a long time since I slept in a bed with you."

Orrie glanced at her in the mirror and smiled. "You was about ten, I do believe. You and Cecille both slept in my room during a storm."

"After you told us a horrendous story about ghostly riders who appeared during thunderstorms," Lily recalled. "We couldn't possibly sleep in our room that night. Not after that story." She removed her bonnet and smoothed a hand over her hair, checking the loose chignon. "Devil's Den. Ominous sounding, isn't it?"

"Sure is. Like something out of my stories."

Lily sprayed some toilet water across her throat, then checked her appearance in the mirror.

"Isn't this excitin'?" Orrie asked.

"What?"

"Going to eat in a restaurant with gentlemen," Orrie said. "It's been a month of Sundays since I've eaten any food but mine."

Lily felt a stab of pity for the faithful maid. Orrie draped a shawl around her shoulders and pinched her cheeks to put color in them.

"You're having a grand old time, aren't you?" Lily smiled, touched by Orrie's exuberance.

"Of course! I'm itching to look this place over. You ready?"

"I suppose I'm presentable enough for a place called the Lucky Spoon."

"Why, honey, you could take tea with the queen." Orrie linked arms with her and they left the room to join the men downstairs.

* * *

Sheriff Mac looked like a bullfrog to Lily. Slumped behind his desk, he studied her and her companions with bulging eyes.

"So, y'all are *all* planning on parading out to the Jeffers place?" he asked, a smile displaying a row of brown teeth.

"Yes," Lily said.

"No," Griffon said, cutting his eyes in her direction in a blatant warning. "We're going out there." He indicated Balthazar with a nod. "The ladies are here because Miss Lily felt the trip would settle her nerves. Naturally, she's been distraught over her cousin's disappearance."

"Naturally," Sheriff Mac said, clearly mocking the way Griffon talked. "What makes you think her cousin's out at the Jeffers place?"

"Just a feeling," Lily spoke up, gaining another sharp glance from Griffon.

"We have reason to believe that she and one of the—"

"Their name came up," Lily interrupted Griffon. "The Jefferses were in Fort Smith and Cecille was seen with them."

"Lily, why don't you and Orrie take yourselves off and do some shopping?" Griffon looked from her to the open doorway. "Leave this business to me and Zar."

"I want to talk to you—privately." Lily stood up and marched outside, then waited for Griffon to follow more slowly.

"What is it?" he almost hissed at her.

"I don't think it's necessary to air dirty laundry in front of that man," she whispered, glancing inside to the sheriff.

"I'll tell him what I think he should know. This is his town, his territory. I might need his help before this is over."

"But if you tell him about Cecille seeing a married man, he'll think she's fast company."

"What do you care?"

"I care because she's my cousin." Lily tried to check her temper. "I don't want her reputation damaged any further."

"Listen to me, Lily." He grasped her forearm and leaned close so that she could take note of the anger flaring in his blue eyes. "I've been hired to investigate this, not you." His fingers bit into her arm when she started to interrupt. "And I know your family hired me, so save that particular speech. I allowed you to tag along—"

"Allowed?"

"Correct. All I had to do was to tell your uncle I didn't want you underfoot and you'd be pacing the floors in Fort Smith right now. You know it. I know it."

"Take your hand off me," she said, trying to escape his hot, hard hold.

"Not until I'm finished. Now shut up and listen."

"You can't speak to me in that manner!"

He stepped in front of her, blocking her view of the sheriff's office and the sheriff's view of her. "I'm in charge. I'll fill you in when I find out anything. Until then, I want you to let me do my job. You and Orrie go shopping or go back to the hotel. I shouldn't have let you come with me this morning, but I thought you'd keep quiet. I should have known better."

"I won't be excused like a child."

"And I won't be supervised like one. Either you make yourself scarce for a while or I'll head back to Fort Smith today and tell your uncle I can't work with you hovering over me like a buzzard. Now what will it be?"

"A—a buzzard!" She narrowed her eyes. "You'll pay for that."

He released her by pushing her away from him. "I'm waiting for your decision."

Lily ran the flat of one hand along the side of her hair, then fussed with her bonnet. She scowled briefly at him before stepping sideways to motion for Orrie.

"Let's leave this business to the men, Orrie."

"Yes'm." Orrie bounded from the chair and joined her.

"I want a full report," Lily said before striding off, Orrie in tow.

Griffon went back inside and took his chair. "Sorry for the interruption, Sheriff. Miss Meeker is rather headstrong." He glanced at Balthazar. "Where were we?"

"You were telling the sheriff why you think the Jefferses might be involved with the disappearance of Miss Cecille."

"Ah, yes. We gather she's been trysting with one of them."

Sheriff Mac pulled his bushy brows together. "Trying? Trying what?"

"Trysting," Griffon repeated, sounding the word more clearly. "Romancing, in other words."

"Oh, I follow you." Sheriff Mac chuckled, leaned forward, and spat brown juice into a rusty can. He seemed more at ease with the women gone. "Which one was she giving it to?"

"The eldest son. He's married, I'm told."

"That'll be Anson. Yup, he's a good-looking devil. Most of them Jeffers boys are, though. But they ain't no-'count. Lazy layabouts like their old man. They got some kind of family band and they bring in some money that way. Otherwise, they do a lot of nothing."

"How many of them are there?"

"There's old Butch and his wife, Eva. Six or seven sons. Got some grandbabies out there, too, I think. And a few in-laws. Anson, Ham, and Jasper still live with Butch and Eva, I do believe. The other boys married and moved to their own shacks." He spat again. "You got any experience with hill people, son?"

"Very little," Griffon admitted, which he thought was just what the sheriff wanted to hear.

Sheriff Mac lounged back in his chair and hooked his thumbs behind his suspenders. "Well, let me educate you. They're tight-knit. Don't cotton to anybody snooping

around their places. Some of them marry cousins and
throw off their share of idiots. They got their own law and
order, and they'll shoot atcha if you come ridin' up on
their property without an invite. Gotta call out to them,
let them know you're coming and that you ain't looking
for trouble. Otherwise they'll wing ya. I sent one of my
deputies out to the hills after one of them once—not a
Jeffers, a neighbor of theirs—and he come back with three
bullet holes in his hat. Scared the peewaddlin' outta him.''
He laughed, and tobacco juice oozed down the corners of
his mouth. He wiped it off with the back of his hand and
spat again into the can.

"Sounds a little like Gypsies," Balthazar noted.

"You Gypsies?" the sheriff asked, looking from one to
the other.

"I am," Griffon said, then pressed on, not giving the
sheriff a chance to question him about his background.
He'd learned that most people thought of Gypsies as problems, and he wanted to keep his dealings with Sheriff Mac
friendly. "Could you give me directions to their place? I'd
like to talk with them."

"Sure. I'd go with you, but my deputy quit last week
and I'm shorthanded. Somebody's got to stick close to the
office in case there's trouble in town."

"I understand. I don't suppose you've seen any visiting
women around in the past couple of months. Cecille
Meeker is a young woman of marrying age. She has blond
hair and blue eyes. Quite fetching, I'm told."

"You don't know know her personally?"

"No, I've never had the pleasure of meeting her. I've
been retained by her family to find her."

"And that feisty miss, she's this gal's cousin?"

"That's right." Griffon smiled. "Feisty" was a good
word for Lily, he thought. Feisty, and at times exasperat-
ing.

The sheriff sat forward, resting beefy arms on the desk

top. "Hasn't been anybody fitting that description around here that I know of."

"And no reported deaths since the first of the year?"

"No woman . . . well, I take that back. There was one death I heard of. Found out about it just last week from the fella who runs the dry goods store. Said a couple of them Jeffers boys came in to buy some two-penny nails. They had to build themselves a coffin."

Griffon felt Balthazar stiffen beside him, but he kept his attention riveted to the sheriff. "A coffin for whom?"

The sheriff smirked. "You don't talk like a Gypsy. Where you from?"

"I used to live overseas. The coffin, Sheriff Mac?"

"I'm told it was for Anson's wife. She died. Sudden. The story is she had a stillbirth and it done her in."

Griffon looked at Balthazar and knew he was wondering the same thing. Did that coffin hold Anson's dead wife or the body of Cecille Meeker?

Chapter 7

❝ C oming with them was a mistake,❞ Lily fumed, striding along the main street's boardwalk and making Orrie trot to keep up with her. ❝I should have known he'd try to shove me in a corner and make me be his idea of a good little girl. Oooo, men! Why can't they see that women have minds and we don't need them to think for us? When will they learn that we have intelligence beyond—❞

❝Lord have mercy!❞ Orrie said, gasping for breath. She snagged Lily's sleeve and made her shorten her stride. ❝What's so terrible about being sent off to do some window shopping? I'd rather poke around that milliner's shop up ahead than sit in that smelly sheriff's office.❞

❝Griffon led me to believe that he was different, that he was a champion of equality for the sexes. That two-faced vagabond. He no more would support women's suffrage than he would ride a horse backwards down Main Street.❞

❝Lily, you should watch that talk. You've driven away beaus by spouting that nonsense. Men don't like ladies who want to stand shoulder to shoulder with them. You got to be more sweet-acting. You got to keep those wild opinions to yourself. No harm in thinking them, mind you, but you won't catch a husband by telling him you're not about to love, honor, and obey.❞

Stopping outside the feed store, Lily faced Orrie. ❝Don't you think I've tried to be more like Cecille?❞

"Cecille?" Orrie's brows met above her nose. "And who's talkin' about Cecille, I ask you?"

"Oh, I know the family thinks she's perfect, and heaven knows she's always had more gentlemen callers than me, but it goes against my grain to demur when I think someone is talking nonsense." Lily straightened Orrie's bonnet, which had slipped askew. "Cecille has a knack for getting what she wants by flattering and cajoling. I just can't do it, Orrie."

"You could if you put your mind to it. Sometimes it's the only way to get a man to listen to you. It's all men understand from a woman."

"Really?" Lily considered this, then shook her head. "I'd feel like a cheat. I'd certainly appear counterfeit. I've tried to follow Cecille's example, but I . . ." Her voice trailed as her spirits drooped. For a moment, she'd thought about enticing Griffon to cooperate, but she'd never be able to pull that off. He'd laugh in her face, and he'd done that enough already!

"Honeypot, I never said Cecille was perfect or that you was any less than her." Orrie placed her hands on Lily's shoulders. "How in the world did you ever come up with such a thought?"

"Well, Father certainly has made no bones about it. He's told me often enough that I should be more like Cecille. When I announced that I wanted to attend college, he almost swallowed his tongue! He said I'd do well to school myself by studying how Cecille attracted promising young men. Father says I try too hard to be different." Concern tainted her mouth with a frown. "But I don't try, Orrie. If anything, I've tried all my life to be like everyone else. Like Cecille."

"Listen to me, missy. Your papa was wrong to ask you to be something you're not. Besides, there's nothing wrong with being different."

"Oh, yes there is." Lily leaned back against a stack of feed sacks. "Look at Griffon. Everyone he meets stares

at him, and I'm sure many shun him. Being different is
his curse.''

''Some would say it's his blessing.''

''No, not when—'' Lily was interrupted by the taunting
calls of some boys who had just come out of the feed
store.

Three adolescents circled a chubby, round-faced boy,
poking at him, shoving their laughing faces close to his.
The boy looked stricken. He reminded Lily of a cornered
rabbit.

''Hey, idiot boy,'' one bully jeered. ''Jasper the dummy.
His sister's his mummy. Jasper the dummy. His sister's his
mummy.''

The others took up the hateful singsong and pranced
around the frightened boy like imps. The victim's mouth
quivered as he tried not to cry. Unable to stand another
moment of their cruel recitation, Lily rushed forward. She
grabbed one of the boys by the shoulders and flung him
aside, then rocked her hip against another, sending him
off balance. The third she thumped in the back of the
head, hoping to make his ears ring.

''Stop this! You boys get away! Don't you have anything
better to do than this? Shame on you!''

''He's an idiot,'' the leader of the pack said, giving the
chubby boy a shove.

''And you're a numbskull,'' Lily shot back, lifting her
parasol in a threatening gesture. ''Get away before I cane
you.''

''Me, too,'' Orrie said, waving her own parasol. ''Y'all
get.''

''Are you deaf? Scat!'' Lily charged at them. They scattered and raced down the street like turpentined cats.
''Heathens! Your folks ought to wallop you good!''

Lily turned back to the victimized boy. He was grinning
ear-to-ear. ''Are you all right?'' Lily asked, and he nodded enthusiastically.

''Looks like you got yourself a friend,'' Orrie said.

He wasn't as young as Lily had thought. Close up, she saw that he was in his late teens, probably older than his attackers. He was her height and shaped like a barrel. He looked stout and could have easily beaten off those boys if he'd tried. His dark brown hair was already thinning. His brown eyes were childlike, trusting.

"Jasper." He jabbed a thumb at his chest, then offered his hand shyly. "Jasper Jeffers."

"So happy to meet you. I'm Lily Meeker and this is Orrie—" She gasped, clasping his hand more tightly. "Did you say 'Jeffers'?"

"Yas'm."

Lily glanced at Orrie's shocked expression, then back to Jasper. "Do you live out at Devil's Den?"

"Jasper lives in da woods with his fam'ly. You shore are purty."

"Thank you. Is Anson your brother?"

He nodded. "One of 'em. Jasper gots lots." He looked past her and pointed. "Him Jasper's brudder, too. Him's named Ham."

Lily turned to confront a satanic face; long, narrow, and pointy-chinned. Ham was older, taller, with no innocence in the slanty-eyed gaze that swept Lily and missed nothing.

"Ham Jeffers?" Lily started to hold out her hand, but decided she didn't want to touch him. "I'm Lily Meeker from Fort Smith." She watched carefully and was rewarded by the tightening of the skin around his mouth. The name and the town obviously meant something to him. "I'm here looking for my cousin, Cecille. You know of her, don't you?"

Ham was carrying a sack of feed over one shoulder. He motioned for Jasper. "Here, take this to the wagon."

"Cecille Meeker. You know her," Lily repeated as Jasper took the feed from his brother.

"Yup. I heard the name."

"And do you know where she is?"

"Nope. Told the lawman we didn't."

"What lawman?"

"Some man from Fort Smith come out to our place asking about that gal you mentioned. We don't know her and we shore don't know her whereabouts. Told him that."

Lily's hopes sank. "Your brother Anson knows her. I'd like to come to your home and talk to him."

"Anson ain't around no more." He started past her toward the flatbed wagon hitched to a couple of swaybacked mules. "Be wastin' yore time an' ours."

"Wait!" Lily swept in front of him, heading him off. "Where's Anson?"

"He took off. Don't know where he is. Maybe Texas. Maybe not." He ran a hand down his long face, the lower part darkened by two days' growth of beard. "You got yourself a mister?"

Lily ignored that question. "Could you give me directions to your family's home? I'd still like to talk to your father and mother."

"You jist stay away." He would have walked over her if she hadn't jumped out of his way. "Git up in that wagon, boy," he ordered Jasper.

Jasper scrambled onto the flatbed, wedging himself between two feed sacks and tins of molasses and lard. He waved like a baby, stretching his fingers out straight and then curling them into his palm.

"Bye-bye, purty gal," he called. "Bye-bye."

Lily waved back, wishing she could produce a horse and follow that wagon. "He knows something," she said to Orrie.

"That boy is too simpleminded to know squat."

"Not Jasper. The other one. Ham. He knows something. I saw it in his face when I said Cecille's name."

"Wonder if Cecille went off with Anson?"

"I doubt it, Orrie."

"Too bad Anson has flown the coop."

Lily shook her head. "Something's not right. Didn't you notice Jasper when Ham said that?"

"No, I wasn't looking at him."

"Jasper looked confused."

"Honey, that boy looks confused all the time. Like I said, he's light in the brainpan."

"Look, there are Griffon and Zar." Lily was already moving toward them. "Come on, Orrie." She met the men halfway down the block. "Griffon, see that wagon? The one with the boy sitting in the back of it beside the feed sacks?"

"Yes," he said, turning and locating the vehicle.

"That's two of the Jeffers boys and they're heading back to their home. Grab a horse and follow them." She pushed him. "Go on. Hurry before they're out of sight."

He swatted aside her hands. "Quit that. I'm not your personal servant. And I'm certainly not going to steal a horse and land in the Van Buren jail."

"If you won't follow them, I will!" She moved swiftly to the nearest hitching post and started to untie the reins of a saddled bay.

"Go right ahead and make a fool of yourself, Lily. You seem adept at it." He folded his arms and watched her hike her skirts and fit one shoe into the stirrup.

Lily hesitated, struck by the expression of dismay on Orrie's face. Sighing, she removed her foot from the stirrup and tried to ignore Griffon's smirk. "Are you or are you not going to question those Jefferses?"

"I am, but not this minute."

"How do you expect to find them? They live in the middle of nowhere."

"The sheriff gave us directions," Balthazar said. "Explicit directions."

"Oh." Lily smoothed wrinkles from her skirt. "Why didn't you say that in the first place? When are we leaving?"

"Zar and I will ride out in the morning."

"Why wait?"

"Because it's a day's ride."

Lily held up a quieting hand. "Don't tell me that you expect Orrie and me to remain here while you and Zar go to Devil's Den."

"That's the plan," Griffon confirmed. "And arguing would be a waste of breath."

"It's my breath." She took a deep one. "I'm tired of being dismissed by you. I'm a grown woman and I intend to do exactly as I wish, and I wish to go with you tomorrow. So that's that." She wiped her hands together three times in a gesture of finality, then she tipped up her chin and glanced at Orrie. "Come along, Orrie."

She would have swept past the two men in a swish of petticoats if not for Griffon's firm hand at her elbow. He spun her around and into him, making her gasp at being handled in such a way on a public street. His dark face moved within inches of hers.

"I'm not a man to make idle threats, Lily, so pay heed."

"Let go of me. Are you mad? We're on a city street!"

"You mistake me for a gentleman. While I might on occasion dress like one, speak like one, and appear to behave like one, I'm not one. I'm a maverick, a lone wolf, and I live by my own standards, which include not allowing anyone to speak to me as if I'm an indentured slave." His teeth flashed white in contrast to his dark skin. He released her and pointed a finger in warning. "Leave this business to me. When I need your help, I'll ask for it."

"Mr. Griffon?" Orrie spoke up, her tone properly deferential. "That oldest boy said Anson wasn't around anymore."

"Where has he gone?"

"He said he didn't know for sure."

"But he was lying," Lily said.

Griffon slanted her a quizzical glance. "You sensed this?"

She started to rephrase his question, then shrugged.

"Jasper—the youngest one—was surprised when Ham said Anson had gone."

"The sheriff said Anson's wife died recently."

"She's dead?" Lily bit her lower lip. "Then he'd be free to go off with Cecille, wouldn't he?"

"Yes, or—" Griffon moved aside to let several men pass, their arms full of feed and flour sacks. He opened his pocket watch to check the time. "I want to talk with the owner of the general store here. We'll meet you ladies in the hotel dining room about four, where I'll give you a full report." He cocked a dark eyebrow. "Is that fair enough, Lily?"

"Fair enough. Why do you have to talk to the proprietor of the general store?"

"I'll tell you later. Come along, Zar." He touched the brim of his hat, then set off, boot heels tapping smartly. Balthazar took two steps to Griffon's one. Others stepped aside, letting them pass and then staring after them.

"Griffon can certainly part the waters," Lily noted, dryly. "See how the people stare, Orrie? 'Odd' might as well be branded on his forehead. Zar's, too."

"Lily, take some advice from an older, wiser woman," Orrie said, placing an arm about Lily's waist and giving her an affectionate squeeze. "You'll catch more flies with honey."

Lily sent her a baffled glance. "What are you talking about?"

Orrie smiled and stared after Griffon and Balthazar. "It means you'll get your way more often with Mr. Griffon if you talk sweet to him. Be nice, Lily."

"Orrie Dickens, are you suggesting that I be familiar with that man?" Lily demanded.

"Land sakes, no!" Orrie said, but she was grinning like a jack-o'-lantern.

Griffon swirled the amber liquid in the glass and glanced around at the other diners. Only a few people dawdled

over desserts of sponge cake or peach cobbler. Three men
ambled into the hotel's dining room and made for the piano at the back wall.

"The hardware salesman recalled when the Jefferses
purchased those coffin nails. It was two weeks after Cecille's disappearance," Griffon said, taking up his narra-
tion of what he and Balthazar had learned that day.

"Oh, dearie me." Orrie pressed a hand to her heart.
"You don't think they . . . that sweet Cecille is . . . Oh,
dearie me."

"But they said they were burying Anson's wife, didn't
they?" Lily asked. "They made that quite clear?"

"Yes, that's what they said." Griffon finished the shot
of brandy in one smooth gulp, then set the glass down
solidly. "And that's what we must believe. I'll question
them about this tomorrow, naturally, and until then we
must all assume that Cecille is alive and waiting to be
rescued."

"Sound thinking," Balthazar agreed. He tugged fitfully
at his pointed beard. "No use dwelling on bad thoughts."

"She's alive." Lily's gaze met Griffon's briefly, and she
saw the light of understanding in his silvery blue eyes. It
was a comfort, and her nerves settled as if they'd been
stroked by a gentle hand. She leaned back in her chair and
gave her attention to the three men near them at the piano.
The tall, thin one sat on the piano bench and flexed his
spindly fingers. The youngest, with red hair and freckles,
pulled a guitar from a gunnysack and dropped his hat to
the floor, its crown ready to receive coins. The third, who
looked as if he might be the redhead's father, removed a
violin from a battered black case.

"Looks as if we might be serenaded," Balthazar said.
"I'll wager that man can't play the violin any better than
you, Griffon."

"You play the fiddle, do you?" Orrie asked, and Griffon nodded. "A Gypsy violin is the prettiest. Nobody can

play them like Gypsies. They make those fiddles cry, they do.''

The trio proved entertaining, obviously enjoying their making of merry music. Orrie clapped in time and the others fell in. Griffon flipped a coin into the hat and received gracious thanks from all three musicians.

"I'm reminded of my own troubadour days," Griffon told them.

"Are you a music maker, too, sir?" the guitar player asked.

"I am." Griffon glanced at the fiddle player. "I can pick out a tune on a piano, but my favorite instrument is the violin. It's been a while since I've played."

"Please." The violin player held out the instrument. "Be my guest."

"Well . . . I . . ."

"Yes, I'd like to hear you play," Lily said, and only then realized how much she meant it. While the trio's music had been lively and homespun, Lily had a feeling Griffon's music would be melancholy and exotic.

Griffon shrugged. "Very well. But don't expect too much. You should know by now, Lily, that Zar tends to exaggerate."

"Not about this," Balthazar insisted.

Griffon stood and removed his jacket. Then he rolled up the sleeves of his white, gauzy shirt. Taking hold of the violin, he tested its strings, listening for perfect tonation. He adjusted one string, then tucked the violin under his chin and placed the pads of his fingers upon the frets ever so gingerly. In the other hand he held the bow between thumb and forefinger as if it were made of spun glass. His heavy gold ring caught at the lantern light overhead.

Lily held her breath, waiting for the first notes. The room was silent, as if everyone dared not breathe. The bow stroked the strings and the notes were born and took wing, soaring into a tune of romance that squeezed the heart.

She was immediately swept up in it. Memories of Gypsy tales, campfires, and folklore trailed through her mind. She glanced at Orrie, but Orrie had eyes only for Balthazar, so Lily returned her rapt attention to Griffon. While she'd known of his ancestry, this was the first time she'd seen him wear it so boldly. He fit her imagination's portrait of a Gypsy wanderer down to the smallest detail— that circlet of gold glinting in his earlobe.

Never had she seen anyone play an instrument with such passion, such verve. He poured his soul into it. Beads of perspiration dotted his forehead and upper lip. He tossed his head, trying to fling a thick curl of hair off his forehead, but the lock proved tenacious. With his hair in his eyes and his skin glowing with the sheen of exertion, he exercised a wizard's skill. Lily's heart hammered and her palms became moist. She tucked her fists beneath her chin and hunched her shoulders as delicious chills raced up her arms and across her breasts.

Griffon's expression told the story of love found and love lost. He took a few steps in her direction until he was standing directly in front of her. She saw that his lashes were wet, his eyes luminous, as he caressed the final stanzas from the violin strings. The notes quivered, sobbed, cried. The final chord hung in the air and then diminished by degrees into silence.

The other musicians broke into spontaneous applause. Griffon handed over the violin reluctantly, and its owner patted him on the back.

"Where'd you learn to play like that?" the other man asked.

"On my grandfather's knee," Griffon answered, affording the man a mere glance. His gaze rested on Lily and asked for her approval.

"Wonderful," she whispered, letting her hands float back down to her lap. "I've never heard such music before. It seemed to have a life of its own. So sad . . . so fraught with emotion.'' Only a man of depth could conjure up such sounds, she thought, gaining insight to the one standing before her, legs braced apart, black hair hanging in damp curls across his forehead.

''You a Gypsy fella?'' the youngest of the trio asked.

''Yes,'' Griffon answered, but kept his gaze on Lily.

Receiving his sole attention unnerved her, and she glanced sideways to find that Orrie and Balthazar were no longer seated at the table. She looked around the dining room, finding them nowhere in sight.

''They slipped away,'' Griffon said. ''Perhaps they went upstairs.''

''How could they leave? I was spellbound. A fire couldn't have budged me from this chair.''

''I believe the dining room is closing.''

''Oh.'' Lily stood, flustered by the tumult of her feelings.

''May I see you upstairs?''

''Yes, thank you.'' She allowed him to take her hand and tuck it in the crook of his elbow. ''You'll be leaving quite early, I imagine.''

''Just after sunrise.''

''And when will you return?''

''The next afternoon. We'll be back before you know it.''

Lily made no comment. She climbed the stairs beside him as a plan formed in her mind. She'd toyed with it through dinner, hardly listening to the conversation flowing around her. Whether Griffon agreed to it or not, she fully intended to go to Devil's Den tomorrow. She hoped to obtain his permission, but she certainly didn't require it. However, the ride would be ever so much more pleasant if they could all travel together, instead of her and Orrie having to trail behind, keeping out of sight.

''Good night, Lily.'' Griffon seemed uncommonly courteous.

"Good night." Lily wanted to waylay him, but words failed her. She knew he was waiting for her to go inside her room before he retired to his, so she bobbed a curtsy and crossed the threshold.

The room was dark. Lily felt her way to the bedside table and the oil lamp. "Orrie?" she whispered, running her hand across the bed where the woman should be slumbering. "Orrie?"

The wick lit and cast a glow, showing Lily that she was alone. Crossing to the window, she looked out in search of the familiar figure. The pale moonlight illuminated the street below. Orrie and Balthazar strolled arm in arm down the center of it. Lily sucked in her breath when Orrie tipped her head to rest it against Balthazar's shoulder. On a public street, no less!

"Uncle Howard and Aunt Nan would give you a tongue-lashing if they could see you now," Lily whispered to Orrie's distant figure. "And if I'd done such a thing, why, you'd never let me hear the end of it!"

Lily turned slowly from the window and stared in the general direction of Griffon's room. Orrie's suggestion about treating Griffon more sweetly drifted back to her. Could she entice him to take her with him tomorrow? Would she dare?

She moved briskly from her room to his and tapped smartly on the door. It was ajar and opened under the slight pressure. Lily swallowed hard as the muscles in her throat contracted.

"Griffon? I spotted our companions outside. Would you like to—" The rest of the words failed her, stolen by the realization that Griffon's shirt hung unbuttoned, exposing a darkly furred chest. "Ex-excuse me."

"No need to apologize. You're always welcome in my room." His smile teased her. He propped his fists on his hips, his arms sweeping back his shirt to expose even more of himself. "What were you saying?"

"N-nothing." She found she couldn't concentrate; her

thoughts scattered like dandelion fluff. She'd only seen such masculine beauty carved in marble and displayed in museums. But this was no statue before her. He stood close enough that she could smell his musky scent. A queer sensation corkscrewed in her stomach, not unpleasant, not unexpected.

"Don't worry about Orrie. She's a grown woman. Zar's courting her, and I believe Orrie likes the attention." His heavy-lidded eyes explored her. "Mutual attraction has its advantages."

"How's that?" Lily asked, finding nerve enough to look at him again.

He ran one hand absently down his chest to his flat stomach. "It is easier to milk a cow that holds still. That's an old Gypsy proverb." He gestured toward the lamp table and chairs near the window. *"Besh."*

"Pardon?"

"Sit. Please." He gestured again, and smiled this time.

"No, I should—can't." But at the door, she hesitated and turned back to him, suddenly remembering her mission. How would Cecille handle this man? she wondered. In the inconstant light from the oil lamp, he seemed ethereal, a vision from one of Orrie's tales. The memory of his searing kiss flooded her mind, reminding her that she could arouse him. But could she control him?

He made an impatient sign. "In or out? Make up your mind, Lily."

"You speak the Gypsy language?" she asked, blurting the first thing that came to her while she bartered for time. "You're fluent?"

"Yes." He shrugged. "Anyway I used to be fluent. It was my first language. I speak Rom rarely these days, so I'm probably rusty."

"Say something for me in Gypsy—Rom." Lily offered a smile, remembering that Cecille usually flattered a man until he was dizzy-headed with his own self-importance. "I think it's wonderful that you know more than one lan-

guage, and the Gypsy tongue sounds lovely. So romantic.''

"Gorgios usually think so.'' He noticed her confusion.
"Outside the Rom. Outsiders,'' he translated. "You all
think our speech is pretty, that we're fascinating creatures,
but you don't want us to get too close. We're *creatures*,
after all. Animals.''

Lily shook her head. This certainly wasn't going ac-
cording to plan. In fact, he seemed to be on the brink of
anger, just the opposite of where she wanted him.

"When I was a *tikno* I learned to use the Rom to my
advantage. My mother taught me. She taught me to beg.
She'd say, 'Leave the white people alone, child. Don't ask
them for money or food. They can't be bothered by the
likes of you.' Then she'd say, *'Mong, chavo, mong,'* which
means, 'Beg, boy, beg!' '' He laughed, but the sound held
little humor.

"Your mother taught you to beg?'' Lily asked, appalled.

"My mother and grandmother taught me many things.
I could *dukker the vast* with the best of them.''

"Dukker the. . . ?''

"Read fortunes,'' he clarified, holding out one hand,
palm up. "I could see the future in these lines and creases.
And, of course, that became my downfall. I was too good
at it. I scared my own people. They cast me out.'' He
stared at his palm, dropping into a moody silence. He ran
his other hand up and down his chest in a lazy motion that
awakened something primal in Lily. "We were close—my
clan was all I knew. Then suddenly they turned their backs
on me and I was utterly alone.'' His voice dipped, grew
more hoarse than usual. "I remember the cold . . . and
the hunger in my belly.''

Lily sank her teeth gently in her lower lip. Her heart
ached for the frightened boy he'd been. She wanted to tell
him that she knew what it was like to be shunned by those

who were supposed to love you, but then he blinked several times and cleared his throat, breaking the mood.

"So, you like *cigannyal mulatni*?" he asked.

"I don't know. What's that?"

He pondered the question. "How do you say . . . dancing with Gypsies . . . no, reveling with Gypsies. You like that?"

"I . . . I can't say. I've only heard about them or . . . or seen them from afar. I never really knew any."

"You do now." Then, with one long stride his body came against hers. Flattening his hand against the door, he closed it. Lily looked up into his slumberous blue eyes and wondered when he'd turned the tables on her. "Such hair. The Gypsy word for it is *bal*." When he said the foreign word his breath came with it to caress her face. It smelled of brandy and sweet seduction. He reached behind her and plucked a comb from the russet mass before she could stop him. "Like autumn leaves. Dark fire. Beautiful."

She shied from him, twisting away and ducking under his arm. Lily clung to the bedpost, her knees shaking. Just who was enticing whom? She gathered her senses and strove to take control of the situation again. Flattery, she reminded herself. Drown him in flattery.

"You—your hair is beautiful, too. It's like midnight without stars or moon. And your eyes are a fetching color of—"

His hand settled over hers on the bedpost. He circled her waist with his free arm and trapped her against him. Lily's mouth was so dry she couldn't even swallow.

"What's the word for . . . for nose?" she babbled, finding her mind scrambled with him so near.

"*Nak*." He rubbed her lips apart with his thumb and touched her teeth. "And these are *dand*. Your face—your lovely, flushed face—is *mui*." His lips bussed her hot cheek. "I know the Gypsy words for all the parts of the body. Want me to continue?"

"No . . . no." She laughed lightly, haltingly. "Thank you, though."

"*Nais tuke*. Thank you." He smiled and dipped his head. His mouth found a spot just beneath her ear. One by one, her combs slipped free and fell to the bed. Her hair cascaded to her shoulders in curling profusion. Griffon combed his fingers through it, then lifted one strand to his nose.

"Ummm," he growled. "I bet you smell this good all over."

"We make quite a pair, don't we?" she murmured, enjoying the feel of his lips on her skin.

"You're so beautiful tonight. While I played the violin, I couldn't take my eyes off you. Your skin glowed. Your eyes spoke of love to me. You wanted me then. Do you want me now?"

Lily steeled herself against the longing churning in her and kept her objective front and center. "It's a pity we must be apart."

"This"—he brought her more firmly against him—"is not apart."

'No, but we shall be separated tomorrow and the next day."

"That's tomorrow. What about tonight?"

Lily gathered her nerve and pushed her fingers through his hair, lifting his head so that she could see his face. "How can you leave me behind? Don't you think you should reconsider?"

One corner of his mouth tipped up. "Maybe I should."

She smiled, relieved that her feminine wiles were up to the challenge. She couldn't recall the last time she'd tried to put stars in a man's eyes.

Rising on tiptoe, she whispered close to his ear. "Take me with you and I'll make you ever so glad you did."

He tipped his head sideways, giving her a peculiar look. "Lily Meeker, what are you up to?"

"I'm trying to make you see how much more enjoyable the trip will be with me along."

"You'd let me sport with you?"

"You'd like that, wouldn't you?" She ran her fingertips across his shoulders. His arms tightened like bands of iron around her waist. "You do something for me"—she smiled suggestively—"and I do something for you."

"We're talking about making love, yes? You'd remove your clothes, I'd remove mine, and I'd fondle your breasts and—"

"Hush!" Blood scalded her cheeks and she pushed at his arms, trying to break his hold. He let her go and his shoulders shook with laughter. Lily smoothed wisps of hair from her hot face. "That is no way to talk to me and you know it! I'm not . . . not common!"

"I do believe you're trying to turn my head. Are you? Is that what this is all about?"

She glared at him, then gathered her hair combs off his bed. "You're the Great Goforth. Read my mind."

"I don't have to. You're transparent."

Lily couldn't tolerate him laughing at her. She threw the hair combs at him, so furious she couldn't control her fit of temper. He turned a cheek and they bounced harmlessly off him.

"Stop this foolishness and tell me the truth." He collected the combs, grabbed one of her fists, and pried her fingers open to receive them. "Why are you so desperate to go with us tomorrow that you'll make promises you have no intention of keeping?"

Reluctantly, she brought her gaze to his, knowing she was bested in this battle of wills. "I just know Cecille is there—in that Devil's Den country. I want to see her. That boy—Jasper—he likes me. I can get him to tell me where to find Cecille. I'll be more use to you there than here."

He smoothed his fingertips down her cheek. "If Cecille is there, I will find her and bring her to you." He pressed his fingertip to her lips, preventing her next words. "Zar told me that I wouldn't be able to think clearly with you along, and he's right. It might be dangerous out there, Lily, and I won't be able to concentrate if I fear for your safety.''

She jerked her mouth away from his damming finger. ''Oh, posh! You sound as if you're marching off to war.''

He smiled. ''Will you keep a candle burning in the window for this soldier?''

''Certainly not! I'll go back to Fort Smith before I keep vigil for the likes of you. I think you're vile.''

He searched her face with an intensity that sent an uneasiness through her, then he shook his head. ''No, you don't.'' With that, he took her by the elbow and steered her to the door. ''Good evening, Lily. See you again in a couple of days. Stay out of trouble, won't you.'' His mouth came down hard on hers as he stole a kiss from her. Before she could slap him, the door closed in her face. His laughter floated to her in the hallway.

''Go ahead and gloat, Mr. Goforth. Enjoy your meager victory while you may!'' She whirled, skirts billowing, and went to her own room. The door slammed behind her with a satisfying boom. Lily folded her arms tightly against her rib cage, warding off her seething anger at being laughed at, at being treated like a child, at her own failing. She should have known better than to try and be coy with him. Batting her lashes and fashioning inane bits of flattery were as foreign to her as a sidesaddle was to a cow.

Setting aside her anger, she busied herself with packing her bedroll. Tonight he'd been the victor, she thought, then smiled slyly. But tomorrow's spoils would belong to her.

Chapter 8

Lily tugged on the reins and brought the buggy to a stop beside the two horses tethered beneath a weeping willow. Saddles and blankets were nowhere in sight, and Lily assumed they'd been hidden somewhere close by.

"Where do you reckon they got to?" Orrie asked beside her. "Think they stopped to rest?"

"I believe they've gone on afoot." Lily maneuvered the buggy closer to the grazing horses and set the brake. "Help me unharness the team. We'll leave them with these others."

Orrie stared at her, dumbstruck. "You're not figuring to follow them on foot into the woods!"

"Griffon and Balthazar have obviously forsaken their mounts, and so shall we. We haven't any choice, Orrie. As you can see, the woods are quite thick here. We couldn't get the buggy through." Lily bent at the waist to peer into the tangle of leaves and branches. "I wouldn't be surprised if this road meanders into nothing a few yards ahead."

Orrie remained in the buggy even as Lily lighted from it. "I'm not about to tramp through that wilderness. And neither are you. I won't allow it. I'm your chaperone, and I got to watch out for you." She crossed her arms over her bosom. "We'll wait right here for them."

"You can wait here. I'm going." Lily began loosening the rigging. "At least help me with the team."

"Honeypot, listen to old Orrie. You can't go following after those men. This isn't for young ladies. We'll be in enough trouble when they return and find us here waiting for them. We shouldn't flirt with more woes by venturing into those—"

"Stake them securely, Orrie," Lily interrupted as the buggy's tongue dropped and she freed the team. "We might not get back here until morning."

"Morning!" Orrie's dark eyes widened. "Girl, what must you be thinking?" She squinted at Lily. "You're not thinking. That's the problem. The sun's too hot and it's bled through your bonnet and scalded your brains. We're not highwaymen. We're not wilderness trackers." Orrie threw back her shoulders and ran her hands down the front of her plain dress. "We're city-bred ladies, who won't last two minutes out there in that overgrown wilderness."

"I'll take one flask of water and this tin of biscuits, and I'll leave the rest for you. Your bedroll is tucked beneath the seat."

"Lily Jane Meeker!"

Lily looked up from the basket of food and other essentials they'd packed for the trip. "Yes, Orrie?"

Orrie stared at her for several tense seconds, her frown deepening. Finally, she released a long breath. "Better bring that buggy whip. No telling what kind of varmints we might have to fight off, and we sure as shootin' can't fight 'em with discouraging words."

Lily allowed herself a secret smile of triumph, averting her face so Orrie couldn't see, and grabbed the buggy whip. "Sound thinking. I'll carry this, my bedroll, and the basket. Can you manage the other things?"

"I suppose." Orrie scooped them into her arms and set her face in lines of discontent. "I'll lead the way."

"No." Lily held Orrie back with one hand. "I will. And don't fret so. This isn't the jungle."

"It's not Main Street, either."

Lily set off. The road, as she'd predicted, ended abruptly

no more than fifty paces into the woods. She paused to get her bearings. They'd traveled deep into the Ozark Mountains, and the air was thin and cool. The ground under her feet angled up, which meant they were still climbing the mountain where it was said the Jefferses staked their claim. Lily yanked the hem of her split skirt from a barbed bush and wiggled her toes inside her stylish boots. At that moment, she would have gladly traded the high-arched footwear for a pair of sturdy cowboy boots. Why did women's attire have to be so impractical?

"Changed your mind?" Orrie asked. "Ready to go back to the horses and sit pretty while we wait for the men?"

"No. I'm merely adjusting to the elements." She pulled her hanky from her cuff and dabbed at her upper lip. "Come along, Orrie."

"How far up ahead you think they are?"

"Oh, not too far. But be as quiet as possible. Sounds travel great distances in the woods. We don't want to tip them off." She whispered the last, taking her own advice.

"What if we're going in the wrong direction? What if we get lost? Then what?" Orrie whispered.

"We won't get lost. They're up ahead, I tell you."

"And how do you know that? I don't see no signs of it. No tracks. Looks like nothing's come this way."

"I know what I'm doing," Lily assured her. "Now hush. I must concentrate."

"On what?"

"Hush!"

The woods closed around them, thick and green and full of noise. Crickets chirped, toads sprang and rustled leaves, birds cried in alarm and flapped noisily overhead. A low growl sounded to their left, and Orrie shrieked and grasped the back of Lily's blouse.

"Orrie, you're going to tear my clothes," Lily scolded, shrugging off the frightened woman.

"What in merciful heaven was that?"

"Probably a dog."

"A dog? I never heard any dog that sounded like that. It was a wildcat. He's up some tree, getting ready to pounce and tear us limb from limb."

"Spare me your scary tales," Lily begged as a shiver teased the back of her neck. "Just keep close to me. You'll be fine."

"This is madness, us being out here. I never thought I'd meet my end being attacked by wild animals. There won't be nothing left of us but bleached bones. Nobody will know what became of us. No Christian burial, no—"

"Orrie, please don't go on. You're trying my patience. Do you want Griffon to hear us?"

"Yes!"

"Well, I don't. So button your lips, if you please." Lily glanced around to issue a stern frown. It was imperative that they keep quiet. She had an inkling that Griffon and Balthazar were close by. Very close by.

Holding a branch, Lily let Orrie pass in front of her, then she released the limber obstruction and it whistled back like a whip. As Lily turned to continue her trek, she sensed Griffon's presence a heartbeat before his hand tightened on her wrist and brought her up short. Her bonnet slipped to one side, blocking her vision for an instant. Shoving back the brim, she smothered a cry of alarm and found herself staring into stormy blue eyes. Orrie's shriek was quickly followed by a prayer of thanks.

"Griffon!" Lily gasped. "You scared ten years off me."

"Good. Just what the devil do you think you're doing out here?"

"Following you, as you well know." When he released her, Lily righted her bonnet and adjusted her short-waisted jacket. She glanced around at the shadow-dappled area. "Have you stopped for a respite?"

"No, we haven't stopped for a respite," he mocked her in a higher register, squinting his eyes and wagging his head in an exaggerated imitation. "We stopped to ambush you." He shared a victorious smirk with Balthazar.

"You . . . you knew . . . how did you know we were behind you? Did you hear us? I told Orrie to be quiet. I suppose we made such a racket that we telegraphed our passage to you."

"Sure, that's how I knew you were right behind us," he agreed, albeit too readily.

Lily dropped the bedroll and buggy whip to pass the back of her wrist across her perspiring brow. Assessing his smug expression, she knew she was being coddled. "You've known since early this morning . . . since the first mile out of Van Buren," Lily accused, and Griffon's slow grin affirmed her suspicion. "You've been letting us creep behind you, letting us think we were unnoticed, when all the while you knew . . . how?"

"Luck."

She shook her head. "No. More than that."

He narrowed one eye. "Are you admitting that I'm psychic, Miss Meeker? Is *that* what you're admitting?"

Glancing around at the others, Lily saw expectancy everywhere. She knew when she was beaten. "Yes. But I think you were cruel to play this silly game. Why did you wait until now to . . . to ambush us?"

"If you were so keen on being sneaky, who was I to spoil your fun?" His brows lowered threateningly. "But the fun is over, Miss Meeker."

"I wasn't having any fun."

"Me neither," Orrie joined in, edging closer to Balthazar's bulk. "I'm terrible glad to join up with y'all. I told Lily we shouldn't be hiking in these woods on our lonesome."

"What's this?" Balthazar picked up the whip. "Your weapon?"

"Orrie thought it might come in handy," Lily said, not missing the humorous glances between Balthazar and Griffon. She took the whip from Balthazar and retrieved her bedroll. "Shouldn't we be on our way?"

"I was so afraid we'd get lost and never find you men.

And my feet are killin' me! Climbing these mountains is torture.'' Orrie fanned her face and sent a smile of gratitude to Balthazar when he placed an arm about her shoulders.

Griffon ran a thumb along his jawline. ''How *did* you track us?'' he asked Lily.

''How does anyone track anyone?'' Lily hedged.

''By following prints, broken twigs, disturbed brush.''

Lily shrugged. ''We did the same.''

''Uh-uh.'' Griffon shook his head slowly. ''Not in these woods. We were careful not to leave prints or any other signs of our passage.'' He curled a finger under Lily's chin and forced her gaze to his. ''You sensed me ahead of you as I sensed you behind me. I was fairly *drenched* with you. I could almost taste you on my tongue, smell you on my skin, see you with my mind's eye. That's how it was for you, too.'' He nudged her chin with his knuckle. ''Isn't that right, Lily Meeker?''

''Don't be ridiculous.''

He dropped his gaze to her feet. ''You wished for better boots.''

Lily gasped. How could he . . . ? Recovering, she angled her chin from his touch. ''While I will admit you have an uncanny sense of perception, I will not burden myself with such an absurdity.''

''You're as stubborn as a mule.'' He aimed a finger at her. ''And that's *not* a compliment.'' Heaving a sigh, he snatched the whip and bedroll from her hands and tossed them under a tree.

''What are you doing?''

''You're not going anywhere. Zar, you stay with these ladies. I'll go on and—''

''No,'' Lily protested. ''I won't stay behind and—'' She released a garbled sound when Griffon seized her upper arm and brought her high and tight against his chest. She struggled briefly, and her bonnet slid off and dangled by its ties down her back. Staring into his eyes, she witnessed the flames of rage and bit back a whimper. "Y-you're hurting me, Mr. Goforth."

"And you've pushed me beyond endurance. Because of your blatant disobedience, I'm forced to leave Zar with you and visit the Jefferses by myself. That, Miss Meeker, makes me infinitely more vulnerable. Happy now?"

She chewed on her lower lip, fighting off a wave of guilt.

"Griffon, you shouldn't face them alone," Zar said, his brows forming wings above his troubled eyes. "The sheriff said they're trigger-happy and completely uncivilized."

"I'll be careful."

"Why can't we all go?" Lily asked. Griffon's scowl intensified, and she edged her head back, cringing from his blast of anger.

"Because I'm the one hired to find Cecille. Not you. Not Orrie. Not Zar. Me. Now, kindly stay out of my way and allow me to do my job." He shoved her aside, showing so little regard that she stumbled and nearly fell.

"You let me come to Van Buren because you think Cecille and I have some kind of mind connection," Lily said. "Perhaps I do feel a strong bond, but distance won't help it. If I come with you, I might sense if Cecille's around."

"We were warned to stay away, remember? The Jefferses won't beg us to stay for dinner." He spotted one of the water flasks. Uncapping it, he tilted it to his mouth and drank deeply. "Zar, you have my permission to bind and gag Miss Meeker if you must to keep her quiet and keep her here." He pointed to the ground for emphasis, then handed the flask to his friend. "If I'm not back before sundown, take the ladies back to town and get the sheriff."

Balthazar clamped a hand on Griffon's shoulder. "Tread lightly, *Borossan.*"

Griffon nodded, smiling jauntily. "There should be a creek a few yards that way." He pointed to their right. "You can fill the flasks there and refresh yourselves."

"I'll make camp here while you're gone." Zar directed a baleful glare at Lily. "And there won't be any trouble, so don't waste a worry on our account."

"Don't chance a campfire," Griffon warned, and gave a quick salute. "I'm off then."

Before any of them could offer further advice or instructions, Griffon ducked beneath overhanging foliage and vanished amid the green, gold, and brown of the woods.

"What did you call him?" Orrie asked Balthazar.

"When, dear woman?"

"Just now. You called Mr. Griffon some strange-sounding name."

"Ah, that was the Gypsy language." He laughed when Orrie breathed a sound of awe. *"Borossan* means 'Gypsy king'."

"Is he a king?" Orrie asked, clasping her hands under her chin in excitement.

"No, but he might have been. His grandfather was king of his Gypsy clan. The word is one of respect for men who are leaders, men who are brave and wise." Balthazar dug into a canvas satchel and withdrew a length of rope. Lily stiffened when his eyes pinned her.

"That won't be necessary," Lily said, settling on the grass under a shade tree.

"Just in case." Balthazar dropped the rope beside his bedroll, within easy reach. "Just in case."

The sheriff's directions proved accurate. Griffon smelled woodsmoke before the ramshackle log cabin came into view through the jumble of foliage. He had only a few seconds to survey the slanting roof, woodpile, and boiling pot set over a low fire when the first shots ripped past him in an explosion of leaves and shattered wood. Griffon ducked and felt a projectile part the air beside his ear. Too close, he thought, cowering behind an elm tree. Much too close.

"Hold your fire!" he called, putting steel in his voice.

"I'm not armed and I mean you no harm." That was only partly true, he thought, touching the hilt of the knife inside his right boot. Another hung from his belt. While his aim with a gun was little more than adequate, he'd been a lethal knife-thrower since he was barely out of short pants.

"Who goes thar?" a voice boomed, deep as a bear's.

"Griffon Goforth. I've traveled from Fort Smith to speak with you."

"This here's Jeffers land," someone else shouted off to his right. Griffon glanced around, wondering if he was surrounded. "You best haul ass, mister, 'fore it gets shot full o' holes."

"I want to talk to the head of the Jeffers family. It's about Cecille Meeker."

"Who?"

"Cecille Meeker. She's a friend of Anson's."

"Anson ain't cheer. You git!"

"That gal ain't here." The deep voice came again, straight ahead of Griffon and closer than it had been before. "I tole that detective feller. He said nobody else'd be out here asking a bunch of durn-fool questions. I don't like strangers trespassin' on my property, ya hear?"

"Mr. Jeffers?" Griffon called. "Mr. Butch Jeffers?"

"That's right."

Griffon jerked, realizing that the booming voice was now behind him. He whirled on his haunches to stare up at a barrel-chested man holding a hatchet. Gray, fuzzy hair covered the lower half of Butch Jeffers's face. Above the full beard and unruly mustache poked a beaked nose, separating beady eyes. Slowly, Griffon stood to confront him.

"Anson is gone? Where to?"

"None of your blamed business."

"Did he take Cecille Meeker with him?"

"He didn't take nobody with him. Just took off." He projected a stream of tobacco juice that splattered Griffon's left boot.

"And he didn't tell you where he was headed?"

"Why should he? He's growed."

Griffon focused his attention solely on the man, blocking out the danger of the others he knew watched him from cover. Deceit hung in the air, thick and cloying. Griffon sensed something else: a skittishness that quivered around Butch Jeffers. He's hiding something . . . someone, Griffon thought. He concentrated, tried to delve into the big man's thoughts, but came up empty.

"I don't like the way yore lookin' at me," Butch said, showing gaping holes where teeth had been. He narrowed his eyes, looking Griffon over as if he were a bull at auction. "You a Gypsy feller, ain'tcha?"

Surprise socked Griffon, rocking his head back. How would this Arkansas woodsman know Gypsies by sight? He cleared his throat, hearing the rustle of leaves as the others tightened the circle around him.

"If you don't mind, I think I'll look around. I'm quite sure Cecille Meeker was here recently."

"She ain't been, and yore lookin' is done over. Boys!"

Voices rose up around Griffon. Four, five, maybe six. Outnumbered! Butch Jeffers hoisted the hatchet and grinned. Griffon tensed and his mind scrambled for a way out of a bad situation.

"This here feller needs y'all to help him skedaddle off our land." Butch gave a nod. Rifles belched and bullets tore grass and dirt at Griffon's feet.

Charging directly at Butch, Griffon knocked the man off balance and sent him sprawling. Scrambling to his feet, Griffon made a dive toward the thickest underbrush. Twigs and thorns tore at his clothing to find skin. A bullet burned past him, shaving off flesh and leaving him with fiery pain. Blood oozed and then ran freely down his cheek, splashing on his shoulder, staining his shirt. Forcing the agony from his mind, he dodged among trees and leaped over bushes. Thrashing and grunting, he swiped at low branches, clearing a path for himself.

Dazed, he ran headlong into a small clearing and collided with a chunky body. He struggled, trying to dislodge the hands that gripped his upper arms. A moon-shaped face with kind eyes floated before him.

"Looky, Maw-Maw. It's the feller Jasper seen with the purty gal in town!" The boy/man laughed with delight and hugged Griffon to him. "Is that purty gal here widya? Didja brung her?" His dark eyes clouded and his upper lip quivered. "Uh-oh. Maw-Maw, him leaking blood. Him got hurt."

Griffon looked at the woman. Her dark hair was gathered into twin braids that fell over her jutting breasts. Black eyes stared at him and then softened, smiled. She was a stranger, but familiar. Griffon sucked in a breath, stabbed by recognition.

"San tu Rom?" he asked, and she nodded, her black eyes beginning to sparkle.

"I'm Rom," she said, moving closer to gently pry her boy's hands from Griffon's arms. "What clan are you from?"

"Goforth and Tshurara. In England. And you?"

"Davidovitch and Kalderasha. Russia, but some of my people came to this country. Up east. What are you doing here? Why have my men shot you?" She untied a scarf from her neck and held it to his wound.

"Is the purty gal widya?" Jasper asked again. "Maw-Maw, make him tell. Make him tell."

"I'm trying to find Cecille Meeker," Griffon said, pressing the cloth to his throbbing head. "That's the pretty girl's cousin," he told Jasper, and received a gleeful grin. "Anson knows Cecille."

The woman shook her head, worry dulling her eyes. "What are you called?"

"Griffon. And you?"

"Eva." She glanced nervously behind him. "You go now. My husband and his sons will be looking to make sure you've run. Go or they'll kill you."

"How did you get here . . . with Jeffers? Where is your

Rom family?'' Griffon asked, letting her guide him from the clearing. He saw that she and Jasper had been picking berries before he'd burst into their lives.

"He took me from my family when I was thirteen. They didn't know he lived so far away." She shrugged off her history. "The deed was done. It was a long time ago. Go now. Go! You're too handsome a Rom to be shot like a coyote."

"Which way is the creek?" Griffon peered through the slanting shadows. His head ached so fiercely that it distorted his eyesight.

"Yonder way," Jasper said, pointing east.

"Eva Davidovitch . . . Jasper . . ." Griffon turned back to them, sensing comrades among this hive of hostility. He offered Eva the blood-soaked scarf, but she pressed it back to his temple. "Thanks. Thanks to you both." He smiled at her, then at her son. "I'll be back. I know she's here. Dead or alive, she's here."

"Paw-Paw's coming," Jasper whispered, giving Griffon a mighty shove that sent him reeling into the thick woods.

Griffon regained his footing and grimaced against the pain shooting through his head. For a few moments, he couldn't focus on a plan. He stood, rooted to the spot, his mind blank, the pain overtaking him. Then he felt her . . . Lily. Her thoughts came so clearly to him, he felt as if she'd spoken his name, her lips brushing his ear. He blinked and held his head, warding off his stupor to let Lily's shining spirit guide him in the right direction.

Over and over again, he heard her sound his name. Her worry reached out to him, pulled him along, propped him up when he would have fallen, prodded him into a run when his energy began to sag. Her thoughts of him were so strong, they carried him to her.

Lily had been dozing, but she came to her feet in a rush of fear. She plastered one hand against her right temple and squeezed her eyes shut, nearly passing out from the tearing talons.

"Lily, what is it?" Orrie asked, hurrying to her. "Honeypot, why are you crying? Are you hurt?"

"Yes!" She pulled her hand away and stared at her palm. Where was the blood? Hadn't she been shot?

Orrie ran her hands over Lily's hair. "What is it, child? Where do you hurt?"

"No . . . not me." As the pain subsided, she began to understand. This wasn't her pain. "It's Griffon."

"What about him?" Balthazar asked, leaping to his feet.

"He's hurting. He's been shot, I think." Lily paused to decipher the messages whirling in her mind. She pressed her fingertips to her temples and closed her eyes.

"What are you saying, Miss Lily?" Balthazar demanded.

"I feel . . . he's coming, but he's wounded." She began to pace as a chill overtook her. It had been the same with Cecille. The cold, the dread, the nerves unraveling until she thought she might go mad. "Griffon . . . oh, Griffon." She blinked back tears. "Come on, Griffon. Come to me. Hurry. Hurry."

Balthazar scratched his head. "Has she gone daft?"

"She's no more daffy than your Griffon Goforth. Can't you see she's in the grips of something terrible?" Orrie stood back to watch helplessly as Lily continued her pointless journey, going nowhere, but unable to stand still. "She knows things about people she loves. Don't ask me to explain it. She just knows. Always has. Before I ever knew her, she had the knowing. Her own mother would be alive today if she'd listened to Lily's warnings."

Lily stopped, assaulted by the ghastly memory Orrie had exposed. "I told you never to talk about that!" she snapped.

"Yes, honey. I'm sorry." Orrie bowed her head, contrite.

Balthazar studied first one woman, then the other. He

shook his head and squatted by the basket of food. "I'm going to have some supper because I think you've both taken leave of your senses. That's what *I* think."

But it wasn't an hour later that Griffon came stumbling into camp, one hand clamped against his bloody head.

"Lily!" The name fell from his lips before he dropped to the ground.

Lily rushed to him, cradling his wounded head in her lap. "I told you he was injured," she said, looking up at Balthazar. "Now do you believe me?"

Balthazar touched the side of Lily's face with gentle fingertips, and his eyes shone with wonder. "I believe." He caressed her right temple with his thumb, and his gaze moved to Griffon's matching wound. "I believe Griffon is right about you. You're bloody miraculous."

Chapter 9

Resting Griffon's head in her lap, Lily skimmed her thumb over the tips of his thick lashes and thought about what Balthazar had said to her when Griffon had stumbled into camp. Miraculous, she mused. Balthazar had said Griffon had described her as "bloody miraculous."

Sweet gratitude seeped through her. No one had ever thought of her in such terms. She was used to being chastised, ostracized even, when voicing her hunches. Only Orrie and Cecille had encouraged her to reveal her inner visions. Around all others, she stifled herself. She'd learned to block out the "knowing" and tell no one of her waking dreams. But Griffon had seen within her and had not shunned her. He had called her "miraculous."

Lily adjusted the makeshift bandage, made from a length of Orrie's petticoat, wrapped around his head. They'd all doctored him, working together to cleanse the wound where a bullet had burned through his skin. Balthazar had determined that Griffon wasn't as badly hurt as they'd all feared when he'd staggered through the brush, blood staining his head and his shirt. Head wounds bled profusely, no matter how slight, Balthazar had assured the frightened women. They'd stopped the bleeding and bandaged his head. Balthazar had removed Griffon's blood-soaked shirt, and Orrie had taken it to the creek and washed it. Now it hung over a tree branch, drying in the evening breeze.

They'd all realized that Griffon was their focal point. He lashed them together. Without him, they'd never find Cecille. That had become crystal clear to Lily as she'd washed the blood from Griffon's face, neck, and shoulders. Perhaps she could help, but it would take Griffon to find Cecille. Griffon, who could channel his powers. Griffon, who had no fear of those powers.

"You're the miraculous one," she whispered, dousing her hanky with water from the flask and cooling his face and throat with it. "Your powers of perception are so strong, th-they scare me."

It was true. When she'd heard his name the first time, she'd been frightened. The word *psychic* sent dread through her. Hadn't she rejected that word and others like it her whole life? Yet, over the last few days, she'd become less afraid and more intrigued. Her fingers touched her temple with the memory of the pain she'd endured—a ghost pain, Griffon's pain. She'd known the exact moment when the bullet had plowed through his hair, taking a flap of skin with it. She had felt him running, diving through the woods, trying to reach her.

"I'm here," she whispered, bending over him to press her lips to his bandaged forehead. Remembering she wasn't alone, she glanced toward Orrie and Balthazar and was relieved to see that they were deep in whispered conversation, their backs to her.

Balthazar had decided to chance a small campfire. He and Orrie had rolled out the bedding, placing the women's on one side of the fire and the men's on the other.

Griffon stirred and mumbled something, giving Lily a start and causing both Orrie and Balthazar to spin around.

"Griffon?" Lily cradled his chin in her palm and pressed her fingers and thumb gently into his lean cheeks. "It's Lily. Wake up, Griffon. Come back to us."

Cloudy blue eyes stared at her through plentiful, black lashes. His lips moved and he swallowed with difficulty. Lily tipped the flask to his lips and he drank deeply, sputtered, then drank some more. Balthazar came to crouch beside them. Orrie stood next to Lily and squeezed Lily's shoulder.

"See? Told you he'd come around soon," Orrie said. "He's going to be feelin' fine by tomorrow."

"Take a swig of this. It'll kick the life back into you." Balthazar produced a small flask from his inner coat pocket and uncapped it. Amber liquid trickled into Griffon's mouth. Griffon choked, mostly in surprise, then gulped greedily. "That's the way, my friend. Drink it all."

"What is that?" Lily asked.

"Whiskey."

"He shouldn't drink that!"

"Why not?" Balthazar asked.

"Yes, why not?" Orrie echoed.

"It's spirits. He . . . he's ill enough already."

"Don't you fret," Orrie said, patting her shoulder. "Whiskey is medicine to the ill. Look, his color's already comin' back. See that flush in his cheeks?"

Lily caressed his flushed cheek with her finger. Griffon smiled lopsidedly. "I think he's getting drunk."

"Who's getting drunk?" Griffon asked, his voice foggy, his words sliding together.

"Griffon?" Lily held a lock of inky hair off his forehead. "How do you feel? Are you in much pain?"

"Not much." He lifted a hand to explore the cloth wrapped tightly around his head. "Feels as if there's a blooming blacksmith in there hammering away at what's left of my brain."

"Poor thing," Lily crooned. "Those Jefferses will pay for hurting you. I swear it."

"What are you going to do?" Griffon asked, still wearing that crooked grin. "Scold them to death?" His grin grew when Balthazar barked a laugh and Orrie giggled.

"I can see you're feeling much better," Lily said, trying to sound miffed but failing. "And I'm ever so glad. We've been on pins and needles."

"Can you put something in your belly?" Balthazar fit an arm beneath Griffon's shoulders. "Sit up, Griffon."

"Don't hurry things. He's weak and—"

"He'll feel much better on his own power," Balthazar said, overruling Lily's qualms. "We saved you a pork chop, a hunk of bread, and an apple." He propped Griffon against a tree trunk. "Got some hot coffee here, too. I went ahead and built a small fire."

Lily sat to one side, letting Balthazar and Orrie fuss over Griffon. Weariness washed over her, and she suddenly found it hard to keep her eyes open. Now that Griffon was awake and in good hands, she felt utter, deflating relief. Using every shred of energy she had left, she went to her pallet, removed her shoes, unbraided her hair, and curled onto the thin pad of bedding. It felt as good as a feather mattress to her tired body, and sleep had no trouble finding her.

Coming awake slowly, Lily realized it was still dark. Her name, spoken by Griffon, jerked her to full wakefulness, but she didn't move. Balthazar's voice rumbled. Parting her lashes a fraction, she saw Griffon and Balthazar on the other side of the fire, sitting side by side, talking quietly. Orrie's soft snoring sounded near her. Having finished eating, Griffon looked better. Natural color had returned to his skin. He propped an arm on his bent knee and laughed at whatever Balthazar had said. Lily strained to hear the conversation, telling herself she had a right to eavesdrop since they seemed to be discussing her.

"She did that, did she?" Griffon asked, and Balthazar nodded.

"Grabbed her head like she'd been shot and said you were hurt. It wasn't an hour before you came bleeding into camp. You don't seem surprised by this."

"I'm not."

"You did tell me that you thought she was special, but I thought you were thinking with what you've got between your legs instead of what's between your ears. What happened tonight convinced me otherwise.''

Lily was glad for the cover of darkness, for she was sure she'd blushed clear up to the tips of her ears. Even her scalp tingled. She turned her face into the lumpy pillow, closed her eyes, but kept her ears open for every sound, every word or sigh.

"The first night we stayed at the Meeker house something happened that disturbed me,'' Griffon said. "I had a dream, but it didn't seem to have any connection to my own life. Usually, as you know, Zar, my dreams are puzzles I can solve. But not this one. Not until I spoke with Lily later did I discover the reason why.'' He fell silent and only the crackle of the dying fire competed with night crickets and croaking frogs. "I dreamed her dream, Zar.''

Lily frowned into the pillow. What on earth did *that* mean?

"What say?'' Balthazar asked, obviously as puzzled as Lily. "Her dream? I don't understand.''

"Somehow, her dream entered my unconscious mind. Visions of dolls, one with ink stains. I couldn't figure out why I'd dream such a thing, but then Lily mentioned *she'd* dreamed it. It was a childhood memory about her and Cecille. That's never happened before, Zar, and I began to realize the power of her mind.''

Initially, Lily rejected the story, but common sense gradually won her over. Why would he make this up? Besides, she remembered that morning when he'd seemed so interested in the recollection of her dream, of the swing outside her bedroom window, of the doll she'd ruined. At the time, she'd wondered about his strange reaction. Now it was clear. But that didn't make it any less disturbing. The man could not only read her mind, he shared her dreams! The men's voices wove through her shocked thoughts.

". . . a witch burned at the stake,'' Balthazar was saying.

"Yes, that's true. Witches and warlocks; that's what we used to be called."

"Some still believe you're spawned from the devil or from some evil place."

"Do you think that's why she resists me so?"

"Who?"

"Lily, of course."

"She resists you, does she?" Amusement colored Balthazar's rumbling bass.

"Much to my eternal regret, yes."

"That wasn't what she was doing earlier. Why, she hovered over you like a guardian angel. She was absolutely *possessive* of you!"

Lily cringed, wishing Balthazar was less theatrical and more truthful. She'd shown concern, that's all.

"She'd never admit it," Griffon said, sounding depressed. "Did you notice that once I was conscious again she put as much distance as she could between us? She doesn't hold me in high regard, Zar."

"You're foreign to her, that's all. Your accent, the way you dress, your background . . . she's never known anyone like you. She'll warm up. I bet she's different toward you by morning even. I tell you, Griffon, she was frantic when she thought you were near death. Frantic."

Griffon heaved a sigh. "No. She looks down on me. She's afraid to get too close. She thinks I'll soil her."

Lily bit her lips to keep from crying out in protest. Her mind yelled to him that he was wrong . . . wrong! It was that stupid Gypsy goat remark—*thought*—and he'd never forget it. Never forgive her for it. It wasn't fair for him to snoop into her mind and find things he wasn't meant to find, and then punish her for them. She didn't think he was beneath her. She just felt vulnerable around him. She'd always been able to fold into herself for protection, but she had no shield from him. There wasn't anywhere she could go that he couldn't follow.

Eyes tightly shut, she sought courage, but couldn't find

enough of it to tell Griffon what was in her heart. Yet, she had to find a way, she knew. When he'd been wounded, she'd realized how much she'd come to care for him. Against her own counsel, she'd put her trust in him. She admired him, found herself wishing to be more like him. It must be wonderful to simply be one's self, she thought. To admit all frailties, all strengths, all problems and peculiarities, and not flinch when others laughed at you or turned their backs on you. Yes, she must tell him that she cared and didn't fancy herself his superior.

Opening her eyes, she smothered a gasp when she saw a tall silhouette standing over her. The shape moved sideways so that the firelight fell upon his face. Griffon! Her heart floated from her throat to its rightful place in her chest.

"You . . . you." She held the blanket high against her throat. "You gave me a start. Is something wrong?"

"Thank you, Lily."

"For what?"

"The kind words . . . thoughts." He came down on one knee. His eyes were a shade of blue that made her think of heaven. "I needed them. It pained me—more than this gash in my head—that you thought of me as filth. I still don't entirely understand why you reject me and what I offer, but it's a comfort to know that you hold some regard for me."

Lily propped herself up on her elbows and scowled at him. "Griffon, you simply must stop intruding on my *private* thoughts."

"Even when they make me feel wonderful?"

"Well . . . I'm glad you're feeling better. And if I've helped in some way, then I suppose I'll forgive you this one time for stealing my thoughts."

"I'm not stealing them, only sharing them." He bent closer until his lips brushed her temple. "She's there, Lily," he whispered against her hair. "They're hiding her."

Lily clutched at the collar of his shirt. Linked as they were, she knew he was talking about Cecille being held captive by the Jefferses.

"Griffon, did you see her?"

"No, but I felt her."

"She's alive? You think she's alive?"

"That I can't say for sure. I only know that she's been there—recently—and the Jefferses don't want anyone to know about it." He nuzzled her ear, blowing softly. "I saw your secret admirer. Jasper Jeffers? And I met his mother. She's Gypsy."

"A real Gypsy?"

"Yes. I think she and Jasper might help us if they can."

"They'd betray their own family?"

"Perhaps." He sighed and rocked back to look into her face. "I think we should go back to Van Buren tomorrow and tell the sheriff about our misadventure."

"Why not go back to the Jefferses and demand that they—" She didn't bother to finish since he was laughing silently at her. "They'd kill us, wouldn't they?"

"They'd try, and we don't have any weapons to use against them. Besides, I could use a day or two's rest before I meet the Jeffers clan again on their territory. It's best if we enlist the sheriff." He placed a hand on her shoulder and pushed her back onto the bedding. "Go to sleep." His lips were cool upon her brow. "And try not to dream. I need a good night's rest."

She slapped playfully at him, and he caught her hand and kissed it before moving to his side of the campfire.

By midday the sparkle of the rushing water proved too tempting for them as they traveled toward Van Buren. When Balthazar suggested they stop for a while beside the creek, the others readily agreed. During the night, clouds had rolled in to block the morning sun. The air was unseasonably heavy, making the return journey considerably less comfortable. Although they'd left shortly before sunrise, Lily estimated they were several hours away from Van Buren.

As she stepped down from the buggy, the muscles in her legs, shoulders, and back complained and she released an audible groan. Orrie laughed and echoed the sound of fatigue.

"I'm going to sit my weary bones down someplace soft and stationary," Orrie declared, rubbing her backside. "How about you, honeypot?"

"Not me. I'm tired of sitting. I think I'll stroll along the creek bank. Maybe I'll even dip my hands into the cold water." Lily touched the back of her wrist to her forehead, which was warm. "It's so terribly oppressive today."

"Part of me wishes it would rain and part of me prays it won't, at least not until we get to Van Buren." Griffon handed the reins of his horse to Balthazar. "Zar, I believe I'll accompany Lily on her stroll. Will you see to the horses?"

"Most assuredly." Balthazar began loosening the saddles.

Lily experienced a tiny thrill when Griffon's hand closed on her elbow. She smiled at him, then directed her gaze to the carpet of mossy grass and wildflowers. She was struck by how her feelings toward Griffon had changed since yesterday. On the way to Devil's Den, she'd thought of him as her adversary. His brush with danger had educated her to how foolish it was to thwart him at every turn. Orrie was right. Being friendly toward Griffon made more sense. Her trepidation had nothing to do with him, but more to do with her aversion to the inexplicable. Simply put, her battle wasn't with him but with herself. For as long as she could remember, it had been so. The two parts of her at war with each other. The sensible, rational part had been the victor until lately. Since meeting Griffon, Lily had felt that fanciful, irrational half of herself getting stronger and stronger. That's what scared her. Not Griffon, but that other half of Lily Meeker. That pacing, restless beast inside her.

Looking back, she knew she'd found Griffon attractive from the moment he'd swept into the Meeker home on that stormy, blustery night that seemed so far past but, in fact, had been only a handful of days ago. Still, a part of her cowered from him even as her heart galloped from the brush of his body against hers as they walked side by side along the creek bank.

The water moved swiftly over jutting rocks. It was shallow, deepening in the center where the water flowed unimpeded, foaming and white-capped. It made a gurgling, sucking sound. Lily stopped to watch the hectic water swirl around a smooth rock. Uneasiness began to chew at the edges of her peacefulness. She glanced around, looking for a reason, finding nothing but greening grass and budding trees. But there was something about this place . . . something *not right*. She chalked it up to being on a creek bank, which usually reminded her of her mother's accident. Horror crept into her heart and she turned her thoughts away from that hideous memory.

Griffon walked a few paces past her to a cypress that grew crazily over the creek. He touched its smooth trunk and examined Lily from the corners of his eyes. She crossed her arms and rubbed her hands briskly up and down them. He sensed her troubled undercurrents.

"Lily? Are you feeling unwell?"

"No." She laughed breathily. Bright color stained her cheeks. "It's the weather, I think. That expectancy in the air before a rain often makes me edgy. Does it you?"

"Sometimes."

"How's your head? Still pounding?"

He rested his fingertips gingerly against the scrap of Orrie's petticoat. "Pounding away, but not quite as ferociously."

"I hate that you're in pain. I wish I could do something for you."

"I'm not in pain," he corrected. "Just a headache. Nothing serious. I've had much worse injuries, I assure you."

The faint scar curving at the outer corner of his eye drew her attention. "How'd that happen?" she asked, running a fingertip along the corresponding part of her face.

"A jealous lover?" he said, false hope twinkling in his eyes. He scowled playfully when she shook her head. "Don't believe that one, eh? Ah, well." He sighed heavily. "I suppose I'll have to tell the truth, although it's not nearly as romantic." He squared his shoulders, staring straight ahead at the gunmetal-colored creek. "This was a warning from my half brother to stay away from the family."

"Your *brother* did that to you? Why?"

"I told you I was outcast."

"Yes, you did."

"I got homesick and tracked down my family. I thought my mother and grandmother wouldn't be able to turn me away again. I was wrong." He smiled to ward off the bitterness. "My cousins and half brothers greeted me with knives and threats. It got . . . nasty, and I was lucky to escape with only this." He traced the scar, remembering his confusion and panic. "I never bothered them again. That night convinced me that I was no longer a son, grandson, brother, or cousin to them. When they looked at me, they saw a monster."

Seized by a vision of him as a lost, lonely boy, Lily went to him and slipped her arm around his waist. His arm circled her shoulders. "A monster, indeed," she chided. "How could your mother turn you away?"

He kissed the top of her head. "How could your father do the same to you?"

Lily jerked away from him. Hot, bitter words rushed to her tongue, but she held them back by pressing her lips together so tightly her teeth drew blood. She wrestled for control and drew a curtain across her mind to block Griffon out. To her amazement, it worked. She saw the evidence in his face: narrowed eyes, frowning mouth, an air of bewilderment. Good, she thought. I *can* escape you, after all.

"My father has never turned his back on me." She turned hers on Griffon.

"Never?" he challenged, his voice softly doubting. "You're going to stand there, Lily Meeker, and tell me that you've never felt abandoned by your father?"

She wanted to tell him just that, but she couldn't. She thought too much of him to lie. So she shrugged nonchalantly. "What child hasn't felt moments of abandonment?"

"That's not what we're talking about."

Lily whirled and picked her way carefully along the bank where tree roots snaked along the ground and burst up through the mossy earth. The going became rougher and Lily angled farther from the bank. She heard Griffon's soft tread. A glance located him several paces back, hands clasped behind him, eyes trained on the flight of a kingfisher. The bird dipped toward the creek and speared a small fish with its long beak. It climbed the sky on strong wings and disappeared through the lacy fronds of a willow. Lily, too, watched the bird's showy hunting expedition, her steps slowing. When the bird left her eyesight, Lily found she had wandered farther up on the bank where tangles of brush and low tree limbs created an impassable wall. She started to veer away and seek the coolness of the creek again when something clutched her throat and began to squeeze.

A few feet behind Lily, Griffon struggled with hindsight. Shouldn't have barged into her past like that, he scolded himself. She'd come to him, hugged him around the waist, let him embrace her, and then he'd rubbed salt into a particularly bloody wound from her past. How would you like it if she did the same to you, old boy? a voice sneered at him. You'd tell her what's what! You'd tell her to mind her own blooming business, eh? But it's perfectly fine for you to tromp on her past, dig up her old skeleton bones, and rattle them in her face. Apologize, you pompous bloke. How the hell do you think you'll win her affections if you can't even keep yourself from batting aside her—

A strangled sound whipped Griffon's head around. His gaze collided with a sight that made his blood run cold. His body turned in the direction of his head, slowly, numbly. All his awareness fastened on Lily's odd pantomime. She clutched at her throat—no, at something that seemed to have hold of her throat. Her watery eyes ballooned from their sockets. Her tongue lolled out, and that sound—that warbling, garbled sound—emerged again from her throat. Her lips formed the word *Help*, but she didn't . . . couldn't . . . voice it.

"Lily!"

She didn't acknowledge him in the least. Kicking backward, one foot and then the other, she seemed to be trying to damage shins. She clawed, twisted, but her movements grew less and less frantic as the seconds ticked by.

My God! She's dying! Galvanized, Griffon sprinted to her. He tried to pry her hands from her throat, but her strength was superhuman. From the glaze of her eyes, Griffon knew she was totally immersed in the fugue. He grabbed her shoulders and shook her violently, trying to release her from whatever demon had dragged her into someone else's nightmare.

"Lily, he's let you go. Lily! Listen to me. The hands around your neck are gone. Breathe, Lily, breathe!"

She drew a short, vibrating breath and then wilted like a plucked blossom in his arms. Her sudden weight drove him to one knee. He draped her over his thigh and brushed the hair from her face and neck. Her neck!

Horrified, he saw the red marks appear on her white skin; marks left by the vise of invisible fingers. Grasping her frail body to him, Griffon lowered his face, positioning his cheek near her mouth and nose. Her sweet breath fanned his skin and he swallowed a sob of gratitude.

"Thank you, thank you," he murmured, glancing up at the gray sky, his fear beginning to subside. She's alive, he told himself, drawing comfort from that. She'll be okay. Just get her to the buggy and get the hell away from here.

Even as he tucked his arms beneath her and readied to lift her and rise, he saw the angry, red marks begin to fade. Her lashes fluttered and she moaned. He kissed her, coaxing color into her lips.

"Lovely Lily," he whispered against her temple. "Don't scare me like that again, do you hear? I swear, you're going to learn to control your power instead of letting it control you. It's too dangerous to allow it free rein, don't you see? It will trample you to death."

She made no response, dropping deeper into unconsciousness. Griffon stood with her in his arms and headed for Balthazar and Orrie.

Chapter 10

A lullaby from her childhood wandered through Lily's consciousness. Within, she hummed along, snuggling into the comfort of the tune and the voice singing it. Safe. She felt so safe and loved. Gradually, her senses came back to her. Her mouth, she found, was quite dry. She tried to swallow and couldn't. Her throat burned, ached. Lily opened her eyes a fraction, letting her lashes filter the light until her pupils could adapt. Orrie's face swam into focus. She was singing.

Lily moved her hand slightly and her fingers touched Orrie's knee. The last note of the lullaby jolted from Orrie and she issued a cry of joy.

"Glory be! Lily, how you feelin', dear heart? Sakes alive, you've been out like a light for hours and hours. I thought you'd never let me see those pretty brown eyes of yours again. Mr. Griffon said you'd come around, but—oh! I promised to tell him the moment you did."

"Wait," Lily managed to rasp. "Water. Drink, Orrie."

"Of course, darling girl. I'll fetch you a glass of water." Orrie moved away but came back within a minute with the water. "Can you sit up a wee bit?" She tucked one hand at the back of Lily's head and helped her raise it. The water cooled Lily's mouth and throat, dousing the flames and washing away the bitter taste of ashes.

"Was I in a fire?" Lily asked, her voice emerging as a hoarse whisper.

"No, honeypot. You . . . had a bad spell and fainted."
Orrie knitted her brows. "Don't you remember?"

Lily started to shake her head, but the tendons in her
neck protested and she froze the motion. "I was walking
along the creek with Griffon."

"That's right. I'd better go get him. He's been pacing
the floor with worry, he has. I do believe he thinks you're
sweeter than fresh milk."

"Where are we?"

"Back in the Van Buren hotel."

"How . . . ?"

"Mr. Griffon put you in the buggy with me and off we
went, riding fast as we could back here to town. You never
so much as whimpered. Just lay there in the seat, dead to
the world."

"What time . . . what day?"

"It's late evening," Orrie said, sandwiching one of Lily's
hands between her own. "Ten or so. None of us could rest
until we was sure you'd be all right."

A soft knock sounded on the door and Orrie went to
answer it. "Oh, Mr. Griffon," she said, stepping back to
let him enter. "She just now woke up. I was on my way
to get you."

Griffon stepped into the room and knelt swiftly beside
the bed. He held Lily's hand to the side of his face and
closed his eyes for a moment as if overcome. *"Gula
devla."*

"Huh?" Orrie said, blinking in confusion. "You say
something, Mr. Griffon?"

"What?" He glanced at Orrie, then dismissed her with
a shake of his head. "No, I was . . ." He smiled at Lily.
"I was only giving thanks for your recovery. How are you
feeling, Lily? Any phantom pain?"

His strange question brought it all back, moving across
her mind like the dark sweep of a cloak. Her hand sought
her throat and she expected to feel welts.

"Someone tried to strangle me," she said, but that

wasn't quite right. Her mind picked through debris and uncovered another chunk of the truth. "No . . . that is, someone strangled somebody." She looked questioningly at Griffon. "Is my throat bruised? It burns, like I've breathed in smoke or hot air."

"There were marks, but they've disappeared. Would you like another drink? Perhaps some warm tea," he said, directing the last suggestion to Orrie.

"Yes, yes." Orrie bobbed her head, setting her tight curls to bouncing. "I'll trot downstairs and rustle up a tray. Honey and lemon tea will cure what ails her. You'll watch over her while I'm gone?"

"It will be my pleasure." Alone with her, Griffon gave Lily his full attention. "You rest, Lily. Don't tax yourself. I daresay a spot of tea will have you dancing a jig."

She smiled as his English accent and phrasing pleased her ear. "Do you miss your home?"

"My home?"

"England," she said, her voice a bit stronger.

Still on his knees, he propped his elbows on the edge of the feather mattress and held her hand between his. "If the truth be known, I have no real home." He winked. " 'Tis the Gypsy in me. Scotland, England, Ireland, America, it's all the same to me. I don't get attached to places. Only to people."

"Like Balthazar."

"And Thurman Unger . . . and you."

She discovered a deep peace while gazing into his eyes. She allowed herself the luxury of simply admiring the beauty in him. If she were artistically blessed and asked to illustrate *exotic*, it would be his face she'd sketch. A bar of shadow slanted diagonally across his fascinating features, leaving his left eye and part of his wide mouth illuminated, the rest dark. His hands were large and gentle on hers, and his thumbs massaged the inside of her wrist.

'You and I have become friends, haven't we?" He pressed a kiss to her palm when she nodded. "And you've grown to trust me?'' Another kiss was her reward when she agreed. ''Are you ready to open up your petals to me, Lily? Going to bloom and allow me to see your full beauty?''

''I don't know what you mean.''

''No?'' He quirked his brows. ''I mean, are you finished hiding from me? What I saw today, what you went through, it shook me to the soles of my feet, so it must have literally knocked you off yours. It doesn't have to be that way, Lily.'' He kissed her knuckles. ''We're only afraid of what we can't understand. Once you learn how to use your gift—just as you learned to use a fork or ride a horse—why, then you won't have to be hiding from yourself. You can *be* yourself, once and for all. Isn't that what you want, Lily?''

''I don't want to talk about this.''

''How long do you plan to avoid—'' He turned as the door opened and Orrie came in with a tea tray. ''Ah, good.'' Getting to his feet, he moved aside to let Orrie fuss over Lily. He sat in a chair against the wall, waiting for Lily to drink the steaming herbal tea laced with honey and lemon.

The warm liquid coated Lily's raw throat. Orrie helped her sit higher in the bed, propping her against the pillows and headboard.

''Feeling more like yourself?'' Orrie asked, tucking the bed linens around Lily's hips and waist. ''You were as white as this sheet when Mr. Griffon carried you to the buggy. I couldn't figure out what could have happened to you. What made you faint like that, honeypot? Can't you talk about it? You can tell old Orrie, can't you?''

''I'm not sure what happened. It's fuzzy in my memory.'' Lily glanced from Orrie to Griffon. Although she couldn't see his face—it was hidden from her by the room's shadows—she could feel his disbelief. ''I remember walking along the bank.''

"That's right," Orrie said, patting her arm in gentle encouragement.

"And it felt as if someone grabbed me from behind. Grabbed me by the neck and squeezed hard." She rested a hand protectively against her throat. "I couldn't breathe. I tried to get away. She kicked at him. She twisted, but his hands closed more firmly on her neck."

"She? She who?" Orrie asked.

"He killed her!" Lily's spine straightened as the certainty of the heinous deed slammed into her. "He murdered her!"

"Oh, dearie me!" Orrie wailed and covered her face with trembling hands as she rocked back and forth. "Poor Cecille. Not our Cecille! How I've prayed she still drew breath. That man . . . some horrible man throttled our lovely Cecille."

"There, there," Griffon comforted, rising from the chair to help Orrie into it. He examined Lily's calm demeanor and knew something was amiss. "Lily? Is she right? Was it Cecille you felt at the creek bank?"

She shook her head as the memory stepped into full light. "No, it wasn't Cecille. A woman, but no one I know."

"Wh-what?" Orrie uncovered her face and wiped glistening tears from her chubby cheeks. "Not Cecille?"

"I knew the man." Lily closed her eyes, seeing that face, feeling his brute strength, cringing from his madness. Blindly, she reached out and clutched Griffon's shirtsleeve as an anchor. "It was the same one, Griffon. The man I saw in the barn, remember?"

"Yes, I remember."

"That's who strangled the woman at the creek. He mur-murdered her!"

"And you sensed nothing of Cecille?" Griffon asked, hope rushing his words.

"No . . . wait." She paused, the fingertips of her mind exploring the edges of the ghastly trance she'd been caught up in. She knew she was staring straight ahead, lost to the others in the room, but she also knew she needed every shred of her concentration to be sure. Cecille. Hadn't she *felt* Cecille? For a few moments before she'd blacked out, hadn't Cecille been near? "Yes, yes! She *was* there!" Her mind hooked the flash of recognition and reeled it in for her. "Cecille was watching. Cecille was standing nearby. Cecille . . ." Her voice faded, diluted by shock. She had to swallow hard. Her throat ached again.

"Go on," Griffon urged, "Tell, tell!"

Turning wide eyes on Griffon, Lily made herself say the words. "Cecille stood and watched him murder that woman. She witnessed that horror and she did nothing— she did *nothing* to prevent it." A shudder rattled through her. "How could she, Griffon? How could Cecille do such a thing?"

"Glory be," Orrie cried, sobbing once again. "What are you saying? How could you say such a thing about Cecille? She wouldn't just stand by and let something like that happen!"

Lily shook her head. "Of course she wouldn't. Don't listen to me. I'm mad. I'm going insane!" She clutched her head and squeezed her eyes shut, rejecting the visions as she had so many times before. "I fainted. That's all. I . . . I must be ill or something."

"Lily, you're not ill and you bloody well know it," Griffon said between clenched teeth. "What you experienced is real. Maybe it's not clear—maybe the motives are hazy—but what happened is real. You relived an act of murder. Red welts marked your neck as if fingers *had* closed around your throat. Maybe you can try to deny reality, but I know what I saw. I know that you couldn't breathe. That's why you lost consciousness."

"Please, no more." Lily slid lower into the bed and brought the covers to her chin. "Leave me be. I'm tired. So tired."

Orrie flicked her hands in a shooing motion. "Mr. Griffon, if you'd be so kind? She needs rest. Please, Mr. Griffon?''

"Very well." Doubt and derision rode on his glance at Lily. "We'll sort all of this out when you've regained your strength." He closed the door softly behind him and felt Lily's relief flow through it. She thinks she's off the hook, he thought, shaking his head. But she's not. He refused to let her wriggle from the truth.

Griffon stood at the bar, sipping a whiskey that tasted faintly of sawdust and staring at his reflection in the mirror behind an array of bottles and shot glasses. Behind him a serious game of poker continued among five players. A saloon girl, squeezed into an indecent black corset, filmy skirt, fishnet hose and garters, flitted from one man to the next in a guileless search for stray coins.

Sheriff Mac entered through louvered half-doors and sauntered toward Griffon, his gait pitched as if he walked on a slant board. Observing him in the mirror, Griffon realized the man had a peg leg. His left one. The sheriff swept off his hat and whacked it against his pants' leg, releasing clouds of trail dust.

"Gimme a shot of whiskey, Curly," he told the boyish barkeep with the mop of orange hair. "I'm dry as a desert bone. Hotter out there than you think."

Griffon slid a coin across the wooden bar. "On me. How did it go out at the Jeffers place?" He knew before he asked that the answer would be as disappointing as the sheriff's trip.

Downing the drink, the sheriff motioned for another and wiped his mouth on his sleeve. He shook his head and grinned like a possum. "Them Jefferses are about as accommodating as a bale of barbed wire. 'Course, they said you had no business on their property and they fired a warning shot that must have ricocheted and hit you." He leaned on one elbow and fished a tobacco pouch from his shirt pocket. "I asked them about Cecille Meeker, but they gave me the same story as before. They don't know nothin' 'bout nothin'.'' He tucked a pinch of tobacco behind his lower lip. "Sorry, partner. I did what I could."

"Did they let you look around?"

"Sure they did." He finished off the second drink. "Didn't find anything. Didn't 'spect to. If that gal is around there, they got her well hid. 'Course, I figure she's gone off with Anson or she's met with her demise. Either way, wasn't much chance in me finding out anything. I tell you, Goforth, them Jefferses stick together like an old maid's thighs."

"Well, thanks for trying." Griffon drained his own glass and shook off Curly's offer to refill it.

"You figuring on goin' back there or are you heading for Fort Smith?"

"I'm not ready to return to Fort Smith." He rested one boot on the footrail. "If I go to Devil's Den again, I'll go on cat's feet."

"What you got to remember is that them Jefferses know that area better than anybody. You go snooping around, they'll find out and they won't be firing any warning shots. Next time, you'll be a hunting accident." He turned and nodded to the poker players. "How y'all? Hey there, hon." He grinned at the saloon girl, then heaved a sigh. "Well, I guess I'll be gettin' home. The missus will be waitin' supper for me."

"What do you know about Jeffers's wife? She's Gypsy, isn't she?"

"Yep, sure 'nuff." He fit his grimy hat back on his mostly bald head. "Eva's his second missus. The first one died some time back—before I come to town. I hear tell she was an Indian squaw. Them older boys is hers. Jeffers come to town and tried to get him a gal to help raise his brood, but nobody was interested." He paused to direct a stream of brown juice at the spittoon. "The way I heard it, he went to a livestock auction somewheres up by Poplar Bluff and there was a band of Gypsies milling around.

Jeffers spotted a pretty one—Eva, and she couldn'ta been more'n thirteen or fourteen at that time—and he just snatched her.'' Sheriff Mac lifted a beefy hand and grabbed a pocket of air. ''Tied her up and blindfolded her, threw her in the back of his wagon, and made for home. Just like that. Like he had a right.''

If that's true, Griffon thought, then Butch's sons might want to imitate their old man.

''You think you might know her people?'' Sheriff Mac asked.

''I doubt it. Why?''

The sheriff shrugged. ''Thought maybe you could tell them what went with her all them years ago. They've been wondering, I reckon.''

Griffon started to tell the sheriff that Eva's people wouldn't be interested or want her back, because it was too late. Eva had wed a *gadjo* and bore his child. She was tainted. *Marimay*. Outcast forever. Just like him, but for different reasons. Griffon held his tongue, sensing that the sheriff was anxious to take his leave, having wet his whistle and done his duty.

''Say now, I really gotta be goin'. My old lady will pitch a fit if'n I don't.'' He held out a hand and pumped Griffon's. ''Sorry, young fella. Maybe somethin' will turn up for ya.'' Then he swaggered across the floor, and Griffon saw that the peg leg was stuck into an old boot.

Griffon turned back to the mirror to watch the half-doors flap like wooden wings. His thoughts lingered on Eva. Did she like her place with Butch? He had sensed sadness in her. She seemed to him a caged bird. She knows more than she's willing to tell, he thought. Butch Jeffers had kidnapped himself a wife after his first one had died. Had his son done the same?

''Pssst!''

Griffon shifted his gaze to the saloon entrance and saw half a face. Wide, moonish eyes stared at him above the scrolled, latticed doors. He glanced over his shoulder. The boy motioned for him to come outside. Cautiously, Griffon answered the summons. He didn't recognize Jasper Jeffers until he faced him on the boardwalk fronting the saloon.

"Jasper cain't go in thar." Jasper rolled his big eyes toward the whiskey palace. "Maw-Maw would whup Jasper if'n he did." He tugged at Griffon's cuff. "Is that purty gal all right? That flower gal?"

"Lily?"

"Uh-uh." Jasper smiled, showing ivory rows. "Lily, that's her name. She didn't get shots by Paw-Paw, too, did she?" He tipped his head and studied Griffon's bandaged head. "You mending?"

Griffon nodded. "I'm okay. Lily is resting. I'll tell her you asked about her."

"Tell her not to come to Jasper's place again. Paw-Paw don't like it. Paw-Paw don't like that star man comin' 'round neither."

Griffon had to think a moment before he understood that Sheriff Mac was probably the star man, since he wore a silver star on his chest. "Lily and I are looking for another pretty girl, Jasper. Have you seen her? Have you seen Cecille?"

Jasper glanced around nervously. "Jasper likes Lily," he murmured.

"Anson likes Cecille. Do you remember Anson bringing home a pretty girl?"

"Anson is bad sometimes." Jasper ran the heel of his hand across his runny nose. "Him don't want nobody around neither."

"What about the girl, Jasper? Where'd he put her?"

"In the ground."

Griffon's heart lurched. "Cecille?"

Jasper whimpered and started to turn aside, but Griffon caught his shoulder.

"Who? Anson's wife?"

Jasper bobbed his big head. "Doralee! That's right! She's gone to heaven."

"Doralee? Is she Anson's wife?"

"Maw-Maw says Doralee rode up in a gold chariot pulled by six white horses. It's a long way to heaven." He started to turn away again. "Gettin' dark. Gotta go."

Griffon blocked him. "After Doralee left for heaven, did Anson bring home another wife?"

"Maw-Maw says you and her gots the same blood. You her brudder? Jasper's got lots of brudders. But no sisters. In-laws and girl cousins, but no sisters. Jasper's the baby. Jasper will *always* be Maw-Maw's baby." He threw out his chest, proud as a peacock with his rung on the family ladder.

Griffon couldn't help but smile. The boy/man nurtured a pure spirit. Several inches shorter than Griffon, he looked up with shining eyes, his thin hair blowing in the breeze. He wore pants that were too short and patched at the knees, frayed suspenders, and a faded red shirt with no sleeves. His arms were big, but going to fat. However, he was probably as stout as a young bull. Griffon sensed in him a tame soul that wouldn't put up much fight, if any at all. Having a soft spot for the lost lambs in the world, Griffon knew a moment of yearning to wrap his arms around Jasper in a protective hug. His was a simple heart that loved the beauty in all things. What a pity he had been born into such a dark, mean pocket of the world.

Laying a hand on Jasper's shoulder, Griffon tried to probe his thoughts, but found them too unfocused and jumbled to make sense of them. "Jasper, Lily misses her cousin very much. She's unhappy because her cousin has disappeared. If you help Lily find Cecille, Lily would love you forever and ever."

Jasper stared solemnly at Griffon for long moments. "And if Jasper don't, will Lily hate him?"

The mercenary in him told Griffon to say yes, but his decency won out. "No. She won't hate you."

Jasper released a long, sighing whistle. "Good, 'cause Jasper don't got time to look fer nobody. Jasper gots to get home and do his chores come mornin' or he'll get whupped."

Griffon squeezed the side of Jasper's neck affectionately. "Go then, and take care."

"You, too." Jasper pulled his pale brows together in a fierce frown. "You keep Lily away. Away from Paw-Paw and Anson and all of Jasper's brudders. They don't love her like Jasper does." Then he shuffled to a chunky white horse and hauled himself onto its bare back. He grabbed the length of thick rope that had been fashioned into a halter and kicked the horse into a jarring trot down the middle of the street.

Griffon waited until Jasper was a smudge against the twilight before he turned to stroll back to the hotel. As was his custom, he reviewed the conversations with both the sheriff and Jasper, investigating each for anything he might have missed. One thing became clear to him: Eva and her baby Jasper were the weak links in the Jeffers chain.

Lucky for Jasper that he'd not been born in a Gypsy clan. More often than not, disabled children were either abandoned or put to death. In his own clan when it was determined that something wasn't right about a child, the babe was left on the steps of the nearest orphanage, church, or convent. If a child was disabled after birth, he stayed in the clan. Only those born with defects were shunned or abandoned. They were a blight on any marriage and could curse the union forever if allowed to grow. Cast him out! That was always what the elders ordained when asked for counsel after the birth of such a babe.

Griffon guessed that, since evil and insanity seemed to run rampant among the Jefferses, Jasper's deficiencies had most likely seemed insignificant. So Eva had been allowed to raise her simple son. Her simple, honest son. That honesty lent Griffon hope. He won't lie, Griffon thought. Not even to a stranger.

Another thought brought him to a standstill. He stared across the street at the hotel while he went over his conversation with Jasper once more. Yes, yes! Jasper hadn't talked as if Anson was gone. He spoke as if Anson was still around, which confirmed Griffon's own belief. Anson's there, he thought. He's there and hiding—or hiding someone. If Griffon could get Eva and Jasper alone, he felt certain he could charm, coax, or rattle the truth out of them. At the very least, he could steal through their thoughts and find something useful.

Suddenly, he heard his name. Clearly, distinctly, but in his head. The voice was husky, musical. He looked up to a window of light on the second floor of the hotel. A silhouette wavered within the light—slender, full of grace. Griffon felt Lily reaching out to him, urging him to cross the street and come upstairs to her.

So, now you want to talk, do you? he asked her silently, but she sent no reply. Just that static sense of urgency. Hurry. Hurry. He felt fingers poking his back, so real he stumbled into a walk and crossed the street. God, she had no earthly idea of the extent of her power! And she didn't want to, he added. That, however, deterred him not a jot. For he was bound and determined to make her accept herself—her *whole* self—or be damned for trying.

Griffon entered the hotel parlor, nodded at the bespectacled man behind the registration desk, and stopped at the bottom of the staircase. Lily's eager anticipation poured over him like warm honey. His heart hammered and sent a tide of blood to his groin. A grim smile rode his mouth. Blimey, he had a bad case for her.

He'd had his share of women—good women, wild women, hookers, and virgins—and he'd lusted for a few, but never as he lusted for Lily. Just the thought of her aroused him. Lily Meeker. What a misnomer! Lily was no delicate posy, although sometimes she gave that appearance. No, this Lily, *his* Lily, was tempered with fire and brimstone. Again, her voice wove through his mind, calling his name in an urgent, pleading way. *His Lily.*

"You want me?" he whispered, grinning like a predator with prey in sight. "You got me."

He took the stairs two at a time.

Chapter 11

Peeking out into the corridor, Lily waited impatiently for Griffon. What was keeping him? She'd seen him cross the street and enter the hotel a minute ago, so where was he? A shadow fell on the landing a second before he filled the corridor.

"Griffon!" Lily motioned him forward, and when he was close enough whispered, "I was hoping to catch you before you retired this evening. Orrie told me that you'd gone to the sheriff. What's happened while I've been asleep?"

He glanced past her into her room. "Orrie isn't in there?" He already knew she wasn't, sensing no other presence.

"No. She and Balthazar went out to some church wingding. An ice cream social, I believe." She flopped a hand. "I didn't pay much attention. So, tell me what—" She swallowed a yelp when he shouldered past her into the room. Recovering, she sent him a cross frown. "Come right in, why don't you? I'll just leave this open," she said, moving away from the door and pulling the sides of her wrapper tightly together at her throat. "Wh-what are you doing?" By the time she voiced the question it was pointless, since he'd already shut the door. She looked at him—*really* looked at him. It seemed she'd stepped into the middle of Act Two of an unfamiliar drama. Griffon's skin harbored a slight flush and his eyes glittered strangely.

If she had a role in this play of emotions, she didn't know which or why.

"I'd like some privacy." His gaze flickered over her like twin blue flames, then he occupied the chair set against the window. "Sheriff Mac performed his duty. He went out and spoke with the Jefferses."

"And?" Lily prompted, keeping her distance until she could get a better grip on his mood.

"And what do you think?" he asked, dryly. "They lied, let him look around their place, and then he galloped happily back to town."

"Piffle!" She stamped one bare foot against the thin carpet. "Why didn't you go with him?"

"He wanted to go alone." Griffon shrugged one shoulder. "I didn't think my being present would matter one way or the other."

"So, that's it? That's all the sheriff can do?"

"For now, yes." He picked at a loose embroidery thread in the scarf covering the table at his elbow to keep from staring at her like a man craving a bite to eat. Had she any earthly idea how tempting she was in that formfitting wrapper with her russet hair framing a face that haunted his every waking hour? His heart thumped in his chest and his body, below the waist, began to tighten, twitch.

"I don't know what I expected," Lily said, pulling fretfully at her lower lip. "But I feel crushed . . . defeated."

"I just spoke with Jasper Jeffers about you. He came into town to check on your well-being." His gaze shifted from the scarf to her. "You have an admirer in him. That might be to our advantage. We could use a friend in the enemy camp."

Having gained some equilibrium, Lily closed some of the distance between them and sat on the side of the bed, facing Griffon. "He's like a child. I'm surprised he was in town this late at night."

"I believe he crept away and plans to be home by morning, before anyone misses him. I got the impression he took quite a chance in seeking us out."

"Sweet boy."

"We spoke briefly of Anson, and Jasper talked as if Anson was about somewhere."

"Did he?" She hitched one shoulder. "You're surprised?"

"Not really. I never believed that Anson left for parts unknown. The Jefferses are as thick as thieves and wouldn't let one of their own stray too far without knowing where to and for how long."

"Yes, that never washed with me, either."

"Have you noticed how in tune we are? It's uncanny how alike we think. For instance, when I was outside"—he jabbed a thumb over his shoulder at the window—"I heard you calling my name."

"But I didn't." Her gingery brown eyes smiled at him. "You imagined it."

"I heard you, here." He tapped his temple and gave a wink. "You were so anxious to talk to me, to find out what I'd learned from the sheriff, that your feelings reached me, practically dragged me across the street and into the hotel. It was just like in the woods when I could feel you behind me."

Her laugh was breathless. "What else did Jasper have to say? Be serious."

"I *am* serious." He sat forward, hands on knees, elbows akimbo. "Let's talk about what happened to you at Devil's Den, about what happened to you in the barn back in Fort Smith. Let's talk about you being psychic."

"No." She shook her head so violently that her fiery hair fanned out around her shoulders. She crossed her legs, her arms, folding into herself.

"What are you afraid of? I'm not leaving this room— not giving you a moment's peace—until you tell me, Lily."

His expression was implacable, and Lily knew stalling would do no good. "Me. I'm afraid of me." She spread a hand above her breasts and fought against the burn of emotion in her nose and throat. "Tell me, Griffon Goforth, how can I go on like this? How can I live with so much fear writhing inside me? I'll go mad. I'll end up in one of those horrible asylums!" She pushed all ten fingers through her hair and rocked back and forth, trying to dispel the anxiety. "God, what a curse."

"That's where you're wrong. It's a blessing."

"Is that how you live with it? You fool yourself into thinking you're normal by telling yourself you're blessed? Well, I don't see it that way. I don't want to be out of control. I don't want to drop off into a void, unable to come back until whatever evil that has a hold on me lets go. Someday that evil might not let go, and that's when the madness will take me over for good. That's not a blessing, Griffon." She hiccuped a sob and began to tremble. The burning switched to her eyes, but she fought the tears. "I'm so fr-frightened."

"I know, but that's only because you don't understand what you're dealing with." He sat beside her on the bed and took her into his arms. She leaned into him, letting the tears come. "Whoever made you think your gift is a sign of madness should be horsewhipped. But I do understand your confusion, Lily. After all, I've know it firsthand, haven't I? I was cast out by my family because I knew things, felt things, understood things they couldn't. My grandmother was psychic, but even she feared it showing up in me. Only women were supposed to be so blessed."

"I don't feel bl-blessed." Lily made herself sit upright, although a part of her wanted to melt into Griffon's arms and let him make everything better. "Sometimes these . . . these things hurt others. Do you like being shunned, being pointed at as if you're two-headed or a horned monster? I don't want to go through life like that."

"Usually, I don't feel that people are pointing fingers

at me. Unless I tell them, they don't know that I have special gifts. It's not seen with the naked eye, you know."

She shivered. "I don't want to talk about this."

"But you must. You can't live your life in hiding. How long do you think you can dodge this bullet?"

"I believe that if you don't cultivate this . . . this strange seed, it will die. It's a phase I'm going through. Don't look at me as if I'm already daffy. I know myself."

"You are what they call a gilded lily." He smiled at his own cleverness. "Yes, that's it. You have a beauty all your own, but you don't trust it, so you've coated yourself with something you think is more attractive. But that's what it is, Lily. It's a coating—a veneer that will rub off over the years. There will always be people like me who see through the veneer to the more beautiful you. It's not a bad seed. It's . . . magic, mystic, a rare flowering."

Something broke loose inside her and sailed off, wild and free. Lily touched her fingertips to one corner of his mouth, lightly, wonderingly. "How is it that you can look through my clothing, skin, muscle, and bone to see the very heart of me?" she asked, her fingertip tracing the lush curve of his lower lip and his cupid's bow upper one. His face reflected a myriad of cultures, ethnic characteristics, the best of everything. From his bold, Roman nose to his heavenly blue eyes, he was male beauty, gathered from every corner of the wide, wonderful world. Even his accent was not entirely British, but foreign, taking from the many tongues in his colorful family history.

Lily released a little sigh. "I have tried so often to be like someone else. Oftentimes like Cecille. Gay, high-spirited, caring nothing of the ways of the world other than what frock is in fashion, which hat to buy, and what type of jewels to wear with each gown." She wrinkled her nose in distaste. "But I find that all so trivial."

"And so you should."

He laughed, and she liked the feel of it against her fingertips. His breath smelled faintly of liquor, and she wondered if he'd been drinking alone or with someone.

"Could you study anything you wished at Oxford?"

Again, his laughing breath beat against her fingertips. "Yes. Whatever made you think of that?"

"That's one of the things I've tried not to wish for—going to college. At one time, I wanted it."

"You should. You'd enjoy it immensely. It would be good for you."

"You don't think it would be . . . well, unseemly of me?"

The black slashes of his brows met. "How so?"

"You know, a young lady going to an institution of higher learning and all. It's a waste, don't you think?"

"What's important is what *you* think."

She kept her gaze steadfastly on his mouth, unable to meet his eyes when she answered in a small voice, "I think it would be heaven on earth."

"Then you should, by all means, enroll at college. A woman with your intellect would excel."

"Do you think I'm intelligent?"

"Extremely, and so do you."

It was her turn to laugh, for he'd spoken the God's truth. Her laughter died, struck down by what she knew was reality. "Father would never consent. He told me I couldn't go to college."

"Why do you need his permission? If you want, I'll help you to enroll. I have a few connections. Or you might want to attend one of the colleges outside Massachusetts. There are quite a few outstanding ones for women."

She couldn't help but smile, although she knew this was all a dream. She'd never enroll, never take college classes. But she was ever so grateful for Griffon's support of her dream. "Dreams should be nurtured," she said, speaking her thoughts aloud. "Not dashed. Not ridiculed."

"I couldn't agree more."

Slowly, she lifted her gaze to his. In the twilight of the

room, his eyes glittered with stardust. He directed his attention to her mouth. Warmth imbued her, sent that wild, free spirit soaring inside her again. She didn't have to read his mind to know his wish.

"Yes," she whispered. "I would very much like it if you would kiss me."

His thumb and forefinger at her chin tipped her head just so a second before his lips brushed hers. She smiled. So did he. Again, a butterfly's kiss, honeyed and oh, so sweet. On a sigh, she let her lashes flutter down. His mouth closed over hers in a succulent kiss. Lily placed her hand at the side of his head, her fingers dancing lightly over the square bandage that covered his wound. When his lips released hers, she moaned softly.

"You kiss so divinely," she whispered, eyes still closed.

"This isn't kissing. This is merely a rehearsal, a prelude." Then he claimed her mouth again, but this time his tongue slipped between her lips as neatly as a hot knife through butter. He filled her up and she felt his body surge against her.

Suddenly, it was hard to breathe, hard to think, hard to be conscious of anything but the rapaciousness of his mouth and tongue. He ravaged her, slanting his mouth first one way, then another, never giving her but a fraction of a second in between. Lily realized that both her hands were occupied with him now, one raking through his midnight hair, the other gliding along the shelf of his shoulder to his nape, where his hair felt damp. Tendrils curled around her fingers. She pressed her breasts flat against his chest. She wore no corset, only a silk chemise under her nightgown and wrapper. Her nipples puckered, responding to the proximity of his male flesh.

He captured her head between his hands and pulled back to gaze intently, ardently, into her face. His breath, ragged and intoxicating, fanned the fine hair at her temples.

"I want you. So much that I ache. *I ache.*"

No man had ever spoken so to her, and Lily couldn't help but gasp and stare, wide-eyed, at him.

"Do you hear me? Do you understand what I'm telling you? I want you body and soul, Lily Jane Meeker. Oh, what a preposterous name for such a woman as you. You're not Lily the Meek. You, my fiery-headed witch, are Lily the Bold. Lily the Lionhearted."

She smiled at his foolishness, but loved it all the same. "Shall I roar now?"

"Just kiss me again."

This time the kiss had a fire to it, and Lily felt it catch hold and blaze through her to dissolve her bones. Griffon embraced her, angling her across his chest. Her hand rested on his breastbone, and she could feel the feverish beat of his heart through his clothes. He tore his mouth from hers.

"If you hate convention as much as I, then you're ready to snap its leash and do what your heart and body command. You want me, too, don't you, Lily? From the moment I saw you, I felt at one with you. Spiritually at one. But I want more. So do you. Tell me, Lily. Say it. Say that you do."

Her mouth was as dry as kindling. *Yes*. It burned in her mind, scalded her tongue. Her body sizzled with wanting. He's right, of course, she thought. Convention and society's two-faced rules of conduct were totally boring! Here was a man who knew her heart, her mind, and her deepest secret, and he wanted her—not in spite of it all, but *because* of it!

"You're a woman ahead of your time, Lily." His lips flirted with hers again. "So why be shackled by antiquated social behavior?"

"Oh, Griffon," she whispered, trailing her fingers along the bold, exotic planes of his face. The man certainly possessed arguments that swayed her to follow his suggestions. "You've awakened in me such—"

Footfalls sounded in the corridor and then the doorknob

rattled. Griffon and Lily had only a moment to right themselves. Lily's hands flew to her hair, attempting to tame its curling profusion. Griffon shot up from the bed, face flushed, eyes bright with unrequited passion. Orrie stepped inside and her accusing glance fell first on Griffon, then on Lily.

"What goes here?" she asked. "It's too late for a gentleman to be calling on a lady—especially in a hotel room with the door closed!"

Lily ducked her head, appalled that she had an overwhelming need to grin. Being caught in such a fashion should alarm her, shame her! Instead, she was amused, happy that Griffon wasn't a gentleman in the strictest sense. The ones she'd known were about as interesting as a bucket of hair.

"Right you are. I do apologize." Griffon smiled teasingly at Lily and squeezed her hand, releasing her slowly. "Good evening, Lady Lily." He strode to the door. "And good evening to you, too, Lady Orrie."

"Go on with you, you jester you!" Orrie pushed him outside and shut the door. "Lily, you should shield your honor with tougher stuff. What did you think you were doing just now?"

"Being seduced, and I'm quite sure of it." Lily lifted herself from the bed, feeling light-headed and overly warm. She opened the window to let in a breeze.

"Your aunt would faint dead away if she knew what you were letting Mr. Griffon do to you."

"He was only kissing me. He wouldn't have gone any further. Not tonight, anyway." She arched a brow when Orrie gasped. "Oh, come now. Don't preach to me when you can hardly stay away from Balthazar for more than a few hours at a time."

"Mr. Zar is a gentleman and treats me with respect."

Lily tipped up her nose at Orrie's assertion. "Don't you tire of the restraints placed on us? Men can flit from saloon to brothel with nary a blemish on their reputations, but women aren't allowed to even *think* in bold colors! Our world is white and pastel. We sit upon our pedestals and wish to join the gamboling below, but we can't because only painted ladies can kick up their heels and dance jigs with gentlemen, who are usually bored with their ladies waiting at home. It's not fair. Sometimes I want to cast off the rules and codes of conduct and run barefoot in a field of clover, streaming scarlet ribbons behind me, and with nothing but sunlight to cover me.''

"Hush such talk!" Orrie placed a hand over her heart. "Here I am trying to chaperon you and you're talking trash. Did Mr. Griffon put such ideas in your head? Honeypot, don't you know that he'll say anything to satisfy his lusting? And later he'll say you misunderstood. Believe me. I've been down this road. I know from whence I speak.''

Laughing, Lily draped an arm around Orrie's shoulders and pulled her sideways in a fond embrace. They stood at the window, looking up at a star-pocked sky and a half-moon surrounded by hazy light.

"I shan't tell Aunt Nan about you gallivanting with Balthazar if you forgive my indiscretion with Griffon.''

Orrie was a silent for a span of seconds. "Deal." Then she slipped an arm about Lily's waist and gave her a hug. "You scamp. You're getting to be a handful.''

"I'm becoming your friend instead of your responsibility. That's good, isn't it?''

"Yes, but I'll always feel maternal toward you." She hugged Lily again. "No matter how unfair society's rules are toward young ladies, you can't change them. They're around to protect you. Don't make a hasty decision you'll regret later when your head clears. And remember, I was sent along to chaperon you. I mean to, no matter that we've become friends. Hear me?''

"I do believe his eyes are the color of the bluebells in our backyard." At Orrie's squeak of distress, Lily laughed and kissed the woman's rosy cheeks. "Now, now, Orrie.

Haven't I always had a sound head on my shoulders? Don't you fret. I'm not a starry-eyed scatterbrain.'' Then she returned to her stargazing, feeling positively giddy.

Yes, the same color as those bluebells, Lily decided, gazing into Griffon's eyes across the Lucky Spoon breakfast table. He didn't seem to mind her staring at him, so she continued as Balthazar and Orrie carried on a gay patter.

"Griffon . . . I say, Griffon!" Balthazar bounced a fist against Griffon's shoulder to get his attention. "Gathering wool?"

"Yes, 'fraid so.'' Griffon cleared his mind of thoughts of ravishing Lily. "What is it, Zar?"

"I asked if you planned to go back to the Jeffers place today or if you've some other agenda."

He took a sip of coffee before he answered. "Actually, I think we all deserve a day of relaxation. Lily's just back on her feet, and it wouldn't hurt if I didn't do anything terribly strenuous for another day. That'll give my head a chance to right itself completely before I use it again to block another projectile."

"Don't even joke about that,'' Lily said with a shudder.

"Careful, Lily. You'll make us think you care,'' Griffon teased.

"I do . . . care.'' She glance at him through her lashes and caught his pleased grin.

"Tomorrow is soon enough to hound the Jefferses again.'' Griffon looked at each one in turn. "Sound fair?"

"Fine with me,'' Balthazar said. "I'd feel much better if you're good and mended before you court danger. What are your plans for once we set foot on the Jefferses' land?"

Griffon finished his cup of coffee and fished for coins in his pocket. "Let's talk of that later.'' As he flipped the dollar onto the table, he passed a message with his eyes to Balthazar, getting a sage nod in return. "For now I believe I'll pack a noonday meal and head for the river. Should be relaxing there. Anyone care to join me?''

Lily held her breath and prayed the other two would extend their regrets. She rolled her eyes in the direction of Orrie and could almost feel the woman's mind whirring.

"Uh . . . ummm . . .'' Orrie stared at Balthazar for a moment, then said in a rush, "I can't, Mr. Griffon. I got mending to do. Somehow I ripped a hole in my traveling skirt. I must repair it, don't you see. And then there's a few things I should launder.''

"Yes, and I brought a book that has caught my interest,'' Balthazar said. "I can hardly put it down. I believe I'll stay in the room today and finish it, if you don't mind, Griffon.''

"Don't mind a'tall,'' Griffon said. Then his bright eyes found Lily. "And what about you? Do you have a torn dress or a good book to keep you from an outing to the river?''

Leg irons and chains couldn't keep me from going with you to the river, she thought. "I'd love to go,'' she said, and barely kept from lowering one lid in a wink.

"Fine, fine. Shall I ask the café owner for a few food items and a bottle of wine while you don your riding outfit?''

"Yes, I'll only be a few minutes,'' Lily promised, ready to spring from her chair and dart outside toward the hotel, but Orrie intervened.

"Pardon me, Mr. Griffon, but I don't think it would be proper for you and Lily to go off alone—without a chaperone.''

"Orrie, don't you recall our talk last night? We're friends, aren't we?'' Lily asked.

"True enough. But people would get the wrong idea if you and Mr. Griffon rode out of town together, pretty as you please.''

"What people?" Lily asked too sharply. "I don't care what these Van Buren people think of me!"

"These Van Buren people often cross the river to Fort Smith, Lily, and word would surely reach your aunt and uncle—word that you don't conduct yourself as a lady. I promised the Meekers that I'd keep an eye on you." Orrie looked miserable when Balthazar cleared his throat and sent her a stern what-the-devil-do-you-think-you're-doing glare. "I gave my word, don't you see."

"Then come with us," Lily said. "I don't want to dawdle in town."

"But my mending . . ." Orrie's dark eyes reflected lost hope as she gazed longingly at Balthazar.

"Hang your mending!"

"Lily, behave yourself." Griffon's mild reproach stunned them all, but no one more than Lily.

During the past few years she'd honed a sharp tongue and had usually gotten her way. Even her uncle had begun to throw up his hands in dismay when she resorted to stamping her foot and putting iron in her tone and steel in her eyes. But Griffon's softly spoken request had gone straight to her heart. Shame clipped the wings of her high-and-mightiness, and she sought Orrie's hand with her own.

"Forgive me, Orrie. I shouldn't speak to you like that. But I want to go to the river with Griffon. Can't you bring your mending with you?"

"Orrie, might I try to put your mind at ease?" Griffon asked. "Would it make you feel better if I point out that it will be broad daylight, we'll return before dark, and that I'll behave myself?"

Orrie looked from him to Lily, back to Griffon, then to Balthazar, who was nodding as if his head were attached to a loose spring.

"Please, Orrie? I'll be good," Lily said, adding her promise to Griffon's.

Orrie threw up her hands. "I'll rue the day, but go on with you." She wagged a finger in Lily's face. "But keep in the open! And if anyone asks, you tell them that Mr. Griffon's your cousin—better yet, your brother.''

"Orrie, are you telling me to lie?" Lily asked, feigning shock but laughing under her breath.

"I'm telling you to guard your reputation! It's all a lady's got worth anything in this world." She regarded Griffon with serious intent. "I'm trusting my Lily to you, Mr. Griffon. You haven't seen mad until you see me once my Lily's been wronged."

"I believe you," Griffon assured her. "She'll be safe with me." He kissed the back of Orrie's hand, then the bluest eyes—the color of bluebells—found Lily. "Meet you in front of the hotel in an hour."

Lily sent him off with a smile. Somehow she felt as if she was on the brink of a dizzy adventure, one by which she would return a new person.

"I don't like this," Orrie muttered as she and Lily left the Lucky Spoon. "I'll fret all day."

"Oh, Orrie, don't be such a fussing hen." Lily glanced back, checking that Balthazar was far enough behind them that he wouldn't hear her next remark. She whispered just to be sure. "I won't let Griffon do anything to me that you wouldn't let Balthazar do to you."

Orrie eyed her with rank anxiety, then she threw back her head and laughed. "You scamp! You just remember that I'm a woman of years and you're a fair maiden. There's a big difference! And I'll know if something goes on behind my back." She touched a finger under one eye. "You aren't the only one with a seeing eye, little lady."

Chapter 12

The barge, anchored at the shoreline, bobbed gently on the Arkansas River. Flat-bottomed, its sides were no more than three feet high. Reclining as she was, Lily was hidden from any passersby, who were few and far between. In the hour since they'd happened on the barge, she and Griffon hadn't seen a soul. Chattering squirrels, songbirds, and delicate butterflies were their companions. *Idyllic* was the word that kept drifting through Lily's mind. She realized it had been weeks since she'd known such peace. Tensed muscles relaxed in her shoulders and neck. For a while, her cares slipped from their moorings, leaving her trouble-free.

Griffon had spread two blankets on the rough barge floor, and there they'd commenced on their noon meal of cherry wine, a loaf of banana nut bread, boiled eggs, and a jar of sweet pickles. An odd assortment of foods to be sure, but they all tasted unbelievably good to Lily. It was as if her senses were heightened so that she appreciated, *relished,* every taste, every aroma, every texture.

Stretched on her side with one elbow propping her up, Lily watched a striped bumblebee float from blossom to blossom along the shore and thought that the nectar it gathered couldn't be any sweeter than the cherry wine. Griffon hadn't remembered to pack glasses, so they drank right from the bottle. That, too, seemed inordinately pleasurable. The wine was deep crimson and deceptively intoxicating. Like no beverage she'd ever tasted!

Glad she'd dressed comfortably, Lily tipped her head to the side to fully enjoy the lick of a breeze up her neck and across her cheek. She'd even forgone her corset, something she rarely did, and she reveled in the freedom of movement. Only a chemise and legged petticoat touched her skin, none too confining. Over them she wore her split riding skirt and a calico blouse.

Griffon, too, had opted for comfort, choosing black trousers and a loose, collarless shirt. He eyed the river over his shoulder, then sat up as if coming to a decision.

"I'm going to wade in. It looks so bracing, I can't resist." His blue-eyed gaze glittered with mischief. "Want to join me?"

"I can't! I'll get my clothes wet."

He shrugged. "So will I. They'll dry. We won't wade out too far. It isn't too deep near the barge." He held out a hand, wiggling his fingers. "Come on. It'll feel wonderful."

The outing had been memorable, and a dunk in the river didn't seem out of hand, so Lily sat up to tug off her boots. Griffon followed suit, yanking off his high boots and heavy socks. He rolled up his pants legs to the knees, then hopped over the side of the barge, laughing like a boy. Droplets leaped into the air all around him.

"It's great," he assured her. "Take my hands."

Slipping her hands into his, Lily held her breath and jumped. The water was breathtakingly cold. It swirled around her. She lost her footing, and Griffon supported her weight until she found it again. Laughing, she shivered.

"It's c-cold!"

"Your body will adapt to it." He flung back his head. "I think it feels wonderful. That old sun is heating the air. Spring is getting long in the tooth early this year." He looked around at the leafed-out trees, most a budding lime green, but some had already changed to summer emerald.

"It's the rain. We've had more than normal." A rainstorm had brought Griffon to her doorstep, she recalled. She slicked her wet hands over her hair, taming curling wisps and directing them to her chignon. The river swept up under her skirt, and she kept her legs together so that the full halves wouldn't float up to her waist. "I haven't jumped into a river since I was ten or twelve. Somewhere along there I decided or was told that it wasn't ladylike to splash about, clothed or not."

"It was at a river where I suffered my first case of puppy love." He smiled hugely at the memory. "Her name was Zola, and she was twelve or thirteen years old. Coal-black hair and eyes. Coffee-colored skin. She was washing clothes with her mother and sisters at the riverbank, and I was watering a couple of horses. She was a Carranza."

"Carranza family, you mean?"

"Yes, and I have no doubt she would have been selected as my wife if I'd stayed in the family. I often wonder who she ended up with after I was sent away."

"Selected . . . there are arranged marriages among Gypsies?"

"Most always."

"And I suppose the girls have no say in the selection." Lily skimmed her palms over the water's surface. She felt something small and scaly brush the calf of her leg and tried not to think about it.

"The girls have as much say as the boys." He laughed and splashed water into his face. "Which is little or nothing."

"So I thought."

"It's a little different with the Gypsies. Most cultures, I've found, require that the maiden come with a dowry. With us Gypsies, the female is the jewel. A family never gives up a jewel without being paid well. The more beautiful the jewel, the heftier the price."

"You mean the boy's family *purchases* the girl?"

He made a face, not liking her phrasing. "Yes, in a manner of speaking."

"That's slavery, and it was abolished in this country years ago."

"It's compensation, and Gypsies have no country, so they don't follow any country's laws." He brought a handful of water to his face again. "The girl joins the boy's family. Her family should be left with something. After all, they've lost a wage earner." His grin was kind, not bitter. "The women support the families. The men—" He shrugged helplessly. "Well, Gypsy men are good for two things: spending money and making babies."

"In that case, maybe it's fortunate that you were forced out to be on your own. You would never have received a good education or learned a trade if you'd stayed." Holding on to the side of the barge, she began to pick her way across the riverbed, her feet sliding on mossy rocks. "Is it true that Gypsies marry when they're but children?"

"Gypsies grow up fast. The boys are married by the time they're sixteen, the girls when they're thirteen or fourteen."

Lily shook her head, dismayed. So young. Children marrying and pretending to be adults, she thought.

"There's a good reason for them marrying young," Griffon said, his voice muffled.

"What, pray tell?" She looked back at him and found that he'd stripped off his shirt. He'd waded out to where the water pooled around his lean waist. Wadding his shirt into a ball, he tossed it toward the barge. It would have fallen short if Lily had not plucked it from the air just before it hit the water.

"Thanks," he said when she dropped it onto the barge. "Orrie should see us now, eh?"

Lily shuddered as an image of Orrie's wide eyes and gaping mouth flashed through her mind. *Don't think about that,* she instructed herself. *It'll only ruin the magic of this day.* "Tell me why the Gypsies marry so young."

He shrugged smooth, coppery-colored shoulders and ran a hand down his chest, a chest bulging with muscle and lightly sprinkled with fine, dark hair. "We must come to the marriage whole—virgins."

"I know many young women over the age of sixteen who can and do enter into marriages pure and untouched."

"But how many young men can you say the same about?"

She faced him, bracing her arms and back against the barge. "None, actually. Unless, you're . . . ?"

"No." A smile hurried across his face. "But you are."

For reasons she could not name, she felt her face flush with embarrassment and her voice emerged whispery. "Of course."

That wandering hand of his smoothed over his jutting breastbone and then hung on the opposite shoulder. "But you don't necessarily want to be—a virgin, I mean."

"W-what?" She tried to laugh. "What a thing to say! Of course, I want to be . . ."

"It's wearing thin, losing its appeal, outliving its time." Again, he clarified unnecessarily, "Your virginity, that is."

"Yes, I know the subject matter. You don't need to keep repeating it." Her tone was sharp, too shrill.

"I've upset you, and that wasn't my intent."

"No, it's just that . . ." She bobbed her shoulders. "This is a strange conversation. We shouldn't even be discussing this. It's far too personal."

He shifted from one foot to the other, and the water shifted with him, swirling around him and then flowing smoothly again. "It is personal, but since I was hoping to relieve you of your virginity this afternoon, I think we should discuss it."

If she had been called upon to spit or die, she'd have been doomed to take her last breath. With her mouth as dry as a desert and the rest of her body throbbing with a blistering heat while she stood thigh-high in river water, Lily stared at him. His pulse rang in her ears like church bells—*bong! bong! bong!* Somewhere in the echoing depths of her body, she found her voice.

"You were hoping that, were you?" Where had she uncovered that voice of sanity? If her tone had matched her disposition she would have squawked like a frightened chicken.

Never had his eyes seemed so richly, robustly blue. "Weren't you?"

A weak laugh trilled from her. "Hope would be too strong a word. I hadn't *hoped*. I *considered* the possibility. But you must know, Griffon, that a woman can't make this kind of decision lightly. This will, undoubtedly, affect the rest of my life."

"Undoubtedly. And the decision is yours, Lily. I want to make that clear. I'll gladly seduce you, but only after you've given me permission." A smile, crooked and charming, bloomed on his heart-stoppingly handsome face. "Or, if you'd rather, I'll grant *you* permission to seduce *me*."

She released another of those nervous laughs. "I would be atrocious at that, I'm afraid."

"I beg to differ. I would be a willing partner and that would make the task far easier."

Because she was afraid her face would burst into flame, Lily lifted handfuls of water to it. Drops rivered down her cheeks, nose, chin; streamed into the valley between her breasts. The cherry wine, heated by her body, sent fumes to her head that made her thoughts hazy and meandering. Suddenly, nothing seemed too ridiculous or too scandalous to ponder . . . to permit.

"And if I allowed you to *relieve me* of my maiden's burden, would it be our private business, or would you hire a bragging wagon and ride it through the streets of Van Buren and Fort Smith?"

He made a face. "I'm sorry you had to ask that. Of course, it would be our private business. While I would be proud and pleased, I would share this only with you."

"And you wouldn't think of me as your property afterward, nor would you be *familiar* with me in front of others?"

He made a cross upon his chest. "On my honor."

"Oh, dear." She pressed her fingertips to her lips and felt her eyes widen with alarm.

"What is it?"

Her hand fell away to release her voice. "I'm actually considering this, aren't I? I'm shocked!" Giggles bubbled past her lips before she could stopper them with her hand again. A thought blasted through her, and she drew herself up with alarm. "Do you think Orrie or Aunt Nan and Uncle Howard will be able to look at me and tell?"

"Tell what?"

"Tell that I'm no longer—a l-lady." The last word was hard to expel. It stuck in her throat, a last vestige of propriety.

"Lily," he whispered, sadly shaking his head. "Being a lady has nothing to do with this. You know that, don't you?"

She nodded with reticence. "But will they be able to tell?"

"Of course not. Not unless you go about grinning from ear to ear and reciting my name."

"I shall refrain from that, I'm sure." She decided the river was too strong for her suddenly weak knees. Moving cautiously, she went around to the open end of the barge and sat on the smooth planks. Her skirts hung soddenly against her legs. She slapped the soles of her feet against the water. The sting cleared some of the fog from her brain. "I might become pregnant. That wouldn't do."

"You won't. I'll take care of that."

She glanced at him sharply. "You can do that? You can keep from making me pregnant?"

He folded his arms on his chest and nodded. "Of course."

"You know a lot about this, don't you?"

"Well . . ." He glanced down at the rippling water, then back up to her. "Let's just say I know more about it than you."

"Such humility!" She threw up her hands and laughed, then she plucked at her skirt, her mind in a whirl. "I suppose it's good that one of us is experienced." An errant thought nudged her. "If you'd stayed with your family, you'd be married with children by now."

"Many children by now, I imagine," he agreed. "I'm glad it worked out this way. Otherwise, I wouldn't be here with you."

"You'd be faithful to a wife, would you?"

"As faithful as she to me." He waded toward her, his muscles bunching and flexing as he fought against the river's flow.

Sensing his approach, Lily couldn't suppress a moment of alarm. It sent her sliding off the barge and splashing near the shore where heavy-headed blossoms bowed their heads as if taking an afternoon nap.

"Look," she said, bending over to pick one. "It's a tiger lily. I don't know which is prettiest—these or water lilies."

"I prefer these." He stood behind her and reached around to pluck the reddish orange flower from between her unresisting fingers.

"But water lilies are so delicate, so serene floating upon the surface," she said, only managing a whisper. She closed her eyes as her conscience did battle with her desire. She wanted Griffon to sweep her off her feet and decide her fate for her, but she knew he wouldn't. The path she took would be of her own choosing, and she couldn't stand at the crossroads the rest of the afternoon and discuss flowers!

"My grandmother called these fire lilies." He smoothed

the petals down the side of her face. "They grow in great
numbers along riverbanks, and from a distance they make
the banks look as if they are covered in orange flames,
especially when the wind blows and sets the flowers in
motion. 'Look, *chavo*, look,' my *yaya* would say. 'Even
the mighty river cannot tame the fire lilies. Still they burn
along the wet banks, *chavo*. Still they burn!' " His voice
had grown low and foggy. The flower teased her skin,
floating down her neck. "Do you burn, Lily? Do you
burn?"

Like a firestorm, her passion raced through her, and she
whirled to face him. "Yes," she said, flinging her arms
around his neck. "Yes. Oh, yes!"

The next minutes seemed to pass in a blur. Griffon's
kisses consumed her, blotting out rational thought. She
floated on surface feelings, governed only by Griffon, for
she had no will of her own. He picked her up and carried
her to the barge, his eyes smoldering, his muscles tightening under his teak-colored skin. On the barge again, she
reclined on the blankets, content to watch him stand over
her like a great beast who had run his prey to ground, his
chest lifting and falling from the exertion of the chase.
Droplets of water licked paths down his arms and chest.
A few fell to splash on her upturned face.

He shook his head, flinging fat droplets that burst into
tiny rainbows, then he drove his fingers through his hair.
He'd removed the bandage, insisting that the wound would
heal faster if exposed to air, and she noticed that his hand
skimmed lightly over that place. His eyes glowed with
embers of desire as he continued to gaze at her. "You are
the most exquisite thing I've ever seen," he said, smiling
when she gasped. "Why does that surprise you?"

"I . . . I was thinking the same thing about you," she
admitted, then boldly raised one hand, beckoning him to
join her instead of keeping himself apart from her. "Will
you be patient with me? I'm quite ignorant of this part of
life."

"I will be your guide." He came down beside her on one knee. "And I'm in no hurry, *gula devla.*"

"What's that mean?"

"Sweet goddess." He cupped her chin in one hand and swooped to claim her waiting lips.

His mouth sealed over hers, and his tongue explored her in a way she wasn't sure any kind of lady would allow, but she had wanted this, and having chosen this pathway, she yearned to explore it fully. Unfurling her tongue, she touched the tip against his slick teeth and then crept tentatively inside his mouth. He tasted like cherry wine, but twice as potent as what had been in the bottle. He was intoxicating, especially when he moaned appreciatively and the sound reverberated in her head.

His body weighted hers. She ran her hands wantonly over his smooth, sun-warmed shoulders and explored the indentation of his spine. Her wet clothes tangled with his, impeding them until they became such a nuisance that it was only right that they shed them.

Lily's hands began to tremble, and she was tempted to yank at her clothes and send buttons flying, fabric tearing. But Griffon sensed her frustration and her uneasiness. His hands gentled her, pushing hers aside to unbutton her skirt and blouse, to unlace her chemise, to work the damp clothing off her quivering body. She glanced around, nervous as a fox with the hounds baying in the distance.

"Perhaps this isn't the place . . . if someone comes along and finds me like this, I'll just . . ."

"Shhh." His mouth silenced her, and she didn't feel so exposed with his body shielding hers again. He set her hair free and lifted a handful to his nose. He nuzzled it as if her auburn hair was a nosegay. "I am a lucky man today. The stars have blessed me. Good fortune has showered me with moments that most men only dream of."

"I've never known a man like you . . . a man so full of poetry and so willing to share it." She felt him unfastening his wet trousers, but she couldn't find the courage to glance any lower than his breastbone. He buried his face in the side of her neck, moistening her skin with his tongue, nipping playfully at her tender skin.

She was so caught up in him removing his own clothes that for a moment she paid no attention to his deft release of her breasts from her chemise. Suddenly, cool air bathed her breasts, and she looked down to see them peeking at her like rose-tipped globes. The chemise lay open, freeing her breasts to Griffon's feverish eyes. Without the slightest hesitation, he fastened his mouth to one like a hungry babe.

"Grif-fon!" An intake of breath divided his name. She found that she'd buried her hands in his hair and some shred of reason made her loosen her grip for fear she might harm his wound. Her trembling hands wafted over his inky locks, and she could barely breathe as he suckled gently on her breast. Pleasure radiated from her nipple and throughout her chest. She felt her other nipple pucker as if begging for his attention. And then his mouth relieved it, his tongue scraped its sensitive surface, and Lily closed her eyes tightly as the world began to spin out of control.

Slowly, her hands traveled down his body to encounter his muscled hips. His body texture was so different from hers, all jutting bones and knotting muscle, his skin tougher and covered with fine hair, which teased her own sensitive bare skin. His fingers hooked on the loosened waistband of her petticoats and pulled. She thought for a moment to resist this final stripping, but then his tongue whorled around her nipple, and all thought was lost in that tiny whirlpool. The air touched her virgin skin, and again she was glad for his blanketing body, which shielded her abject nakedness.

"Griffon, I'm afraid," she admitted, and he kissed her mouth until her lips throbbed and her belly ached with a sensation she'd never known.

"Don't be afraid," he whispered in her ear. "This isn't just happening to you. It's happening to us."

Somehow she took comfort from that, no longer feeling like a stranger in a strange land. She acquainted herself with the territory by way of touch, for she couldn't bring herself to look at that part of his body that seemed to possess a life of its own. It branded her inner thigh, and she would have sworn she could feel it move, twitch, pulse of its own volition. It felt much larger than she'd imagined it to be, and that made her doubly afraid to look at it. She was already apprehensive enough.

Snatches of an overheard conversation burst unbidden into her mind. She'd been in the general store a couple of years back when she'd heard two women whispering. She'd never forgotten their words, for they had creating a stumbling block for her.

". . . and when I saw *it*, well I nearly fainted!" one woman had confessed.

"Me, too. On my wedding night, I screamed when my bridegroom stood before me in his altogether," the other had confided.

"Why, I told him, 'You ain't putting that enormous thing in me! It'll kill me!' But he just laughed. I swear to you, it nearly did slay me. I was afraid it'd made me cross-eyed!"

Then they had laughed, and Lily had trembled with fear. So that's what it's like, she'd thought, then wondered why women submitted to such torture. Love must be a strong force, she'd figured. So strong that you'd risk your good health just so your mate could derive a moment's pleasure from your pain.

That memory swam in her mind, and her body stiffened. Griffon must have felt her tension, because his kisses slackened, and he made her look him in the eyes.

"Don't fold your petals, sweet Lily." His lips caressed her nose and cheekbones. "I won't hurt you."

Lily felt the flat of his hand smooth over her belly and then his fingertips delved into the delta of her femininity. Again, she gasped and tension radiated from her.

"Ah, now," Griffon scolded softly. "Go on the journey with me, Lily. Give me a moment and you'll bloom under my care."

He breathed into her ear, and warmth seeped into her. Her muscles unknotted a fraction. His fingertips explored and then found their treasure. A different kind of tension began to build within her, and she cried out in sublime pleasure. It came in waves of exultation and in rivers of long shudders. She heard herself chanting, "Oh . . . oh . . . oh!" But the rest burned away like morning fog, leaving only the heat, only the shimmering light of a new dawning.

"What I take from you, I'll press between the pages of my memory forever," Griffon suddenly whispered in her ear, and his voice sounded tight, as if he spoke from strain. "I'll store it inside me. I'll keep it like the rare flower you are."

And then he took it . . . took her . . . transformed her from a girl of trembling anxiety to a woman of raging passion. He tore through her virginity swiftly, and she knew only a moment of discomfort before emotion—white-hot and conquering—ruled her. He hooked his hands under her knees and brought her legs up to embrace his hips, then he drove deeper into her.

Griffon flung his head back and shut his eyes tight. Veins stood out in his neck and ropes of muscles ran down his chest and upper arms. He pulled her to him, then angled back, pull, push, pull, push, rocking and sending flash after blinding flash of desire bolting through Lily. A band of sunlight fell across his face and made his gold earring twinkle. In that instant he looked incredibly beautiful, and tears of joy pricked her eyes.

"Griffon," Lily whispered, her heart overflowing with words. "Griffon, I lov—" Her feelings crested and shook her voice to pieces. Griffon groaned, and she felt his hips buck against hers, then he enfolded her in a tight embrace and his body melted against her.

It wasn't until a few moments later that she realized he hadn't spent himself inside of her. She marveled that he could remember his vow to leave her without child.

She didn't know how long it was before she heard her own panting breath and opened her eyes to stare at leaves and clouds. The barge beneath her rocked gently on lapping waves. The man sprawled over her spoke her name as if it were part of a prayer. Her body throbbed in a thousand secret places. She'd never felt more alive in her life.

Griffon bent over and kissed her navel, then rained light kisses across her stomach. He looked at her beneath lowered brows and through thick lashes, and his eyes held sparkles like sunlight dancing upon the flowing river.

"I have dreamed of you so long," he said, his voice hoarse. "And I have known you all my life." He smiled. "Thank you, Lily. From the bottom of my heart, I thank you."

She released a sob of longing and reached for him, bringing his mouth to hers. He made love to her again, and in his arms she was beautiful, she was wild, she was an exotic Gypsy flower blossoming along the riverbank. In his arms she burned.

Chapter 13

Fastening the last button on her blouse, Lily glanced over her shoulder at Griffon. He tugged on his boot and caught her eyeing him.

"It's getting late," he noted. "I guess we should start back." But instead of leaping to his feet, he leaned on stiff arms and tipped his head back to admire the blue canopy of sky. "I'd like to save this day and call it back whenever I wished."

"Me, too." Lily leaned against him, and he wrapped an arm about her. She rested her head on his shoulder. "I feel so *wanted*. Like I really belong."

He rubbed his face in her hair. "I do want you. Now more than ever. That's a feeling you've craved ever since your father turned you over to his brother to raise, yes?"

She fell silent, wishing he hadn't mentioned her father. It spoiled her good mood. She wriggled from his embrace and sat up to begin taming her hair into a bun.

"I said something wrong?" he asked.

"We should be leaving for Van Buren."

"Lily," he said, his voice honeyed, his hand solicitous on her shoulder. "After this afternoon, I should think you and I could share our thoughts, our feelings, our fears and disappointments. You were hurt by your father's indifference, weren't you?"

"I'll have you know that my father loves me." Unable to wrestle her hair into a bun, she began braiding it in-

184

stead. "Just because I live with my aunt and uncle doesn't mean that Father deserted me. After Mother died, he simply thought my childhood would be happier spent in Fort Smith than in the stuffy confines of a college setting. Father's teaching keeps him very busy."

"Not so busy that he couldn't find time to court and wed another woman."

She sent a barbed glare over her shoulder. "Why are you so intent on maligning my father? What has he ever done to you?"

"What has he done to *you*? That's what I'm interested in." He sat up, looping his arms around his bent knees. "You didn't feel the tiniest bit abandoned when he brought you to live with the Meekers?"

Abandoned, yes, she thought as the memories swarmed and darkened the landscape of her mood. She remembered the unhappy child she'd been, having lost her mother and then her father when he walked out of her life. Oh, he'd visited, he'd sent presents and letters, but he hadn't been around to see her grow and change, to listen to her problems or to help her over the rough spots in life. Lily felt the intensity of Griffon's gaze, and she was surprised to see the glimmer of emotion in his eyes.

"What is it?" she asked, concerned. "You look so sad."

"Such loneliness, such confusion," he whispered. "You should have told him, Lily. You should have expressed your feelings to him. He might have listened and let you back into his life again if he'd known how much you missed him, how much you needed him."

She dropped the heavy curtain over her mind. "Griffon, my thoughts and memories are mine—and mine to share if I wish. Stay out of my head, if you please."

"I'm sorry." He looked away from her. "It's habit—as natural as breathing."

Flinging her braid back over her shoulder, she stood

unsteadily and hopped off the barge before Griffon could offer a helping hand.

"You'd feel differently if I could crowd into *your* head and poke around. It's as if . . . as if I'm transparent!"

"As a matter of fact"—he leaped over the side of the barge to land nimbly in front of her—"you *can* read me pretty well. You'd be better able to do so if you'd harness your abilities instead of letting them stampede at will."

"Griffon, let's not spoil the day by discussing this. You know how it upsets me." She laid a hand on his chest. "Please?"

He shrugged, giving in but not liking it. His gaze strayed, and he pulled his brows together. Kneeling, he picked up something from the grass. "If only we could shed our problems as easily as this," he said, holding up a discarded snake's skin for her inspection.

The skin, silvery white in the slanting sunlight, drew her for a reason Lily could not fathom. Her hand lifted, as if it had a will of its own, and her fingers trembled, straining for a touch. The moment the pad of her middle finger touched the skin, the daylight dimmed to gray, then black. She heard Griffon speak her name, but she was lost to him as her consciousness sent her back to another day along another river.

She saw herself as a child, skipping among field flowers, scaring up butterflies and honeybees. Her father, so young she hardly recognized him, knelt and opened his arms to her.

"Come on, baby," he said, beaming, and she raced across the field to him. His arms felt like home, and he smelled wonderful—like the woods after a spring rain. "That's my pretty baby," he cooed in her ear. Then louder, "Sweetheart, she's the spitting image of you. Every day, she reminds me of you more and more."

Laughter, melodic and oh, so angelic, floated to Lily. Hearing it, her heart surged and she trapped a sob in her chest. Mother! She turned slowly, still held by her father, and stared with liquid-filled eyes at the woman who personified love itself to her. Mother!

I do look like her, Lily thought, her vision clearing so that she could see the dark red luster of her mother's hair and the copper color of her eyes. Her mother was of a more delicate build, barely reaching five feet in height and weighing no more than one hundred pounds. She moved with a dancer's grace. Her voice was more than sound to Lily—it was love.

"Want to take a walk with Mommy while your father catches us some fish for supper?"

Father fishing? Lily couldn't believe it, but then she saw her father with a cane pole. He worked a wiggly worm onto a hook and cast it into the river. In his rolled-up shirtsleeves, his beard showing no gray, Lily studied him, amazed that he could be so relaxed and youthful.

"Lily? Want to come with Mommy?"

Lily felt herself nod and start toward her mother. Oh, yes! She wanted to walk hand in hand with her more than anything she could imagine. She'd often wished she could see her mother one more time. Lily reached out from her child's perspective, her chubby hand lifting toward her mother's delicate one.

"Let's go over there by that big old oak and pick primroses. I'll show you how to make a flower necklace." Her mother's hand felt cool and gentle. "Won't that be fun?"

Lily nodded, entranced. She looked from her mother's lovely face to the split trunk of the oak. Its heavy lower limbs nearly touched the ground. Beneath it stretched a carpet of pink and coral primroses. For a moment the place exuded peace and tranquility, but then Lily remembered walking near it earlier. Something bad had risen up like a black cloud. She had shied away, pulling her mother and father from it and toward the riverbank, where it felt safe. Her mother had started to veer toward the flowers, and Lily had hugged her around the legs to stop her.

"No, no!" She'd looked to her father for help.

"Mommy can't go there, Father. Tell her! Tell her she can't go there."

Her father had laughed and motioned for them to join him near the river. The bad cloud had disappeared.

"Come on, sweetie." Her mother tugged on her hand.

Lily stiffened, planting her bare feet firmly and curling her toes in the baby-soft grass. Shaking her head, she pulled back. "Uh-uh, Mommy. Not there. Don't go there." She managed to free her hand and looked toward her father for help. "Father . . . Father!"

"Want to stay with him? Okay, go along. Maybe you'll bring him good luck and he'll catch a huge trout or cat-fish."

Lily skipped toward her father, glad the danger had passed them by again. She thought her mother was right behind her. Reaching her father, she turned to find that she'd been wrong. Her mother approached the bed of flowers beneath the towering oak.

Terror sank its claws into her heart, and Lily let out a shriek.

"What is it, baby?" her father asked, even as her mother whirled in her direction and lifted one hand to shade her eyes and see what had frightened Lily.

"Mommy, no!" Lily pointed a shaking finger. "Father, get Mommy. Go get her." Sobs of panic shook her voice and then closed on her throat.

Her mother retreated a few steps. "What's going on?"

"Nothing. Lily's just being a mommy's girl. She can't stand it if you're out of her sight," her father called.

Then her mother jumped as if startled and let out a cry of alarm. She looked down at her feet. Lily felt her mother's horror and screamed.

"Oh, no!" Her mother stamped her feet and flailed, trying to keep her balance. "Eddie! Eddie, help! Sn-snakes!"

Her father dropped the fishing pole and dashed across the uneven ground. He kicked viciously and plucked his

wife from the field of flowers. Lily saw a triangular head
lift from the blossoms and strike at her father's boot. Her
mother lay limply in his arms. He carried her to the buggy.

"Come, Lily. We must get the doctor. Hurry, baby.
Hurry!"

Her mother was pale, and there were flecks of blood on
her ankles. She moaned and her eyes rolled back in her
head, showing white. Lily cried all the way to town.
Somehow, she'd known that her mother wouldn't get well.
She had known that the bad thing had wanted her mother
and had taken her.

"Lily? It's Griffon. Can you come back to me?"

The voice invaded, separating the past from the present
like the parting of draperies to let in the sun. Why couldn't
she see him? she wondered, feeling drugged. Then she
realized her eyes were tightly shut. It took a huge effort to
lift her lashes off her cheeks.

She was lying on the barge again. It rocked beneath her.
She heard the lapping water along the sides. Her face felt
damp, and she realized she'd been crying. Griffon laid the
back of his hand against her cheek in a gentle caress.

"Hello, love. Where did you go? Back to the day your
mother died?"

She turned her face away from his touch, away from his
probing eyes. "What's happening to me, Griffon? Maybe
it's you. Being around you seems to bring on these . . .
spells."

"If you were tested at the Society, I daresay they'd find
that you possess a strong tactile memory. Has nothing to
do with me, and it's not a witch's spell."

Lily struggled to sit up, feeling weak as a kitten, and
Griffon helped her. She braced her back against the side
of the barge and picked bits of grass from her long braid.

"I haven't thought of that awful day in years," she
said, after a long silence. "That day changed my whole life.
Before it, I was a happy child with two loving parents.

After it, I had lost my mother. And my father . . . well, I lost him, too.''

''Does he refuse to discuss that day with you?''

''We never talk about it. I'm sure he doesn't know what to think about me.'' She fetched up a sigh. ''How much do you know about her death? I assume you robbed my memory of it.''

He winced. ''I wish you wouldn't put it that way. I gather your mother was bitten by a snake.''

''Snakes. She wandered into a nest of water moccasins. I kn-knew they were there.'' She shook her head. ''That is, I knew *something* was there. Something terrible. I tried to make her stay away from that place, but she walked right into them.'' She covered her face with her hands for a moment, waiting for the old ache to subside. ''After the funeral, Father seemed distant around me. He looked at me . . . well, in a peculiar way. Almost as if he didn't know me anymore or didn't trust me. He was uncomfortable around me. Still is to this very day. He never touches me unless it's absolutely unavoidable. And he's forever telling me to be normal—to act normal—to *pretend* to be normal.'' She crossed her arms against a sudden chill that emerged from her bones. ''He makes me feel like a freak.'' She caught her lower lip between her teeth to keep it from trembling. ''Maybe I am,'' she murmured, mostly to herself, for hadn't she just emerged from an eerie trance?

''Damn it all, you are *not* a freak!'' Anger pumped through Griffon's voice.

Lily knew a moment's thrill at his championing her. ''What is tactile memory?''

He sat cross-legged on the barge. ''It's when a person can get a sense of what has happened or will happen by touching something connected to the event or persons involved. When you touched the snakeskin, it transported you back to your mother's death. When you touched that beam in the barn back in Fort Smith, you recalled moments between Anson and Cecille there.''

"It seems farfetched.'' She looked over her shoulder at the glistening water. "I would imagine witches were hung for less in Salem.''

"Some of those so-called witches were our ancestors— our gifted ancestors. At the Society our research indicates that sensory perception might be hereditary.''

She hardly registered this because the memory of her father's reaction to her after her mother's death still poisoned her mind. Her need to talk about it grew too strong to fight. "After my mother died I lived with Father for six months before he made arrangements for me to move in with Uncle Howard and Aunt Nan. Uncle Howard came to visit once, and I heard him and Father arguing about me. Uncle Howard was terribly angry because my father had said he thought I might have known of those snakes and suggested that my mother walk in that direction.''

"Good God!'' Griffon stared at her, his brows pinched together, his eyes a stormy blue. "The man couldn't have thought that an innocent child would do such a thing. His own daughter!''

Lily covered the lower half of her face with one hand, hiding the telltale tremble of her lips and chin. "H-he didn't understand. He meant only to find an answer to the puzzle I'd presented.''

"But to think that his little daughter would send her mother into death's jaws?'' Griffon shook his head, his eyes tightly shut. "No, that's crazy thinking. No wonder you felt ill at ease around him.''

"I didn't. He felt that way around me. I think I scared him.'' She blinked the sting from her eyes. "Can't blame him. I scared *myself*. That's when I decided to curb these odd tendencies, and that's why I've been rude to you at times. It's nothing to do with you, Griffon. But I feel I must protect myself. You embrace what I have spent my whole life dodging.''

"Well, at least you now admit that much." He sighed as if relieved of a burden. "You've shunned me for another reason, as well."

"And what's that?"

"Because I am the embodiment of your girlhood fantasies." He essayed a rapscallion's grin. "Isn't that right, my fire lily?"

She tipped up her chin, partly amused and partly appalled that he'd exposed another of her deep secrets. "You fancy yourself a fantasy figure, do you?"

"You and Cecille cut your teeth on stories of Gypsy caravans. You told me yourself that you thought Gypsies were romantic. I suppose, after today, you no doubt think we're legendary lovers as well."

"How you go on," she scoffed, mildly amused at his bragging.

"I'm glad we're closer." He took her thick braid in hand, rubbing his thumb over it, involved in his own thoughts for a minute. "Now we can begin channeling your energy. A few simple techniques will help you tame your psychic powers and utilize them to their fullest."

She chose her next words carefully. "I, too, am glad we . . . well, we're closer, as you said. But just because I reached out to you doesn't mean I'm reaching out to the psychic world, too. I have no desire to live my life as you do."

His expression changed minutely from friendly to wary. "And how do I live my life—as you see it?"

"By flaunting your . . . abnormalities. By exposing them to the world and thus courting the contempt of others." She could tell he didn't approve of her assessment.

"Better than how you live your life."

"And how is that?" she demanded, already insulted.

"I am who I am. You live your life pretending to be someone you aren't and can never be." He thrust his face close to hers and gripped her upper arms. "You aren't average, Lily. You are special.'' He spoke the last sentence slowly, stressing each word.

Lily supposed he meant to compliment her, but she had lived too long avoiding her differences, and she wasn't ready to give them a pretty name. She wriggled from his grasp and sprang to her feet. The barge rocked as she leaped off it to the soft ground.

"I want to go back to town," she said, already folding one of the blankets. "It's been lovely . . ." She paused, hearing how inadequate that sounded. Her gaze skittered to Griffon and her smile, she hoped, added to her words. "More than that. Today you have changed me forever."

"And I trust you aren't disappointed or regretful?"

"No, not at all." She held out one hand to him, and he took it to kiss her palm and each fingertip. "Griffon, please don't be angry because I won't bend to your every wish, your every suggestion. I know that women should be flexible, swaying like willows in whatever direction a man blows them, but I feel this isn't necessary with you."

"Lily, I will never ask you to be less than you are. On the contrary, I want only that you be yourself—your whole, glorious self." He pulled her forward. Their bodies collided a second before their open, seeking mouths.

She was immediately lost in his lovemaking. Clinging to his broad shoulders, she experienced a kiss that set off small fires at her pulse points. Lily raked her fingers through his thick hair, giving herself up to the mastery of his flicking tongue. His lips nibbled hers. His hands cupped her hips. In those moments she belonged to him and was glad of it. Griffon Goforth was more than her lover. He was her Gypsy. Yes, her fantasy come to life. Cecille had thought she'd found the same in Anson, but her dream lover had become a nightmare. That realization disturbed Lily, and she gently disengaged herself from Griffon's embrace.

"If we don't leave soon, it'll be dark before we return to Van Buren and Orrie will be frantic," she explained, swaying sideways to elude his persistent mouth. She patted his chest. "You promised Orrie you'd behave, remember?"

"I remember, and this is the way I behave around a ravishing woman."

She laughed huskily. "You sly fox. Seriously, though, I don't want to worry dear Orrie."

"Very well." He backed away from her, each step labored, reluctant. "I don't want to get on Orrie's bad side."

"Yes, it's better if she continues to dote on you."

He chuckled, bending to retrieve the blanket she'd dropped. "Dote on me, does she?"

"She does, and you know it." Lily turned in a half circle, searching for her bonnet. The breeze had sent it skipping across the grass to the edge of the woods. "Ah, there it is."

She went to fetch it before the pesky wind could blow the straw creation into the tree limbs and thorny bushes. Within a few steps, she realized it was not the bonnet that drew her, but some other powerful force. The knowing engulfed her, driving her to her knees on the soft grass. She balled her hands into fists over her heart, feeling its frantic pounding, aware of what was happening to her. Instead of fighting it off, she rose to her feet again and let the force guide her as if she were a paper boat gliding upon the mighty river.

"Lily, what is it?"

She flapped one hand, silencing Griffon and letting him know that she was aware this time of her actions. She sensed him behind her, moving cautiously. Slipping between two slender dogwoods, she picked her way a few feet into the dappled sunlight. The burning expanded in her chest and gripped her mind more fiercely. Using herself as a divining rod, she turned this way and that, finding the right direction by the strength of her intuition. Her gaze focused on a distant point, and she knew it for her destination. She hurried toward the plot of overturned earth. The moment the toes of her boots touched the loose dirt, an absolute dropped into her mind.

"A woman is buried here," she said, her voice as firm as her conviction. "Recently. She . . . she was murdered."

"Yes, I feel it, too." Griffon's eyes seemed flat, glazed. A tangle of vines and brush marked one end of the rectangular plot. Amid them stood a crudely constructed cross. Griffon walked to it, then turned his head to look at Lily. "Let's try to channel your energies this time. Take a deep breath, Lily. That's it. Now let it out slowly and imagine that smoke is curling out of your mind with that breath, leaving your thoughts clear and unobstructed." He squatted beside the grave and took from it a handful of dirt, which he pressed into one of her hands. "What can you tell me now, Lily?"

She shut her eyes as her fingers closed around the soft clod, and sensations, impressions, random thoughts flickered in her mind like fireflies against a dark night. Then the lights brightened. She didn't flinch from the light, but let herself examine it, unafraid.

"This is the woman Cecille saw strangled by a swarthy man," she said, as certain of this as she had been when she was a child and had known the primroses hid an awful fate meant for her mother. "She was an attractive woman, older than me, very unhappy. No! She's angry. This man is scaring her, making her realize he means to kill her. She fights him, but he's strong, ruthless." The soil grew cold and lifeless in her hand. She dropped it and brushed the rest from her palm as the impressions faded.

Griffon tore the vegetation from the cross. "There's a name scratched here," he said, peering at the uneven lettering. "Dora . . . Doralee Jeffers."

"Anson's wife!" The import of that stunned Lily for a moment as her gaze met Griffon's. "Oh, my God! He killed his own wife."

Griffon nodded. "And Cecille saw it all. That means, if she's still alive—"

"She is," Lily affirmed.

"Yes, I believe so as well. Therefore, she's in great danger. I don't think she had anything to do with this, do you?"

"You mean, that she approved or wanted this to happen?" Lily shook her head, rejecting the idea. "No, not Cecille. At first, I was confused. I couldn't imagine why she'd allow such a heinous act to occur before her eyes and do nothing, but I understand more now. I've seen some of the Jefferses. Ham Jeffers is not a man I'd want to tangle with. If Anson is anything like him, then he's evil to the core. I didn't mention this to you before, but Ham gave me the jitters. The way he looked at me . . . well, it was horrible. He looked at me as if I weren't a human being, but property—less than an animal. A thing."

"Take it easy," Griffon said, pulling her into his arms. "Don't work yourself into a lather over this."

"Anson has more finesse," she said, grabbing at another spark of intuition. "He's a smooth operator, but down deep he's like his brother. It's hard to explain . . . but one doesn't see the danger in him at first."

Griffon ran light fingertips around the outside oval of her face. "One might admire the grace of an eagle in flight, but the field mouse knows the terror of its talons."

"Exactly," she agreed. "Cecille has seen those talons. And that poor woman . . ." Her gaze drifted to the grave. "Doralee was their victim."

Griffon put his arms around her, and Lily rested her cheek on his chest and closed her eyes. His heartbeat beneath her ear calmed her. When he led her away from the tainted place, she went gratefully.

Chapter 14

"**M**aybe that grave doesn't hold that Jeffers woman," Orrie Dickens said. She sat by the window, where a reading lamp cast sufficient light on the book she held in her lap. "I don't want to put bad thoughts in your head, but it might have been a grave to make nosy people think that woman is dead and buried."

Sitting in the middle of the bed, Lily glanced up from the game of solitaire she'd fanned across the spread. At first, she didn't understand where Orrie was leading, then she caught on to her meaning. "Cecille isn't dead, Orrie. She wasn't in that grave."

She and Griffon had arrived in Van Buren less than an hour before dusk, winning Orrie's scolding. After a quick dinner, they'd all retired to their respective rooms. It was still too early to go to bed, so Orrie had picked up a book, and Lily had tried to engage herself in a card game. But her thoughts kept straying to the afternoon on the barge where Griffon had made her his lover. *Lover.* It didn't have the secure ring of *wife* or *betrothed,* but it had a charm all its own, she decided. It hinted at passion, bright and hot and undeniable.

"Did you hear me, Lily Jane?" Orrie's voice rapped on her private thoughts.

"What? No, I . . . was concentrating on this card game. What did you say?"

"I asked you how you can be so certain that grave contained the Jeffers woman. Did Mr. Griffon sense it?"

Lily placed a queen upon a king. "Yes." She weighed her impulse to tell Orrie that Griffon hadn't been the only one sensing things and found it a burden she wanted to share. "Orrie . . . remember how we loved to play hide-and-seek?"

"Sure I do. You always found us. Me and Cecille couldn't hold a candle to you. I swear you were better at finding us than any bird dog would've been."

"That's right. I could usually find missing objects. Sometimes I could even know things about people. Remember how I knew what was in the boxes before I opened the presents on Christmas morning?"

Orrie closed the book and set it on the table. "Lily Jane Meeker, what's come over you?"

For a moment, Lily thought Orrie meant she'd noticed a change brought on by the afternoon of lovemaking, but her heart settled into a normal beat when she realized Orrie was talking about her knowing things before others.

"I used to ask you about this way you had . . . how you could guess right most of the time and how you mostly knew what was under the Christmas tree before lifting the lids off the boxes. I used to think you snooped and found those presents before they'd been wrapped, but then I suspected you just *knew*." Orrie clasped her hands in her lap and angled closer to Lily. "When I tried to get you to talk about it, why it was like trying to talk to a hoot owl. You'd just blink those big eyes at me like I was plumb nuts."

Lily caught her lip between her teeth in a moment of sympathy. "I'm sorry, Orrie. Was I a rascal?"

"A loving one, so it's okay."

Holding out one hand, Lily grasped Orrie's and squeezed. "You've been my mainstay, Orrie, and far better to me than I deserved."

"Stuff and nonsense!" Keeping Lily's hand in her own, Orrie moved from the chair to sit on the edge of the bed.

"You want to tell me how you always found me and Cecille when we played hide-and-seek?"

Lily examined Orrie's age-spotted hand, thinking how many times that hand had comforted her. "I'm not sure I can. I just knew. When I wandered near you, I felt it. Like today when I felt that grave before I saw it, and then I knew who was buried there before I saw the name scratched in the wooden cross." She laughed self-consciously. "Griffon thinks I'm like him. He says I have tactile memory."

"What in tarnation is that?"

"From what Griffon says, it means I can touch things and sense things about them. For instance, I can hold this card"—she held up an ace of hearts—"and sense that Balthazar's held it recently."

Orrie released a squeak worthy of a mouse and plastered her hand over her mouth. Her eyes were big and startled above her hand. Lily dropped the card to rest her hand on Orrie's shoulder.

"Dear me! Don't get so upset." Lily pulled Orrie's hand away from her mouth. "You've known for years that I was overly sensitive. You're right, I hid it because it scares me. Evidently, it scares you, too."

"I'm not scared . . . exactly." Orrie sucked in a breath. "You shook me up, that's all." She screwed up one eye. "How'd you know that Balthazar was in here today showing me a few card tricks? Did that nosy hotel clerk flap his lips?"

"No, I haven't spoken to the clerk. I knew because I touched this card, and when I did I saw Balthazar in my mind." She tipped her head, listening to herself. "I certainly sound addlepated."

"Oh, honeypot, I don't mean to make you feel that way. I just never figured you could know so much or how you knew it. I always felt you were a sensitive child, but I hadn't thought of you as a psychic."

"I'm not."

"But I thought that's what you've been trying to tell me."

"I'm not . . . psychic. I'm . . ." She paused, searching for a word that didn't rankle her. "Observant."

Orrie clucked her tongue against the roof of her mouth. "Now, Lily, you know good and well it's more than that. I've seen your spells. Whatever you've got, it's getting stronger. That's why you're finally talking about it to me. Isn't that right?"

Lily gathered up the cards. "It's his fault, I think." She glanced at Orrie and clarified. "Griffon. He poked a hole in this dam inside of me, and that hole is getting bigger and bigger, letting more and more out."

"You don't like that?"

"No, I don't. A person should be in command of her faculties. If you can't control yourself, then you end up in a hospital for the insane."

"The insane?" Orrie laughed lovingly and smoothed a hand over Lily's hair. "Dear girl, your imagination is running away with you. Why, you're not insane or anywhere close to it."

"But if my emotions run away with me, that's what will happen, don't you see? It's better if I keep these . . . these quirks under wraps. They shouldn't be encouraged, and that's what Griffon does every chance he gets." She tapped the cards in her palm. "He's exciting and interesting and intelligent. But he doesn't understand my world. He sees no complications in encouraging such odd behavior. His own family turned their backs on him, but I suppose he doesn't think that will happen to me."

"It won't."

"It already has . . . once."

Orrie took the deck of cards from her hands and placed them on the bedside table. Holding Lily's hands, she waited until Lily looked at her before she spoke again.

"You mean your father, honeypot?"

Lily nodded.

"You think he left you with your aunt and uncle because of how you acted?"

"I know he did."

"Oh, now you don't know any such thing. You're only guessing. I told you that your father thought you'd be happier in Fort Smith than growing up around a boring old college."

"Yes, I know that's what you told me, but I always knew better. I knew in my heart that Father didn't trust me."

"Trust you?" Orrie laughed softly. "What are you talking about, dearie?"

Lily faced her squarely. "You know what I'm talking about, Orrie. Father is a no-nonsense man. He doesn't believe in magic or wizardry or psychics. Why, he told Uncle Howard about Griffon in jest! I'm sure he never expected Uncle Howard to actually *hire* Griffon. Don't you see? I warned Mother away from the snakes, and Father couldn't rationalize that. The only answer he could come up with was that I must have *seen* the snakes there and didn't tell him or Mother about them. I know that for a while he thought I told Mother to walk in that area and then got upset when the snakes bit her."

Orrie shook her head emphatically. "Don't say that, Lily. Your father would never think such evil of you."

"He did think it, Orrie. He no longer believes that of me, but he's uneasy around me. The day Mother died he stopped loving me." She slid off the bed and crossed to look out the window. "That's why I can't let these feelings I have run amok. I couldn't bear it if I lost your love or Aunt Nan's or Uncle Howard's."

"Now listen here," Orrie said, bustling to her and grasping her shoulders from behind. She laid her cheek between Lily's shoulder blades. "Nothing you could do would make me stop loving you. You're my sweet honeypot. Always will be."

Lily drew back one panel of the sheer draperies and

sighed. "I never would have thought I could lose Father's love, but it happened." She recalled the vision she'd had of that day long ago when her father had been so young and her mother so achingly beautiful. She had felt her father's unconditional love in that memory, and the beauty of it was now bittersweet in her heart. "Griffon seems to think I might be able to find Cecille more easily than him."

"That makes sense. You and Cecille have always been so close. Lily, maybe you should listen to what Mr. Griffon says. He knows about these things and he—"

"No, Orrie." Determination firmed her voice. "And don't talk about this to anyone else, especially Aunt Nan and Uncle Howard. I couldn't bear it if they spurned me as Father did."

"Honey, they won't. They love you."

"So did Father," Lily whispered, losing her voice to emotion. She managed a tremulous smile. "Someday he might again. I hope so."

"I'm thinking of going back to Fort Smith tomorrow."

Griffon lowered the newspaper slowly and looked across the breakfast table at Lily. She didn't seem to be joking, but he found it difficult to believe she was serious. After yesterday, after their day of making love, how in the world could she be thinking of leaving him when all he could think about was how to get her alone? He shifted his gaze to Orrie and saw that the announcement had surprised her as well.

"When did that thought spring into your head?" Orrie asked. "You didn't say anything last night about wanting to head back."

Lily bobbed a shoulder. "I came along because I wanted to keep an eye on Griffon and Balthazar. I didn't trust them, but I do now. There's no reason to stay." She smiled stiffly at each man. "I'm sure you two can carry on quite well without my interference."

Balthazar stroked his pointy beard. "It might be best. If we're to tangle with those Jefferses again, it could get nasty." He winked at Orrie. "Of course, we'll miss your lovely faces and gracious company."

Griffon folded the newspaper and cleared his throat. "Zar, Orrie, would you be so kind as to allow me some privacy with Lily?"

"There's no need to dismiss them," Lily protested. "Say what you have to say." She laughed, but the sound carried little humor. "After all, we have no secrets to keep."

He knew she was trying to cover, needlessly, their more intimate relationship. "Nevertheless, I'd like to talk privately with you."

Balthazar stood and cocked an eyebrow at Orrie. "Shall we?" He extended his hand and she took it. "Might I suggest a morning stroll?"

Orrie patted Lily's shoulder before she left. "Whatever you decide is fine with me."

Griffon moved to the chair Orrie had vacated, which put him beside Lily. "Now what's all this business about you leaving tomorrow? And be careful, you might hurt my feelings."

Lily dabbed at the corners of her mouth with a napkin. "I should think you'd be pleased with my decision. After all, it proves that I've grown to trust you and Zar. It's time I returned home and let you and your assistant concentrate solely on finding my cousin."

The graceful motion of her hand attracted him, and he captured it and smoothed his thumb over the top. Her skin felt delicate, soft as a petal. "I rather enjoy being distracted by you."

"But you were sent here to find Cecille, not court me." She gently but firmly, disengaged her hand from his. "Please, Griffon." Glancing around the crowded hotel restaurant, she gathered her mouth into a bud of censure. "You promised not to treat me differently in public."

"So I did." He inched away from her with effort. "So, why this sudden decision to run?" He grinned when his arrow found its mark and made her eyes blaze. "That *is* what you're doing, Lily. Tie all the pretty bows and tails you want to it, but you're still a kite flying far, far away. Was yesterday so traumatic?"

"This hasn't anything to do with yesterday."

He bit back an epithet. Absently, he fingered the scar at the corner of his eye. "I want to make love to you again, Lily. How can I do that if you're in Fort Smith and I'm stuck here in Van Buren?"

"This proves my point. You should be devoting yourself to finding Cecille. I daresay that if I weren't here you'd be riding to Devil's Den this very moment to scout that area. Instead, you're keeping me company." She placed the napkin in her plate. "Once Cecille is located, then you and I can commence with our lives." She glanced at him from the corner of her eyes, and pink color tinted her cheeks again. "Why are you looking at me like that?"

"I was remembering how lovely your skin is—all over. Cream-colored, but with a bit of peach across your breasts and stomach."

"Griffon!" She glanced nervously from side to side, and her voice sounded like the hiss of a cat with its back up. "You swore you wouldn't treat me this way! Excuse me. I must pack."

"No." He caught her wrist, and the pressure of his fingers stayed her. "You're not going anywhere until we talk to each other—honestly. Now tell me the reason why you've decided to scamper back to Fort Smith. If it's not what happened between us, then it must be your psychic energies spooking you."

"You don't need me here."

"I *want* you here." He linked his fingers with hers. "Honestly, I believe you can help. You have a special connection to Cecille that I lack. You might be the key we need to locate her."

"You're just saying that to keep me here."

"Lily, look at me." He waited for her to comply. "I won't lie to you—ever. I ask nothing of you but the truth. Are you running from me or from yourself?"

She turned her face aside. "Both."

Sighing with regret, he released her hand and sat away from her. "And I thought yesterday was a breakthrough."

"It was, but perhaps not the one you thought. I accept that I have certain—well, for lack of a better word, powers. That, for me, is a breakthrough because I never admitted it before. But admitting it to myself is all I want. I'm not going to tell the world or explore these powers any further."

"Why not?"

"Because it won't accomplish anything. It will only cause more pain."

"More pain? Who's been hurt?"

"My mother."

He made a face. "You don't believe that. Your mother died of snakebites."

"My father suffered great pain. We'll never be close again."

"That's his loss. If he's too narrow-minded to see that you're a walking, talking miracle, then he doesn't deserve to be around you."

She gave a short sigh. "You are making this very difficult. When I came downstairs this morning I was sure of what I was doing and what I was going to say to you, but then . . ."

He smiled. "Then what?"

Her gaze slipped to his. "Then I saw you and all my good intentions went up in smoke."

"What brought this crazy idea into your head, Lily? Why did you decide to put distance between us? Yesterday was beautiful, but you make me wonder if perhaps you're disappointed."

"No, it's nothing to do with that." She glanced around

again and lowered her voice to a bare whisper. "I shall treasure that memory forevermore. The thing is, I came along to make sure you and Zar were what you professed to be. I'm satisfied that you're working with my family's best interests in mind. I didn't come along to—to fall into stupors and scare up old ghosts. I know you want to explore my—my quirks, but I don't want that. I like myself and my life, and I have no desire to change either."

He couldn't say he entirely believed her, but he thought better of voicing his doubts. Before he could fashion a response, a rotund woman dressed in a plain dress with a white pinafore over it approached their table.

"Begging your pardon, but are you Miss Lily Meeker?" she inquired.

"Yes, I am." Lily turned in her chair to face the woman.

"I work for the Victor Fishbine family. Mr. Fishbine is the bank president here."

"Yes, I believe the Fishbines dined in my uncle's home last year."

"That's right, miss." The woman curtsied. "Mr. and Mrs. Fishbine asked that I give this to you, miss. It's a dinner invitation. Should I wait for a response or come back later?"

"Wait just a moment, please." Lily opened the envelope and withdrew a single sheet of scented stationery that bore Mrs. Harriet Fishbine's signature. "Oh, the dinner is tonight?"

"Yes, miss. In your honor, miss."

"Oh, dear. I was planning on leaving soon. Today, tomorrow morning at the latest."

"Should I tell them you can't attend, miss? They'll be so disappointed. They would have planned the dinner sooner, but they learned you were in town only last night. A wire arrived from your uncle."

"I see." Lily looked to Griffon. "Just like Uncle Howard to alert any friends or acquaintances so that they, too, could keep an eye on me." Then she turned back to the

woman. "Please accept on my behalf and thank the Fishbines for their thoughtfulness."

"And tell them she's bringing a guest," Griffon cut in.
He grinned at Lily's wide-eyed surprise. "Any objections?"

"None." She nodded at the maid. "Mr. Griffon Goforth will accompany me."

"Fine, miss. I'll tell them." After another curtsy, she
left them.

"Changed your mind again, I take it," Griffon said.
"You'll be staying another day or two."

"Yes. I couldn't be rude and refuse the invitation. Not
after Uncle Howard went to the trouble of letting the Fishbines know I'm in town." She shifted to face him again.
"And what are you going to do about finding Cecille today?"

"I'm going to talk to the sheriff again and let him know
I'm going out to the Jeffers place again tomorrow. The
sheriff and I are going to talk with a few saloon girls who
have serviced the Jeffers boys. Maybe one of them in-
dulged in pillow talk. Women of ill repute usually are the
most informed. Maybe they even saw Cecille if she was
ever in town."

"You're going to Devil's Den tomorrow?"

"That's right. Bright and early. But that won't keep me
from escorting you to the dinner tonight. You won't be
ashamed to be seen with this vagabond Gypsy, will you?"

"Don't be silly." She laid one hand alongside his face.
"I never felt that way about you. And don't look at me
that way—calling me a liar with those damning eyes of
yours. Maybe I had one or two unkind thoughts about you,
but I never felt those things in my heart. You must believe
me, Griffon. I objected to your way of making a living,
but not to your heritage." She snatched her hand away as
if suddenly realizing that she was in a public place.

"Do you still object to the way I make my living?" he
asked, sensing her answer before she gave it.

"Yes . . . but not as strenuously. I know now that much of what you do helps other people."

Griffon lounged in the chair, crossing his arms and extending a smile that felt cool on his lips. "How magnanimous of you."

"Now, Griffon, don't get your hackles up. I was complimenting you."

"You were patronizing me," he corrected. "How can you sit there in judgment of something you know so little about? You have no earthly idea what my work at the Society entails. I don't gallivant across the country advertising myself as a human bloodhound, you know." He squinted one eye, struck by a thought. "Or do you? Do you actually think that this"—he extended both arms to indicate his surroundings and situation—"is what I do for a living?"

She turned her head, doing a slow survey of the room. "Isn't it?"

"Of course not!" He brought one hand down flat on the table, giving her a start. "I'll have you know, Miss Meeker, that I lecture, I write scientific articles, I research, and I tutor other psychics. I'm a scholar, Lily Jane Meeker. Not a supernatural detective."

"Then why did you volunteer to find Cecille?"

"I didn't; I was enlisted. Your father asked Thurman Unger to help if he could, and Thurman turned to me." He drummed his fingers on the table top, recalling his resistance to leaving his work at the Society for the wilds of Arkansas. "I can't refuse Thurman. I owe him too much."

"But now you're glad you accepted because you met me."

He regarded her saucy smile and his pulse quickened. Witchy woman, he thought, who could cast a spell on him as easily as casting a net over a submissive animal. "Do you feel different today, Lily? Did Orrie suspect you'd changed?"

"Orrie suspects nothing, but I *do* feel different."

"How so?"

"Wiser, more mature." Her lashes lifted briefly to reveal the glimmer in her brown eyes. "Liberated."

The restaurant walls closed in, and the drone of the other conversations battered his ears. Griffon captured one of Lily's hands and pulled her up from the chair with him.

"Come on. Follow me."

"Griffon, where are we going?"

"Somewhere private." He glanced around, looking for just such a place. He recalled a hallway, dark and narrow, giving access to the office and storage rooms in the back of the hotel. He led the way, pulling Lily along, turning a deaf ear to her protests.

The hallway was as he remembered: dark and secretive. Halfway down it, he grabbed Lily's shoulders and pressed her back against the wall. Her eyes seemed enormous, full of brassy highlights. He drew his thumbs over the arch of her brows, sensing her mixture of anticipation and puzzlement.

"You are a beautiful creature," he murmured, absorbing each feature and locking them firmly in his memory. "Do you know what agony it is to sit near you and not be able to do this?" He rubbed a kiss upon her soft lips. "And this." He filled his hands with her breasts, but the layers of her clothing thwarted him. "Wearing your armor today, are you?"

"What armor?"

"That bloody corset." He plucked at the places where her nipples were hidden beneath three or four layers of fabric. She flung back her head and moaned, revealing that he'd found them. Twin flames burned in her eyes.

"Oh, what you do to me, Griffon." She lowered her voice, giving it a purring quality. "Keeping my hands off you is a sweet torture. My behavior is shameful."

He laughed at her for thinking she had tarnished her morals. "Your behavior is delightful." Then he took her mouth as he'd wanted to take it ever since she'd seated herself at the breakfast table. He buried his fingers in her lustrous hair and angled her to slant his mouth more fully across hers.

Her tongue touched his, quivering. He delved deeper, familiarizing himself with her taste and smell. He felt her hands roaming his back and one of her legs slipped between his. Her thigh rode up, rubbed his hardness, made him groan and want her more feverishly.

"Mmm, Lily," he muttered, dropping his face to the curve of her shoulder and nuzzling her sweet-smelling skin. "There is so much I want to do to you."

She laughed and raked her fingers through his hair. "Such as, Mr. Goforth?"

"I want to wrap your lovely legs around my waist, and I want to join with you and take you to the brink of passion. Then I'll worship your honeyed breasts with my mouth, and I'll go deeper and deeper until I touch off a flood of—"

"Hush, hush," she begged, shaking her head, eyes closed. "You torment me."

He caressed her ear with his lips. "Let's go to your room and lock the door."

"No. We can't."

"My room then."

"No." Suddenly her hands weren't gentle, but strong and insistent. "Griffon, no."

He raised his head slowly and regretted that the fire had died in her eyes. "Why not?"

"You were going to speak to the sheriff, were you not?"

"I can do that later."

"Do it now." She stepped sideways, escaping him. "Cecille must be the priority. Besides, while I don't regret my time with you yesterday, I'm not entirely sure we should continue in that vein."

He propped his hands at his waist. "Is that so? Then why were you kissing me just now and rubbing against"—

he dropped his gaze to the body part that ached the worst—
"me?"

She covered her embarrassment with a spate of laughter. "I love kissing you and being held by you. What I meant is, I'm not sure I should make love with you again . . . that is, it's *morally* wrong. Lovely as it was, my conscience is calling me all kinds of vile names."

"What happened to your being liberated?" His Gypsy blood revolted against her attempt to make him play by *gadjo* rules. "Why do you follow standards set by a society that doesn't even regard you as equal to men? You have no voice, no vote."

"That's true, but it's where I live, and I can't fly in the face of those standards and expect to benefit."

More arguments sprang to mind, but he shook them off. "This is a fight you must wage against yourself. It's really nothing to do with me." He bumped into her, flattening her against the wall again. "Know this, Lily. When the battle is over, and if the victor is truly liberated and wants her reward, then you come to me." He captured the lower half of her face in one hand. "With regard to you, my conscience is clear. I'm going to keep my appointment with the sheriff, but I'll be back this evening in time to escort you to the Fishbines' dinner." He pressed his mouth to hers and licked the seam of her lips. "I love kissing you and holding you, too. But it's not enough for me, Lily. Now that I have tasted jam, don't expect me to be satisfied with only bread and butter."

Chapter 15

❦❦**O**h, my!'' Lily stood back to admire Griffon's dark suit and the red rose gracing his lapel. She took the three white roses he offered shyly, overcome by his powerful masculinity. ''You look like a dark knight,'' she told him. ''I think I'll place these in my hair.'' She went to the bureau mirror to position the roses in the soft waves of her upswept hairstyle.

''You're quite dashing,'' Orrie agreed. ''And isn't Lily a vision in that peach-colored dress? I packed it for her just in case there was a social occasion. Got a mite wrinkled, but I borrowed a flatiron from the hotel and touched it up right quick.''

Griffon fingered his wide tie, checking to make sure it was straight. ''Zar talked me into packing one good suit. I'm glad he did. What will you and Zar do with yourselves this evening, Orrie?''

''Oh, nothing much,'' Orrie said, turning Lily to face her. She secured the flowers and fussed a moment with the puffy sleeves of Lily's gown of peach satin and pale pink lace.

''They'll read poetry to each other,'' Lily teased. ''And they'll retire to their rooms directly after dinner and lose themselves in their books. Is that about the size of it, Orrie?''

''You hush your sassy mouth.'' Orrie gave Lily a gentle

212

push. "Off with you. Remember your manners and thank your hosts for the invitation."

"Yes'm." Lily essayed a curtsy. She linked her arm with Griffon's and let her pleasure shine in her smile. "Shall we take our lovely selves out onto the drab streets of Van Buren, Mr. Goforth?"

"Let's." He waved to Orrie and winked at Balthazar, who was standing outside their room, then escorted Lily from the hotel.

"I see that you're wearing a hat again," Lily noted. "Your wound is less tender?"

"Nearly healed. I'm tough as boot leather."

She tucked her free hand in the crook of his arm. "Anything to report? Are you still planning on your trip to Devil's Den tomorrow?"

"Yes, and I have little to report. The saloon girls say that Anson is charming and dangerous. Oddly, he never slept with any of them. He just flirted. They seemed to think he was faithful to his wife."

"That is odd. It's not the image I have of him."

"Nor mine. Perhaps he really fell in love with Cecille and broke his marriage vows for the first time with her."

"What did the sheriff have to say?"

"Nothing new. He warned me again to go armed to the teeth. It's hostile country, as we well know."

"You will be careful, won't you?"

He squeezed her hand on his arm. "I will."

"I've thought of Cecille all day," she confessed. "Even when I took a nap, I dreamed of her."

"What did you dream? Tell me everything you remember of it."

"Why? Surely, you don't give credence to dreams."

"I do, and so should you. Dreams are wishes or fears. Often they are the most honest revelations, the most naked. If you care to study them, they'll guide you over life's bumps." He patted her hand and smiled his encouragement. "So, tell me, Lily."

She watched the motion of her skirt as she walked, heard the whisper of satin and silk. Around her the town of Van Buren had lowered its voice to a murmur. The street was dark, lit only by lantern light spilling from the windows of the hotels and saloons. She thought of the figure they cut on the boardwalk. Griffon, tall and darkly attired, his face set in pleasant lines as he looked at her. She, petite beside him, avoiding his ardent gaze because it brought a blush to her cheeks.

"It wasn't a dream, actually. It was a nightmare." She pressed her shoulder against his, needing to be close to him while she recalled this bit of horror. "I was walking in the woods and a hand shot up from the ground, grabbed me by the ankle, and pulled me right down through the ground and into a dark, cold place. I saw Cecille. She looked so sad. She was crying. Tears glistened on her cheeks. I asked her where we were, and she said we were in hell. Then she pointed to one side and introduced me to the devil. But I was too afraid to look at him. I heard him laughing and that was enough. It was horrible. Then I woke up."

"Vivid," he said after a few moments. "When dreams are that vivid they are most certainly a message. I wouldn't be surprised if that particular nightmare came from Cecille."

"Came from . . . You mean, you think Cecille sent me that nightmare? Sent it with her mind?"

"Not exactly." He frowned, deliberating. "You caught it. Like a cold. It was out there, floating from Cecille, and you caught it."

"Are you joshing?"

"No." He dipped his head to arrest her gaze. "You're a magnet, just like me. You receive thoughts and feelings without courting them or asking for them. Haven't you ever felt that? Haven't things dropped into your head, things that weren't any of your business but there they were suddenly, bouncing about in your mind?"

"Yes, sometimes." She shook off the uneasiness such talk created in her and checked her stride. "Isn't this where we turn?"

"So it is. Another three blocks to their house, isn't it?"

"That's right. How shall I introduce you? Do you want them to know you're investigating Cecille's disappearance?"

"I'm not ashamed of it. But if you'd rather make up a pretty lie about me—"

"No, that's not what I meant. I'll let you introduce yourself." She lengthened her stride. "I wonder what I must do to convince you that I'm not ashamed to be seen with you. You should be less defensive, Griffon." A blur of movement drew her attention, and she leaned forward to look past Griffon in time to see Jasper Jeffers loping across the street toward them. "Griffon, look who's following us."

"Hey, purty gal." Jasper grinned at Lily, then bobbed his round head at Griffon.

"Good evening, Jasper. What are you doing in town this late?" Lily asked.

"Lookin' at you." He blushed and giggled.

"We're going to dinner at the Fishbines'."

"Can Jasper walk a ways with you?"

"Well, I . . ." Lily looked at Griffon inquiringly.

"Of course." Griffon placed an arm around Jasper's hunched shoulders, and the boy/man fell into step with them, his bright eyes trained on Lily. "Have you been following us, Jasper?"

"Naw, not much. Jasper was worried about the purty lady and wanted to see that she was feeling fine again."

"As you can see, I'm quite fit," Lily assured him. "It was sweet of you to be concerned. How's your family? Everyone well?"

"Sure. They's healthy as hogs."

"Even Anson?"

"Sure, him too." Jasper's eyes bulged, and he darted a

scared look at Griffon and Lily. "Far as Jasper knows, he is. Anson's not at home no more."

"Where did he go?" Griffon asked, but Jasper only shrugged and pressed his lips tightly together. "Jasper, do you know that it's wrong to lie?"

"Uh-huh. Maw-Maw tole me."

"Have you ever lied?"

Jasper shuffled to a halt, and his eyes seemed big and sad in the fading light as he trained them on Griffon. His lower lip quivered slightly. "Jasper's a good boy."

"Of course you are," Lily said, touching his shoulder. "Poor dear. Griffon, be careful. He's sensitive, vulnerable. Can't you see that?"

"Jasper, you want to be Lily's friend, don't you?" Griffon asked.

Jasper nodded, smiling shyly at Lily.

"Friends always tell their friends the truth."

"Griffon . . ." Lily frowned, trying to veer him from this tack.

"Fam'ly more better than friends," Jasper said, pushing out his lower lip. His dark, unwashed hair hung over his forehead and into his eyes. "Got to do what fam'ly says or Jasper gets whupped."

"We don't want you to get whipped," Lily said, pushing the hair from Jasper's eyes. "We only want the truth, Jasper. But if you can't tell us the truth, then that's all right. Don't you fret."

"Lily, quit coddling him. Jasper knows right from wrong. He knows the difference. He knows it's wrong to lie and it's wrong to steal people from their homes. Lily's cousin has been stolen, Jasper. How would you like it if someone snatched you from your mother and wouldn't let you go back home to her?" Griffon leaned down to be at eye level with Jasper. "Wouldn't you want someone to find you and get you back home safely?"

Jasper nodded. "Uh-huh. Maw-Maw would cry if Jasper went away."

"Lily's been crying because her cousin Cecille went away."

Jasper looked from Griffon to Lily. "You been cryin'?"

"Yes, I have. I'm frightened for my cousin." She untwisted the strap of his overalls. "I'm very sad, Jasper. If you really like me—"

"Jasper does," he cut in, his head bobbing like a horse's at a fast clip. "You chased those bad boys away from Jasper."

"That's right, and I'd do it again for you. We're friends." She laid a comforting hand along his chubby cheek. The prick of whiskers felt odd since she thought of him as a child instead of a grown man. "Friends help friends, Jasper."

"Don't cry, purty gal. Jasper is your friend." Concern clouded his eyes. "Anson done gone and—"

"She is mighty pretty," someone drawled from across the street, making all of them jump guiltily.

"Who's there?" Griffon called.

Ham Jeffers stepped into the light thrown from the second-story windows of a boardinghouse. He sauntered toward them, hands thrust in the pockets of threadbare pants. He wore no shirt, only a plaid vest left unbuttoned to expose a muscled chest. He was shorter than Griffon, but probably outweighed him by ten or twelve pounds. A slouch hat hid the upper part of his face, but his mouth sneered at them. Jasper scrambled toward him, ducking behind his big brother, not for protection but to show submissiveness. The action infuriated Lily, and she gritted her teeth to keep from hurling insults at Ham.

"You're right, little brother. She sure does look purty tonight all gussied up, prancing down the street like a proud filly with roses in her mane."

Griffon stepped forward. "I thought you Jeffers boys hardly ever came to town, but it seems you're always hanging around."

"Jasper here was worried about this gal, and I had a

hankering for some female meat, so I brought him in to town tonight.'' He lifted his head enough for the light to reach his eyes. They reminded Lily of a snake's, slanted and mean. ''Not that it's any of your business, Gypsy.'' He said the last word like a curse.

Lily shivered at his reference to women as something to devour. ''Griffon, we should go. We'll be late.''

''Y'all going to a party?'' Ham asked. His laughter added more insult. ''I thought y'all was looking for a lost relative. Guess you're not so worried that you can't take time to kick up your heels.'' He winked at Griffon. ''Never pass up a chance to rub up against decent folks, do you, Gypsy?''

''Eva is Gypsy,'' Griffon pointed out.

''She's his blood, not mine,'' Ham said, jerking a thumb over his shoulder at Jasper. ''I got no use for Gypsy trash.''

''You'd do well to watch your mouth,'' Griffon said, pitching his voice low to a near growl.

Lily plucked at his sleeve. ''Come on, Griffon. Please.''

''Go along, Griffon,'' Ham mocked, flicking his hands at them. ''If you mind her, maybe she'll give you a look under her skirts later.''

''Why, you—'' Griffon pounced, quick as a cat.

He took Ham by surprise, barreling into him and knocking him flat. Jasper dodged them and brought his fists to his mouth. Sounds of fear escaped him, and he looked from the two men rolling and grunting on the ground to Lily, as if she should intervene. Lily considered it for one second, but the flying fists and powerful punches dashed that foolish notion. She placed an arm about Jasper and pulled him clear of the fight. Griffon had taken her by surprise as well. She didn't think he was the kind to start a fight. Finish one, yes. But he usually held himself in rigid control, and a few hateful words couldn't send him into a rage. Until now. Did he attack to defend her honor?

''Make them stop,'' Jasper whined around his fists, stirring Lily's pity enough to make her step closer to the fighting men.

"Griffon! Please, stop!" Her words were useless. Looking up and down the street, she spotted the sheriff swaying toward them, favoring his good leg, dragging his peg leg along. She glanced skyward in relief. "Sheriff, please do something!"

Sheriff Mac grabbed the back of Ham's vest and hauled him off Griffon. Ham held on to Griffon's jacket sleeve long enough to tear it from its shoulder seam before he let go. The rose boutonniere flew off Griffon's lapel and landed in the street. Ham crushed it with the heel of his boot. Griffon leaped to a crouch, ready to attack.

"Hold off there, fella, unless you want to go to jail." The sheriff flung Ham toward Jasper. "You Jefferses get out of town. I don't want any more trouble from you. You might rule the roost at Devil's Den, but this here is my chicken coop, and what I say is law. Now vamoose!"

"He jumped me," Ham said, pointing at Griffon. "Just ask my brother."

"Asking him is like listening to an echo. Heard it once, heard the same thing twice." The sheriff raked the back of his hand across his mouth. "I don't care who jumped who. All I want is peace and quiet. I don't cotton to men fighting like stray dogs in the middle of a public street. Am I gonna have to haul y'all in to jail or are you goin' your separate ways?" He eyed Ham, then Griffon. "Well, what's it gonna be?"

Griffon rose to his feet and turned his back on Ham, letting his body language speak for him. Lily left Jasper and went to his side.

"Are you all right?" She touched a drop of blood on his lower lip. She picked up his dusty hat and handed it to him.

"Ain't that touchin'?" Ham drawled, and Griffon whirled, ready to do battle again.

Lily clutched his torn sleeve. "No, Griffon. Please."

Sheriff Mac gave Ham a push. "Get goin'. You, too, Jasper. I'm short on patience with you two. Get on back where you belong."

Jasper put his hands against Ham's back and propelled his brother in front of him. "Paw-Paw won't like it if Ham and Jasper land in jail. Let's go, Ham."

"I'm going. Get your hands off me." Ham batted Jasper aside. His eyes glinted as he turned them in Lily's direction. "I'll be seeing you again, purty gal. You can set your clock by that."

"You're this close to getting arrested." The sheriff held his thumb and forefinger a fraction of an inch apart. Ham sauntered away with Jasper trotting a little ahead of him. "I know you folks got troubles, but I don't like you adding to mine," Sheriff Mac said, directing his warning at Griffon. "I make myself clear?"

Griffon nodded. The sheriff touched the brim of his slouchy hat and headed in the direction of his office. Griffon slapped his own hat against his thigh to dislodge the dirt.

"Are you hurt?" Lily asked.

"No." He glanced at his dusty, torn clothing, then noticed the dots of blood on his tie. "I certainly can't go anywhere looking like this."

"We'll go back to the hotel so you can change."

"Into what? I have nothing else to wear to a dinner party." He smoothed his hair into place. "I'll escort you the rest of the way, and then I'll come for you at nine to walk you back to the hotel. Is nine okay? Should I make it ten?"

"Nine is fine. Won't you change clothes and join me later? A shirt and trousers will do. We'll explain the circumstances."

"No. I'd be poor company now." He breathed in deeply and let the air out in a rush. "I wouldn't mention this to your hosts. Word might get back to Fort Smith and add to your uncle's worries. You're right about Ham. He's dangerous.

I want you to be careful, Lily. I don't want you to venture outside the hotel alone—ever.''

"You don't think he'd . . ." She laughed, shaking her head. "You're scaring me."

"Good. I want you to be scared of that man." He gripped her upper arms and held her gaze. "Never go out alone. Do you understand me?"

"Yes, relax." She wiped the blood from his mouth with her thumb. "I'm worried about you."

"I'm okay." He plucked a white handkerchief from his pocket and handed it to her. "Wipe your hands on that. Can't have you supping at the bank president's table with bloodstains on your fingers."

She used the handkerchief and gave it back to him. "Did you tell the sheriff that we think Anson killed his wife?"

"No." He cupped his hand around her elbow and pointed her in the direction of the Fishbine residence.

"Why not?"

"He'd ask me for evidence."

"That's *his* job, getting evidence."

"Lily, when you accuse someone of murder you should have a shred of evidence to support your claim."

"But we both felt—"

"I don't think the sheriff puts much faith in feelings or psychic impressions. I didn't tell him about our theory because I would like him to take us seriously. If I tell him about your fugues and my mind reading, he'll laugh us out of town."

"Yes, I imagine he would." She peeked at him from beneath her lashes, wondering how often he had to protect himself from howling laughter at his expense.

"Here we are." He stopped before a picket fence gate and held her hands lightly. He plucked one of the white roses from her hair and sniffed it, closing his eyes for a moment. "You're a vision, Lily. Have a good time and extend my regrets. Tell them I remembered a previous engagement. Make up a suitable excuse for me."

"I will." She turned her cheek for the brush of his lips. "See you later. Be sure and eat something."

He smiled. "Yes, ma'am." Then he strode away, his torn sleeve flopping forlornly, the white rose clutched in his hand.

At the hotel, Griffon went upstairs to the room he shared with Balthazar and changed clothes. Balthazar was nowhere to be found, so Griffon went downstairs and outside, thinking he'd stop at the saloon and see if Zar had decided to play a few hands of poker.

"What are you doing here?"

Griffon turned to see his friend striding toward him, a bottle of spirits in one hand and a bouquet of wildflowers in the other. Griffon laid a palm over his heart.

"For me?" he asked. "How sweet of you, Zar. But you shouldn't have, really, old boy."

Scowling, Balthazar stopped in front of him and surveyed the remaining evidence of Griffon's street fight. "I gather that Lily finally got her fill of your theory that she's psychic and she boxed you."

"No, this fat lip is the work of one Ham Jeffers. We scuffled and I ruined my suit, so I dropped Lily at the Fishbines' and came back here to make repairs. I'll forgo the dinner and fetch her in a few hours." He reached for the bottle. "Champagne? What's the occasion? Shall we drink it in the dining room or upstairs?"

"*We* shan't drink it anywhere." Balthazar removed it from Griffon's easy reach. "I'm taking this upstairs to Orrie Dickens."

"Those, too?" Griffon indicated the daisies, marigolds, and bachelor buttons.

"These, too. We're having cold chicken, fruit, and this champagne. I'd invite you to join us, dear chap, but I'd have to check with Miss Dickens first."

Griffon nudged a shoulder against Balthazar's and grinned. "I should insist that you ask Orrie if three's a crowd, but I won't put you through that. Go ahead, Zar. Give her a kiss for me, too.''

"Oh, you!" Balthazar puffed out his chest. "We're having dinner, Griffon. Why must you exaggerate everything?''

"Something I learned from you, old fox.'' He buttoned the cuffs of his fresh shirt. "Go on with you. Don't keep the lady waiting.''

"Before I trundle off, are you okay? That heathen didn't damage your goods, did he?''

"Ham?'' He shook his head. "Not likely. But I didn't fancy what I felt when he looked at Lily.''

"Jealous, were you?''

"N-o-o,'' Griffon said, drawing out the word. "I was concerned because Ham's feelings toward Lily are anything but chivalrous. He thinks of women as property.'' Griffon fingered his lip, which had swollen slightly but now seemed to be returning to normal. "Why did you jump to the conclusion that I'd be jealous?''

"Well, because you care for that girl.'' Balthazar tucked the bottle under his arm and transferred the flowers to that hand. "You're not going to stand there and deny it, are you? Believe me, it would be pointless.''

"I don't deny it. I told you I thought she was special.''

"You're falling in love with her.'' Balthazar heaved a pained sigh. "I admit I don't exactly approve of you getting all dreamy-eyed over this girl, especially when we have important work ahead of us, but I'm resigned to it. There's nothing I can do to reverse it, is there? Therefore, I've decided to step aside and not offer any dire warnings or ill-timed advice. I've never seen you in love before, but I imagine you'll be as bullheaded as any besotted man.''

"You stand there with flowers and champagne and have the audacity to call me besotted?'' Griffon rested his hands at his waist and swayed back to issue a bark of laughter. "That tops everything.''

"Miss Dickens and I are good friends. Since you and

Lily were going out tonight, I, of course, offered to keep Miss Dickens company.''

"Always the gentleman." Griffon made a slashing motion. "Cut the bull, as they say here in the south. You're courting that woman," Griffon accused, jutting his chin at Balthazar.

"And you're in love with Lily Meeker," Balthazar shot back.

"What if I am?" Griffon heard the sharpness in his tone and shook his head. "Listen to us. We sound quite daft."

Balthazar chuckled, one hand riding his round stomach. "So we do. Is the feeling mutual between you and Lily?"

Griffon leaned against the outside wall of the hotel and tucked the tips of his fingers in his front pockets. "Not in the same degree, no. I have no chains holding me from her, but Lily is chained by her need to be accepted by everyone.''

"She'll outgrow that. Most of us come to realize we can't make everyone like us.''

"No, it's more than that." He stroked his tender lip again, and the tingle of pain was nothing compared to the ache in his heart. "I represent everything she has rejected her entire life.''

"Come on, dear boy," Balthazar said, seeking to comfort him. "She'll come around. Don't be so impatient. Ladies have to be courted and chased. They don't give in to a man as easily as the women we've run across of late.''

Griffon laughed shortly. "No, that's not what I mean, Zar." He ticked off his reasons finger by finger. "I'm an outsider, an outcast, an oddity, a man facing the very thing that she has turned her back on since she was a toddler. She's denied her psychic ability for years.''

"Oh, I follow you now." Balthazar placed his hand on Griffon's shoulder. "But I'm afraid I can't help you.''

Griffon smiled. "Go meet your lady friend, Zar." When the other man hesitated, Griffon jerked his head in a silent command. "I'm okay. Have a nice evening.''

"Cheerio, then. When will you be coming back to the room tonight?"

Griffon eyed Balthazar, reading his thoughts with no trouble. He reached into his pocket, found a folded bill, and tucked in into Zar's hand. "Why not secure another room tonight? My treat."

"No, really, I couldn't—"

"Zar," Griffon interrupted. "Don't press your luck. Take the money and rent the bloody room." He lowered one lid. "Have fun."

Color dotting his cheeks, Balthazar took the money and gave Griffon a smile of gratitude before hurrying into the hotel. Griffon saw him flag the hotel clerk and place the money on the registry desk, then he turned away to take a seat in one of the rockers in front of the hotel. He checked his pocket watch, mindful of the time. He didn't want Lily to wait for him or start back to the hotel alone.

Rocking, he found bitter humor in his predicament. Priding himself as a man who didn't require anyone's approval, he was obsessed with gaining Lily's. His teeth grazed his lip and he winced, but the pain brought his thoughts back to Ham.

Danger flooded through him, making him freeze for a few moments. His sixth sense told him that something was afoot, but he couldn't pinpoint it, other than knowing that Ham was at its center. He supposed Zar was right. He should concentrate on keeping Lily safe and finding Cecille quickly. But he knew his good intentions would turn to ashes the moment he saw Lily again.

Hadn't he lectured himself like this countless times since he'd met the lovely Lily Meeker, only to listen to his beating heart when he was near her? He was like the town drunk, who was sincerely sober only when a bottle wasn't in easy reach. Lily was his bottle of spirits, and he couldn't quench his thirst for her.

He set the chair to a lazy motion again. Conversely, a tiny part of him hated Lily Meeker. Hated her for making him feel unworthy of her, for making him a trifle uncomfortable with his psychic power. He balled his hands into fists atop the wide chair arms, and the rocking motion increased with his agitation. While he could understand the painful episode in her past, when her mother died and her father rejected her, he couldn't understand her refusal to accept her talents. She was a grown woman, yet she was still vying for her father's attention . . . his stingy love.

Lily, you're a fool, he thought. *You're trying to be something you're not so that a man will love you, and* this *man loves you just the way you are.*

His mother and grandmother would be pleased to know of his current lot in life, he thought. On the day he was born, his grandmother had read his fortune. He would be a lantern, she'd predicted, to shed light on life's mysteries. He would hold himself apart from others and, ultimately, his destiny would be linked to a *gadjica.* Of course, his mother had taken steps to make sure that didn't happen. She'd picked out a wife for him as soon as possible and had raised him to despise the *gadjo* ways. As it turned out, he hadn't held himself from his family, they had thrown him away like so much slop.

Sighing, he closed his eyes and counted his blessings. True, the early years had been hell, but fate had sent him two angels named Balthazar and Thurman Unger. Two *gadjos* who had embraced a sullen Gypsy boy and given him a better life. Instead of punishing him for his keen sixth sense, they had helped him hone it and appreciate it. Once, his "knowing" had frightened him, just as it frightened Lily, but he'd shone a bright light on it, examined it thoroughly, and had seen there wasn't anything to fear.

I am a lantern, he reminded himself. *I will shine my light on Lily's dark pocket of fear and make it go away.*

First he'd have to find Cecille.

"Cecille," he whispered, opening his eyes and staring

in the direction of Devil's Den, knowing he would find her there.

But what would he find? Lily was certain Cecille was being held captive, but Griffon couldn't share in her staunch belief. If Cecille had been so enchanted by Anson that she'd slip off to meet him in secret places, telling no one of their affair, then wouldn't she run away with him? It made sense. Maybe not to Lily, who had been shocked to hear that her cousin had carried on behind her back. In fact, Griffon suspected Lily couldn't allow herself to think that Cecille might have made love to Anson in that barn outside Fort Smith. He, however, sensed that Cecille's attraction to Anson was carnal, white-hot, obsessive. There was a chance that Cecille might not want to be rescued. She might resist, along with the other Jefferses.

Griffon sat straight and gripped the chair arms, stabbed by the blade of fatalism. He had been thinking that Lily was the *gadjica* his grandmother had prophesied. What if Cecille was the link to his fate? It was entirely possible he'd misinterpreted his grandmother's reading of his future. She might not have been speaking of his love life, but of his life, period. He might very well come face-to-face with his destiny—with his death—in the wilds of the Ozark Mountains.

Chapter 16

⁓⁓⁓

Victor and Harriet Fishbine's daughter, Emily, sat beside Lily on the front parlor settee. The dinner of roast duckling and vegetables had been meticulously prepared, and Lily had enjoyed both it and the conversation. The other guests—two bank employees and their wives—had left shortly after the dinner, leaving Lily time to converse with her hosts before she, too, took her leave.

Lily glanced at the mantel clock. Eight-thirty. Griffon would be collecting her soon.

"I'm so sorry your friend couldn't make it," Victor Fishbine said. He was her uncle's age, but with nary a hair on his gleaming head. His mustache, however, was luxuriant, curling and waxed at the tips. "Rumors are abounding about town concerning him."

"Oh? I had no idea." Lily looked from him to his pretty, chubby-cheeked wife and then to Emily, two years her junior. Emily's green eyes sparked with interest, and she nodded, causing the dark ringlets at the back of her head to dance.

"Is it true that he's from overseas?" Emily asked.

Lily laughed. "That is true. He has an English accent. Actually, it's more than that. It sounds European. He's lived all over the world, mostly in Scotland."

"How exciting!" Emily looked across the small parlor to her parents. "Isn't it, Mother?"

"Yes. We don't often get foreigners visiting here."

"He's a detective, is he?" Mr. Fishbine asked, striking a match to light his thick cigar."

"My family hired him," Lily said, hedging. She didn't think of Griffon as a detective. He was so much more than that.

The maid who had delivered the invitation to her at the hotel restaurant entered the room pushing a tea cart. Besides aromatic tea, the top tray held a delicious-looking assortment of frosted cakes and jam-filled cookies.

"This is too much!" Lily leaned forward, her mouth watering for one of the petit fours. "After such a wonderful dinner, you tempt me with these scrumptious cakes and cookies." She smiled mischievously. "Of course, I'll have to sample them just to be kind." Her comment illicited laughter as the maid handed her a cup of tea and one of the white-frosted cakes. "Seriously, it was terribly kind of you to invite me to your home for the evening."

"We thought you might like a change of scenery from the hotel. How much longer will you be in town?" Mrs. Fishbine asked.

"I'll leave soon, I think, and it is nice to have someone to visit outside the hotel. I hadn't realized how much I needed to get away from everything until I sat down at your lovely dinner table. Since my cousin disappeared, my social schedule has been nonexistent." She noticed the pattern on the china plate: orange and red flowers similar to lilies. She smiled, remembering the riverbank and Griffon's loving mouth and hands. "Of course, I'm not alone here. There's Griffon and his assistant, Balthazar, and my own maid, Orrie." Glancing at the Fishbine's maid, Lily added, "Orrie's been with my family since I was a child. She practically raised me and my cousin."

"It must be a nightmare not knowing where your cousin is," Mr. Fishbine said, shaking his head at the maid's offer of tea. "I'll stick with my cigar, thank you," he told the domestic, and the woman left them to their chatter. "How did you trace her here?"

"We think she's friends with a . . . a family near here." Lily bit into the sweet cake, chastising herself for fabricating a lie. Somehow she hated to tell what might be the truth—that Cecille had foolishly carried on with a married man.

"Which family? I probably know them," Mr. Fishbine said.

"They don't live in town," Lily explained. "They live outside of Van Buren." She noted that he still waited to hear their name, and she couldn't see a way around it. "Jeffers." She was relieved when the Fishbines displayed no recognition. "They're related to a family in Fort Smith."

"Have you spoken to them?" Emily asked. "Did they know where she is?"

"They say they don't, but their eldest son isn't home. We're hoping he might know something."

"Jeffers." Mr. Fishbine snapped his fingers. "That simple boy that comes into town now and again . . . you remember, dear. You think he's pitiful. He's probably in his twenties, but he acts as if he's no more than ten. Ah . . . what's his name? Isn't he a Jeffers?"

"Jasper," Mrs. Fishbine supplied. "Yes, his last name is Jeffers. Is he related to that family?"

Lily cringed inside. "Yes." Suddenly, she knew how David Jefferson and his mother felt when they'd had to admit to being related to such a clan. Jasper was the best of the bunch. He had an innate goodness the others lacked. "Jasper is the youngest child. He's a sweet man, isn't he? I feel sorry for him."

"They live in the wilds," Mr. Fishbine said. "Somewhere out in the part known as the Devil's Den."

"Yes, they do." Lily brushed crumbs from her skirt. Her mind whirled, trying to find a different subject. "This has been a wonderful respite from my worries. You have a beautiful home, Mrs. Fishbine. You must be so very proud of it." Not sparkling conversation, she allowed, but it had done the trick if Mrs. Fishbine's beaming smile was any evidence.

"We've lived here for twelve years. I've taken great care in selecting the furnishings."

"You have a marvelous eye for detail," Lily said, leaning back in the settee. She sipped her tea, surveying the intimate room with its subdued lighting and flocked wallpaper.

"Didn't I hear something about the father of those Jeffers boys marrying a Gypsy woman?" Mr. Fishbine asked, and Lily gritted her teeth in consternation.

"Where in the world would he find a Gypsy wife around these parts?" his wife asked.

"Dear, every town has its riffraff."

Lily stiffened and examined the Fishbines' twin expressions of disapproval.

"Mama, Papa, I think Lily's friend is a Gypsy," Emily said, looking at Lily from beneath fluttering lashes.

"Oh, no!" Mrs. Fishbine's hand flew to her gaping mouth.

"That's not so, is it?" Mr. Fishbine demanded, his mustache twitching with agitation.

Lily took a deep breath. "Actually, yes. He is a Gypsy."

"Well, it's no wonder that your aunt sent a chaperone along with you," Mrs. Fishbine noted.

"I'm surprised Howard Meeker would allow you to be in a Gypsy's company, regardless of the number of chaperones surrounding you. Why, I'd no sooner allow our Emily here to consort with such people than I would trade my wife in for a pair of mules!"

Mrs. Fishbine glanced at her husband, clearly miffed at his comparison. "That goes without saying, I hope! A pair of mules . . . Where do you hear such things? I should hope and pray I'm worth more to you than that!"

"Dear, you are missing the point, as usual," Mr. Fishbine said, puffing furiously on his cigar. "Would you want Emily anywhere near a Gypsy?"

"Glory be, no!"

"That, my dear, is the point I was making." He trained his damning eyes on Lily. "You trust this man? You trust him to walk you around town after dark?"

Lily laughed, trying to insert humor and perhaps get them to laugh at themselves. "He's not a monster. In fact, he's a perfect gentleman, educated at Oxford and graduated with honors. He knows several languages and makes the average man feel downright ignorant." She made sure to stare at Mr. Fishbine.

"How could a Gypsy receive such an education?" Mr. Fishbine asked, almost scoffing. "I think he showed you a marble and told you it was a jewel, dear girl."

"I think I know the difference, sir." She realized she was sitting ramrod straight and that anger burned the edges of her voice. "He has a benefactor . . . someone who believed in his abilities and made sure he went to the best schools."

"Still, he's Gypsy." Mrs. Fishbine shrugged helplessly. "No amount of education can erase that."

"I shouldn't think he'd want to wipe out his ancestry." Lily cautioned herself not to insult her hosts or to engage them in a verbal battle. "He's been kind to my family. In fact, he's not even taking a fee for helping to find my cousin."

"But has he made any progress?"

"Some, and he's risked his life doing it," she added. It struck her that she was hotly defending him and was hurt because they were judging him by his race and finding him unworthy. Shame coated her. Only days ago she had prejudged him. How did Griffon remain so courageous, so courtly in the face of such prejudice? she wondered. She doubted she would be able to stand up to such adversity day after day. It would beat her down and make her want to surrender her life.

"Where did your family hear of him? Does he work for

Pinkerton's or some other detective outfit?'' Mr. Fishbine asked.

Lily clenched her teeth and found herself searching for another white lie. She stopped herself, knowing that Griffon wouldn't lie to these people if he'd been here to speak for himself. Still, it took every bit of daring for her to answer Mr. Fishbine's query.

''Griffon is a psychic and was recommended by a professor back east. My father suggested we give him a try, since the conventional detectives and local authorities had turned up nothing.''

The Fishbines traded incredulous looks.

''What's that?'' Emily asked. ''Sigh—what?''

''Psychic,'' Lily repeated. ''That's someone who has special powers of perception. For instance, Griffon can determine if people are lying to him. Sometimes he . . . well, he can read minds.'' Saying it aloud made her feel silly, although she had come to accept Griffon's unusual talent.

''That can't be true,'' Emily protested, laughing as if Lily had told a joke. She looked to her parents for support. ''Nobody can do such things, can they?''

''Of course not.'' Mr. Fishbine flung his head back and laughed. His wife and daughter joined in. ''It's like that magician who came through town last year, Emily. There is no magic. The man was only pulling the wool over the gullible's eyes. These so-called psychics are the same sort. They make their living off simpletons.''

''Victor,'' Mrs. Fishbine cautioned, petting his hand, ''the Meekers hired this man, dear. Howard Meeker is no simpleton.''

''Oh, yes.'' Mr. Fishbine sucked on his cigar for a moment. ''Sorry. Meeker must be desperate, to engage an impostor.''

Lily selected another cake and filled her mouth with a bite of it, giving herself a reason not to reply. Her thoughts scurried back to the hours before Griffon had arrived in

Fort Smith. She'd thought of him in just such uncharitable terms. In fact, he'd read her thoughts and had been wounded by them. Perhaps he'd never admit to it, but she knew it to be true. She'd mentally called him an arrogant Gypsy goat and she'd seen the pain in his eyes. He said he'd adjusted to his life, to what he was, but she wasn't convinced. How could he ever adjust to people laughing at him, calling him a liar, branding all who believed in him simpletons? How could anyone be happy with such a life?

"Leave it to a Gypsy to make such outrageous claims," Mr. Fishbine said. Smoke curled around his head in a hazy halo.

"I detect scorn in your tone," Lily said. "He's quite civilized, I assure you. Besides, I always thought of Gypsies as rather romantic."

"Romantic?" Mrs. Fishbine's hands fluttered with agitation. "They're baby-stealers and thieves! I remember when I was a girl and a band of Gypsies came into town. By the time they left, they'd not only stolen livestock, money, and every other item they could lay their hands on, they also took a six-month-old baby boy! Some men in town tracked them down, but when they caught up with that bunch they couldn't find the child. The Gypsy men— vicious as wild dogs, they were—wounded two of our men and killed one of them outright! Oh, it was terrible. And that poor mother! To have your baby stolen. It would be too, too horrible to bear."

"Yes, I've always heard that Gypsies steal babies and sell them," Emily said. "Isn't that awful? Do you think your friend has ever stolen children?"

Lily stiffened, insulted by the question. "Certainly not. Those are old wives' tales, I'm sure. Perhaps those who would believe such behavior of Gypsies are the true simpletons." She cared not a jot that she'd offended her hosts. They stared at her, then shared their affront with each other.

"It seems that this young man's charm has blinded you to reality," Mr. Fishbine said. "I can certainly understand why Howard contacted me and asked that I look in on you."

"My uncle is overly protective. I assure you I'm fine. My family is thankful for Mr. Goforth's efforts in trying to find my cousin. He isn't taking advantage of us. As I said, he isn't even asking for a fee."

"He's going out of his way for free?" Mr. Fishbine asked, clearly unbelieving.

"He asks only that we consider making a donation to the American Society of Psychic Research."

"The what?" Mr. Fishbine chuckled. "I've never heard of such a thing. Obviously, young lady, it's a front. This donation will go right into that Gypsy's money pouch."

"My father works with Mr. Goforth's benefactor, who happens to be on the board of the Society. I'm told it's quite respected in England."

"Well, it would be. Those Brits are mad for any kind of tomfoolery." Mr. Fishbine laughed again, then set to relighting his faltering cigar. "No matter . . . how civilized this man . . . appears to be," he said between puffs, "keep in mind . . . that he is a Gypsy . . . and not fit company . . . for a lady of your standing." He pulled the cigar from his mouth and pointed it at her. "I tell you this as someone older and wiser and watchful of your reputation. The Meekers have been more than kind to us, and I couldn't hold my head up around them again if I didn't caution you about this Gypsy, dear girl." He must have seen the flash of anger in her eyes, for he hastened to add, "Now, now, don't get agitated over this. I'm not insulting you or those around you. I'm only pointing out that in polite society Gypsies are not tolerated."

"He's right, dear," Mrs. Fishbine agreed. "You should be sure that your chaperone is present when he's around. Otherwise, people will talk."

"Tonight, for instance," Mr. Fishbine said. "He escorted you here."

"He did, and he plans to escort me back to the hotel," Lily said, glancing at the mantel clock again and wishing the minutes would fly by.

"It would have been wiser of you to summon your chaperone. What did you call her?"

"Orrie Dickens is her name," Lily replied. "I assure you I'm quite safe with Mr. Goforth."

"We're talking about your reputation, dear." Mrs. Fishbine selected a straw fan from a holder near her and began stirring the air in front of her face with it. "A girl can't be too careful. Husband hunting is serious business, and a good match takes careful planning."

"I'm hunting for my cousin, not a husband." Lily forced herself to smile, thawing the ice from her tone. "It's been a lovely evening, but I should prepare to go. My escort will be here shortly."

"First I want to show you my doll collection," Emily said. "They're in my room. Won't you come and look?"

"Yes, I'd love to." Anything to get away from your parents and their unwelcome advice, Lily thought, rising to follow Emily from the parlor to the back of the house, where the bedrooms were located. Emily's room was decorated in pinks and grays. A bureau sat against one wall, and the top overflowed with dolls, at least twenty of them.

"I've kept every one since I was two." She touched the porcelain head of one. "This was my first. Her name is Amy Sue."

"She's sweet." Lily straightened the apron on a dark-skinned doll. "This one is unusual. I've never seen a colored doll before."

"Mama got that one for me two years ago. It's a mammy doll. Funny you should pick that one out."

"Why?"

"Kind of points out how you're attracted to the unusual, the forbidden." Emily clasped her hands behind her back and swayed to and fro, a naughty smile flirting on her mouth.

Lily saw in her eyes something she had missed earlier: the gleam of experience. Emily might be younger, but she was more seasoned than Lily and much more bold than her parents would ever believe.

"I'm not attracted to the forbidden," Lily protested, laughing a little. "If you think I'm a rebel, you are mistaken, Emily. On the contrary, I've always obeyed the rules and have no desire to shock anyone."

"Gypsies don't interest me." Emily picked up the nappy-haired doll. "But darkies . . . well, I've always thought they were pretty." Her eyes sparkled fiercely, and she lowered her voice to a whisper. "There's this boy at McDonald's stables. He's almost white, I swear. His skin is light brown, like a white field worker's. And you haven't seen muscles until you've seen his. They just ripple all over his body. I love to go to the stables and watch him saddle horses, hitch them to buggies, and the like. He knows I like to look at him. He's noticed. He's got to taking his shirt off when I'm around so I can get a good look at him."

"Emily, you shouldn't be telling me this. We hardly know each other and I—"

"But we're two of a kind. I can tell. It feels good to talk about him. You know, to tell someone else how he makes me sweat when I look upon his beautiful skin." Emily hugged the doll to her small breasts and closed her eyes as if she were making a wish. "His name is Truman. Sometimes I dream about how he looks all over. I dream that he's loving me . . . like men and women love each other, you understand. I hear tell the darkies are huge. Much bigger than white men." Her eyes popped open. "You think there's anything to that?"

Openmouthed, Lily seized another few moments of stunned silence before she made herself reply. "I doubt it, although I honestly have never given it a thought."

"Ooo, I have." Emily squeezed the doll and twisted from side to side. "I think about it all the time. You think Truman ever thinks about me and wants to see me in my altogether?"

"Emily, you shouldn't be talking about this." Lily shook her head. "Not to me."

"But you know what it's like to want a bite of the forbidden fruit. We know what Adam and Eve went through, huh?" She winked slyly. "I hear tell Gypsy men want it all the time. They keep their women pregnant year after year because they can't keep their hands off them. They get married when they're children because they develop quicker than most, and they go around"—she leaned close to whisper in Lily's ear—"*hard* all the time! Is that true? Is he ready night and day? Is he after you all the time to give him some?"

"Emily!" Lily rocked back, shocked and unsure of how to handle the situation. "I can't . . . *won't* listen to another word of this nonsense!" She went to the door and opened it, but glanced back at the younger girl. Emily showed not an ounce of remorse. On the contrary, she put the colored doll back on the bureau and grinned. "Emily, you should rein in your—your fantasies. They're going to get you in big trouble."

"You don't have any fantasies, huh?" The younger girl arched a brow. "You never dream about the Gypsy? Ha! I've seen him around town. He's the kind of stud dreams are made of, Lily Meeker."

"Shhh!" Lily shook her head and swept from the room, suddenly eager to have the Fishbines' company again. What a family!

"Ah, Lily," Mr. Fishbine said, striding toward the front door. "I believe your . . . that Goforth fellow is outside. I was just going to call to him that you would be out in a few minutes."

She started to speak her mind and tell him that she thought it petty that he wouldn't invite Griffon in to wait for her but would shout to him as if he weren't allowed in the front entrance and should remain outside. Mrs. Fishbine brought Lily her purse and light shawl, and Lily took them and decided to rise above their behavior by being gracious.

"Thank you, Mrs. Fishbine," she said, letting the woman slip the shawl around her shoulders, then retrieving her purse. "And thank you, Mr. Fishbine. As I said before, the evening has been a welcome respite." Sensing Emily's approach, Lily barely afforded the girl a glance. "Good-bye to you, too, Emily. Your doll collection is . . . unique." She smiled as Mr. Fishbine held the front door open for her. "Good evening, and thanks again for—oh, Griffon."

Griffon removed his hat and nodded at her, then at the Fishbines. "Lily, have a good time? Hello, I'm Griffon Goforth. You must be Mr. and Mrs. Fishbine."

"Yes." Mr. Fishbine stared at Griffon's hand, then turned to his wife, placing his hands on her shoulders. "We're the Fishbines. Good night, Lily. *You* are welcome in our home any time."

"Good night." Lily slipped out the door, shouldered past Griffon, and stepped lightly along the walk that led to the street. She heard Griffon's tread behind her, then beside her. Only then did she examine the pinched expression on his face. He'd put his hat back on, but she could see beneath the brim. "The dinner was wonderful, but the company could have been better." She tucked her hand in the crook of his arm. "I'm afraid they've taken to heart my uncle's suggestion that they keep an eye on me. They don't approve of my being alone with you. They think Orrie should have tagged along with me as a chaperone."

He slanted her a quick glare. "It's more than that. Mr. Fishbine thinks I'm dirt under his feet because I'm a Gypsy."

"Now, Griffon, don't go—"

"You don't think I felt it?" he asked, chopping off her attempt at placating him. "You don't think that man's thoughts didn't blast me in the face?" He sighed, shaking his head. "Don't worry, Lily. I'm not shattered by the experience. I'm used to it."

"How can that be?" she asked. "How can anyone ever get used to that kind of treatment? I don't think I could bear being the brunt of everyone's scorn."

" 'Everyone' is too broad a term. Only those who are too hard-headed or too hard-hearted brand me without giving me a chance."

"I don't think I could live with such a heavy burden. To prove yourself over and over again." She shuddered at the thought. "It would get weary."

"I don't have to prove myself to imbeciles." His tone was brusque. "People accept me or they don't. If they have preconceived ideas about who I am, that's their burden, not mine."

"Griffon, do you have a . . . a craving for that which is forbidden?" She was thinking of Emily's strange fantasies and finding them hard to shake. Could Griffon have the same affliction as Emily? Did he crave the forbidden? Did his Gypsy heart yearn for a *gadjica?*

"The forbidden? What's forbidden?" Griffon asked.

"You know . . . things or people you've been brought up to consider out of your reach."

"No. I have no such cravings. If I want something, I reach out for it. I don't think anything is impossible—forbidden. Other than crimes or out-and-out sin, you understand. Murder, lies, cheating on your betrothed; those kinds of things, if not forbidden, are certainly things I couldn't live with." He tipped his head toward her. "Why do you ask?"

"The Fishbines' daughter is fixed on a colored boy who works at the stables. She's daffy about him! All because she's been brought up knowing such a union would get her and him killed.'' She glanced at Griffon and was surprised to see his smile. ''You find this amusing?''

''The Fishbines have a stick of dynamite on their hands and don't know that someone has touched a flame to its fuse. Serves them right.''

''Yes,'' she agreed, seeing his point. ''While they fret about me being with you, they have a bigger problem right under their noses!'' She smiled at him and noticed the cut on his lower lip. ''Oh, dear! I completely forgot about that fight you had with Ham. You're hurt. Your lip is—''

''Fine. Not even sore. It was swollen for about an hour, but it's back to normal now. My clothing took the worst beating. I'll have to have the jacket mended and the whole outfit cleaned. Do you think Orrie might be able to get those bloodstains out of my tie?''

''Lye soap and Orrie Dickens can remove any stain,'' Lily assured him. ''Orrie can mend your jacket, too. She'll be happy to do it.''

''So you won't be leaving tomorrow?''

Lily slowed, making him check his stride. ''I'll stay until you get back from Devil's Den. I want to be sure you return in one piece before I head back home.''

''You're still wanting to leave me, I see.''

''Not you. I swear, I don't understand you. Shouldn't you be glad that I've grown to trust you?''

''Have you?''

''Of course I have, as you well know, Griffon Goforth.''

''But?'' he prodded.

''But our relationship has changed, and it's not right for me to stay and chance idle talk about us. Don't laugh at me,'' she ordered when she heard his low chuckle. ''A girl's reputation is sacred! Why, if anyone found out that you and I . . . well, what happened on the barge . . . I couldn't hold up my head in the whole state of Arkansas!''

''Is that so?'' he said, continuing to take her stand lightly. ''It's a mite too late to worry about that, isn't it? What's done is done.''

"But no one except you and me must ever know that, Griffon. Remember, you promised not to talk about it."

They reached the hotel and Griffon walked with her to her room. Outside her door, he waited for her to go inside and light the lamp.

"Orrie's not here," she told him, staring at the untouched bed.

"She might not be back for hours, Lily." He shrugged. "You should have been around to chaperon her."

"Where is she?" Lily held up her hand. "No, don't tell me. I don't want to know."

"And it's none of our business, is it?" He caught her hand and brought it to his lips. "You are a vision in that gown, Lily. I shall never forget how you looked tonight."

"Oh, Griffon." Her heart hammered, but her mind carried the taint of the evening's conversation. The Fishbines' contempt for Griffon and his special abilities had brought home to her again that Griffon's expectations of her were too lofty. She knew he wanted her to admit that she, too, had a certain power of the mind, but she didn't think she could stand up to the ridicule such an admission would bring. He was strong and could take it. More than ever, Lily didn't want to face a life of being looked at as if she were a sideshow attraction.

"What's wrong, Lily? What happened at the Fishbines' tonight that makes you draw away from me?"

She realized he was probing her mind, sifting through her feelings, and she shuttered her thoughts from him. "Griffon, I'm not drawing away from you. It's just that . . ."

"Yes, what?" He trapped her hand against his chest.

"You've brought so many new experiences into my life, not all of them pleasant, and I don't know whether to kiss you or slap you for it." She smiled, letting him see that she was only partly serious.

"I'll take the kiss, thank you." He pressed his lips to hers in a warm caress that set her pulses pounding. "Good night, Lily. If you need anything, just call. I'm only across the hall.''

Lily stared at him for a moment, shocked that he was going to settle for only one kiss. She had half a mind to grab him and pull him down to her burning lips, but then he turned away and crossed to his own room. Feeling foolish, she moved inside her room and closed the door. Disappointment tugged at the corners of her mouth. Evidently, Emily is dead wrong about Gypsy men, she thought. Griffon wasn't wanting her every minute of every hour. One kiss was all he'd wanted tonight, and he'd been satisfied when he'd received it.

Unfortunately, she couldn't say the same for herself.

Chapter 17

The corridor was dark, intimate, but light streamed in from someplace, enough to let her see the naked desire blazing in Griffon's eyes. Panting, she raked her hands through his hair and forced his eager mouth to where her breasts surged above the tight bodice of her dress. His mouth was warm, moist, erotic.

"Do you burn, Lily?" he asked against her soft flesh. "Do you burn?"

"Yes! Yes!" She flung her head back, giving herself over to the wild passion. He pressed kisses up the column of her throat, over her chin, and then on her trembling lips. She opened her mouth to the bold strokes of his tongue. Hers imitated the action of his. Each surge and retreat increased the throbbing low in her womb.

Somehow he exposed her breasts. Her nipples nestled in his palms while he kneaded her pliant softness. He nudged her with his pelvis and she felt him, hard as steel.

"Not here, Griffon!" she whispered, glancing around frantically. "Anyone could walk into this hallway and discover us."

"What do we care? I want you now and now is when I'll have you." His hands swept down and her clothes ripped, torn from her trembling body. "I can't help myself. I'm a Gypsy."

"What has that got to do with it?"

"You know. . . ." He smiled and violins began to

play, heartrending Gypsy violins. She knew the song was about carnal love, forbidden passion, a sweet tragedy. "We Gypsy men can never get enough. We keep our women either tired and happy or pregnant and pampered. And we're never satisfied. We go night and day, day and night."

She realized it wasn't Griffon's words coming from his mouth but Emily Fishbine's! She pushed at his shoulders, but his lips had fastened around one of her taut nipples and tugged mightily. She swayed. Her knees buckled. She didn't protest when his hand swept under her dress to cup her feminine mound.

"Want it right here?" he asked, almost growling.

"Yes!"

"Are you burning, Lily?"

"I'm on fire," she cried. "Please, Griffon. Now, now, now. Put out the fire before I'm nothing but ashes. Put out the fire. . . ."

Disjointed words and whimpers rattled in her throat, jolting her from the dream. Lily thrashed in the bed, then shot up, eyes open, unfocused.

"Orrie?" she croaked out, but no one was in bed with her. She flung the hair out of her eyes and realized she was dripping with perspiration. Moaning, she threw off the sheet and escaped the damp confines of the bed.

"What a dream," she murmured, stumbling to the window to look out at the deserted street. Deserted, except for . . . She craned closer to the pane and squinted to make out the figure near the hitching post across the street. The man ducked into the shadows as if he knew she'd spotted him, and Lily retreated, feeling exposed. She drew shut the draperies and lit the lamp, turning the wick key until the light was an amber glow.

Staring at the bed, she wondered if she should worry that Orrie still wasn't back. It must be three or four in the morning, she guessed, but reason told her that Orrie probably wouldn't tiptoe into the room until dawn painted the

sky with pastel strokes of pink and lavender. Orrie, no
doubt, was doing with Balthazar what Lily had been
dreaming of doing with Griffon. For a few moments, envy
sent its knife through her. Lucky Orrie. Lucky, lucky Orrie. At least someone was happy tonight.

She felt sticky. Perspiration trailed between her breasts,
tickling her and making her gown cling to her skin. The
washstand tempted her. She poured water into the shallow
bowl, then set the pitcher to one side. Wetting a sponge,
she ran it down her arms from wrist to shoulder and sighed
with pleasure. The sponge bath cooled her. She removed
her gown and washed all over, then slipped into her ivory-
colored wrapper. Belting it loosely at her waist, she wandered aimlessly around the bedroom, feeling trapped and
restless. The dream—so raw, so real—had left her edgy,
bored, wide awake.

"It's Emily Fishbine's fault," she grumbled, falling like
a rock into a chair near the window. "All that crazy talk
of hers upset me."

Upset, perhaps, was the wrong word. *Manic, aching,
frenzied.* Emotions foreign to her. She rubbed her arms
and sprang from the chair, her bare feet slapping on the
wood floor, then muffled on the woven circle rug. Griffon's face, his eyes hooded with passion, kept floating past
her mind's eye. Her skin recalled the caress of his hands.
Her lips throbbed for the touch of his. She groaned. Stopping in the middle of the room, she shut her eyes and let
thoughts of him surround her until she trembled with longing.

You've tasted the jam, a voice in her mind whispered.
*Bread and butter aren't good enough anymore because
you've tasted the jam.*

"I've got to get out of here." She flung open the door
and stepped into the corridor. Immediately, she was reminded of the dream she was trying to escape. Leaning
against the wall, she let the passion play out in her mind.
Her pulses thrummed with the memory. She moistened

her dry lips with the tip of her tongue and ran her hands lightly down the front of her wrapper. Her breasts felt heavy, full, tender.

Staring at Griffon's door, she wondered if she could insert another dream into his head. She'd done it once, unwittingly. That dream hadn't been nearly as powerful as the one she'd just experienced. If Griffon Goforth was so uncannily hitched to her mind, to her dreams, to her every emotion, then why was he still in his room while she stood in the corridor outside, panting as if she'd run a mile, throbbing with a divine longing?

When the door swung open, so swiftly the hinges had only a moment to squeak, Lily thought she was imagining it. But the reality of Griffon standing on the threshold dispelled that notion. His chest rose and fell with his labored breathing. He stood before her, dressed only in a pair of black trousers. Sweat glistened on his chest and arms; it ran in diamond drops down his cheeks and wide neck. His tousled hair lay across his forehead in damp curls. Wild, boundless desire widened his eyes and changed their color to royal blue.

"You're driving me crazy," he said, his voice breathy, raspy.

"I . . ." She swallowed hard and placed her hand to her throat. "I was standing out here because . . . I can't sleep. Have you seen Zar or Orrie? I thought I'd—"

"I *know* what you've been thinking, and it has nothing to do with Zar or Orrie, and everything to do with me and you."

She felt herself blush to the roots of her hair and didn't bother to deny it. She'd wished he would grab onto her dream, and her wish had come true. When he held out his hand to her, she grasped it and he pulled her across the threshold of his room and into his arms. His skin was slick under her hands, and his tongue was slicker, parting her lips to stroke the sensitive places within. He reached out and closed the door behind her. Lily clasped her hands at the back of his neck and bowed her body into his. She hadn't known until that moment how ravenous she was for him. The afternoon on the barge had whetted her appetite and the hot kisses in the hallway that morning had been a potent aperitif, but she was hungry for the main course.

His room was semidark. The draperies were open, letting starlight spill in. Hazy light hung over his bed. Lily looked past his shoulder at the rumpled bed, a twin of hers, and smiled. She wove her fingers in his hair and pulled his face away from the side of her neck. Looking into his eyes, she visually feasted on the tantalizing torment swimming in them.

"Poor Gypsy," she crooned. "Did my dreams punish you? It's your fault that I crave the sweet jam of you." She arched a brow, thrilling at the low growl he emitted. "You've turned this kitten into a tiger. Now you must tame me, Griffon." She showed her teeth and snapped at him. "Think you can?"

"Will you scratch and claw?"

"Probably," she purred, then laughed when he swept her into his arms and swung her onto the bed in one dizzy motion. In a blur, he removed his trousers, and in the next blurring second he was astraddle her on the bed. "Griffon! I . . . I . . ."

"You asked for it." He bowed over her, cupping one hand at the back of her head and lifting so that her mouth met his halfway.

His lips flirted with hers, bestowing plucking, juicy kisses. He found the knot in her belt and loosened it. Her wrapper parted and his hands covered her bare breasts. He sucked in a breath and glanced down, his face registering surprise.

"I didn't think you'd be nak—" He met her gaze, and a feral grin leapt to his mouth. "I'm so-o-o grateful." He flicked the robe all the way open and stretched out like a big cat beside her. His warm mouth slipped across her breasts. He curled his tongue around one of her sensitive nipples.

Lily hitched in a breath and let it out in a long sigh of contentment. Her heart swelled and beat rapidly. Tension built by degrees in the center of her chest. Her gaze, filtered by her lashes, drifted lazily down his body, over wide shoulders and silky-skinned ribs, along slim hips to thick, muscled legs. And then she saw it. That part of him she'd been too timid to appraise before. Turgid with desire, it strained from his body, seeking hers. Before she could analyze her action, she grasped it lightly in her hands.

"My God!" Griffon ceased all movement for a few seconds. He was a statue, head thrown back, ecstasy written in his face and in every tensed muscle in his body.

She moved her fingers a fraction, and his whole body jerked. Lily marveled at the reaction. She caressed him and he shivered.

"Lily, oh, Lily." He moaned and rolled his head forward. Beads of perspiration dotted his brow. "That's right. Touch me. Hold me. I won't break. The only thing breakable about me is my heart."

The poetry in that sent a ribbon of sentiment through her. "Your heart is safe with me, Griffon," she assured him, still stroking the rod of flesh. Why had she been so afraid of looking at it? she wondered. It was beautiful. Nothing to fear. Every part of him was boldly masculine, but this erect extension was the essence of maleness, and her femininity longed for it.

Some of the mysteries about men and women fell away, replaced by cleansing knowledge. As if born to lovemaking, she manipulated his erection, rubbing the pad of her thumb across the dewy tip. He moaned again and angled his body over hers. His mouth roamed over her breasts, leaving fiery kisses and reshaping her nipples into tight, throbbing buttons of flesh. His fingers tangled in her long hair, holding her head in place as he made love to her mouth with tongue thrusts and tender nibbles. Eagerly, she parted her thighs to accommodate him. He shifted and she felt the hot tip touch her, press for a moment's resistance, and then slip inside.

Buried in her, he released a pent-up sigh while she sucked in a gasping breath. For a full minute, neither one of them moved. Their gazes locked and their eyes worshiped what they beheld. The liquid movement of their bodies began slowly, picking up speed as their flesh grew slicker, hotter. Lily clutched his shoulders and locked her heels behind his thighs. Her release from desire's clutches came quickly, like a lightning stroke. It burned through her, making her cry out in mindless pleasure. A part of her noted that Griffon paused to experience her climax before he set the pace again. His thrusts slowed, but went deeper and deeper until she was sure she felt the tip of him in her belly, in her empty womb. He filled her up, giving her supreme satisfaction, and then he gave a final surge and spilled his seed into her.

A cautionary voice whispered to her that even Griffon had been completely overtaken by passion.

Pregnant, she thought. *I might be pregnant after tonight*.

Amazed that such a possibility didn't send her into a mind-numbing panic, she realized this man had become more important to her than even she had acknowledged until this moment. Having his baby would pose problems, but it would also present an undeniable joy.

Their child would not only be physically beautiful; their child would inherit an acute sensitivity to those things elusive to others. And their child, no doubt, would not be accepted in polite society.

"Lily, what I feel with you is beyond my experience," he murmured against her throat. His breath was warm. "I want to stay inside you forever."

He was still within her, and made no move to break the connection.

"I admit my experience is little or nothing, but I do believe you did nothing to prevent a pregnancy, Griffon Goforth."

His head bobbed up and his gaze held pure startlement. "You're right!" He closed his eyes and his shoulders sagged. "I can't believe I forgot. I'm always careful . . . so careful not to . . . See what you do to me?" He opened his eyes, and they were the color of heaven again. "You go to my head like spirits, and all my good intentions go up in smoke."

"Good intentions?" she repeated, touching her fingers to his lean cheeks. "Did you intend to leave me alone in my bed tonight, Griffon?"

He dropped his gaze. "I did."

"But you heard me calling you?"

"Yes, in your dreams and outside my door. I couldn't stand it another moment. I had to have you."

"I'm so glad." She crossed her wrists at the back of his neck and kissed him. He moved, bowing his back, and she felt him slip out. "Good-bye, sweet prince," she said, sadly, and he chuckled. "Promise you'll come again?"

"That's a promise." He kissed the tip of her nose. "Sure you'll want me again?"

"Why even ask such a question?"

He trailed a fingertip down the side of her face to her collarbone. "I sensed confusion in you tonight, Lily. Whatever happened at the Fishbine house sowed seeds of doubt in your mind, in your heart." His fingertip traced the skin above that beating organ. "Did their contempt for me make you question our alliance?"

"Oh, Griffon." She raised her head to rest her forehead against his for a few moments, then let her head drop back to the pillow. "I admire your bravery, but I don't think I'm made of such strong stuff. You're asking a woman who has spent years hiding her light under a bushel to suddenly expose herself to every sort of scorn."

"I am asking only that you accept yourself and take

pleasure from it. Lily, you'll never be free until you free every part of yourself.''

She gathered her robe around her and tied the sash. "You see, that's what troubles me.'' Scooting off the bed, she went to the window and gazed at the cold stars as her body began to cool. "I think it's dangerous to allow yourself every whim.''

"This is not a whim,'' he corrected, his voice taking on an edge. "This is a personal trait. Once you see it as such, you'll understand that to deny it is the same as trying to deny that your eyes are the most beautiful shade of brown known to mortal man.''

Giving him a sideways glance and heartfelt smile, she laughed. "Smooth talker,'' she chided. "It's not the same thing, though. Brown eyes are accepted. Dropping into trances is not.''

"Both are acceptable to me.''

"Ah, but you are a gold nugget among drab stones, and twice as rare.''

"Now who's the smooth talker?'' He draped the sheet haphazardly across the lower part of his body and shifted to his side, propping his head in one hand. "Talk to me, Lily. Tell me your deepest fear.''

Releasing a shaky breath, she let the truth fly. "I'm afraid I'll go mad if I let this . . . wild thing loose inside me. I've always thought of it as an animal—like a tiger— pacing back and forth and looking for a way to escape. Once it does, Griffon, what would keep it from swallowing me whole? I'd end up in an insane asylum.''

"My, my,'' he whispered. "Your fears are ferocious. Come here, lamb.'' He held out his hand to her. "Snuggle against me and let me assuage those fears.''

She crossed to him. Propping himself against the headboard, he wrapped his arms around her as she curled on her side against him.

"Lily, the pacing beast is you,'' he said, his voice rumbling against her ear, which was pressed against his chest. "You've got to stop being afraid of it—afraid of yourself. When you love that beast, explore that beast, you tame it. Once you've tamed it, you train it. Just as I have trained my beast to work for me instead of against me."

"But what good would it do me, other than disrupting my life and confusing the people who love me? My knowing things didn't help my mother, did it? All my knowing did was alienate me from my father." She rubbed her cheek against his chest, enjoying the touch of the springy hair growing there.

"What happened to your mother isn't your fault," he said, his tone brooking no argument. "She was warned and she ignored the warning. You did what you could. As for your father's inability to accept *all* of who you are, it points to his weakness. He refuses to face that which he doesn't understand, and there isn't much you can do for him, Lily. He must find courage within himself."

"Me, too."

"Yes, but where he is weak, you're strong."

"I don't feel strong."

"*I* feel it. Would you reject a God-given musical talent?"

"No, but that's hardly the same as what I've been given. People like musicians."

"But what if, as a four-year-old, you sat down on your first piano bench and began playing Bach? People would be amazed, shocked, skittish. They'd look for a logical answer. They'd investigate to see if you were a fraud. If they found nothing, then they would explain your talent as a miracle God has brought to your life and theirs. Once you reveal your talent, Lily, the people who love you will embark on this same process and will come to the same conclusion. Trust me."

She was silent, taking it all in, assembling and sorting

through his explanation. He curled a finger beneath her chin and brought her head up until her gaze found his.

"Lily, do you trust me?"

"Yes." The answer came from her heart.

"Then let me help you over the rough spots ahead. If you decide to be yourself, let me help you train that tiger in you just as Thurman Unger and Balthazar helped me bring mine to hand."

She nodded and pressed her mouth to the center of his chest. His heart pumped, making the skin flutter.

"The Fishbines are like your father. They scoff at anything they don't understand."

Running her hand across his coppery skin, she recalled the blatant hatred the Fishbines had for Gypsies. Griffon caught her hand and held it still against his heart. She knew then that he'd picked that pocket of her thoughts. She peeked at him through her lashes. His gold earring glinted in the muted light and she touched it.

"When did you get that? Is it symbolic?"

"In a way. I don't remember having my ear pierced. Must have been done when I was a babe. But I wear the ring because it links me to the Rom. Although they rejected me, they can't expel me altogether. Their blood runs in my veins. I was raised on their standards, their legends, their customs." He shot her a glance down the straight bridge of his nose. "On what did the Fishbines base their hatred of Gypsies?"

"Mrs. Fishbine said she remembered when a band of Gypsies came into town and kidnapped a baby boy."

He barked a laugh. "God save the queen! What rot!"

She smiled at his British euphemisms. "I take it you think this highly unlikely?"

"Gypsies think any family of eight or less is a small one, so why would they be stealing babies? And a *gadjo* baby at that! The child would *never* be accepted by the Rom." He held up one finger. "And there's another telling clue here. She said a baby boy was stolen?"

"Yes."

"*If* a demented Rom decided to snatch a babe, it wouldn't be a boy baby. A *girl* would be selected. Girls are far more valuable, far more cherished by the Rom. We pray for girls. The greatest wish one can bestow on a newly married couple is that they have a family full of girl children." He curled his upper lip. "Baby stealing. That's something the *gadjo* made up to cover his own crimes against his children. More likely that poor baby died by the hands of its own kin."

"I rather like the way the Gypsies treasure females." She sat up on her knees beside him. Supine and lazy-eyed, he reminded her of a big cat sprawled in the bed, a bed the same size as the one she shared with Orrie in her room, but there was precious little room left with Griffon in it.

"Women are treasures," he said, trailing a fingertip along the side of her face.

"But in my world—the *gadjo* world"—she smiled when he smiled at her careful pronunciation—"the female is considered less than the male. We are shunted to one side, not allowed to think or vote or offer an opinion on anything outside cooking and child rearing." Slamming a fist into the mattress, she let out a sigh. "How I hate it! Orrie says I should be resigned to my position in life, but I loathe being treated as some imbecile."

"If only you were as passionate in defending your psychic gifts." His tone was sad. "But I agree, Lily. You women must change things if you want a say in what goes on in society. I can assure you that men will never give you any power out of a sense of fair play." He laughed at such an idea. "You'll have to beat it out of them. You must harp and harp and harp until they get sick of hearing your collective voices and hand over some equality just to shut you up. That's the only way you'll get anything from your menfolk."

"How did Gypsy women get the upper hand?"

"They've always had it." He shrugged. "Gypsies are more wise than the *gadjo.*"

Gathering her hair over one shoulder, she drew her fingers through it, combing out tangles. "You sound proud of your people."

"That surprises you?"

"Well, they weren't proud of you," she pointed out.

"And your family isn't proud of you."

She frowned, hating the truth in that. "Yes, we're two of a kind."

"Are we? Are you a Gypsy now?"

Laughing, she snuggled into his arms again. "I wouldn't mind."

"Liar."

"Why do you call me that? I was raised on Gypsy stories! Remember, I'm the one who thinks they're romantic."

"Hmmm, and look where that kind of thinking led your cousin."

They fell into a few minutes of silence, each thinking of Cecille and wondering where this journey to Van Buren would ultimately take them. Would they find happiness or sorrow at trail's end?

"Let me go with you tomorrow to Devil's Den," she whispered, looking at him with pleading eyes.

"No." He shook his head decisively. "No, absolutely not. You will stay here."

"Maybe I'll be gone when you get back. I might head for Fort Smith."

"If so, hire a buggy driver. Don't you and Orrie try to go back by yourselves." He kissed the top of her head. "However, I hope you'll be here when I return."

"Why?"

"Because I'll be thinking of you while I'm gone, and by the time I get back I'll be starving for your touch, your kiss, your body."

She rolled onto her stomach, half on and half off him. "What's become of me? My reputation is shot to pieces because of you. How will I be able to hold my head up in the streets of Fort Smith?"

"From my vantage point, your reputation is unchanged, Lily. You're still, and will always be, a lady in my eyes."

Dragging a finger across his lower lip where a tiny cut marred the left corner, she puckered her brow in a frown. "You'll be careful, won't you? That skinned place on your head and this cut on your lip—"

"Won't hinder me in the least. I'll be fine, and I will be careful. Balthazar and I will look out for each other as we always do." He kissed her brow. "Don't fret."

"I should be getting to my room. If Orrie comes in and finds me gone, she'll have a hundred questions I won't want to answer."

"I'll return you to your bed in due time." He wrapped his arms tightly at her waist. "No need to be in any hurry. Orrie won't be back in the room before dawn."

"How do you know that?"

He shrugged. "I'm psychic."

She narrowed her eyes, doubting his explanation. "Yes, but I repeat, how do you know so much about Orrie's comings and goings?"

"A hunch." He smoothed his hands over her hair. "While I'm away, I want you to stick close to the hotel and remember not to go out alone. Take Orrie with you if you must venture out."

"Yes, Griffon," she said, nodding in a bored way.

"I'm serious, Lily."

She glanced down at his telltale organ, bobbing under the sheet. "So you are!"

Laughing, he rolled with her so that he ended up on top of her. "You vixen! One look from you sets my blood afire. I can't get enough of you, Lily. Can't . . . get . . .

enough.'' He punctuated the statement with drugging kisses.

Lily closed her eyes and opened her lips. Maybe the precocious Emily Fishbine's right, she thought before passion fogged her mind.

Chapter 18

O rrie took great pains at opening the door sound-lessly. Poking her head around the edge of it, she peeked in. The lantern was lit and turned down low, but the light was sufficient for her to see Lily sitting in bed, staring straight at her.

"Glory be!" Orrie stepped inside, one hand flying to cover her heart. "I didn't expect you to be up at this hour! Is something wrong, honeypot?"

Lily managed to keep from grinning. "I was on the verge of asking the same of you, Orrie Dickens. Are you aware of the hour? It's five, I'll have you know."

"Five, is it?" Orrie closed the door, caught the hem of her skirt in it, and turned her back to Lily to jerk the material free. "I've been out. Thought I'd . . ." The rest was a jumbled collection of mutters.

Lily leaned forward, cocking an ear. "Pardon? Didn't catch that."

Orrie pivoted slowly. Crimson colored her cheeks an even rosier hue. "I said I couldn't sleep, so I took a walk."

"For eight hours? You've been walking aimlessly around the hotel all this time?"

Orrie flung off her shawl. "I fell asleep on the couch downstairs."

"I didn't see you when I came in. Griffon hasn't seen

hide nor hair of Balthazar this evening either. I don't suppose you ran into Zar during your all-night stroll.''

Orrie propped her hands on her hips. ''What's with all these questions? I'm the older one here. I'm the chaperone. I should be askin' you what you're doing sittin' up at this hour. You should be asleep, girl! Why, you won't be fit for nothin' today. You'll have dark smudges under your eyes and be as cross as an old bear.''

Lily pursed her lips to keep from laughing. She was enjoying this turning of the tables. ''I wouldn't have lost sleep if my older chaperone had been here with me in the first place! I returned from the Fishbines' to find you gone without a trace. How could I possibly sleep?''

''You shouldn't have worried about me.''

''That's what Griffon said.''

''Zar said Mr. Griffon didn't go with you to the Fishbines'. Said Mr. Griffon got in a skirmish of some sort.''

''Ah, so you *did* see Zar this evening,'' Lily said, feeling like a half-pint detective.

Orrie plopped into the nearest chair to unlace her shoes. ''Yes, yes. I saw him. What happened to Mr. Griffon this evening?''

Lily traced the band of lace stitched onto the edge of the white sheet. ''We ran into Jasper, which wasn't too bad. But then Ham butted in and things got ugly fast. Poor Jasper might be simple-headed, but Ham is downright crazy!''

''He didn't try to hurt you or nothin', did he?''

''No. He's just . . . vile.'' She shoved aside all thoughts of Ham Jeffers, returning to her good-natured joshing with Orrie. ''So, what did you and Zar do all night?''

Orrie, bending over to remove her shoes, swung up to glare at Lily. She must have seen mischief in Lily's eyes, because her burst of anger died and she shook a finger at her. ''None of your business, missy. How was your evening at the Fishbines'?''

''Pleasant enough.''

"Too bad Mr. Griffon couldn't go with you."

"Actually, it's just as well."

"Why is that?" Feet freed from her shoes, Orrie sprawled in the chair and wiggled her stockinged toes.

"They don't have a very high opinion of Gypsies."

"I see." Orrie nodded. "I always thought of Gypsies as beautiful, wild, free people. I know, though, that many don't share my view."

"It must have been awful for him growing up," Lily said, plucking at the lacy band on the sheet again. "To be cast out by his family into a world that treated him like human compost." She sighed. "Sometimes I glimpse such sadness in him, Orrie, that it clutches at my heart." When Orrie made no comment and unbroken minutes stretched between them, Lily looked up from the lace pattern to witness Orrie's keen regard. "Don't you think he's led a lonely, bittersweet life?"

"I'm thinkin' that you might be falling in love with that blue-eyed Gypsy. You know where he got those blue eyes?"

The first statement startled her, but Orrie's follow-up won Lily's response. "No, do you?"

"Zar says they showed up—out of the blue, you might say. Nobody could figure it out. His mother swears she didn't mess with anybody but his father. His folks finally marked it up to fate. They said he was singled out somehow."

"He's certainly one of a kind."

"So you *are* in love with him?"

"I'm attracted to . . . Oh, I don't know, Orrie. I can't think straight. Not until Cecille is found. I will say that I've never felt like this before about any man."

"Honeypot, are you still a good girl?"

Lily couldn't meet Orrie's gaze for a few moments, then a voice within her told her to hold her head high when she answered. So she did. "I am still a good girl, Orrie, but I am not a virgin."

Orrie clasped her hands and stared up at the ceiling. "Oh, I have failed! I knew in my heart, but I kept telling myself it wasn't true. I kept telling myself that my sweet Lily had been raised right and wouldn't ruin her life on a whim. First, Cecille. Now you. What have I done wrong, Lord? What could I have done better?"

"Oh, Orrie, stop it." Lily flung aside the bedclothes and swung her feet to the floor. "I'm fully grown, and you are no longer responsible for me."

"I'm your chaperone!"

"When it suits you," Lily noted, then regretted the hasty words when Orrie's eyes filled with tears. "Don't cry," she begged, dropping to her knees in front of the woman. "Be happy for me."

"H-happy? Why would I be happy? You got a ring on your finger? No. You got a proposal of marriage offered to you? No. You ruined for any other serious suitor? Yes. What have I got to be happy about?"

"Be happy that mine was an experience beyond measure and that I have no regrets."

"Now you have no regrets, but what about later when you have a fine young man wantin' to marry you, and you know it'll break his heart when you tell him he's not your one and only?"

"I'll face that when the situation arises."

"You should have thought about that before you let Mr. Griffon have his way with you. Didn't I teach you better, girl?"

"Mrs. Pot, are you calling me, Miss Kettle, black?"

"Don't you sass me, Lily Jane Meeker. You're in a heap of trouble. Mr. Griffon should be horsewhipped!"

"No. It was my decision, Orrie. Do you think Uncle Howard and Aunt Nan would ever be able to accept him?"

"As what?"

"Family, of course."

Orrie fell back, aghast. "Are you sayin' he has asked for your hand in marriage?"

"No, he hasn't. But he might, you know. I should be ready with an answer, one way or the other. Do you think my family would receive him?"

"I think you might be headed for heartache, Lily. The man would have asked for your hand *before* he bedded you if he were interested in you as wife material."

Orrie's words stung. Lily popped to her feet and went to sit on the bed again.

"He might still ask me. I think he cares for me. I believe he cares deeply."

"Honeypot, listen to me. Don't go wishin' on a star and expectin' miracles. Mr. Griffon might be different, but he's still a man. Men bed women, but when it's time for a man to seek a wife, he looks for a lady."

"I am still a lady, Orrie." Lily tipped up her chin, refusing to let Orrie storm her defenses. "Griffon would be the first to tell you that!"

"In this arena, I've had more experience. I might be sportin' with Zar, but I don't hold any hope of him askin' me to marry him. We've had our good times and I don't regret them, but I'm not a young thing lookin' for a husband and holdin' out for children either. A man wants a lady for a wife and not someone who he can sport with before any mention of marriage. Why do you think ladies of the evening make so much money? But do you see them gettin' married and takin' their places in society? Heavens, no! Everybody knows they aren't ladies. They're soiled."

"Orrie, are you saying that I'm dirty?" She bit her lower lip to keep it from trembling.

"If this gets out, you'll be ruined, Lily."

"I won't tell and neither will Griffon."

Orrie nodded. "That's all fine and good. But what about your eventual betrothed. How you going to explain Griffon to him?"

"I won't have to. I just won't discuss it."

"And on your weddin' night, he'll know he wasn't your first. Then you'll have some explainin' to do."

"I'll tell him I rode horses. Wild horses. Without saddles!" She rammed her fists into the mattress. "Don't go on, Orrie! I won't regret my time with Griffon. I won't! I won't!"

"Fine. Suit yourself." Orrie folded her arms and looked off to one side in a pouty fashion. "I'm beginnin' to think you might be right about that man."

"What?" Lily gathered in a deep breath and tried to lower her temper. "What do you mean?"

"You know, about him being stuff and nonsense. Think about it." She shifted her wizened gaze to Lily. Lily was reminded of an enchanted troll. "What has he done *magical* in finding Cecille? You're the one slippin' into trances and not actin' yourself at all. He's just been sniffing around here and askin' an occasional question or two."

"And getting ambushed and shot!" Lily reminded her hotly. "Just what are you getting at, Orrie Dickens? Are you telling me that you've now decided that Griffon Goforth and your beau, Balthazar, are two frauds taking us for suckers?"

"You tell me. What otherworldly hocus-pocus has Mr. Griffon done?"

"He can read my mind."

"How does that help us find Cecille? What has he done to find her? Seems to me all he's done is sniff around you like you was a bitch in heat."

"Orrie, I won't allow you to speak to me that way!" She stood, her body trembling with affront, her eyes stinging with unshed tears.

Orrie shrugged and gathered her mouth in an unattractive moue. "I'm disappointed in you, is all. I thought you were raised with better sense."

"You're mad at me, so you're taking it out on Griffon by saying awful things about him," Lily charged.

"I'm waitin' for you to answer me, Lily Jane. How has Mr. Griffon used his so-called powers to find Cecille?"

"He led us here, didn't he?"

"The Jeffersons led us here and that other detective y'all hired. All Mr. Griffon did was retrace that man's steps after the Jeffersons fessed up to lying." She cocked a brow. "Anything else?"

"He . . . he has told me that he feels Cecille around the Jeffers place."

"We all have feelings," Orrie scoffed.

"He's shown me that he can tell the Jefferses are lying and that he's confident he'll find Cecille at Devil's Den."

"Then why isn't he out there this very minute?" Orrie sat straight to better aim her arrow.

"He's recuperating from his head injury," Lily rejoined. "Would you have him face those hill-bred heathens at only half steam?"

"He don't seem to be in any hurry to continue his search."

"He's leaving tomorrow morning after breakfast," Lily informed her haughtily. "There goes your theory."

"Not entirely. So he goes out there for the day again. He'll come back with nothin' just like the other trips. He'll love up on you again and then probably get feelings that Cecille has left this country and is headed someplace else." Orrie sighed. "Balthazar never pretended to be anything but a former carnival barker. But Mr. Griffon has set himself up on a high pedestal. Sooner or later, honeypot, he's goin' to fall. Then you'll be just another in a long line of soiled doves, and he'll be off on his next virgin hunt."

"Those are horrible things for you to say!" Lily paced, releasing some of her anger in long strides. "What's gotten into you? You're just like the Fishbines—like every narrow-minded person! No, you're worse. You're maligning Griffon because he's my lover. You're trying to make me believe that he's a scoundrel. I'm shocked, Orrie. Shocked, that you would think for a moment I'd fall for such a pitiful act.''

''It's no act. I think it's best if we head back home tomorrow morning. We'll hire us a buggy driver.''

''I don't want to leave until Griffon returns.''

''You either come with me or I'll wire your uncle to come fetch you. Which will it be, Lily?''

''You wouldn't!''

''I will.'' She squared her jaw. ''I came here as your chaperone and I've done a poorly job, but I won't turn the other cheek and betray the Meekers any further. You're comin' home with me tomorrow or I'll send that wire.''

Lily measured the determination in Orrie's eyes and deemed it fierce. She bobbed a shoulder in a partial surrender. ''We'll see about hiring a buggy driver after breakfast. But I'm not doing this because of your puerile threat. I'm doing it because Griffon mentioned only this evening that he found it difficult to concentrate on his task of finding Cecille with me around. I'll go home for Griffon, not for you!''

''Who's bein' childish now?'' Orrie tossed back with a supercilious smile. ''Time we tucked ourselves in. We can grab a few hours of sleep before breakfast.''

''I told Griffon I'd meet him downstairs at eight.''

''Eight?'' Orrie rolled her eyes and began loosening her clothes. ''Then let me at that bed, girl. Scoot over and wipe that hateful look off your face. You know I said what I said for your own good. Nobody loves you as much as me, Lily Jane. Not even Griffon Goforth.''

Lily turned onto her side away from Orrie, but she couldn't keep herself from wondering if that weren't true. After all, Griffon had never said anything about loving her.

The heavy gold ring on the middle finger of Griffon's left hand caught the sunlight that streamed through the window of the Lucky Spoon restaurant. The Lucky Spoon had a lighter breakfast trade than the hotel restaurant, mainly because service was slow and coffee cups sat empty too long before the only waitress in the joint could get around to refilling them. The waitress also owned the five-table eatery and was the cook and dishwasher.

The hotel restaurant had been so busy and noisy, Balthazar had suggested they take their trade down the street. Now seated at the table in front of the street window, Lily admired Griffon's ring: a free-form griffon of hammered gold. She tried to forget that Orrie was glaring at her, her way of ordering Lily to tell Griffon of their travel plans.

Griffon peered over the top of the newspaper he was reading and his brows arched. "It's a gift from Thurman." He wiggled his fingers. "The ring. You were wondering about it? A Christmas present . . . two years ago."

"Three," Balthazar corrected.

"Ah, right you are. Three. Anyway, it's one of a kind."

Lily laughed lightly, shaking her head. "You're reading my mind again, Griffon. No fair."

"I knew you were thinkin' about that ring, too," Orrie said, an edge to her voice. "I saw you looking at it with a question written all over your face. Sure didn't take a mind reader to figure it out." She turned her attention sharply to Griffon. "Unless I've suddenly growed a third eye."

Griffon's smile stopped short of warmth. He folded the newspaper carefully and laid it beside his plate. "I didn't say that I'd read Lily's mind, Orrie. I noticed she was scrutinizing my ring, as well. Being observant is often nearly as good as having that third eye, as you call it." He winked, then scowled when Orrie didn't respond to his teasing as she usually did. "Hello, what's this? Now I *am* sensing something, and it's not at all pleasant. Are you mad at me, Orrie?" His gaze shifted to Lily. "And you. What's on your mind this morning besides my ring's origins?"

"Tell him, Lily, or I will." Orrie set her mouth in a firm line.

Lily sighed and glanced upward for effect. "Orrie and I have decided to go back to Fort Smith today." She poked her tongue into her left cheek and stared at the ceiling, sending Griffon blatant body language.

"I see." He cleared his throat. "I also see that your resolve is firm, so I shan't attempt to talk you out of it. Perhaps it's for the best."

"Perhaps," Balthazar said, brows inching together, snappy eyes trained across the table at Orrie. "What brought this on?"

"Since you two will be traveling to Devil's Den today, Orrie and I didn't see any reason to hang around," Lily explained. "It's better if we're out of your way."

"Whoever said you were in the way, dear girl?" Balthazar asked.

Lily delivered a dry smirk. "When I decided to come along, you practically pitched a fit, as I recall. I won't ask what—or who—has softened you up. The answer might be indelicate for so early in the morning. Ouch!" Lily grabbed her stinging shin under the table and sent Orrie an injurious glare. "That was uncalled for, Orrie Dickens!"

"What's wrong?" Griffon asked.

"She kicked me," Lily said, rubbing her bruised shin. "It's true what they say about the truth hurting."

Griffon clucked his tongue in mild reproof. "Actually, we're not going to Devil's Den today, after all."

Orrie gave a loud *hurrumph* sound and folded her arms against her pillowy breasts. Her eyes said I told you so to Lily. "Not goin' anywhere, huh? Another day of doin' nothin'. What a surprise."

Balthazar sputtered on the tea he had been sipping. Bewilderment lined his face. "I say, Orrie, what's going on with you two females this morning? That last comment sounded as if you think we're fleecing you. Do you think

I'm a crook, Orrie Dickens? Is that what you're telling me this bright and shining morning? After an evening so divine it brought tears to my eyes?''

"There, there, Zar." Orrie reached across the table to pat his arm. "This has nothing to do with you. Just close off your ears."

"If this has nothing to do with Zar, I can only surmise it has everything to do with me." Griffon drummed his fingers on the folded newspaper, and the mythical animal atop his ring danced. "Shall I read your mind, Orrie, or will you kindly tell me why I've been placed on your enemy list?"

"You know why." Orrie fussed with the napkin in her lap. "Don't play dumb with me, Mr. Goforth."

"Stop this deplorable behavior," Lily said, hating to be left out when she was at the center of Orrie's surly attitude.

Griffon narrowed his eyes. The half-moon scar trailed white across his dark skin. "I see. Yes, I understand now."

"You made me a promise," Orrie muttered. "And you broke it."

"I told you I'd behave and I did."

Orrie's eyes looked like pieces of coal stuck in her face. "You tricked me with words, you did. But you know what I meant and that I didn't want Lily hurt and you went right ahead and ruined her."

"He did not!" Lily gritted her teeth and clamped a hand on Orrie's arm. "Orrie, I told you I'd go along with you to Fort Smith. That is my pound of flesh, paid to you in full. I owe you nothing more. Certainly, I don't have to sit here while you soil my name and reputation. It's mine, after all, and I shall tend to it."

"I'm your chaperone."

"Yes, but first you are my friend. My best friend. The woman who loves me as dearly as if I were her daughter. So don't do this to me, Orrie. Some wounds are too deep to heal. I'm asking you to withdraw your saber before it's too late."

Orrie curled back into her chair. Her lower lip trembled, but she nodded her head. "So be it. I've said what I want to say. I'm done talkin' about it."

"Good." Lily drew in a breath. "As you can see, Griffon, it's best that we leave. Will you or Zar see about hiring us a buggy driver?"

"I'll be glad to oblige," Zar volunteered.

"Unfortunately, I don't think there'll be a driver to be found. Not until tomorrow, anyway. Possibly for a couple of days."

"Why, Griffon?" Lily asked.

"For the same reason I've postponed the trip to Devil's Den until tomorrow." He held up the newspaper, pointing to a headline. "Tonight's the barn dance in Alma Hollow . . . rather, Alma Holler." He winced at the odd pronunciation. "I spoke with the hotel proprietor this morning before you ladies came downstairs and was told that everybody goes to this dance since it's the only festivity until the cotillion at the end of summer."

"How does that keep you from Devil's Den?" Orrie piped up. "You going to the dance instead of trying to find Cecille?"

"Sadly, dancing is not one of my talents." He tapped the newspaper again, this time with purpose. "What's a dance without musicians? I give you the Jeffers Gypsy Band."

Orrie craned her neck to view the paper sideways. "I'll be. They'll be playing there."

"All evening. Probably won't go back home until the next day."

"Then why in tarnation don't you go snoop around their place while they're gone?" Orrie asked, clearly exasperated and intent on painting Griffon in shifty colors.

"Because I want to speak with Eva Jeffers."

"So, talk to her when she gets back," Orrie said. "Sneak a peek while she's gone. Would it hurt you to scout the area?"

Griffon's lips twitched but stopped short of a smile. "I believe you want me out of town, Orrie."

"I think it's high time for some results, is all."

This time Griffon's smile seemed genuine to Lily. "You two have traded opinions of me." He glanced at Lily and then Orrie. "How about this? I'll see about hiring you two a driver first." He held up his hands, palms out. "I doubt if I'll be in luck, but I'll make inquiries. Then Zar and I will pack up and start toward Devil's Den later today so that we might spend the night under the stars and then arrive at their place by morning. Suit you, Orrie?"

Orrie shrugged indifferently. "Guess it'll have to do."

"What more do you want? You said something about results. Will I be in disfavor until I produce Cecille for you?"

"That'll certainly restore my belief," Orrie allowed.

Lily batted a hand at Orrie. "Don't mind her. She's got it in her head that you haven't proven yourself. Orrie thinks I'm the only one showing peculiar behavior. You haven't produced enough magic for her."

"I can speak for myself, missy," Orrie said.

"So can I," Lily rejoined.

"Ladies, ladies." Griffon frowned, then snapped his fingers and held out his hand to Balthazar. "Zar, the cards. I shall sprinkle some magic dust in Orrie's direction." His silvery blue eyes sparkled with teasing lights, which were lost on Orrie Dickens.

"Card tricks," Orrie said with a sniff of contempt. "That's not magic. That's pulling a fast one, it is."

"Not this kind." Griffon's smile wore a cloak of mystery. He shuffled the cards, his hands agile and confident. "Perhaps I'll fail, but I want to at least attempt to show you that I'm not a liar and my soul isn't completely black." While he talked, he shuffled the deck, cut it, shuffled it again. "My grandmother used to do this, and I found I could do it, too. It was the beginning of the end for me.

At least, with my family." He set the deck at Orrie's elbow. "Pick any card. Don't show it to me. Just concentrate on it. Please, Orrie."

With a half frown, Orrie picked up the deck and plucked one card at random. She held it in front of her face and stared at it. Lily could see over Orrie's shoulder that it was the jack of hearts. She, too, focused on the card, thinking it would help Griffon.

He smiled. "Jack of hearts. Please, again."

Orrie eyed him cautiously and chose another. Lily glanced at it. Three of spades.

"Three of spades," Griffon said. "Again. Once more."

Orrie selected a six of diamonds.

"Six of diamonds," Griffon said. It wasn't a guess. His tone said he knew the card.

"Card tricks." Orrie shrugged.

"Select five of them, Orrie," Griffon said. "Think of each, then place them face down, side by side." He waited for her to finish. "Queen of clubs, ace of diamonds, seven of diamonds, four of spades, and ten of clubs." He glanced at Zar, and the other man flipped the cards over, just as Griffon had named them.

"Griffon, that's wonderful," Lily said, laughing. "And you're so quick! Orrie, he read your mind as if it were his own! Surely, you don't think that demonstration was an elaborate trick."

Orrie handed the rest of the deck to Balthazar and shoved back her chair. "I think it's time you and me went back to the hotel to pack our things while these men hire us a driver." She flung down her napkin and sliced Griffon with her sharp eyes. "You find my Cecille and I might forgive you for what you took from my Lily." Then she walked away, back stiff, chin tipped up. "Come along, Lily Jane."

Lily closed her hand over Griffon's. His ring felt cold against her palm, but his eyes were warm with emotion. "She'll get over it."

"I hope so."

She squeezed his hand, then stood up. "I suppose it's best that we go home. I can't help you, Griffon. More importantly, you don't need my help." She smiled at him and Balthazar. "You and Zar have earned my trust. I leave you with it."

When Lily was gone, Balthazar nudged Griffon with his elbow. "I thought you were going to tell her about the nightmare."

Griffon shrugged. "Changed my mind."

"Why?"

"It was just a dream."

"But you believe in dreams."

Griffon thumbed his gold ring, watching the sunlight bounce off it. In the dream . . . nightmare . . . Lily had fallen into a dark hole and Griffon had reached out to rescue her. Someone had pushed him from behind and he had pitched forward into a tunnel of black smoke and belching flames. Before he'd jerked awake, he'd seen faces peering down at him from above, and he'd recognized the people who'd pushed him and Lily to their deaths: Anson and Cecille.

"Griffon, shouldn't you tell her that you're beginning to think Cecille is in bed, so to speak, with Anson?"

"I don't want to add to her worries. Besides, I don't think she wants to hear my hazy theory. It doesn't place her cousin in a favorable light."

"But you're worried," Balthazar said.

"Yes." Griffon looked up from the ring to confront Balthazar's wise eyes. "Yes, I am. I'm picking up random emotions linked to Cecille—none of them coated with fear. That worries me. I just hope . . ."

"What?"

"Nothing." Griffon smiled tightly. He'd never say aloud what was in his heart. *I just hope I get out of Devil's Den alive.*

Chapter 19

Bags packed, Lily and Orrie sat in the hotel room and waited. The silence held a multitude of moods ranging from disappointment to suspicion. Lily fluffed the elbow-length sleeves of her dress, a drop-waisted one she saved for travel because it afforded easy body movement. Her hand strayed to her throat and the tear-shaped pearl pendant suspended there by a length of gold chain. Cecille had given her the necklace on the eve of Lily's coming-out party.

"I trust you're going to keep your mouth shut around Aunt Nan and Uncle Howard," she said, matter-of-factly.

Orrie's eyes snapped warnings. "I keep my word."

"Clarify, please. You won't breathe a word of what's happened between me and Griffon?"

"I won't. Mainly because I won't have to. They'll figure it out for themselves."

"How?"

"By the way you're actin'."

"And how is that?"

"Like you think you're the queen of England." Orrie wrinkled her nose in distaste. "It don't become you."

Lily sighed. She wanted desperately to tell Orrie Dickens to go straight to Hades, but she bit down on that impulse. Time would iron out these wrinkles, she told herself. Stay calm. Be pleasant. Don't take anger's bait.

"I certainly hope Griffon and Zar make headway this

time. I have a strong feeling that Cecille is waiting to be found at Devil's Den.''

Orrie shivered and hugged herself. ''I hate the name of that place.''

''Yes, but aside from the fact that the Jefferses live there, it's beautiful country.''

''I'll be glad to see home again. I don't mind telling you that I am mighty sick of this here hotel room.''

''But won't you miss Zar?''

Orrie cut her eyes at Lily, measured Lily's expression, then bobbed her head. ''Sure, but he knows where to find me if he wants to see me again.''

''That's a fatalistic attitude.''

''It's realistic. Once he and Griffon Goforth get back to their world, they probably won't give either of us a thought.''

Lily winced, stabbed by that bitter possibility. ''I prefer to look on the bright side.''

''Then be prepared to cry many tears, honeypot. Buckets of tears.''

At the soft knock on the door, Lily sprang up and opened it to Griffon and Balthazar.

''Yes? Did you find a driver?'' She could tell by their expressions that they hadn't.

''Not for today, no,'' Griffon said, hat in hand. ''But we hired the young lad at the stables to drive you tomorrow.''

''How much did he charge?'' Orrie asked over Lily's shoulder.

''A fair price, which I gladly paid.''

''Let me fetch my purse and I'll—''

''No, please.'' Griffon grabbed Lily's wrist. ''It was nothing. I have peace of mind knowing you and Orrie will be in good hands. The lad is trustworthy and a gentleman. His father owns the stables and vouched for him without hesitation.''

''As we reckoned, there wasn't an honest man to be had

who wasn't going to that barn dance tonight. It must be the event of the season,'' Balthazar said.

"The *only* event of the season,'' Orrie corrected. ''It's like that in farming country. The good times come few and far between, and you're a durned fool if you don't partake of them.''

''A couple of boys still wet behind the ears said they'd drive you,'' Balthazar said. ''But neither Griffon nor I would hear of it. You don't mind awfully waiting until tomorrow, do you?''

''No, I s'pose not.'' Orrie smiled for the first time since she'd learned of Lily's relationship with Griffon. But the smile was brief. She crossed her arms in a militant gesture. ''I hope you men aren't thinking we'll go to that barn dance tonight. I think it's high time we all remembered why we're in this infernal town and quit actin' like we're on a holiday!''

''Orrie, I don't believe any of us have forgotten Cecille, and I sorely resent that veiled accusation,'' Balthazar said, frowning.

''If you'll recall,'' Griffon said with a bemused smile, ''Zar and I have planned to start to Devil's Den this afternoon. Our plans have not changed.'' His blue eyes shifted from Orrie to Lily. ''You'll be okay on your own until tomorrow morning?''

''Of course. But you could stick around if you want,'' Lily replied.

He shook his head and gave a short laugh. ''No. I'd like to arrive at the Jefferses' early in the morning before they scatter to the winds.''

''When they're all under one roof, it makes ambushing less likely,'' Balthazar explained.

''The boy's name is Sam, and he'll be outside at seven with the buggy and horses.'' Griffon stepped back. ''Zar and I have preparations to make, so we'll see you ladies later.''

Lily grabbed Griffon's sleeve. "You won't leave without telling me, will you?"

"Certainly not." He patted her hand. "In fact, might I have a private word with you?"

"Yes." Lily stared hard at Orrie, who had moved to stand at her shoulder. "I'll be back in a minute, Orrie. I want to speak to Griffon alone." Then she stepped out of the room and shut the door in Orrie's face. "I swear, she's on a rip, isn't she?"

Balthazar ducked into the room across the hall and closed the door with barely a click.

"Alone at last," Griffon teased, taking her hand and pulling her to the end of the corridor, where a bench sat before French doors that led to a rickety balcony. He pulled Lily down beside him. "Will Orrie sing like a bird to your aunt and uncle, or do you think she'll show discretion?"

"She won't tell them about us, but she'll expect me to."

"I see. Will you?"

"Well . . . . I don't know if the time is right. Perhaps after Cecille is located, then I'll—" She wondered if she imagined she saw a tensing in his face. "Is there any reason why I shouldn't tell them?"

"I think you're right about waiting until this business with Cecille is behind us." He took both her hands in his and brought them to his lips. "I shall miss you, Lily."

"Then I suggest that you make haste, find Cecille, and bring her to Fort Smith. I'll be there waiting. But you know how badly I wait, Griffon."

"Yes, that's true. And I find your impatience charming." He released one of her hands to curl a wisp of her hair around his finger. "I find so many things about you charming." His eyes darkened to a sultry slate blue. "Do you think Orrie will ever forgive me?"

"I don't care. And I refuse to apologize or appear regretful. That's what she's after, you know. She wants me to admit I've done a terrible thing. But being with you was anything but terrible.''

"Fire Lily," he whispered, sending a delicious shiver down her spine. His gaze drifted to the curve of her neck. "Do me a favor and don't think of me too hard or you'll drive me mad while we're apart."

She smiled. "No matter how many miles separate us, we're linked. Do you think it will always be so?"

"Always is a long time. Too long for this footloose Gypsy to even contemplate." His mouth touched off sparks along the side of her neck.

Lily tipped back her head, giving him ready access. She laughed softly when his lips plucked at the gold chain. "Careful. Cecille gave that to me."

He leaned back to study the pendant. "Lovely." His eyes found hers, and she felt herself slipping under his spell. "You take my breath away."

"Did your mother have blue eyes?" Lily rested her hands against his gray shirt and felt his heart beating steady, strong. Then she felt it jerk, skip a beat, and resume its regular pace. She'd struck a nerve.

"No, she didn't. My eyes are another curse I've had to suffer."

"Curse? I think they're beautiful."

"And unusual for a Gypsy. If I'd had your color eyes my early life would have been smoother sailing."

"So . . . your father? His eyes were blue?"

"No one in my family has blue eyes." A muscle in his jawline spasmed. "What does that tell you?"

"I'm not sure. Another of life's mysteries?"

"Now, now. You needn't coddle me by pretending to believe in every sort of sorcery and miracle. Tell me what you *really* think, Lily."

"Well, I don't know. . . . " She dipped her head, ashamed to be thinking ill of a woman she'd never met and shouldn't judge.

"You can tell me anything, Lily. I'm not one of the boys back home, so speak your mind. Be yourself."

She released a long breath before she freed the thought. "Perhaps your father wasn't really your father." Lily glanced up, startled by his soft laughter.

"How delicately you put that!" A hundred sparkles danced in his eyes. "In other words, my mother might have shared her favors with more than one man? Yes, that's my inkling as well. But no one voiced such a thing. Not to my mother."

"Why not?"

"Because she's a great *boojo* woman. My grandmother has psychic powers, but my mother was the shrewd one. She could convince the queen to give up her crown to save her soul. She was too important to the Rom to even suggest that she might have done something as ghastly as sleeping with a *gadjo*. I heard some gossip once that she was raped by a *gadjo* and that's why no one said anything about my funny coloring."

"There are no Gypsies with blue eyes?"

"Some, but few in my clan. I am what you would call a rarity."

"Yes," Lily agreed, stroking his cheek, touching the scar at the outer corner of his eye. "Yes, you are rare. That's one of the precious things about you."

He laughed and settled his smile upon hers. The spark became a flame, and Lily found herself crushed to his chest while his tongue plundered her mouth. She'd had a notion to leave him with a quick, tender kiss that would make him hunger for more. The memory of that little kiss would be his whip, making him hurry to find Cecille so he could rush to Fort Smith for a more satisfying one. But that plan shriveled and died the moment his tongue separated her lips and stroked the roof of her mouth. She clung to him like a lost love found. He tasted faintly of coffee and dark chocolate. She'd never tasted anything as good. When his mouth finally left hers, she lifted her lashes a

fraction, feeling drained by his prowess, but wanting him
to take more from her.

"Griffon, how I'll miss you. You'll be careful tonight,
won't you? It's dark in that forest."

" 'The darkness of the forest is the light of the
Gypsy,' " he said. "My grandmother used to say that to
me so that I wouldn't be afraid of the dark."

Suddenly, a shaft of fear pierced her heart and she
grabbed handfuls of his shirt and looked directly into his
eyes. "Griffon, you will come back, won't you?"

He heard the tremor in her voice, and concern dimmed
the teasing lights in his eyes. "Of course, my fire lily."
He ran a hand over her auburn hair. "Don't be afraid for
me. You concentrate on keeping yourself out of harm's
way."

She started to tell him that she felt the taint of death,
but decided it would only make him worry about her own
safety. Her safekeeping didn't concern her, but his did.
For a few terrifying moments, she had felt the same overwhelming fear she'd known on the day her mother had
been bitten by the snakes. She debated whether or not to
tell him of her chilling sensation, but then he furrowed his
brow, and Lily realized he'd zeroed in on her thoughts.

"Remember when I told you that I'm a prospector of
feelings?" he asked. When she nodded, he added, "I
know you fear for me, but I'll have Zar to watch my
back." He kissed the pads of her fingers. "Ah, these
hands. These knowing hands. I shall dream of them, of
their touch."

A bubble of strong emotion burst in Lily's chest. She
caught her lower lip between her teeth and shook her head
in wonder. "There's no one like you in the whole wide
world, Griffon Goforth. I have felt the gamut for you—
suspicion, dislike, awe, desire. You are indeed a prospector of feelings." *And I love you with all my heart.* She
didn't say it, but she knew he heard it in that alert pocket
of his mind.

He released her hands and averted his gaze, mumbling something about helping Zar with the saddlebags. Stung by his reaction, Lily managed a brave front, her pride serving her well. But she knew it was child's play for him to see past her facade. If, that is, he wanted to see past it to her bleeding heart.

An hour after Griffon and Balthazar rode out of town, Lily stood in front of the window in her hotel room and stared moodily out at the dusty street. A dull ache persisted in her heart.

Orrie snored softly, curled on the bed with the chenille spread pulled over her. A wall clock ticked steadily. Quiet time, Lily thought. Feeling a bit drowsy herself, she yawned and wished she could keep from reviewing the unsettling meeting with Griffon before he and Zar had packed up and left for Devil's Den. Perhaps he hadn't received her thought about loving him. That would mean she'd misinterpreted his hasty retreat. Maybe, perhaps, what if, could be . . . useless words, useless strategy. She shook her head at her own musings. In her heart, she knew he'd heard her silent admission and that's when he'd acted as if someone had dumped a shovelful of live coals down his trousers.

Orrie would have a field day if she found out that Griffon had turned his back on Lily's vow of love. Lily looked at the sleeping woman and wondered if she should listen to her pessimistic view of a future with Griffon. Was Griffon the grand seducer and Lily the glassy-eyed maiden who couldn't see the difference between love and lust?

Lily dropped her head in her hand and swallowed a groan. "I hope not," she whispered. "I hope to heaven I haven't unwittingly played the fool."

If she had, maybe it was for the best. After all, a life with Griffon would contain more than its share of obstacles. He was a walking, breathing curiosity. That would be exciting for a while—but for a lifetime? And what of their children? The poor dears would have to bear the burden of their parents' impetuosity. Yes, she reasoned. She should treasure the memories and be resigned to the impossibilities of a lasting union with a carefree, mysterious Gypsy.

He had been her dream. Perhaps it was only right that he stay in that venue.

The tap at the door was so light that she thought she'd imagined it, but it came again after a minute. Lily tiptoed across the room, so as not to awaken Orrie, and eased open the door. A chambermaid handed her a folded piece of paper.

"A man asked me to give this to you."

"Thank you." Lily took the note and closed the door. The paper was an old general store receipt for oats, molasses, and flour. On the back of it someone had written in a shaky hand: "Outside. J."

"Jasper," she whispered, smiling at the big block letters. It surprised her that he could write at all. So he wanted her to come outside. Lily grabbed her shawl and flung it over her shoulders. She was glad Jasper had come. Since she'd be leaving tomorrow, she'd have the chance to tell him good-bye.

Glancing at Orrie, she decided not to rouse her. Her talk with Jasper wouldn't last long and she'd most likely be back in the room before Orrie awakened from her nap. She let herself out of the room and went downstairs to the empty lobby. Everyone was getting ready for the big barn dance, no doubt. She'd learned that Alma Holler was a couple of hours' ride from Van Buren. Most people would set out from town before sunset and arrive in plenty of time to greet their neighbors, repeat gossip, and catch up on births, deaths, and illnesses before the Jeffers Gypsy Band struck the first notes.

Outside, she found no sign of Jasper. She waited, looking up and down the street at the few people lingering on the wooden walks fronting the buildings. No Jasper. Not even a familiar face.

She was about to turn and go back inside when she heard a sound, not unlike a hissing snake.

"Pssst!"

Lily stopped, beating down the terror such a sound provoked from her past. "Jasper?"

"Pssst!"

The hiss came from around the side of the hotel where an alley led to a sad, overgrown garden area and a three-hole outhouse. Long shadows tumbled into the alley. Lily stepped into them, at first with anticipation and then with a sense of doom. The hairs on the back of her neck stood on end, and she checked her stride.

"Jasper?" No longer a certainty. Now only a foolish hope. Danger tapped her on the shoulder and she whirled, intent on running it over on her way back into the hotel.

The hand, foul and beefy, clamped over her mouth, and she found herself wrenched backward into an unyielding body. She struggled against the arm wrapped around her waist and tried to use her peripheral vision to identify her attacker.

"Quit your fighting," the man rasped in her ear. His breath smelled rank, like old urine stains.

Lily spied slanty eyes, a feral grin. Ham Jeffers! Her struggles intensified. She kicked backward, finding a shin. Ham grunted, and his hold loosened enough for her to wriggle free. Her escape lasted only a moment. Ham grabbed a handful of her hair and yanked her backward.

She cried out, but the scream coming after it died prematurely when Ham's fist connected with Lily's jaw. The sun set in the blink of an eye, throwing her world into utter darkness. She felt herself floating down, down, down. Her next bubble of awareness alerted her to extreme discomfort. Someone or something shook her over and over so that her breath came in short puffs and gasps. She thought she opened her eyes, but nothing made sense. She saw green and brown. She smelled horseflesh and saddle leather. Her rib cage burned. Something pressed down on the center of her back, and she wished she could find the strength to buck it off. Buck? Was she on a horse? The bubble burst, and she tumbled again into the abyss of unconsciousness.

Jasper Jeffers stepped out from around the barrels fronting the Van Buren dry goods store. Muscles trembled in his tree-trunk-sized legs. He'd been crouched behind the barrels for almost an hour. He felt sick. Perspiration, sticky and cold, clung to him. A sob broke in two in the center of his chest and half of it pushed up into his throat. It came out as a whimper. A child's whimper.

He and Ham had been playing a game for a couple of days now. Looking at Lily, they called it. Jasper liked the game because he could look at the pretty lady all day and all night and never get bored. He liked being her shadow. But the game had changed earlier today. They were supposed to get back home today. There was music to make later tonight. With Anson not playing the banjo anymore, Paw-Paw said he and Ham had to show up for all the music making. Ham played guitar and could pick the banjo pretty good—but not as good as Anson. Jasper played harmonica. Better than pretty good. Maw-Maw said he played harmonica like angels played harps. Born to it, Maw-Maw said.

Jasper had told Ham they had to get if they didn't want to be late for the music making, but Ham had sent him ahead and told him to tell Paw-Paw that Ham would meet them at Alma Holler. Jasper hadn't trusted the look in his brother's eyes. When Ham was fibbing, he got that glint in his eyes—a glint like when the sun hit the barrel of a shotgun. A bad glint.

So he'd only played like he'd left town. Jasper had mounted old Boojo and rode him out of Ham's sight, then he'd circled Boojo back around and found a hiding place.

Instead of playing Looking at Lily, he played Looking at Ham. He'd seen him scribble the note. He'd seen him give it to the woman in the funny dress. He'd seen Lily come outside and call for him.

Only fear had kept him from answering her. He'd been brought up around Ham, and he knew that Ham would bloody him if he found out Jasper hadn't minded.

Jasper plugged up his mouth with both fists just as he'd done to keep himself from calling to Lily, especially when Ham grabbed her, socked her with his fist, and then flung her over the back of Dobbin like she was nothing but a sack of potatoes!

Standing in the dusty street, Jasper stared in the direction Ham had ridden with Lily draped over his saddle. A knot twisted in Jasper's chest. Lily had rescued him. She had touched him like only Maw-Maw had ever touched him. Lily loved Jasper. Jasper loved Lily.

Shame bruised his heart and tears streamed down his face. Ham would bloody him, but he had to make sure Ham didn't hurt Lily anymore. His shame gave way to anger toward Ham. He unplugged his mouth and wiped his damp hands on his pants' legs.

"Ham's a bad, bad boy," he whispered, lower lip trembling. "Him's up to no good." He remembered how Ham had slammed his fist into Lily's face, and he had to bite down hard on his lips to keep from sobbing aloud. His chest hitched and the inside of his nose burned. He glanced around to make sure nobody was staring at him, laughing at him. Then he sniffed and wiped his nose on his shirt cuff.

Jasper hurried along the street, his waddling gait taking him to where he'd tied Boojo to a tree behind Miss Ruby's, a house of ill repute. The house wouldn't open for business tonight. All the girls had gone to the barn dance out at Alma Holler.

"Come on, Boojo," Jasper said, grunting as he lifted himself onto the white horse's back. "Gots to follow Ham.

Him's got the purty lady. Hurry, Boojo, hurry.'' He heeled the horse into a trot. The wind dried the tears on his cheeks and ruffled what hair he had left on his head.

He kept a sharp eye on the prints left by Ham's horse, and it didn't take long for Jasper to figure out where Ham was headed. He was taking Lily home to Devil's Den.

Chapter 20

❦❦ **Z**ar, I find myself on the horns of a dilemma."
Griffon stacked his hands behind his head,
stretched out flat on his back, and stared at the stars peeking at him through the tree branches.

The ride to Devil's Den country had been uneventful.
They'd made camp a safe distance from the Jeffers land.
In fact, they were nearly at the same spot where they'd
camped before, when Orrie and Lily had been with them.
Closing his eyes and concentrating, Griffon could hear the
gurgle of the creek. The sounds reminded him of the river
barge and of Lily and her wonders and woes.

"Do tell," Balthazar said, his back propped against a
tree stump. He held a branch which he used to poke at
the campfire, sending up showers of sparks. "Orrie has
branded you a despoiler of virgins, and I don't think she'll
ever forgive you for what you did to Lily."

"First of all, Orrie Dickens is the family retainer, not
Lily's mother. Secondly, I did nothing to Lily that either
of us didn't want or now regrets. What Orrie Dickens
thinks of me is not part of my dilemma."

"She thinks of Lily as a blood relation. She practically
raised her."

"Zar, you're the one concerned with keeping Orrie
happy, not me." He glanced sideways to observe his
friend's flushed face.

"She blames herself for the trouble Cecille and Lily have landed in."

"What trouble has Lily landed in?"

"You, of course. She's involved with you."

Griffon laughed, but without humor. "Which brings us back to my dilemma."

"How so?"

"That I'm perceived as trouble for Lily Meeker. Even you said it as if it were true."

"Well, what can become of it, Griffon? She lives in Fort Smith. Her life is there with her family. She has no interest in our work. In fact, she eschews it."

"She isn't rooted in Fort Smith, and she happens to be psychic."

"Yes, but being psychic and acknowledging it openly are quite different." Balthazar squinted through the smoky fire at him. "Just because she has come to believe in your powers doesn't mean she accepts her own."

"Don't I know it." Griffon sighed, feeling as if a weight sat on his chest. "I thought that once I uncovered the why of her, I'd unlock her inhibitions. But it's not that simple." He shifted to his side, propping his head in his hand. "Actually, it all seemed possible to me until I went to collect her at the Fishbines'."

Balthazar sent him a baffled glance. "I was under the impression you two got on like bread and butter after that dinner at the Fishbines'."

"We did, but when I went to collect her I was submitted to her hosts' blatant disapproval. It's been a while since I felt that kind of contempt. It's a good thing I didn't go along with Lily that evening, because I doubt if I would have been allowed to sit at their dinner table."

"People with brains the size of peas shouldn't put on airs." Balthazar stroked his pointy beard. "Do you think Lily would have sat at their table if you'd been turned away?"

He started to answer from his heart and tell Zar that

Lily would have refused the Fishbines' couched hospitality. But then his mind tapped in and gave him pause.

"Well?" Balthazar prodded. "What do you think?"

"I'm not sure." Griffon sighed. "And there's the rub, old chum."

"The horns of the dilemma, as it were?"

"Partly. I can't help but wonder if I'm good enough to be Lily's secret love, but not good enough to squire her publicly."

"Maybe it's best, Griffon. We'll finish out business here—satisfactorily, I hope—and then we'll go home. There are several women there who love your company. Besides, you and Lily have so little in common."

"I disagree." Griffon started at the patch of dirt in front of him, realizing after the fact that he'd written Lily's name in it with his finger. "We have much in common. Perhaps that's what makes her nervous. Perhaps, when she looks at me, she sees the part of herself she tries to hide." He swept his palm over her name, erasing it. "If only she'd let me help her channel her powers as I let you and Thurman channel mine."

Balthazar threw back his head and laughed up at the stars. "You let us? Is that how you remember it?"

Griffon scowled at the other man. "I take it you don't."

"I remember a sullen, disagreeable, thieving Gypsy boy who wanted no help from anyone, especially a white man. A *gadjo*. If you'll recall, it was months before you trusted me enough to sit and share a meal with me. You were a suspicious little rat."

"Ah, yes." Griffon stared into the flames, seeing himself back then, feeling the constant fear he'd carried in his gut. "I'd forgotten those early days. I mainly remember the early days of our friendship. It was wonderful to have a friend after years of having no one but myself."

"You didn't trust Thurman Unger one bit either. I had to practically tie you to a chair to get you to sit and listen to the man. All he wanted was to see just how much psychic power you had, but you were such a scalawag that you wouldn't give the man a straight answer. It's a good thing Thurman has a pound of patience.''

"I was afraid of my abilities.''

"Sure, and why not? Your family gave you the boot because of them.''

"Yes, and in a way, that's what Lily's father did to her. Even her aunt and uncle don't know about Lily's talent. She's afraid to reveal her gifts to them for fear they, too, will desert her.'' He rolled onto his back again. "I suppose I'll just have to be patient with her.''

"Pulling her out of her hiding place, kicking and screaming, might not be what the young woman wants. She might hate you for it.''

Griffon considered this, but one thought kept rearing up in his mind, blocking out everything else. "Zar?''

"Yes?''

"I'm in love with her.'' It felt good to say it. "She loves me. She thought it. I was so surprised, I didn't know what to say.'' He laughed, recalling the awkward moment. "Then I decided to say nothing since my reading her thoughts never fails to irritate her.''

"Often a maiden imagines herself in love with her first lover. It eases her guilt, don't you see?''

Griffon frowned. "I don't sense guilt in her.''

"It's there. She's a decent young woman who knows better than to sport with a bachelor. Mark my word; when Lily returns home, she'll wrestle with guilt. She'll think of her future once again and realize she must nurture a lie if she hopes to land a gentleman husband.''

A dagger of jealousy stabbed Griffon's heart at the thought of Lily choosing someone else. "She is still a lady to me. Any oaf who doesn't think so doesn't deserve her.''

"Griffon, if you love her, let her go. I can't see how she'd be happy in Boston.''

"Why not Boston? Her father and stepmother live in Cambridge.''

"Exactly," Balthazar said, his tone dry as kindling. "That's *another* obstacle to face. It might be better to just let her go."

Griffon grunted, not trusting himself to speak. The thought of leaving Lily behind brought a thickness to his throat. He closed his eyes on hot tears of frustration. He endured a restless sleep, struggling under a weight he couldn't lift or identify.

Balthazar handed Griffon a mug of steaming coffee and a cold biscuit-and-sausage sandwich.

"You certainly didn't rest easy last night," Balthazar said, pouring himself some coffee from the pot he'd brewed over the campfire.

"I had dreams."

"The same as before?"

"Yes . . . no." He shrugged, unable to recall the details. "Even now I feel that something . . . something's amiss."

"You're anxious to confront the Jefferses, that's all. You want to end this search, and I don't blame you."

Griffon popped the last bite of biscuit and sausage into his mouth and brushed crumbs from his fingers. He rolled his shoulders under an invisible weight. "Let's pack up our duds and set off. You're right. I'm eager to get this over with." He lifted the saddle onto the black stallion's back.

Balthazar tightened the belly strap around the big chestnut mount. "My feet are itchy, too, but we must tread carefully. That whole Jeffers clan is as nutty as a Christmas cake. I wouldn't put it past them to—" Balthazar cocked his head, struck by Griffon's tense stance and alert expression. "What is it?"

"Someone's coming." Griffon reached into the saddlebag and withdrew a revolver. "Do you hear them now?"

Balthazar nodded. "Sounds like a buggy or wagon."

"Yes, so it does." Griffon moved soundlessly to the

edge of the clearing, gun cocked and ready. Pushing aside underbrush, he peered through leafy camouflage and spotted the springy buggy pulled by two wild-eyed horses. Early-morning mist swirled at ground level, lending an eerie atmosphere. As the buggy drew closer, the driver's round face shone beneath a wide-brimmed bonnet. "Blimey it if isn't Orrie Dickens herself!" Griffon holstered the gun.

"Orrie?" Balthazar shouldered past him, waving his arms above his head to be noticed. "Whoa, woman! What, pray tell, brings you out here at the crack of dawn?"

Orrie yanked on the reins until it looked as if she were lying flat on her back. The horses whinnied and tried to rear. Griffon and Balthazar sprang forward, seized the halters, and settled the horses on all fours. The beasts snorted, blowing out hot air. Sweat hung like lace on their dark hides.

"Thank the Lord, I've found you!" Orrie released the reins and clasped her hands in gratitude.

Balthazar gripped her waist and helped her climb from the buggy. She clung to him as if her knees wouldn't support her.

"What's wrong, Orrie, love?"

Griffon had never heard Balthazar use that particular tone of voice. So soft and loving, he thought. Griffon had known Balthazar to sweet talk women, but never like this. Never with such respect and depth of feeling.

"It's Lily," Orrie said, sobbing.

Panic seized Griffon's heart, and he suddenly knew why it had felt weighted. "What about Lily?" He heard the crackle in his voice, but didn't care. "Speak up, woman!"

"Sh-she's gone!" Orrie's eyes were so puffy they were nearly swollen shut. "I can't f-find her, and th-that stupid sheriff is n-no help a'tall. They're lookin' all over t-town, but she's not there. Sh-she'd tell me if she was goin' somewhere."

"How long has she been missing?" Griffon asked.

"I'm not sure. I was n-napping yesterday and when I woke up, she was nowhere to be—"

"Yesterday?" Griffon repeated, slapping the heel of his hand against his forehead and reeling in a half circle. "She's been gone since yesterday?"

"Right after y'all left, I guess." Orrie sobbed again, her bosom hitching up and down. "Like I said, I woke up and she wasn't there. The hotel clerk said he saw her go outside, but didn't see her come back in." She stuffed one hand into her skirt pocket. "I found this in the alley beside the hotel."

Griffon stared at the pearl pendant, still on the gold chain, its clasp broken. "Lily was wearing this the last time I saw her."

Orrie nodded. "It's hers. Looks like it was yanked off her neck."

Griffon took the necklace from Orrie's trembling fingers. He rubbed it between his thumb and forefinger and closed his eyes.

"Anything?" Balthazar asked.

"What's he doing?" Orrie demanded.

"He's trying to get a sense of Lily off the necklace. Maybe it can tell him what happened."

Griffon shook his head and opened his eyes. "Nothing. Tactile sensations are Lily's domain, not mine."

"I came as soon as I figured out the sheriff wasn't going to do nothing. He's been pokin' into every building in town. Last night I packed up, got this buggy, and headed out. It got dark and I got kind of lost, so I had to stop a while and wait for the dawn before I went on. But I found you." At that, she collapsed in Balthazar's arms. "What are we going to do? Where's my Lily, Zar? If she's hurt or . . . or . . ." She buried her face in Balthazar's shirt-front.

"There, there, dear lady," Balthazar said, using that rare tone of voice as he stroked Orrie's bonnet off her head and kissed her mussed hair. "You've had yourself a time, haven't you? Poor darling woman. Go ahead and cry.'' He looked over her head at Griffon. ''What shall we do now?''

''Give me a moment to digest all of this.'' Griffon turned his back on them and stepped off six paces. Still holding Lily's necklace, he brought it to his lips for cold comfort. He battled the panic that tried to dupe him and forced clarity to his thoughts. Gone. She was gone. He shut his eyes and burrowed into himself to find the hidden truths. His senses awakened and reached out, but he felt no answering tug from Lily. ''Where are you?'' he whispered. ''Call to me, Lily. For the love of God, call to me.''

He waited in vain, feeling nothing, hating the emptiness surrounding his heart. The silence squatted in his mind like an inert monster. Gradually, the monster shifted, letting in weak signals. But not of Lily. Griffon couldn't feel Lily, but he felt someone. Cecille? his mind asked, but the feeling took on a male form. A man . . . a boy, perhaps. Someone thought about him, but who?

''Zar, take Orrie back to town.''

''What will you do?'' Balthazar asked behind him.

''Go on ahead as planned.''

''Not alone!''

''Yes, for now. You can catch up. Bring the sheriff.''

''Griffon, no. I won't leave you in this enemy's land alone.''

''I don't want Orrie here, and I need the sheriff. Do this for me, Zar.'' He turned to face the other man. ''Orrie will be better off at the hotel, safe and sound. By the time you get back here, the sheriff can make some arrests.''

''You don't *know* this,'' Balthazar said, squinting shrewdly at him. ''You're guessing. You can't fool me, Griffon. I've known you too long.''

''I have every faith in finding Lily and Cecille. I believe we'll find them together.''

''Faith? I won't leave you because of misplaced faith.'' Balthazar glanced at Orrie's tear-stained face. ''This good woman can make her way back to town. You need me here.''

Griffon sent his resolve through his eyes, and Balthazar received the message. He blanched, swallowed hard, then nodded.

"I see your mind is set," he said. "Very well. I'll escort Orrie to Van Buren and hurry back here."

"Bring the sheriff."

"I will. Don't you worry." He prodded Orrie toward the buggy. "Come, Orrie. Let's not waste another minute."

"You'll find her?" Orrie asked Griffon. "Do you feel that she's all right? Is she hurting? Is that what's wrong? Is that why you're getting rid of me so fast? Are you afraid I'll find out sh-she's d-dead?''

"She's not dead," Griffon said, almost snapping at Orrie. "I'll find her. Just . . . just go on." He made an impatient gesture, frustrated in his own inability to make any connection with Lily. "On your return, Zar, go directly to the Jeffers place. I'll find you."

Balthazar helped Orrie onto the buggy seat, then hoisted himself up to sit beside her. He took the reins in hand.

"I'll fetch your horse." Griffon strode through the underbrush to the remains of their campsite. "And water those horses at the creek before you head for town," he said, returning. "They're winded, poor beasts."

"Griffon, do be careful," Balthazar cautioned as Griffon tied the chestnut to the back of the buggy. "Don't take any foolish chances."

"When do I ever?" He slapped the rump of the horse closest to him, setting the team in motion. Balthazar turned them in a tight semicircle and pointed them toward Van Buren. "Godspeed!" he called over his shoulder.

Griffon waved. "God save us all."

He went back to the camp, scattered the campfire ashes, and checked his gear again before swinging into the saddle. The image of a boy returned. A boy . . . He shook his head, shut his eyes, and tried to see some reason to the rhyme. The image, like a misty morning, wavered in his mind's eye, then a light tunneled through for a blazing instant to show him a face.

"Jasper!" Griffon whispered, planting his heels in the horse's sides. The big stallion surged forward, guided by Griffon's deft touch. Jasper had somehow abducted Lily. It made sense, Griffon thought, remembering how the man/child had looked at her with calf eyes. His anxiety lessened. Jasper wouldn't hurt Lily. Griffon released a long sigh, glad that Lily was in kind, if misguided, hands.

But, there were the other Jeffers males. If any of them got their claws on her—

"Hiyah!" Griffon leaned over the stallion's neck. The big horse stretched into a full-out run, skimming around trees, leaping over brush, spurred by the urgency in Griffon's voice.

Chapter 21

Jasper had a hidey-hole in the woods.

When he first found the deep hole in the giant oak tree, he'd been a tyke and able to get his whole body into it. He'd sit in the pungent darkness and stare out the almost perfect oval at the brightness beyond. He'd cross his legs, lean back, relax. Plenty of room for moving and thinking and getting away from Paw-Paw and his brothers.

But as the years crept by his body changed, grew, became gangly, then roly-poly. This perplexed him since he didn't feel different inside. Outside, he hardly knew himself. Sometimes he held his hand in front of his face, like a baby making a profound discovery, and stared at the thick fingers and wide palm. Hard to believe it belonged to him. He always thought of himself as little and helpless.

He was never more aware of having gotten big than when he was squeezed in his hidey-hole. Gone was the elbow room. No way could he cross his legs. In fact, his legs stuck out the hole, and Jasper had to double over to fit. Even then, the crown of his head brushed the top of the hole and dislodged splinters. But he loved the hidey-hole. He felt safe in it. That hadn't changed. It was about the only place he did feel safe. The hidey-hole and Maw-Maw's arms were his refuges in a world of loud voices and mean spirits.

Wedged in the hole, he wiggled his bare feet, scaring away a butterfly that tried to land on his big toe. He folded his arms across his chest and rubbed his tender left cheek against his shoulder. Paw-Paw had hit him there last night when he'd shown up late to make music. Ham had come after, and Paw-Paw had walloped him a good one, too. Ham hadn't cried like Jasper. Ham had wiped the red dribbles from his chin and swore at Paw-Paw. Jasper sniffed and pressed his lips together to keep from whimpering. He didn't love Ham no more. He'd never love Ham again. Not never, never, never, he chanted to himself, wagging his head from side to side.

"Jasper? Jasper, boy?"

Jasper clamped his hands over his mouth and felt his eyes strain outward. Then he recognized his Maw-Maw's voice. His hands fell away, and his breath whooshed out.

"Sonny boy, what you doing in that tree knothole with your legs hanging out? You like that rabbit that thought it was hid behind a blade of grass?" Eva peeked inside the oval opening. "What's wrong, baby boy? Did Paw-Paw hurt you again?"

"Not since last night," Jasper said, emotion making his voice quiver. "Jasper's scared, Maw-Maw."

Eva placed her hands on his knees and leaned between his legs. "You scared of Paw-Paw again?"

"No . . . yep." He shook his head, trying to fling his thoughts into order. "Jasper don't love Ham no more. Him's scary."

"What did he do to you?" Eva clutched his knees, her long fingers digging into his flesh. "You tell Maw-Maw what he did. I'll take care of him. You watch. I'll scald his privates and make him wish he'd never laid a hand on my baby boy. 'Member when I did that to your brother Ennis?"

Jasper giggled, remembering. Ennis had tried to put his pee pistol in Jasper's mouth. Maw-Maw had caught him at it and thrown a whole kettle of boiling water across the front of Ennis's pants.

"He been messing with you, Jasper?"

"Naw. It ain't me him's messin' wid."

"Come out here, sonny, where I can see you." She tugged at his pants' legs. "Mind your Maw-Maw. Wiggle out here, wooly worm."

Her warm voice enticed him, and he worked his body from the hole and landed on his bare feet in a patch of blooming clover. Eva licked her palm and ironed his cowlick to the back of his head.

"Now tell your Maw-Maw what's got you in that hole. What did Ham do now? You know anything about him being late last night? And what about you? I don't believe for one minute that you got lost. Why, my sonny boy could find his way from here to China without no compass." She shook a finger in his face. "Don't mess with the truth. Tell me all of it. No pouting either. Push that lip back in place." She pressed her thumb against his lower lip and stuck it under the upper one. "There you go. What's wrong, sonny boy?" Her voice flowed like honey. "Tell Maw-Maw."

Her understanding opened a floodgate in him, and he wrapped his arms around her and pressed his hot face to the curve of her neck.

"There, there," she cooed, stroking his thinning hair. "Maw-Maw's here and will take care of her baby boy. What's got you so upset?" She took his face between her hands and made him look straight into her dark eyes. "Talk to me, Jasper."

"Jasper and Ham were in town yesterday," he said between sniffles. "Watching that purty gal."

"The pretty . . ." She nodded. "Oh, yes. That Lily Meeker."

"Maw-Maw's brudder's looking for Lily's kin and . . . and now him's looking for Lily!" He wailed and felt tears tickle his cheeks. His mother's face swam before him. She held his face tightly.

"Jasper, get hold of yourself. You ain't making sense.

What did you and Ham do in town yesterday? Did you do a bad thing?''

"Not Jasper."

"Then Ham did a bad thing?"

"Uh-huh." He blinked, clearing his eyes. "Him did."

"What?"

"Took the purty lady. Him took Lily. Put her over hims horse and rode off. Him hit her and made her go asleep."

"You saw this?"

"Uh-huh."

"Anybody else see it?"

"Uh-uh."

"Where did Ham take her? Did you follow him?"

"Uh-huh. Him takes her to the bad under place." Just saying it sent a shudder of revulsion through him. "And now your brudder's looking for her."

"My brother? What do you mean, sonny boy? I've got no brothers around these parts."

He batted his eyes owlishly. Often confused, he constantly struggled with frustration. He puffed out a sharp breath and pinched his brows together, which always helped him reason things out. "Maw-Maw said him was her brudder," he said, stubbornly clinging to the memory. "Him looks like Maw-Maw and Jasper. Not like Paw-Paw and the brudders."

Eva released his face to flatten her hands against her chubby cheeks. *"O Del!"* she murmured in her native tongue. "You telling me that Gypsy man is hunting for that girl and Ham took her?"

Jasper nodded. "Him hurt her, too. Jasper saw him dood it. Before him go down thar wid her she woked up. Him shoved his fist in her purty face." A sob broke his voice in two. "Him carried her down thar, Maw-Maw. The bad under place." He whispered the last, afraid to say it much louder.

Eva whirled and paced, her face crumpling into lines of worry. "Crazy fool. What's he thinking? That girl has family. He can't just steal her for nothing like his father took me! That's where he gets it. Thinks he can follow the old man's trail and get away with it. All those boys act like they can do any old thing and not answer to anyone. Well, not this time. That Gypsy—what was his name?''

"Go ahead?'' Jasper asked.

"No. Not that.'' She snapped her fingers. "Goforth!'' Jasper nodded. "That's it, Maw-Maw.''

"He's poking around looking for her? You saw him?''

"No, but I know him's lookin'.''

"How do you know?''

Jasper shrugged. " 'Causin' he loves her like Jasper loves her. Jasper'd be lookin'.''

Eva laid her hand along the side of his face. "My baby loves her, does he? Why?''

"Her runned off some bad boys that scared Jasper.''

"Where?''

"In town. Her's good to Jasper.'' He puckered his mouth, tasting the bitterness of his tears. "Jasper don't love Ham no more. Ham hurts Lily. Ham hurts her bad.'' He gripped his mother's hand. "Can Maw-Maw gets Lily? Jasper can't go down thar. Jasper's scared.''

"Baby, you know I can't go down there either. I'm more scared of that place than you. Why, you learned to be scared of it from me.'' Eva sighed her regret. "Maybe I can talk Ham into bringing her back up. Maybe Paw-Paw will make him let her go.''

"Think so?''

"Maybe. Paw-Paw and the others are sleeping it off. They drank too much grape juice last night. Once they wake up, I'll talk to your Paw-Paw. Come on, baby boy. I've got washing to do and you can help. No use in you hiding in your hole all day. You just stay around me, and I won't let no one hurt you.''

"What if Paw-Paw hurts your brudder again?''

"The Gypsy Goforth has better sense than to get in Paw-Paw's sights again. That one can take care of himself." She winked slyly. "Gypsy people survive. It's our gift from *Del.*"

"*Del* lives in heaven."

"He sure does, baby boy. *Del* is the king of heaven."

"Where is heaven, Maw-Maw?"

"Up there." She pointed to the blue canopy overhead. "A long, long way from here."

Jasper slipped his hand in hers and skipped along beside her to the log house in the heart of Devil's Den.

The pain came back to her first. Constant and searing, it lashed across her jawline and up toward her eyes. Sounds reverberated in her skull as if it were an echo chamber. Sundry aches erupted in her body, mostly in her joints and across her ribs. Opening her eyes to slits took a great effort. Lily expected to be assaulted by light, but grayness greeted her. She moaned. It scratched her throat and resounded in her empty head.

"Orrie?" she whispered, and her voice came back to her three times before finally fading away.

Where was Orrie? More importantly, where was she? Lily wondered, feeling the hard, cold surface beneath her bone-weary body. Not the hotel room, she knew. Had she fallen outside? A memory swam out of reach. She closed her eyes again, intent on catching that flash of recognition. Jasper . . . Jasper had wanted to see her. Had she met with him? She didn't remember . . . wait! A face, not unlike Satan's, branded her inner vision. Lily sucked in a breath that whistled down her throat and blew apart cobwebby images. A scent of damp, dank things sent questions through her tired brain. Coldness seeped into her muscles. She spread her fingers to touch surfaces and realized with a start that she couldn't move. Her eyes flew open, staring into grayness. She struggled, the movements making it clear to her that her wrists and ankles were bound by scratchy rope.

The gravity of the situation bored down on her, bringing

tears to her eyes. Where was she? Why did she ache all over? Was her jaw broken? She tried it, wiggling the lower portion back and forth. Pain erupted like fireworks. A trembling began in her stomach and spread outward. She shook, teeth chattering, thoughts tumbling in her head like pebbles rolling downhill.

Never in her life had she felt so alone, so frightened. She forced herself to look around. Her lashes were wet with tears and felt heavy as she lifted them again. A silhouette appeared like a ghost before her. It moved, writhing along the gray curtain, misshapen, monstrous. Then a head and shoulders took shape above her. Slanty eyes stared down at her. Lips spread to show teeth, some stained, some white. Desperation clawed at Lily's consciousness. She wished she could faint.

"Hiya, sweet thing. Welcome to my lair."

She trembled as the voice triggered a dreaded knowledge. Ham Jeffers was the man staring at her. Ham Jeffers had hit her, slapped her, stolen her. She closed her eyes and whimpered, unable to find any courage in her battered mind and body.

"These here are the caverns. Me and you is gonna spend our honeymoon down here." His chuckle sounded like dry bones clacking together.

"You can't keep me here," Lily said, forcing each word past her parched throat. When had she last eaten anything? What she'd give for a drink of water! "I—I'll scream."

"Go ahead, sweet thing. Scream your purty head off. Nobody down here gives a damn. We uns is way, way down under the ground. This here place is rock-ribbed, so there ain't no way anybody's gonna hear your wailing. So go right ahead and make your female noise." He reached out a forefinger to touch her, and she angled her head away sharply. "You is my wife now, woman."

He laughed at the strangled sound she made. "I picked you and took you just like my big brother took himself a woman. He got himself a better-looking woman than the one he had before. She's a prize, but he'll bust a gut when he sees you. Why, you put that fuzzy-haired gal to shame, you do. That dark red hair of yours drives a man wild. You and me'll throw off some good chillen.'' He rubbed his hands together and smacked his lips. ''I can hardly wait to get started on making 'em.'' He glanced around, then fashioned a huge shrug. ''Hell, why wait? I'm half-way hard and full of seed. Once I see them pert little breasts of your'n, I'll be ready to shoot my wad, I reckon.''

He grabbed a handful of her hair. Lily screamed. The sound rose up and fell over and over and over. It went on forever, even when Ham's mouth closed over hers to squelch her squeals. The front of her dress ripped, torn by his cruel hand. Futility settled over her. She could barely move, so how in heaven could she fight? She struggled to no avail, unable to move more than an inch either way. It was impossible to spit out his tongue and angle her mouth from his. He held her hair so tightly her scalp burned. His other hand poked and prodded, sliding under her torn bodice to knead her breasts as if they were not flesh but unfeeling bread dough. She winced, groaned, hated him with every inch of her soul.

Using the only weapon left to her, she bit his tongue. He howled and released her, hands going to his mouth.

''You bitch!'' His eyes watered. Rage shone in their black centers. ''Now you'll get what's what. I was gonna be careful, but no more. I hope I hurt you. I hope I rip you in half!'' As he spoke, he shrugged out of his suspenders and unbuttoned his trousers. He pushed them down, and his member sprang up, a dark, thick root.

''No, no!'' The words stumbled from her in panting breaths, and she strained against the ropes that bound her. Instinctively, she pressed her thighs together, guarding herself from his evil intentions.

''Yes, yes!'' He sounded like a hissing snake.

Snakes! Snakes! Look out! They'll kill you! Lily's rational mind deserted her completely. Wild thoughts flashed through her, jumbling the past with the present. She struggled and thrashed, dimly aware that she was fighting a losing battle. Her skirt flipped up to cover her face. He ripped her underclothes, then tore the rope from her ankles. She kicked, but connected with nothing but air. He wrapped his hard hands around her thighs and pried them apart. Lily heard her own cries, her shrieks, her protests. They rained down on her in unrelenting echoes.

Then the head of his member touched her, and she thought she'd go mad with rage, with shame, with utter humiliation.

"No!" The word exploded from her like a gunshot. She bucked, using the last of her strength. It was enough to unbalance him. He cursed and held on to himself, then guided his fleshy rod toward her again.

"What in the hell do you think you're doing?"

It was a different voice; a deep, angry voice. Lily sensed Ham's jolt of surprise, then she felt something sticky splash her thighs.

"Aw, hell! You made me miss the target and spill too soon," Ham complained. "What the hell does it look like I'm doing, brother?"

"Looks like you've lost your damned mind. Who is that gal and why is she here?"

Rage had blinded her temporarily, but her sight returned, and Lily turned her head to locate the other man. He stood a few feet away, throwing a long shadow across the rock wall. Lily studied him, certain she'd seen him before. But had she actually met him? He resembled Ham. The same slanty eyes and coffee-colored skin. She gathered in a noisy breath when the pieces of the puzzle fell into place. Anson! This man was Anson. She'd seen him in her visions. She'd seen him with Cecille's eyes. She'd seen him murder his own wife.

"I took me a wife. Just like you." Ham scrambled off her, pulling up his trousers and stretching his suspenders over his shoulders. "I was on the brink of making my first child with her when you busted in."

"Take her and yourself and get out of here." Anson turned to go.

"How come? You don't own these here caverns."

"I got rights. I brought my woman here first. You're trespassing, seeing as how I never gave you permission to come in here. So get." He thumbed the way. "And take that squalling female with you."

"I ain't going. I took me a wife, just like you. I got every right to keep her here, just like you. Nobody gave these here caverns to you, brother o'mine."

"You heard me. I'm through jawing. You get." Anson ran his gaze over Lily, making her aware of her exposed breasts and legs. She hunched her shoulders and turned sideways, away from him. "Where'd you find her?"

"In town. Jasper met her first. She's not from around here."

"Where, then?"

"Fort Smith."

Anson's black eyes tracked slowly to Ham. "Fort Smith, you say?"

Ham nodded, grinning like a jack-o'-lantern. "Yep. Her and your gal is cousins."

"Cousins?" The word bounced back and forth, just like Anson's gaze as it moved from his brother to Lily and back again. "You loco? Why, you dumb jackass! Why'd you snatch her kin?"

"Look at her. You ever seen a purtier gal? She's better-looking than your'n."

Anson whacked Ham alongside the head, making him stumble sideways. "Use your noggin, dumb butt. Me taking the first one has brung all kinds of folks sniffing around this place. Now you go and take another one from the same damned family! Why, these hills'll be crawling with law." He pointed a shaking finger at Lily. "You get that gal out of here. If you got any sense, you'll take her back to town and leave her.''

"Will not! She's gonna have me some chillen." Ham rubbed the side of his head and belligerence set on his face. "You might be my big brother, but you ain't my pa. I don't have to mind you."

"You do if'n I take your head off," Anson said, snarling like an animal. "You get out right now or get ready to fight and lose. I'll send you out of here a bloody stack of bones, I will. I been hiding that gal for weeks, and the law had slacked off looking for her. I ain't about to let you sic them on me again." He held up his fists in a fighting stance. "What'll it be, pipsqueak?"

Ham released his breath, and it looked to Lily that he wilted a little. Then, in a stunning reversal, he let out a howl of anger and charged his brother. His shoulder rammed into Anson's stomach and he pushed him back, slamming Anson against the wall. Anson grunted, groped for a hold, grabbed handfuls of Ham's sticky hair, and pulled. Then the two of them toppled sideways and rolled in a bundle of flying fists and flailing legs.

Lily wriggled and sat up, placing her feet on the cold floor. Where were her shoes? She rubbed her wrists together and felt the rope around them loosen. Twisting and turning, she freed her hands and sprang to her feet. Anson had Ham on his back and was straddling him. He landed a vicious blow to Ham's right cheek, but Ham connected with an upthrust fist that caught Anson in the throat.

Dashing past them, Lily ran headlong across the cavern floor. Around a bend, she found herself in a much narrower space. She flattened herself against the cold rock wall and inched along the ledge. Below was a fifty-foot drop to a pool of black water. Above her, spikes of rock dripped. She hadn't realized the cave she'd been in had been lit by a torch until she moved farther and farther from it. Ahead of her was a blackness she'd never known before. Could she make herself step into that void?

"You jackass! She's gone!" Ham's voice acted like a whip on her. It echoed hollowly around her like a dreadful ghost.

"Get the torch, damn you," Anson ordered, then let loose with a string of foul words. "Stupid sonofabitch. Gimme that light."

Lily felt them bearing down on her before she heard their footfalls and saw the light dancing across the ceiling. Taking small steps, she started forward again, afraid of the darkness, but more afraid of who stalked her. Ham's sticky seed dried on her legs, and she could still taste him, horrid on her tongue. She held the bodice of her dress together with one hand and used the other to feel along the wet, slimy wall.

It was impossible to know how far back Anson and Ham were because the cavern echoes cheated distances. A droplet of water splashed on the back of her neck, and she smothered a shriek of fear.

"I heard her," Ham said.

"Me too. She's right up ahead of us. Better stay put, girlie. You'll fall and break your durn neck," Anson called to her. "If you don't stop right now, I'll break it for you!"

The light behind her vanquished more of the dark. They were getting closer. Something made a whooshing noise above her, and Lily looked up to see the ceiling undulate, flutter, *move!* The black separated to become a hundred bodies, two hundred flapping wings. A squeak, loud and long and earsplitting, rose up. Bats!

Screaming, Lily ran into the pitch blackness. It took her in, closing around her, making her feel as if she were falling, although her mind told her that her feet were still slapping solid rock. Her eyes strained, hungry for illumination. Then they found it. A pinpoint of light, a shaft, an arrow of brightness slanting across the cavern floor. Lily navigated to it like a ship following a lighthouse beacon.

A crack in the wall face let the light escape. The opening was large enough for Lily to step through. She found herself in another cavern room, smaller than the first. Torches stuck in the wall face lit the area and gave a measure of warmth. Blinking, Lily waited for her eyes to adjust and show her something besides bright light and spotty images. A sound turned her head to the right, and she squinted to observe a figure rising from the cavern floor. Lily swallowed another scream. Her pupils contracted, and her vision cleared.

"Lily?"

If the voice had been a chorus of angels, it would have had the same effect on Lily. Tears ruined her vision again, but she didn't care. She knew who had spoken. She knew that face better than she did her own. Sobbing, she closed the space between them and gathered the frail body against her.

"Cecille," she said, sobbing uncontrollably. "Thank God! Cecille!"

Chapter 22

❧◯◯◯❧

Voices raised in song drew Griffon to the creek. He sharpened his mind, forcing the cloudiness from it with a shake of his head. Minutes ago he'd gotten a clear image of Lily. He'd felt her consciousness, and that had relieved him. Before that, he'd received nothing of her, and he'd feared the worse. But she was in the world again, and her spirit tickled his psyche, urging him on; a carrot dangled before a dumb ox.

That's how he felt: dumb, helpless, plodding along on instinct. Never had he known such desperation. If he'd needed any further proof that he had fallen under fiery Lily's spell, he now had it. If he didn't find her soon, he was quite sure he'd go mad.

Moving stealthily, he reminded himself he was in enemy territory and Lily's best hope of rescue for the time being. He half expected an ambush at every turn. The Jeffers Gypsy Band would be home from their dance, and they knew these woods far better than Griffon. The ground was sodden, a mush of dead leaves and new grass, muddy soil and pine needles. His boots left damning prints, but time was too short to bother with covering his tracks, even if he could. Bits of leaves clung to his black shirt and pants. He ducked under a low branch, and the new leaves dampened his hair, robbed of their morning dew.

The voices were stronger, nearer. A woman and a boy.

He knew before he spotted them that it was Eva and Jasper.

Parting the budding underbrush, he peeked through the branches at the mother and son. The two squatted at the creek bank. Eva held a scrub board and rubbed a shirt across it while Jasper wrung water from a pair of long-legged underwear. A basket lay between them, clothing tumbling over its sides. The sun dazzled the water's surface, but clouds were rolling in from the north, pushed by a brisk wind. A few early roses grew on a wild bush near the creek. Some had been picked and lay in a bouquet atop the clothes to be washed. The scene was so peaceful, it struck Griffon an ironic blow.

He was reminded of a poem. "Gather ye rosebuds while ye may, Old Time is still aflying: And this same flower that smiles today, Tomorrow will be dying." The words squeezed from his heart Lily's name. It winged past his lips, a whiff of sound heard only by his ears. He felt her spirit and felt something else . . . her panic, her confusion. Hold on, he thought as hard as he could, then wondered if she could feel him as well. She had once in this woods. She'd tracked him with her mind. Could he track her with his?

Jasper and Eva harmonized, and the song was sweetly familiar to Griffon. He'd heard it on Queen Sofie's knee; a Gypsy folk song.

> Free is the bird of the air,
> And the fish where the river flows;
> Free is the deer in the forest,
> And the Gypsy wherever he goes.
> Hurrah!
> And the Gypsy wherever he goes.

Griffon's mouth formed the words with them, his Gypsy heart gladdened by the tune. Sing, he thought, but the song won't make you free. Eva and Jasper were prisoners of a tyrant named Butch and his band of outlaw sons. Two alone, he thought, watching them working in happy harmony. They stood apart from the rest of the Jeffers clan but were shackled to them, nonetheless. Griffon whistled the song of a thrush, testing Eva's Gypsy roots. She stuttered, fell silent, and glanced around apprehensively.

"What's wrong, Maw-Maw?" Jasper whispered.

"I heard a thrush. It's a sign of company."

"Company?" Jasper dropped the garment he'd wrung out and clapped his hands. "Goody!"

Eva set the washboard aside and dried her chapped hands on her apron. She looked around again and spotted the parted brush Griffon crouched behind.

"Who's that?" she called. "Show yourself or I'll show you the business end of this gun." She tugged a big revolver from her apron pocket and pointed it at the brush.

"It's me." Griffon moved into the open, hands up in the universal sign of peace. "Griffon Goforth. I heard you singing. It's a song I recall from my youth." He smiled, offering friendship.

Eva stuck the gun back into the deep pocket. "I knew you'd come nosing around."

"Lily's missing." Griffon switched his attention to Jasper, who ducked his head and refused to meet Griffon's gaze. "Her necklace was found in the alley beside the hotel."

"There are all kinds of bad people roaming about. Especially in town," Eva said, still wringing her hands in her apron. "I figured we hadn't seen the last of you. Still looking for that other woman?"

"I'm looking for both of them now. Cecille and Lily. Jasper, have you seen them?"

Jasper glanced sheepishly at his mother but remained silent.

"Don't bother him," Eva said. "He don't bother you."

"You don't care if Lily's hurt or afraid?" Griffon persisted, disregarding Eva's warning. Jasper swallowed hard and poked at the soft ground with his big toe. "Have you seen her lately, Jasper?"

Jasper's eyes glistened with unshed tears, and his lower lip trembled. "What'll Jasper do, Maw-Maw?"

Eva hooked a hand behind his neck and hauled him to her side. He buried his face in her bosom. "You make him cry. Happy, *Borossan*?"

"You were stolen from your family and now your sons are stealing women. You'll stand by and let this happen? These girls aren't Gypsies. Their family won't shrug this off. Their family will never give up until blood is spilled. Is that what you want, Eva?"

"They ain't my sons. They didn't come from my womb." She pressed her free hand to her stomach. "Their ma was a crazy Indian squaw. Crazy as Butch, I hear. Butch has poisoned their minds with his wild talk." She ran a hand over Jasper's baby-fine hair. "This one is all mine. His father and brothers make fun of him, but he's my angel. *Del* sent him to me so I'd have someone to love with all my heart, with all my soul." Her black eyes flashed. "He's a good boy with a simple heart. I'll kill anything or anyone that tries to hurt him."

"I mean him no harm, but he might get hurt when the others come." Griffon ducked his head to be at eye level with Eva. "And they will come, Eva. Two girls are missing now. Help me find them and avoid a bloody war."

The sun slipped behind a dark cloud, and the atmosphere cooled instantly. Eva tilted her head to one side and regarded him with suspicion.

"Where'd you get them pale eyes, Gypsy man?"

Griffon flashed a grin. "My mother had many reasons, but none were convincing."

Eva laughed. "Many a Gypsy girl has flirted too often with the *gadjo*. Did your people desert her?"

"No. She was too powerful. She could *dukker the vast* better than anyone and it brought much money."

"Money can make the people forget tradition." Eva

glanced up at the gathering gloom. The wind blew back her dark hair and plain skirt. She shivered and hugged Jasper closer for a moment. Sadness doused the light in her eyes, then she gripped Jasper's chin and lifted his face.

"Tell him, baby. He's right. More and more will come, and there will be shooting and killing. We don't want that. Tell him what you saw." She let go of him.

Jasper swallowed a sob and looked at Griffon with round, babyish eyes. "Ham took her." He rubbed his runny nose on his shirtsleeve. "Jasper seen him. Ham h-hit her."

Hatred twisted in Griffon's gut and set his temples to pounding. "Where did he take her, Jasper?"

"To the . . . the bad under place."

Griffon looked from Jasper to Eva. "The what?"

"He's talking about the caverns."

"Where? What caverns?"

Eva patted Jasper's balding head, calming him, comforting him. "Not far from here. Underground caves, caverns. Nobody sane would go down there. Me and Jasper don't go near them, 'less we have to."

"It's where Satan lives," Jasper said. "It's the Devil's Den!"

Eva nodded. "That's right, sonny boy. Evil lives down there."

"Take me to them."

Eva shook her head. "I told you. I don't go around there. Me or Jasper. I'll tell you how to get there."

"No, I might get lost. You take me." He placed a hand on her shoulder. "Guide me to within seeing distance and I'll take it from there."

"Don't go!" Jasper said. "Hell's fires burn in there."

"Jasper, I must get Lily. You want me to bring Lily back up, don't you?"

"If youse can." Jasper nodded. "Her might be dead."

"No, she's not, but we can't waste any more time. Ham

means to hurt her. Ham goes down there and comes back up top, fit as a fiddle. Lily can, too, if I help her.''

"But Ham's bad. Bad people don't get hurt down under. Only good people like that purty gal.''

"Lily.''

"Uh-huh.'' Jasper wiped the tears from his face. "Jasper and Maw-Maw will show you the bad under place. Lily is Jasper's friend.''

Griffon stroked Jasper's flighty hair. "So am I.''

"You're Maw-Maw's brudder. You're kin.''

Eva flung out her hands, palms up, and shrugged. "I tried to explain how you and me were both Rom, but he don't quite get it.''

Griffon touched a forefinger to the swelling along Jasper's jawline. "Did Ham do this to you?''

"Nuh-uh. Paw-Paw dood it.''

Eva pretended not to notice Griffon's damning glance. "Him and Ham were late getting to the dance last night. Our band played at a big barn dance. Butch lashes out at anybody who don't mind him.''

"Why have you stayed here?'' Griffon asked. "Why not take your son and run? You can't be happy with Butch and this life.''

"Where would we go?''

"Anywhere,'' Griffon said, motioning to the tangled woods.

"With no money, no way to make it?''

Griffon made an impatient gesture. "You're Gypsy. All Gypsies can make money.''

She laughed under her breath. "Maybe so. Jasper, gather up the clothes into the basket. We will take you to the caverns, *Borossan,* but then you'll be on your own.''

Jasper dumped the clothes, lye soap, and scrub board into the wicker basket. He arranged the roses on top, then skipped along behind Eva and Griffon as they plowed through brush, Eva leading the way.

"So, you won't leave?" Griffon said, holding aside a low branch for them.

"He's my husband," Eva said with a resigned sigh.

Griffon shook his head. He'd heard the lame answer before, many times from many women. "Even a dumb dog knows to leave when he's kicked."

Gypsy fire flashed in Eva's eyes. "My life ain't so bad here. Butch and the boys leave me and Jasper alone most of the time. We're happy, ain't we, baby?" she asked Jasper, stopping to look back at him.

"Happy," Jasper agreed, grinning from ear to ear. "Jasper and Maw-Maw are happy as cream-fed cats." He giggled and swung the basket from side to side in childish glee.

"Even when your pa knocks the stuffing out of you?" Griffon countered, and Jasper's giggles died abruptly. "Even when your brothers beat on you?"

"Nuh-uh. That hurts."

"Butch hardly ever lays a hand on me or him." Eva stalked ahead of them, taking her anger out on prickly branches in her way.

"Once is too often," Griffon said. "Where's your pride? Where's your mothering instincts to protect your cub?"

Eva swung around to face Griffon. *"Izjele te vjestice!"*

Griffon laughed at the old Gypsy curse. "May the witch eat me?" he repeated, amused. "Dear Eva." He trailed gentle fingertips down the side of her teak-colored face. The anger subsided with his touch, and she practically purred, closing her eyes and rubbing her cheek against his knuckles. "When this is over, I'll help you get away from him. You and your boy can start a new life, if you want."

"You . . . will help me? A stranger?" She looked at him with eyes as hopeful as a child's.

"We aren't strangers. As Jasper said, we are kin." He pressed her shoulder in a warm gesture. "Now show me this bad under place."

"We're almost there." She led him to a break in the

trees. Ahead was a wooded knoll. "See that bush with the yellow flowers all over it?"

"Yes," he said, squinting at the place. He checked the canopy of storm clouds stretching to the horizon. Soon the heavens would open and drench them. The smell of rain hung in the air, sweet and pure.

"Behind that is a hole in the hill. Just big enough to crawl through. I hear that once inside a man can stand upright. I don't know firsthand, because I've never been any closer than this," Eva explained.

"And you don't have to go any closer. I can carry on from here." He grasped her hand, then impulsively kissed her forehead. *"Nais tuke,"* he whispered.

"Him kissed Maw-Maw!" Jasper giggled, dark eyes wide with surprise.

Griffon chucked the man/child under the chin. "Thanks, Jasper. I'll tell Lily that you helped me find her."

"Kushto bacht," Eva said, sending him off with a blessing and a smile.

"Think about it, sister," Griffon said, already moving toward the knoll. "If you want to be free again, I'll show you the way, just as you've shown me." Then he turned and sprinted to whatever dire fate awaited him under the devil's belly.

"Lily, I can't believe you're here!" Cecille held Lily at arm's length, her gaze falling to the torn front of Lily's dress. "But what has he done to you? He didn't . . . Oh, Lily! Did he force himself on you? How could he? He's been with me until he heard you screaming."

Lily held the fabric over her breasts with one hand. "Ham Jeffers kidnapped me." She pushed Cecille's tangled blond hair from her forehead. "I'm fine. But you poor thing! What's been happening here?"

She seized a moment to assess Cecille's condition. She'd lost weight. Lily ran her hands over Cecille's bare arms, which seemed no more than skin and bones. Her hair straggled around her face and neck, dusty and the color of parchment. Lily caught her lower lip between her teeth, anguished by the sight of her sparkling, brassy, blond cousin reduced to this sorry state.

Cecille's dress hung in tatters, and it was not one from her Fort Smith wardrobe. Her eyes looked like two marbles stuck in a white, doughy face. Dark bruises climbed her arms, dotted the skin above her breasts, and circled her neck. She shivered, and Lily realized Cecille was in poor health.

"Cecille, are you ill?" Lily pressed a hand to Cecille's forehead. Fever burned her palm. "You *are* ill. Have you a cold?"

Cecille nodded. "It's always so damp in here. He lights fires, but I'm never warm. I've thought so often of you, Lily. I've prayed you'd come, but now I wish my prayers had gone unanswered. I'm afraid for you, Lily. I'm afraid he might kill you."

"Hush, now. I'm going to get you out of here." Lily hugged Cecille close to her, trying to warm her cousin's cold body. "Others know I'm in this area. They'll come for us."

"They haven't before now," Cecille murmured, closing her eyes and resting her cheek on Lily's shoulder. "Nobody's been here looking for me."

"That's not true! We hired a detective and he tracked you here. Then we hired another. He's about somewhere . . . somewhere very near. He'll find us. I know he will."

"Anson won't let me go. He means to keep me here."

"Cecille, why did you tempt this man . . . this Anson?" Lily held Cecille's head between her hands and looked into Cecille's lackluster eyes. "We discovered that you were seeing him on the sly. Why, Cecille? Why in God's name would you do such a fool—"

"Now ain't this touchin'?" Anson sneered, striding through the opening.

Lily sucked in a breath and gathered Cecille closer to

her. She recognized Anson Jeffers, the fog clearing from her memory. She could recall his wild Gypsy dance across the flatbed wagon that served as a stage. And she recalled Cecille's breathless wonder of him. Lily had thought him a bit too savage, but Cecille had seen him as a dashing rogue meant to be tamed by her. Lily remembered how George Vick had likened Anson to Griffon, and she shuddered at such a comparison. Griffon was dark-haired and dark-skinned, but there the similarity ended. Anson was clearly a brute.

"It's a reunion, Ham." Anson spoke over his shoulder to his brother. "The Meek cousins are reunited. Ain't it too sweet for words?"

"Meeker," Lily corrected. "And I know who you are. You're Anson. The eldest Jeffers."

"Don't hurt her, Anson," Cecille said, moving in front of Lily. "I'll do anything you say, just don't hurt Lily."

Anson Jeffers stood over six feet tall. His shadow climbed the rock wall and spilled halfway across the ceiling, where formations dripped murky water. He wore a flannel shirt, blue trousers, and black suspenders. His boots were brown, muddy, knee-high. He bore a strong resemblance to his brother, both having sloe eyes, swarthy skin, inky hair. But Anson used his smile to good use. He flashed white teeth, and his black eyes glinted like sunstruck onyx. He'd gathered his black hair into a tail at the back of his neck. A romeo, Lily thought. A ladies' man, rough around the edges, dangerously attractive. She knew why Cecille had dallied with Anson Jeffers. He was the dark Gypsy from so many of Orrie Dickens's romantic tales. But this was reality, and the real Anson Jeffers wasn't a Gypsy and he wasn't romantic. He was cousin to the Grim Reaper with no conscience. Do or Die was his motto, and he cared not which was chosen.

"You'll do anything I say? Will you now?" Anson

chuckled and tucked his fingertips in the top of his waistband. "You'll obey me like a good girl, huh? That's nice. But you'll do that no matter what happens to this here gal."

"No, she won't," Lily said. "And you won't get away with this, Anson Jeffers. The marshals will be here within the hour, and they'll track you down like the dog you are! You, too, Ham."

Anson feigned a shiver. "Ooo, I'm so scared! Ain't you scared, Ham?" He laughed with his brother at Lily's threats. "Nobody's tracked her yet," Anson said, grinning.

"Yes, they have. Butch Jeffers lied and said you'd left home."

"Ain't no lie. I did leave. I live here now with my woman."

Lily curled her lip at that. "Butch said he didn't know where you were. Ham and the whole bunch lied, but no one was fooled. We knew you were still around here and that you were holding Cecille captive."

"Ain't none of your concern no more, girlie. Besides, you ain't staying here." He backhanded his bleeding lip, and his glinting gaze fixed on his brother. "You hear me, Ham? I want you to take this mouthy bitch and get."

"Anson, can't we stay the night?" Ham whined. "I gotta think 'bout where to hide her."

"If'n you use your head, you'll turn her loose and then hide yourself until the law gets tired of sniffing around for you. Paw'll skin you if'n he finds out you messed up my love nest here."

"Love nest?" Lily repeated, seeking her cousin's gaze. "Cecille would disagree with that. One has only to look at her to see that she's been mistreated."

"Bullshit. She loves it," Anson answered, but Lily saw fear rise in Cecille's eyes. "She's my Goldilocks." Anson grabbed Cecille's fragile wrist and hauled her into his arms. When Lily made a lunge toward him, Ham pushed her; she was halfway across the cavern before she regained her balance.

"Murderer!" Lily yelled, angry that she was reduced to hate-filled words, but using them all the same. "I know you killed your wife, Anson. You murdered her with your bare hands and buried her by the river."

Anson stared hard at her, his lips drawn into a white line, then he cut his eyes at Cecille. "Now I wonder who told you that?"

"Cecille witnessed the murder. We'll make sure that you hang for it."

"You whore!" He grabbed the lower part of Cecille's face, and she cried out. "You been flapping your jaws about that? I told you to keep quiet, didn't I?" He raised his other hand to strike her, but Lily was on him in a flash, hanging on to his cocked arm and sinking her teeth into the back of his hand. "Gawldarnit, get her off me!"

Lily tasted his bitter blood before Ham buried his hand in her hair and yanked her backward. She felt some of her hair rip from her scalp before Ham let go to fling her to the hard rock floor. Her knees struck it, spreading hot pain along her thighs. She looked up to give Ham a tongue-lashing, but his palm connected with her cheek and set her head to ringing.

"Don't! Please, don't hurt her!" Cecille screamed, sobbing with hysteria. "Anson, I'll do anything. Anything! Let her go, Anson. She'll promise to be quiet."

"Like hell she will. You told her about Doralee."

"No, I didn't," Cecille swore, shaking her head violently.

"She didn't tell me anything. I found the grave." Lily held the side of her face and grimaced with each movement of her tongue. She'd somehow managed to bite the side of it. She didn't know if it was her blood or Anson's she tasted in her mouth. "You're a filthy murderer. No matter what happens to me, it won't alter your fate. You'll swing, Anson. You'll burn in hell along with all the other killers and defilers.''

Anson pointed a finger at her. ''You got a big mouth, woman. Ham, take her outta here. I got some talking to do with my missus.''

''Missus?'' Lily struggled against Ham's hands on her forearms. He pulled her to her feet. ''What do you mean? You and Cecille aren't married.''

''As far as we're concerned, we are. She's gonna have my babies.''

''No!'' Lily looked at Cecille. ''Cecille, you aren't . . .''

''I don't think so,'' Cecille mumbled, ducking her head, too ashamed to face Lily. ''Save yourself if you can, Lily. Forget about me. It's too late for me.''

''No, Cecille! Stop it. Let go of me!'' Lily tried to shake off Ham's beefy hands, but he was far too strong. He wrapped an arm around Lily's waist and lifted her up to carry her from the cavern room. ''Don't give up, Cecille,'' Lily shouted. ''Griffon will come for us.''

''Who?'' Anson asked.

''I'm not talking to you, you . . . you ignorant jackass!''

Ham plastered his free hand against her mouth and flung her into the darkness. She fell to her hands and knees on the damp rock surface. Her kneecaps and shins ached. Ham and Anson talked in whispers, but she could only catch a few words—*morning, away, hide*. Not enough to make any sense of it. Light pooled around her, and she looked up to see Ham standing over her. He held a torch aloft.

''Come on, purty gal,'' he said, using Jasper's pet name for her. The light played over his face, making it seem all the more sinister. ''Me and you gonna play some poke in the bush.''

Lily swallowed the bile rising in her throat. Balancing

on her fingertips and the soles of her feet, she lunged and sprinted away from the light and into the black maw of Devil's Den.

She'd gone only a few yards when she felt Ham claw the back of her dress. The material ripped. Suddenly, the ground evaporated under her feet. She screamed as she fell into a bottomless void.

Chapter 23

$\mathbf{T}$he hole afforded a man little space. Griffon crawled through it on all fours, keeping his head down. His shoulders and hips scraped the low overhang. Moving cautiously, he strained to see any light ahead, but it only got darker and darker. The space remained close for several yards before Griffon's shoulders stopped bumping rock and he sensed a widening area. He lifted a hand higher, higher still, then released a breath of relief. Getting to his feet, he unbent his body gradually, expecting to bump his head any moment on the cavern ceiling. When he was almost standing straight, the crown of his head touched cold rock. Better than crawling, he thought, crouching a little. Much better.

He started forward, moving like the blind man he was in this world of no light. The toe of his boot struck something, sending it rolling. Griffon squatted, hands outstretched, patting cool air and damp rock. His left hand closed over a long club. He examined it by touch, finding the sticky, crumbling end. He smelled ashes, charred wood. His mind recognized the club as a torch. Feeling about, he found three more. So, someone had left a supply, he reasoned, grateful for the thoughtfulness because the darkness was beginning to gnaw at the edges of his courage.

Patting his own pockets, he located his stash of matches and struck one. He touched the flame to the end of the torch. The fire sputtered, smoked, caught. Griffon waved out the match when he was sure the torch's flames had the strength to carry on. Holding the flaming club aloft, Griffon surveyed the underground world.

"It's immense!" he whispered, and his voice came back to him four times.

The cavern room was as big as a barn, with a flat floor and smooth walls. Stalactites speared the air above him. Calcium deposits created lace of subtle colors around them. Half a dozen stalagmites stood in the center of the area, slowly climbing toward the steadily dripping rock icicle, twice the width of a man, that fed them.

Griffon shook off the eerie feeling that tried to rattle his nerves. Stepping cautiously and lightly so as not to alert anyone to his presence, he traversed the length of the cavern room. At the far end the area narrowed to a space just wide enough for a man but only tall enough for a boy. Griffon doubled over and forged ahead, guided by the gray and black smears left by torches. The dampness seeped into his bones. Feeling totally out of his element, he tried not to think about how terrifying it would be if a gust of wind blew out his torch and threw him into solid darkness.

How far should he go into the belly of this beast? he wondered. Was it possible that this underground maze held captive Lily and Cecille? And what of Anson and Ham? Were they around the next bend, waiting to thrust a knife into his heart?

His nightmare visited him again, reminding him of the prophesy of his own death. Before entering what Jasper called the bad under place, Griffon had been playing a hunch that Cecille might have run off with Anson. His nightmare had tended to confirm this suspicion. But now, as he walked soundlessly in the bowels of the earth, sensations came to him more clearly. He found he could sort them out, and realized this must mean that he was drawing near the sources of these emotions. His heartbeats quickened, and he lengthened his stride.

He'd deciphered Cecille's feelings wrong, he thought. She had not acquiesced, but struggled with guilt. Why did she feel guilty? He emptied his mind of all else to concentrate. He sensed Cecille in the rock walls and corridors. Like leftover odors, he sniffed out her fear, her ebbing strength, her guilt at having placed a bet in such a dangerous game. Her spirit came to him in tatters, bruised, faded, soiled. A knot of anger grew in his stomach as the certainty of her molestation took root.

"Dirty bastard," he hissed between his teeth, anger overriding the creepy sensation spawned by the cavern. He'd been wrong—dead wrong?—about Cecille, and he felt bad for it. He'd thrown her into cahoots with Anson, when all the while she'd been his frightened captive; the thought made him burn with inadequacy. It wasn't like him to be so far off track. But then, this case was very different from any other he'd worked. Lily hadn't been around him during those others. Lily, his temptation. Lily, his sweet distraction.

His shirt grew damp, sopping up the wetness on the walls when he brushed against them. When he reached a forked place, both choices showing smoke marks, he paused to catch his breath.

Which way? he wondered, peering left, then right. Which would lead him to Lily? Lily. He'd been sensing Cecille, but what of Lily? Why couldn't he sense her as well?

Griffon closed his eyes and concentrated in the way Thurman had schooled him. Plastering himself against the cold, wet wall, he spread his hands flat against the slippery surface behind him. He imagined sloughing off his past, his present, his every thought and notion like layers of skin. Finally, he was an empty vessel, ready to receive sensations.

Lily? He sent out the thought, transmitting through his mind, a human telegraph machine. *It's Griffon, Lily. Can you hear me? Can you call to me? Do it with your mind, Lily. Do it now.*

He began to tremble from the exertion. He imagined his senses outstretched and floating. They picked up nothing.

Lily! Are you here? I'm in the cavern. Call to me. Lily!

Nothing.

Lily, talk to me. It's Griffon. Listen to me! Lily Jane Meeker, you call to me this—

Something.

Griffon's eyes popped open, but he stared blindly. All his sensory powers focused on that faint inkling, a frail signal flashing in his brain. His inner receptors flailed, located, investigated. It was Lily. Beads of perspiration broke out on his forehead, but he paid no heed. He concentrated with all his might, grappling for a better hold on that weak signal.

Call to me, Lily. Concentrate so that I can find you. Put all your strength into it and I'll—

Griffon! Help me, help me! I can't hold him off. Griffon!

He was running before his mind comprehended the movement. Racing, panting, whipped by panic, Griffon followed his heart. Lily's frightened voice boomed in his mind. Then he heard her scream and he raced headlong, no longer cautious of a possible ambush, not giving a damn about danger around the corner, death around the next bend. He knew only one thing. Someone was hurting Lily, and he meant to kill the son of a bitch with his bare hands.

Crossing a strip of rock that formed a natural bridge above a basin of black water, Griffon flew, his athletic grace serving him well as the space narrowed again to a ledge barely the width of a man's foot. He needed no directions, guided by Lily's frantic thoughts. Skidding around a corner, he ducked into a small pocket in the rock. Somewhere along the way, he'd discarded the torch, no longer needing it because the area ahead of him was bathed in pale light. A corner of his mind noted that torches, stuck in crevices, lit the area. Shadows danced like imps. His pupils adjusted, revealing Ham Jeffers hovering above Lily, who lay on the floor, her dress partly ripped from her body, her hair tumbling, her face blotchy from being struck by the flat of Ham's hand.

Griffon pounced with a roar, his body colliding with Ham's and knocking them both sideways. Lily scrambled out of the way and pulled the torn material of her dress over her breasts. She crouched in the shadows, a frightened ball of humanity. Shivering, she tried to collect her senses. Things had moved so quickly, it was difficult to know what was safe, what wasn't, what was happening before her very eyes.

When she'd run from Ham, she'd almost slipped off the rock bridge. Ham had grabbed her just in time, keeping her from drowning in that brackish water. But he'd forced her back into this hole and had set about molesting her. She'd fought, but her energy had been sapped. Then she'd heard Griffon calling to her and she'd responded. Hadn't she? Hadn't she called out to him?

The events rotated like the colors in a kaleidoscope until she was dizzy. She closed her eyes. Grunts, groans, the sounds of fists connecting with bone and muscle resounded, and she opened her eyes again. Ham lay on the floor, not more than three feet from her. His eyes bulged in his head, and he made a garbled sound as Griffon, straddling him, squeezed his throat. Griffon peeled back his lips, exposing glinting teeth. He looked wolfish, the predator getting the best of his prey and relishing it.

Lily thought of how Anson had strangled his wife and didn't want to watch Griffon choke the life from anyone—not even someone as evil as Ham Jeffers.

"Griffon, no!" She waved frantically at him.

Griffon paid her little attention, but he did take his hands from Ham's throat to strike him a vicious blow with his fist. Ham's head rocked sideways; he expelled his breath with a groan and went limp. Out cold.

Pushing off him, Griffon extended one hand to touch

the side of Lily's face. "Any bones broken? Can you stand, walk?"

"Yes, yes." She nodded, clutching at what was left of the front of her dress.

"Here. Wait." He yanked his shirt up over his head and handed it to her. "Put this on."

"No, I—"

Cutting through her weak protest, he gathered the shirt in both hands and pushed the neck hole down over her head. He helped her poke her arms in the arm holes and then settled the shirt over the front of her dress, covering her. Gently, he freed her hair from the collar, then arranged it about her shoulders.

"That's better, hmmm? Come on, love. Let's get the hell out of here."

"Not without Cecille."

"You've seen her?"

"Yes." She nodded, winced, placed tentative fingertips upon the bruise blooming on her right cheek. "With Anson. He's vile, Griffon. I'm afraid he's done awful things to Cecille. She l-looks so pale, so lifeless."

"Where is she?"

"Out there somewhere." She motioned in a general direction, unsure of where she was at present. "I hate it in here, Griffon. It's so cold and dark. The dark frightens me."

"You stay here and I'll find Cecille."

"No!" She grabbed his forearms, holding tight. "Don't leave me!"

He recognized the rising panic in her eyes. "All right, Lily. Settle down." Running a hand over her russet hair, he fashioned a smile meant to calm her. "You're safe now. I won't leave you. We'll go together to find Cecille."

"Anson will try to kill us."

"He'll fail." Crouched before her, he took a few moments to examine the cuts and bruises visible on her face and hands. "Damn his soul. He hasn't . . . he didn't . . . ?"

"No. You came in time."

"Thank God." He cupped one hand behind her head and hauled her against his bare chest. The touch of her cheek against him was sweet heaven, and his breath caught in his throat. "Thank God I found you. Did you hear me in your mind calling you?"

She nodded, rubbing her cheek against the silky hair on his chest. He smelled smoky, mossy, musky. Lily ran her hands up and down his arms, feeling the strength in them, grateful for their refuge.

"I'm so tired," she murmured, wishing she could just give herself to him, let him carry her limp body from this horrid place and never look back. But she couldn't. Not without Cecille. "I think I can find Cecille again. She's in another room like this, but even smaller. There are torches in it. We can find the light."

"Let's go." He took her hands in his and pulled her to her feet. "The sooner we get this over with, the sooner we can get out of here."

She went with him, following along behind. He grabbed a torch on the way from the room. A narrow path wound through the underworld. His skin glistened like copper, and Lily inched as close as she could to him, seeking his warmth and the security he represented in this dank, sinister world. Sensing light ahead, she looked past his broad shoulder and squeezed his hand.

"Up there. He's lit a fire. Cecille says he does that. Shhh! Hear them?"

Griffon nodded and placed a finger to his lips, gesturing for complete silence. He transferred the torch to her, freeing his hands for battle. Tiptoeing forward, they approached the place. Griffon let go of her hand and sprang into the chamber. A fire blazed in the center of it, but no one crouched near it or in the far corners.

"Cecille?" Lily called.

"She's not here," Griffon told her.

"Then where? Where has he taken her?"

Griffon gripped her shoulders, heading off her rising panic. "We'll find her. No hysterics now. There's no time." He bent his knees to be at eye level with her. "Lily, don't fight me on this. Just do as I say. Close your eyes and reach out to Cecille with your mind. You can connect with her in a way I can't. Do it. Empty your mind and think only of her. Search for her with your sixth sense." He placed his hands on either side of her face in a gentle caress. "Close your eyes, love. Let your gift guide you."

She obeyed, soothed by his raspy voice and supportive touch. His thumbs traced circles on her temples, erasing the pounding of hysteria and instilling peace. She tried to do as he'd instructed, putting aside her loathing of this underground world, her fear of what lay behind her and what lurked ahead, her tired, aching wounds and bruises. She thought only of Cecille.

Cecille. Cecille. Cousin Cecille.

And in her mind's eye she saw Cecille being dragged along by Anson. Cecille sobbed. Anson cursed. He yanked viciously on her wrist, swore at her, threatened to hit her if she didn't hurry.

"I see them."

"Where?"

"I don't know."

"Can you feel a direction?" Griffon asked.

Lily paused, struck by the notion, then responding to it. "Yes. Yes, this way."

She took the lead, holding the torch and trotting along, drawn by Cecille's flagging spirit. Inky shadows writhed along the passageway. The ceiling dipped. They doubled over, hurrying as best they could until, finally, the ceiling soared and they could straighten their kinked spines. Their breathing and footsteps echoed back to them. Darkness followed in their wake and stretched out before them. But then suddenly another bouncing light flashed up ahead.

"There they are," Griffon said, snagging Lily's shoulder and hauling her behind him. "Let me go first."

"Do you want the torch?"

"No, you hold it. Do you think he has a gun?"

"I never saw one."

"Good. Now stay back, Lily. Let me shield you."

She hung back, touched by his chivalry, his bravery. She wanted to tell him, but it wasn't the time. Later, she would say all those sweet things to him, she vowed, and that thought boosted her energy. Crouching a little, she trailed him, catching sight of the other light now and again. They seemed to be gaining on it when it abruptly disappeared.

"Griffon?" Lily rested her free hand against his back. "Where'd they go?"

"Shhh. Come on," he whispered, moving slowly, caution evident in each step.

Lily clutched the torch tighter. Her nerves tingled, and she thought of all those spooky stories Orrie had whispered in the dark. She'd often said she loved to be frightened, but that opinion changed in the dank caverns. Being frightened was no treat. Spooky things and mysterious people were thrilling from a distance, but up close they lost their appeal. Up close they smelled of rot and decay. Up close they tasted bloody and bitter. Up close there was nothing thrilling in Satan's heartless smirk.

After this, she doubted if she or Cecille would want to hear another scary story as long as they lived. Providing they emerged from these eerie caverns with their lives intact.

Griffon stopped so suddenly that Lily plowed into him. She bobbled the torch but managed to hang on to it. When she'd regained her equilibrium, she saw that Anson blocked their path. He held Cecille in front of him, a knife to her throat. Cecille's eyes glittered in the dimness like chunks of blue glass.

"No, don't!" Lily started past Griffon toward Cecille,

but checked her stride when Anson hitched the knife blade higher under Cecille's chin. Cecille cried out, and a drop of blood trickled down her white throat.

"Another inch closer and I'll lay her open," Anson promised. "I'll gut her like a rabbit. Goldilocks here will tell you I mean business. Tell 'em!"

"Do as he says," Cecille begged, her voice warbling with hysteria. "He—he'll kill me!"

"That's right," Anson agreed. "I'll kill this wife just like I killed my other one. There's plenty of women in this old world, believe you me."

"Did you kill Doralee before or after you kidnapped Cecille?" Griffon asked.

Lily glanced back at him, looking for his angle. He knew as well as she did that Doralee had died after Cecille's disappearance.

"After. She'd be alive today if she hadn't been so danged stubborn and set on having everythin' her own way." He never took his gaze off Griffon. "Doralee was barren. I took up with Goldilocks here thinking she could give me babies. But when I brung her home and told Doralee about my plans, Doralee pitched herself a fit."

"Wonder of wonders," Griffon said, drolly.

Anson skinned back his lips. "I had to kill her to shut her up. She said she wouldn't let me keep Goldilocks. What was I going to do, hang on to a woman who couldn't whelp or keep this one and see if she could do better by me? Answer was clear in my mind."

"Clear in your what?" Griffon taunted. "You mistake that lump of tissue between your ears for a mind."

Anson chuckled. "You're one of them Gypsy curs, ain't ya? My pa married one and she threw off an idiot child. You Gypsies got tainted blood."

"I believe it's your pa whose blood is poisoned. As for Jasper, he's got more sense than you and your other brothers put together."

Anson narrowed his eyes. "Where's Ham?"

"Dead, I hope," Griffon answered smoothly.

"Ever heard of 'an eye for an eye'? Maybe I should settle the score and kill Goldilocks where she stands."

"You do, and you can prepare to meet your maker," Griffon assured him.

Anson laughed and retreated. "Just hold your ground, Gypsy scum. Me and my missus is gettin' while the gettin's good. You follow us again and I'll cut you open, rip out your guts, and strangle you with 'em."

Lily looked to Griffon, expecting him to make a last, desperate lunge at Anson to save Cecille. But Griffon didn't move, except for cutting his eyes in her direction and silently telling her to stay put.

"Griffon, we can't let them go!" Lily protested.

"You keep away," Anson bellowed, dragging Cecille with him, the knife glinting dangerously. Then the darkness gobbled them up.

"Griffon! Go after them!" Lily pleaded, grabbing his hands and trying to yank him into a run.

He placed a finger to her lips and cocked his head as if to hear better. Lily listened, catching the sounds of Anson's and Cecille's labored breathing, scrambling footfalls. Somewhere up ahead pebbles were falling and then leaves were rustling.

"What are they doing?" Lily whispered.

"Escaping," Griffon whispered back.

"We can't let them! Come on!"

"They won't get far. Balthazar has returned with the sheriff. They're waiting for them up top."

"How do you know?"

He rested one index finger below his left eye in the sign Orrie had made when speaking of his ability to see what others couldn't. "I know," he assured her.

Just then men's voices rang out, followed by a volley of gunshots. Lily jumped as if the bullets had found their way below ground to rip through her own skin. She placed a hand over her heart and swallowed a sob. Then she ran in the direction Anson had taken Cecille, racing so fast that the torch sputtered and died, throwing everything into the blackest of black.

"Lily!" Griffon called out to her, blind as a bat now in the smothering darkness. He had to rely on his own inner light to follow in her footsteps.

"Cecille! They've killed Cecille!" Lily cried. She spotted a portal of daylight and dived for it.

Chapter 24

～⌒○○⌒～

Sunlight didn't greet Lily topside. Rain clouds obscured the sun, but the world was still bright in comparison to the darkness from which she emerged. Stumbling like a blind woman, she slipped on the damp earthen mound, falling to her knees, forcing herself back up, blinking owlishly at the figures standing near her. Raindrops splattered her face.

She found herself on a grassy knoll dotted by wildflowers, gray stones, and patches of moss. Three men stood a few feet from her. Balthazar, Sheriff Mac, and another man she didn't recognize.

"Lily, for pity's sake! Lily!" Griffon popped up from the rock-ribbed hole like an angry mole. "You'll get your foolish head shot off!" He, too, blinked at his surroundings.

The stench of gunpowder hovered in the air. Lily looked about frantically and spotted the sprawled body partially hidden by the tall grass and brambly bushes. Anson. The breath whooshed out of her.

"Cecille?" she called. "Where is she? Cecille!"

"Here."

Lily whirled in the direction of the weak voice, which seemed to have come from Balthazar. Cecille stepped from behind the big man, her face streaked with grime, tears, and rain. A fragrant breeze billowed her tattered dress. Lily's heart contracted, and she raced to embrace her cousin, her bare feet slipping on the wet grass and muddy earth.

"Dear Cecille! I was so frightened. I thought you'd been shot." She pushed Cecille's matted hair from her blotchy face. "It's over, Cecille. I'm taking you home to Fort Smith. Home, Cecille. Home!"

Thunder rumbled overhead. Cecille glanced up, trembled, and released a sob. "To Mama and Papa?" she asked, tears streaming down her cheeks.

"Yes! Oh, they'll be so happy to see you. And Orrie is waiting for us in Van Buren."

"Orrie?" Cecille sniffed, and color returned to her cheeks. "Lily, I want to go home." Her mouth twisted out of shape. "I so want to go home." Then horror consumed Cecille's eyes and she screamed. She pointed frantically at something behind Lily.

"Look out! Drop it, Jeffers!" Sheriff Mac boomed, reaching for his gun again.

Confused, Lily whirled in the direction of Anson's body. It was still there, lifeless, harmless.

"Lily!" Cecille shoved Lily to one side and darted around Balthazar, using him as her shield again.

Spinning, Lily watched in terror as Ham Jeffers staggered toward her, his fist raised, the blade of his knife glinting dully. Blood and sweat dripped down his face. His eyes glowed with black rage, and he growled like an animal as he cocked his arm to send the knife into Lily's heart. She ducked, hoping to avoid the blade. She heard a whistle and a thud, but felt no pain herself. Her gaze moved to Ham's hand, still clutching the hunting knife. He wore an odd expression—surprise? His black eyes glazed over. A strange smile tugged at one corner of his mouth.

"Bitch," he whispered, then looked over his shoulder. "You Gypsy bastard! I'll kill you now,' he roared, starting to turn.

From nowhere another knife whistled through the air;

its blade thudded into Ham's chest. Lily screamed at the horror of violent death. The stench of fresh blood filled her nostrils. Ham's eyes widened with shock as he faced his murderer.

"Gypsy bastard," he repeated, and then he pitched forward, face down.

The crown of his head bumped Lily's knee, and she jerked backward, stifling a whimper of revulsion. The ivory-and-onyx hilt of a knife protruded from between Ham's shoulder blades. Lily's gaze tracked up to Griffon, standing a few yards away, his hand still in midair, having released the deadly weapon that had helped to fell Ham Jeffers. Griffon looked over her head and smiled.

"Nais tuke, little brother." He gave a nod of recognition.

Lily twisted around. Jasper and Eva stood in the gray shadows of a stand of saplings. Jasper stared at Ham. Eva patted his shoulder, stroked his hair.

"Jasper didn't want to kill Ham, Maw-Maw."

"I know, baby. You done the right thing."

Jasper's red-rimmed eyes tracked to Lily. His chest swelled with a sob. "Jasper's sorry. Jasper didn't want Ham to hurt Lily."

"Oh, Jasper." Lily pushed to her feet and held out her arms to him. "Come here, sweet Jasper."

Jasper ran awkwardly to her. She enfolded his chubby body and let him sob on her shoulder. Stroking his head, she looked past him to his mother. Eva smiled and nodded, understanding the special bond Lily had forged with her son.

"Ham lied to Jasper." Jasper raised his tear-stained face from Lily's damp shoulder. "Him said he wouldn't hurt you none. Him said following you around town was a game. But him lied. Him a bad boy."

Lily smoothed his baby-fine hair. "It's all right, Jasper. We're still friends. We'll always be friends."

"Jasper loves Lily."

"And Lily loves Jasper," she assured him, tipping his head forward to press a kiss to his wide forehead.

"Griffon, are you okay?" Balthazar asked, and Lily turned to examine Griffon for herself. He was doubled over, his hands propped on his knees, his breathing labored.

"Fine," he said between panting breaths. "I'm just winded." He placed one hand gingerly against his side. "Might have bruised something inside. Hurts like the blue blazes."

"We must get him to town and a doctor." Lily released Jasper and went to Griffon, who offered a shaky smile. She motioned to the man holding the reins of three horses. "Bring one of those horses over here and help him up into the saddle."

While Balthazar and Sheriff Mac assisted Griffon, Lily pulled Cecille over to Jasper. Both looked shy and shaken.

"Jasper, this is my cousin, Cecille. The one I was looking for, remember?"

Jasper nodded and ducked his head.

"Cecille, this is my new best friend, Jasper Jeffers."

"J-Jeffers?"

"Half brother to Ham and Anson." Lily nodded to Eva. "This is Butch's wife and Jasper's mother Eva. I'm right, aren't I? I feel as though we've already met. I'm Lily Meeker."

Eva reached out and plucked Jasper from Lily. "Nice to meetcha." She glanced around nervously. "Me and my boy gotta go. Butch and his other sons will have heard the shots and come running." Her dark eyes moved to take in the two bodies of her stepsons. "Once he spots these two he'll go on a rampage."

"They must go with us," Griffon called from astride one of the horses. He was pale and bathed in sweat. "Lily, don't leave them behind. Butch and the others will kill them."

"We have a wagon through those trees," Balthazar said, pointing to the north. "We'll all go back to town."

"But there is nothing for us there," Eva said, holding tightly to her son.

"There is nothing but death for you here," Griffon said, his voice breathy and fading. With effort, he raised a hand to touch a finger beneath his eye. "I have seen it. Don't leave your boy to those animals. I'll settle you somewhere. You have my promise, Eva."

Eva stiffened. "You have *seen* it? Men can't see such things."

Griffon cursed under his breath, his eyes telegraphing his irritation. "I know men aren't supposed to have—"

"*I* have seen it," Lily piped up. Griffon was fighting a losing battle against Gypsy prejudices, and they both knew it. He flashed her a weak smile of gratitude. "I have the third eye, the sixth sense," she elaborated for Eva. "And I have seen your future. If you stay here you'll die, and Jasper will suffer a horrible fate. You must come with us."

"Maw-Maw, Jasper's scared. Jasper wants to go with the purty gal."

Eva kissed Jasper's cheek. "Okay, baby. We'll do this for you." Her dark gaze moved to embrace Cecille. "We're sorry for all the trouble our family dumped on you."

Cecille cowered near Lily, holding her arm. "Let's go, Lily. I want to go now. Hurry before more of them come."

"Y'all go on," Sheriff Mac said. "Me and my deputy here will stay to tell Butch what happened."

"He'll kill you," Eva said.

"Not likely." Sheriff Mac checked his ammunition chamber, then holstered his revolver. "Even Butch knows better than to shoot a marshal. Besides, somebody's got to tell him what befell his boys here." He motioned to Balthazar. "Take them on. We'll catch up with y'all to-morrow."

"Come along then." Balthazar motioned for Cecille.

"You can ride my horse, Miss Cecille. It's not too far to the wagon. Can you other ladies make it on foot?"

"Yes, of course." Lily linked arms with Eva and Jasper, needing their support as well as their companionship. She shared a brief smile with Griffon and sent up a prayer that he'd fare well during the trip back to Van Buren. "We'll all be fine. We have each other."

Sheriff Mac, having returned that morning from Devil's Den, tipped back his chair, planted his peg leg, and let his other swing back and forth. He eyed the three women—the Meeker cousins and Orrie Dickens—and Griffon and Balthazar. Cecille looked more herself, spruced up in clothes borrowed from her cousin. Although faint bruises marred her face, neck, and arms, color had returned to her skin and her hair shone like gold struck by sunlight.

"I'll relate what you ladies have just sworn to me to the circuit judge next week. That way, you won't have to come back here. 'Course I'd appreciate it if you two gentlemen would hang around and give your stories in person to the judge. We need to get this cleared up and the death certificates verified, don't ya see."

Griffon nodded. "We're at your disposal, Sheriff Mac. I can't travel for a few days anyway." He pressed a hand to his side. "The doctor says I have internal bruises and prescribes rest. I do appreciate you allowing the ladies to return home."

"Sure. I know your family's anxious to see you safe and sound." He let fly a stream of tobacco juice that landed in the spittoon. "In fact, I'll send my new deputy along with you to make sure your journey's safe. I hear you've hired the stable boy to drive them to Fort Smith."

"That's right," Griffon said.

"He's a good boy." Sheriff Mac backhanded his mouth.

"Sheriff, did you see the other Jefferses?" Orrie asked.

"Yesterday, you mean? I did." He nodded, slowly. "Old Butch and his other boys were broke up after seein' the carnage, but they knew better than to start shootin' at me. I told them I could run them in for helping Anson and Ham hide these here gals. That made an impression. I agreed to let bygones be bygones, and they agreed the same. They don't want the law crawling over them hills. They like bein' left to their lonesome. Won't have no more trouble from them, I reckon."

"That's good to hear. I was afraid they might seek revenge." Orrie patted Cecille's shoulder. "I'd hate to look up and see one of them on a Fort Smith Street."

"Nothing to worry about on that score," Sheriff Mac assured them. "They did want to know what become of Eva and Jasper." He pinned Griffon with a sharp glare. "I'd like to know myself."

"I sent them ahead. They're going to catch a train bound for Boston." Griffon sat on the window ledge, careful not to jar his midsection, which had taken a beating during his scuffle with Ham. "My friend, Thurman Unger, will find work for Eva and a home for her and Jasper."

"That's good. I'm afraid they'd come to a sorry end if they stayed around here." Sheriff Mac spit again, making the spittoon *ding*. "Butch don't cotton to betrayal."

"We thank you for your help, Sheriff," Griffon said, herding the women toward the door.

"Just doing my job. Seems to me you gents did all the work. Neither one of y'all would be interested in wearing a star on your chest, would ya?"

Balthazar laughed heartily and shook the sheriff's hand. "I'd just as soon wear them in my eyes, good sir."

"We'll be at the hotel should you need us." Griffon took his turn shaking hands with Sheriff Mac. "When will the judge be in town?"

"First of next week. Monday. Tuesday at the latest. After that, y'all can be on your way."

"By then I'll be ready to travel," Griffon said.

Outside the sheriff's office, Balthazar shoved his derby hat onto his head, all business.

"Shall I go to the stables and see that the buggy is hitched and ready to take these ladies back home, Griffon?"

"Yes, and snag that stable boy while you're at it, Zar. I'll go with the ladies and settle their hotel bill."

"Don't be carrying any baggage," Balthazar cautioned. "Let the hotel clerk's boy do that. No need in injuring yourself further."

"Yes, sir." Griffon fit his own hat onto his head, a black western one with a short brim. "Ladies, shall we?"

"I never thought I'd say it, but I'll be grateful if I have no more adventures in my life," Orrie said, linking arms with Cecille and strolling ahead of Griffon and Lily.

"Same here. I'll be fond of the quiet life from here on," Cecille agreed.

"What about you, Lily?" Griffon asked, resting a hand on Lily's where it lay in the crook of his arm. "Finished with adventure?"

"This sort of adventure, yes. But life is an adventure, so it's unavoidable."

"Quite so," Griffon agreed. "My *yaya*—grandmother—used to say that life is a game where all the cards are wild. You just have to play the cards you're dealt as best you can."

Cecille stopped and turned back to him. "You-you're Gypsy?"

He nodded, the playfulness gone from his face. "I am. Don't be frightened of me. All Gypsies aren't devils, you know. Besides, Anson wasn't a Gypsy. His mother was Indian, I'm told."

"Griffon saved your life, Cecille," Lily reminded her firmly.

They walked on to the hotel. Lily sent Orrie and Cecille upstairs while she lingered in the hotel parlor with Griffon. She perched on the love seat, and he sat beside her. The eventuality of their farewells hung heavily between them.

Lily tried to dispel the gloom in her heart with a bright smile. It felt out of place, so she let it drift from her lips.

"Are you sure you'll be okay?" Lily asked. "Your injuries will mend and leave you fit again?" She wished she wasn't in a public place so that she could fling her arms around him and smother him with kisses. Searching his face, she couldn't tell if he felt the crush of farewell as much as she did. Her chest seemed to cave in on itself.

He held his hat and fingered the crease in the crown of it. Did she know how beautiful she looked with the sunlight spilling over her face in a golden splash? he wondered. If only they weren't in a public place, he would have held her fast and kissed her until she begged for mercy. Griffon cleared his throat, feeling awkward and tongue-tied. "I suppose you're looking forward to seeing Fort Smith again."

"Oh, yes." She fell back in the love seat. "It'll be a relief to get back to my normal life."

A peculiar remorse gripped his heart and twisted. He winced and angled away from her. She wanted her normal life again. Where did he fit into it? *Did* he fit into it? His own tumult of feelings inhibited his ability to know hers.

Was there a chance he might ask her to join him in Boston? she wondered, wishing he'd give her a glimmer of hope. She slid her gaze to him, and her love for him made her tremble.

"Yes, and I have my work to continue," he said, his voice sounding oddly strained.

"I'm sure Uncle Howard will contribute generously to your Society, Griffon. You were wonderful. I can't begin to thank you enough for everything. Without you, I know Cecille would have died at the hands of that madman."

Did she think he cared one jot about the bloody money he might make? He glared at her, saw her surprise at his anger, and stared at his hat again.

"What's wrong, Griffon? What did I say to make you angry?" She laid a hand on his sleeve.

"Nothing. It's nothing." He followed her slim arm up to her lovely face. God, how he wanted to kiss her, to crush her soft body to his. Didn't she know how she acted on him like wine? Didn't she care that he ached for the touch of her? "I'll be thinking of you, Lily. I'll be thinking of the fire lilies growing beside the river and of a barge on a lazy afternoon."

She sat forward, drawn by the memories. He dipped his head, and her mouth melted under his like a sugary confection. His hat slipped to the floor, and he gathered her into his arms, his heart leaping against his chest. His inner bruises ached, but his desire overpowered the pain. Lily parted her lips to admit Griffon's tongue. She sucked gently on it. Griffon pulled away first, the ache becoming a passion so keen he was afraid he might forget himself and try to take her right in the hotel parlor.

"You don't know your own power over me, Lily Meeker," he chided, collecting his hat and placing it strategically over the front of his trousers. "You should go upstairs now." He smiled crookedly. "Please."

She stood, feeling as if she'd been dismissed. A kiss, a smile. Was that all? No mention of tomorrow? Lily angled up her chin, forcing herself to show a measure of pride. She wouldn't beg, wouldn't grovel at his feet. It was his place to make the next move, to make mention of their next meeting, should there be one.

"Take care of yourself, Griffon. I shall always be in your debt."

"No." He shook his head firmly. He wanted to embrace her and hold her forever, but he knew that his only hope was to let her go. Back in Fort Smith, she'd decide her fate. "Anything I've given you was given freely. I expect nothing in return."

Tears filled her eyes. Griffon sensed her pain, but couldn't accurately translate it. He grasped her hand and pressed a kiss to her palm. Looking up into her cinnamon eyes, he wondered if she felt any of the pure love that filled his heart. Probing gently, he felt only her confusion, her uncertainty. She obviously didn't know her own mind or heart. She still didn't know if he was her destiny, her lover, a passing fancy, or a momentary indiscretion. Well, to hell with her! If she didn't want the love that bloomed in his heart, then he wouldn't force himself on her. He wouldn't make a bigger fool of himself over her.

"Good-bye, Lily. Godspeed." He released her and sat straight and stiff.

A single tear rolled down her cheek, and her throat flexed. "Good-bye, Grif-fon." A sob broke his name in half, then she pivoted and hurried for the stairs.

After she'd gone, he sat for a long time in the hotel parlor, his heart so heavy it felt like an anvil in his chest.

Chapter 25

❧

From his office window at the American Society of Psychic Research, Griffon had a view of one of Boston's garden spots. A number of people milled among the mounds of early marigolds and irises, but Griffon's eyes took in nothing of the spring day, save for the bunch of tiger lilies growing near a pond where goldfish flashed amid coins. He made his own wish and tossed a mental coin into the water while his mind traveled lovingly to a day on the banks of the Arkansas River.

"Griffon? Sorry if I'm intruding. I knocked, but . . ."

He turned to his mentor and motioned for him to enter the book-lined office. "Good morning, Thurman. I didn't hear you knock. Guess I was woolgathering."

Thurman Unger came to stand beside Griffon. A short man, Thurman was small-boned and had delicate features which were overpowered by thick eyeglasses. He glanced out the window to see what occupied Griffon's attention.

"Lovely day. May is my favorite month, as you well know. My green thumb is itching. Can't wait to get home to my garden. Eva and Jasper are in it now, I daresay. They said something about spading up that strip behind my greenhouse to plant a few rows of vegetables."

"Thurman, if Eva and Jasper are too much trouble, I can find them other employment."

"Trouble? No, no. Lord knows I needed a housekeeper, and Eva is bloody marvelous at that. As for Jasper, well, he's such a dear boy. We all get along famously."

"That's good. They needed a safe place."

"Don't we all." Thurman clasped his hands behind his back and eyed Griffon curiously. "Why didn't you go with Zar to Fort Smith? Your heart's been there all along. I should think you'd want to collect it."

Griffon smiled faintly. "Thurman, you're a romantic."

"Perhaps. That, however, is not an answer to my query." He rocked on the balls of his feet. "Well?"

"She's not ready to see me."

"Has she written to you? Is that how you know this? Or do you *know* in that special way you have?"

"I *know*. She has written once. The letter was warm, but not all that inviting. It wasn't a love letter."

"Have you written her a love letter?"

"No." He lowered his brows, seeing where Thurman was heading. "I didn't feel she wanted to read one."

"Ah. And you know everything. You know what's best."

"Thurman, it's not like that."

"Then enlighten me." Thurman left the window and sat in the padded chair behind Griffon's cluttered desk. "You're pining away for that girl. I've kept my mouth shut on the subject since you returned, but it's gone on too long now."

"I'm not pining," Griffon objected.

"I thought you'd end your sad vigil when Zar announced he was going to visit his Orrie. I was flabbergasted when you didn't go with him. So, out with it, Griffon. What is your plan of action? If you won't court any Bostonian females, then will you eventually become a priest, a monk, a crusty old bachelor like yours truly?"

Griffon propped his hands at his waist, drawing back his jacket to expose his silver vest. "Finished? That

was quite a speech, Professor Unger. I'll not be courting any other woman until I have this one out of my
system.''

"How will that be accomplished?''

"By giving her time to make up her mind about me.''

"Are you saying she doesn't love you?''

"I believe she loves me, but she has not yet come to
accept me.''

"Ah.'' Thurman tapped his chin with a narrow index
finger. "I was given to believe she was psychic, too.''

"She is.''

"Then what is there for her to accept? Is it your Gypsy
heritage she can't stomach?''

"That and my being psychic. It's hard to put into
words.''

"Try. I want to understand. It's obviously important to
you, and therefore, I want to share it.''

Griffon turned to face Thurman and leaned a shoulder
against the windowsill. "And I will never be able to ex-
press my gratitude for your concern, Thurman.''

Thurman waved aside the sentiment. "We understand
each other, Griffon. None of us can choose our family,
but we can our friends. We've chosen each other. So, tell
me what's in your heart.''

Griffon crossed his arms on his chest and sought the
right words. "It's complicated. I embody all that Lily
rejects and all that she fancies. She has fantasized about
Gypsies, having been told romantic stories about them
by Orrie Dickens. At the same time, she's been brought
up thinking herself above certain people—namely, Gypsies.''

"Not uncommon, Griffon. Gypsies have a bad name.''

Griffon nodded. "But I'd hoped that Lily would rise
above such blind prejudice.'' He shrugged, then removed
his jacket and hooked it on a peg near the door. "She
rejects her own psychic abilities, too.''

"Well, well. She certainly doesn't make it easy for a lovesick chap, does she?"

Rolling up his sleeves, Griffon glanced sharply at Thurman. "I don't much care for the adjectives you keep using. I'm not pining, nor am I lovesick." He curled his upper lip, getting a laugh from Thurman. "You make me sound like bloody Heathcliff roaming the moors."

Thurman laughed again—giggled, actually, like a boy. "That's who you make me think of! Heathcliff! Why couldn't I make that connection for myself? So, tell me, do you have a connection to Lily just as Heathcliff was connected to Cathy?"

Griffon started to tell Thurman to go straight to hell, but then the truth socked him. "Yes," he said, stunned by his own admission. "We do have that kind of unearthly connection. I feel her, Thurman. Here." He pressed a fist to the vicinity of his heart. "All the time I feel her." One side of Griffon's mouth quirked in a semblance of a smile. "I grew up steeling myself against those who looked upon me as unworthy, and I put on quite a suit of armor. I thought myself impenetrable until Lily came along with her fiery hair and gingersnap eyes. Her indecision cuts like a knife, Thurman. Like a knife." He bent a little as if a blade had pricked him.

"Heathcliff wouldn't have stood around and done nothing. If his lady couldn't make up her mind, he'd make it up for her. He'd have stolen her away and made her like it!" Thurman chuckled, enjoying that image.

Griffon looked sideways at him, embracing the suggestion. "Kidnap her, you mean?"

"Yes! Pluck a leaf off the Jeffers family tree." Thurman laughed again, then shook a finger at him. "You should have gone with Zar."

"No, she's leaving Fort Smith tomorrow."

"For where?"

"Cambridge, to visit her father and stepmother."

"So close? Will you stay here when your true love is a stone's throw away?"

Griffon shrugged. "Maybe she'll come to me."

"Damned pride. It won't warm your bed, Griffon." He started for the door, but stopped and turned back to Griffon. "Was your grandmother's prophecy right about you marrying outside the clan? Is Lily your destiny?"

Griffon smiled. "It's kismet, Thurman."

Thurman scowled. "Good God, you *are* besotted!" In the next moment, he joined Griffon in heart-lifting, boisterous laughter.

"Here he comes!" Orrie whirled from her lookout post at the front windows and hurried to the door. "How do I look?" she asked, spinning around to Lily and Cecille.

"Like a woman in love," Cecille said, giving Orrie a push. "Go give Balthazar a big kiss!"

"Stop that! For shame! A lady would never kiss a gentleman in a public street." Orrie's eyes danced with mischief. "I'll wait until I get him alone!" Then she bolted out the door, arms waving above her head.

Howard Meeker reined the team over to the curb, and the buggy jostled to a stop in front of the house. Lily drew a deep breath and smiled at Cecille.

"I think I'll go upstairs. I'm not in the mood for a sentimental scene."

"Chicken," Cecille scolded. "You just wish your Gypsy was in the buggy, too. If you had any sense, you would have written to him and invited him."

"Maybe I should have." Shrieks of laughter floated inside. Lily turned and started upstairs. Cecille followed her. "Go on and welcome Zar, Cecille. I'll be fine. I must pack a few more things, then I'll be down to add my welcome."

In her room, she moved like a sleepwalker, gathering

pieces of clothing, folding them, placing them in her travel bag. Cecille watched, silent, understanding.

"You'll visit Griffon while you're in Cambridge, won't you? You won't be an utter fool and not even try to give love a chance?"

"I'll see him, but I'm afraid. I'm afraid Orrie was right."

"About what? What did she say?"

"That'd he'd forget all about me. Out of sight, out of mind."

"Oh, fiddley-dee! Don't listen to such talk. Listen to your heart."

Lily smiled. "I'm glad your heart is still that of a romantic." She sat on the bed and leaned back on locked arms. "It's been a long time since we've sat on this bed and talked about boys."

Cecille smiled and made herself comfortable beside her cousin. "David Jefferson asked to escort me to the community chest dance."

"You didn't accept, did you?"

"Yes, I did."

"Cecille! After he lied to us! Why, if he'd told the truth, we might have found you weeks sooner."

"Yes, I know, but he lied to protect his mother."

"You mean he lied to protect his precious reputation."

"Speaking of which, I'm not in any condition to cast aspersions on those who still have reputations to protect."

Lily studied Cecille's downcast eyes and tightly drawn mouth. "Cecille? What kind of talk is this? Your reputation isn't ruined."

"Isn't it?" Cecille let go a laugh. "Look again, dear cousin. I've been familiar with a man, as they say. Everyone in town is gossiping about me and Anson. Don't you think I've heard the whispers?"

"Everyone knows he forced himself on you."

"After he kidnapped me, yes." Cecille lifted her lashes

to reveal midnight-blue eyes. "Before, however, I consented. Why do you look so shocked, Lily? Surely you'd guessed."

Lily tried to speak, managed a choked sound, then tried again. "I didn't want to think about that possibility."

"Do you hate me for giving in to him? I didn't know he was married at the time, Lily. All I knew was that he was a dashing, romantic Gypsy. Of course, as it turned out, he wasn't even that." She shrugged, regret lining her face. "I was duped all around."

"I don't hate you, Cecille. I could never hate you." Lily stared off into the middle distance, struggling with her own need to confess. "How could I hate you for doing exactly what I've done?"

"What you've . . . ?" Cecille caught Lily's gaze and held it. "You and Griffon?"

Lily nodded. "That's why it hurts so terribly that he's marked me off as history."

"You don't know that," Cecille protested. "You didn't invite him, remember? Perhaps he's just as disappointed that Zar was invited and he wasn't."

"It's more than that." Lily slid off the bed and went to the window. Outside, a breeze pushed the rope swing. Lily remembered the dream she'd shared with Griffon and how that realization had so unnerved her. "If I reach out to him, then I must be certain I'm ready to fully accept him and his life."

"And you're not certain yet?"

"I'm not sure. I'm going to see him face-to-face, Cecille. I'm going to tell him that I haven't forgotten him and that what I feel for him hasn't diminished."

"Good for you! Then this visit to your father's is only a smoke screen for my folks' benefit?"

"Oh, no. I'm going to stop by and see Father. I have something to tell him . . . something I must tell him." She bit her lip, worrying about how she'd confess her psychic abilities to her doubting father. It would probably sever their frail relationship, but she knew she had to step into the sunlight. She couldn't tolerate the shadows anymore. Not even for her father.

"What are you going to tell Uncle Edward, Lily?"

Lily, who'd been staring out the window, shifted her gaze to Cecille. She took a deep breath before she answered. "That I'm psychic." Lily waited for an expression of shock from Cecille that never came. "Did you hear me? I'm psychic. Griffon made me face it."

"I've known that since we were children."

"You—you have?"

Cecille nodded. "I always wondered why you never admitted it."

"Because it's frightening, that's why. But it helped me find you. Griffon says he can help me use it to my benefit and to the benefit of others. That's what he does."

"Why not let him?"

"Oh, Cecille, it's not so easy." Lily leaned a shoulder on the window frame. "I love him, but pledging my life to Griffon means facing society's scorn. Not only is he a known psychic, he's also a Gypsy. You know how people feel about them. Our children . . . they'd be ridiculed."

"But he makes you happy?"

Lily felt her heart sprout wings. "Oh, yes," she admitted, her voice soaring. "The happiest I've ever been in my life."

"Then why have you waited? Are you afraid of what your father will think?"

"Father and the rest of the family."

"Well, speaking for myself and my parents, we only want you to be happy. We all have the highest regard for Griffon. He certainly doesn't court our ridicule. As for your father, will you let him stand in the way of your happiness your whole life? Lily, you can't *force* someone to love you. They either do or they don't."

"Father loves me!" Lily balled her hands into fists. Her temper spent itself quickly, vanquished by Cecille's arched expression. "Well, he does in his own way."

"And his way stinks." Cecille slipped off the bed. The sunlight burnished her blond hair as she moved to stand at the window with Lily. "Someone loves you and wants you in Massachusetts, and I'm not talking about your father. Go to your Gypsy, Lily. My romantic heart says that he'll be thrilled to see you again."

"I'm scared."

"Oh, stop it. It's time you and I faced ourselves, dear cousin." Cecille grasped Lily's shoulders and marched her to stand before the bureau mirror. "Now, let's take a good, long look."

Lily examined the two young women and their serious expressions. Cecille was several inches shorter than Lily, fair-haired and blue-eyed, with a pert nose and pouty lips. She had changed minutely since her ordeal at Devil's Den. Melancholy shone in her eyes, and her laugh was less carefree.

"I see two young women who are ready to give their hearts to the right young men," Cecille said, placing an arm around Lily's waist and giving it a squeeze. "My father won't be entirely pleased with my choice, and neither will yours. But they are our choices to make, Lily. Oddly enough, I find that I love David. When I returned, he came to see me, bearing a huge bouquet of roses."

"Yes, that was nice of him," Lily allowed.

"That took nerve. He knew we were put out with him, but he came calling anyway because I *mean* something to him. I told him all about Anson, and David said he doesn't care. I'm still his lady. How can I not love a man like that?"

Lily turned and embraced Cecille. "I just want you to be happy. If David Jefferson loves you and you love him, then I think it's wonderful."

"He loves me for what I am. That's how Griffon loves you, too. No other love could be better than that." Cecille dimpled. "And, besides, one of us will realize our girlhood dream of marrying a dashing, romantic Gypsy!"

Chapter 26

Lily sat stiffly in the wing chair beside the empty fireplace in the parlor of her father's house in Cambridge. Books lined the walls. The furniture was dark, old, gleaming from frequent polishing. Her father worried with his pipe, tamping tobacco, striking one match after another. Her stepmother leaned over her needlepoint, tilting it toward the light of the oil lamp.

Thunder rattled the windows, and rain beat on the panes. Lily shifted, feeling out of place and wishing she were in Fort Smith or Boston. She felt like a stranger in this place. Her father and stepmother had been married for ten years, but Lily hardly knew Angela Armbruster Meeker. She didn't think her father loved Angela in a romantic way. Angela had been the theology department's secretary, and Edward Meeker had admired her organization and efficiency. He needed both in his life, and he needed a suitable woman to squire at college functions. Angela was perfect. Their marriage was durable, but not the stuff of dreams and romance. Edward had experienced that with his first wife, but didn't require it of his second. As for Angela, Lily suspected she was pleased with herself, having made a good match. Marriage to a Harvard professor gave her a respected place in the community.

Wind whistled down the chimney and cried around the corners of the brownstone.

"Blowing up out there," Edward said, puffing furiously on his pipe. "How's Cecille? Recovered, I trust."

"Yes. She's thinking of marrying David Jefferson."

"Ah, yes. He has law in his future, doesn't he?"

"Yes, he passed the exam."

"Good for him and good for Cecille! You should have put your hook in that one while you had the chance."

"He was your beau, wasn't he?" Angela asked.

"Not really. We went places together, but his heart always belonged to Cecille. Besides which, I was never taken with him."

"Shouldn't be so choosy," Edward said. "You'll end up an old maid. Who will take care of you then?"

"Actually, I have a husband picked out." She smiled when both Edward and Angela stared at her. "I'm going to see him when I leave here tomorrow. Part of my reason for visiting is to inform you of my decision and receive your blessing, Father."

Edward peered at her through the smoke. "Is that so?"

"Don't keep us in suspense," Angela said. "Who is he? Where does he live?"

"He lives in Boston. His name is Griffon Goforth." Lily smiled, hoping to add sparkle to the news she feared wouldn't be well received.

"Goforth. I'm not familiar with that family name." Angela looked at her husband. "Are you, Edward?"

Edward pulled his pipe from his mouth to fashion a formidable frown. "Goforth, you say? Isn't that the Gypsy psychic who found Cecille? The one Thurman Unger is so keen on?"

"One and the same." Lily nodded, still smiling. "He's a wonderful man, Father. We'll make a good marriage."

"He's already asked you for your hand in marriage?" Angela asked. "Did he ask Howard instead of Edward?"

"No, he hasn't as yet, but I know he will," Lily hastened to add.

"Oh, dear." Angela bit her lower lip fretfully, then

fetched a sigh. "Edward, calm down. No need to be bothered by this. The man hasn't even posed the question. Your daughter is counting her chickens before they've hatched."

"Thank heavens for that!" Her father aimed the pipe stem at Lily. "Use your head while there's still time, Lily. Don't act a fool over some mixed-blooded rake."

"Father, I never thought I'd hear you condemn someone for their heritage."

"I'm not."

"You just did."

"It's more than that. He's a man who lives by hook or crook. A psychic." He curled his lip. "I'd be more pleased if you said you were head over heels in love with the sword swallower in a traveling carnival." He shared a chuckle with Angela. "Really, Lily. Try to act as if you have an ounce of sense."

His condemnation sank like a knife into her heart. "I have more than an ounce, Father."

"Then use it. What kind of life could you hope to have with a man like that?"

"He used his psychic ability to locate Cecille," she reminded Edward.

"Pure chance. He located her as any other man would, by following tracks and clues. Nothing more."

"You're wrong."

"There's no proof he has any such skills, if such a thing as psychic talent exists."

"Father, you've spent your life studying theology. You've investigated and debated miracles and prophecies of the Bible, so how can you sit there and say such things can't happen?"

"Theology has nothing to do with chicanery." Edward gave a sniff of contempt.

"True psychics aren't magicians, Father."

"You sound like Unger." Edward chuckled. "That man is daft about such nonsense. Why, when he asked to get involved in finding Cecille, I agreed only to appease him. I never for a moment believed in his hocus-pocus.''

"I saw proof of Griffon's talent. He made a believer of me.''

"You can't believe in such rot. I won't allow it.''

"Allow?'' She repeated the word and laughed at the silliness of it. In her father's eyes, she identified the fear she'd so often seen when he looked at her. She sensed his hope that she would back down, as she'd always done, and bend to his will. Lily squared her shoulders and imagined her spine to be made of tempered steel. "Father, I, too, am psychic, as you well know.''

All color drained from her father's face. Angela dropped her needlepoint into her lap and gasped.

"Lily, dear, are you feeling ill? Have *you* recovered from that unfortunate business in the Ozarks? Edward, perhaps we should have Lily seen by a physician.''

"Yes, yes. She needs help,'' Edward agreed, bobbing his head. "She isn't well. Never has been . . . not since her mother . . . she's touched.''

"I am not!'' Lily protested hotly. "I'm perfectly sane. The day Mother died is when you turned against me.''

"Lily, your father has never turned—''

"You know nothing about it,'' Lily lashed out at Angela. "You weren't even there. I was. Father was. I sensed danger and I tried to keep Mother from going to that place to pick flowers. Remember, Father?''

"I remember . . .'' He cleared his throat and set his pipe aside. "I remember that you acted oddly that day. I assumed you saw those snakes and didn't warn your mother until it was too late. Now you're making up this preposterous tale about having special powers to ease your own guilt.''

Her hand flew to her throat in a protective gesture. "How can you say such things to me, Father? I was a child, a child who loved her parents. I wouldn't have wanted Mother harmed in any way.''

"I didn't suggest that. You just didn't warn her."

"I didn't see the snakes. I *felt* them. But I was a child and didn't understand the knowing . . . the sense of danger. I understand it now. Griffon has made me see that I can't hide from it. That's like hiding from myself, and I've been trying to do that for too long. I want you to accept the whole me, Father. I want to be loved for my entirety. Can you understand that? Uncle Howard and Aunt Nan are trying to grasp it. Cecille and Orrie already understand and have known—"

"Wait!" Edward held up his hands, stopping her. He squeezed his eyes shut for a few seconds as if warding off a seizure of pain. His muttonchops and beard seemed to bristle. "Are you telling me that you've spouted this gibberish to others?"

"I have." She craned her chin upward. "I believe my family should know this about me."

"What, that you're bordering on insanity?"

"Edward, please. Can't you see that she's unstable?" Angela delivered a smile of sympathy to Lily. "Dear, I think it would do you a world of good to see our private physician. I do believe you're vexed. What you went through in those hills has addled your thought processes."

"I know my own mind. I'm traveling to Boston tomorrow and I will marry Griffon Goforth."

"Will you now?" Edward said, making it a warning. "Without my permission or blessing?"

"If need be, yes."

"Listen here, Lily Jane Meeker. I am still your father and I won't hear of it! What sort of life will you have with this man, cut off from your family?"

"Uncle Howard and Aunt Nan like Griffon."

"Perhaps, but they won't be pleased to have him in the family. He's a Gypsy, a vagabond, a man of no means. If it weren't for Thurman Unger, Griffon Goforth would be in prison or begging on a street corner. I thought you wanted a bright future."

"I do."

"Then don't be rash. Stay here, and I'll look into a finishing school for you."

"I've been to finishing school," she reminded him. "And I finished—with honors, I might add."

"A college for women, then," Edward said with a long, drawn-out sigh. "But I won't give it another thought if you run off and throw yourself at the feet of that reformed beggar. He's poisoned your mind, but it's not too late to set things to right. However, I warn you, Lily, continue with this foolishness and I'll cut you off." He chopped the air briskly.

The gesture made her flinch, but she clung to the hope he'd cast like a fishing line. "You'd send me to college?"

"I said I'd look into it, didn't I?"

"Could I take whatever classes I wish?"

"Providing you're qualified, I suppose so." He glanced at his wife. "Secretary skills might serve you well. They certainly didn't hurt my Angela."

Lily's enthusiasm nose-dived. Being a secretary wasn't what she'd had in mind, and her father knew it. He refused to entertain the notion that, given the opportunity, she might just match his intelligence and learning.

His gaze sharpened as he reached for his pipe again. "I think you should go to bed now, Lily. The trip here has put a strain on you. That's painfully obvious."

"Your room is ready, Lily. You'll feel more yourself in the morning," Angela said, still wearing the smile of pity.

"Yes, we'll speak more of this tomorrow." Edward struck a match and went back to work on lighting his scrimshaw pipe.

Dismissed and dejected, Lily went to her room. She closed the door on the other inhabitants of the cold household and undressed by candlelight. The storm beat against the French doors, lashing the panes and rattling the hinges. Clad in her nightgown of golden silk, Lily slipped between the sheets on the feather bed. A vase of red roses on the bedside table held her interest for long moments, her eyes playing tricks by making lilies out of the roses, whisking her back to a barge on the river. Sighing, she blew out the flickering flames of candle and memory, throwing the room into semidarkness.

She wished Griffon was near to assuage her doubts. Should she divorce herself from her father and stepmother on only the romantic belief that Griffon would ask her to marry him? Perhaps her stepmother was right about counting her chickens before they hatched. Griffon had shown no intention of actually marrying her. He'd never even said he loved her, although she'd felt it and witnessed it in the passionate flames leaping in his blue eyes.

If only she knew for certain that his intentions were tied to forever. If only . . .

A clap of thunder jarred Lily awake, tearing her from a dream of the night Griffon Goforth had first blown into her life. Remnants of the dream clung even as she cast her wide-eyed gaze about the room. She'd left Griffon sitting on the sofa in the parlor of her aunt and uncle's home, smoke curling from his clothes, his knowing eyes probing her. That room and that time sailed away, and Lily recalled that she was in Cambridge in a bed meant for guests, not for family.

She smoothed back her tousled hair with both hands and rubbed the sleep from her eyes. Lightning threw white light into the room, silhouetting a shadowy figure standing on the balcony beyond the French doors. Lily smothered a scream behind her hand and told herself she was imagining things. But even as this thought sought to comfort her, a vision of Ham Jeffers flashed through her mind. She scrambled to her knees and snatched the vase of roses off the table. Holding the heavy vase aloft, she watched as the brass handle on the door jiggled, dipped, sprang back up as the catch gave way. The doors flew open, and the storm clattered into the bedroom, flinging draperies and bedclothes, dampening Lily's nightgown and hair, scattering leaves and debris. With the storm came a man in a black cloak that billowed around him like a thundercloud.

Lily sucked in a breath to scream her lungs out as the figure closed the French doors behind him. She aimed the glass vase and started to fling it at the man's hooded head when something familiar flirted with her senses. She paused, saw the twinkle of the man's eyes below the cloak's hood, and released a shriek of delight instead of a blood-curdling scream.

"Griffon!" She let the vase drop from her hand. It thudded to the mattress, slipped over the side and onto the floor, spilling roses and water. Lily propped her hands at her hips, her relief and joy overridden by anger. "You scared ten years off me! How dare you crash in here after what I've been through! When I saw you standing out there, I immediately thought Ham's evil ghost had followed me here."

"You have an active imagination, Lily Meeker." He swept back the hood to reveal a face that had become the dearest one in the world to her. His eyes were feverishly blue, and impatience threaded through his voice. "Get your things together," he said, making a sweeping gesture. "There is no time to waste."

"M-my things?" She laughed, then shivered as a damp breeze caressed her skin.

"Don't argue with me. It won't do any good. My mind is made up, whether yours is or not, and I'm not leaving here without you. Now, gather your things and toss them into your satchel. Hurry!"

"Where are we going?"

"I have a place in mind. People are waiting for us." He spotted her travel bag and hooked it with one hand. "This is still packed. Good. Just stuff the rest of your things into it, and we'll be off."

"To where? I can't just leave." She took the bag from

him, glancing around at her few scattered belongings in the room.

"Then I'll kidnap you, madam. Put some getup in your backside or I'll take you as you are and leave your belongings behind."

"Kidnap me?" She hooted. "I think not. The last time that happened was the worst in my life!"

He flattened a hand at the back of her head and hauled her into his arms. His eyes glinted mischievously. "You'll love it this time, I promise you." Then his mouth, moist and commanding, swept over hers. Her bones melted, and she hung in his arms, a willing, wilted captive.

She could tell by his first kiss that he meant only to buss her and then hustle her out the door and into the night, but the touch of her lips against his foiled his plan. His mouth lingered, brushing hers back and forth, then with a moan he opened his lips over hers and his tongue slipped into the sweet pool. Lily pressed her scantily clad breasts against his wet cloak, letting it soak the front of her nightdress and chill her nipples into tight buds. She snaked one arm beneath his cloak and around to his back. Oh, how big he felt . . . strong, wide, manly. That he hadn't said those three important words to her mattered little as her hands traced his shoulders, the indentations of his spine, the tautness of his hips.

His lips nibbled hers in love bites. His whiskers burned the delicate skin of her neck, her throat, the swell of her breasts above her nightgown. He rubbed the gown off her shoulders, pulling the fabric taut to outline her pillowy breasts and budding nipples. With a groan, he bent and tongued one throbbing peak. Passion shot through her like wildfire.

"Griffon, I've missed you," she whispered, flinging back her head and trying to keep her knees from buckling. "I wanted you to come to me. I wanted you to tell me you couldn't live another day without me."

"I'm here." He kissed her again, hard. His tongue

plunged into her mouth over and over again until her body was swaying and her knees began to melt.

Lily pulled at the cloak, trying to make him join her on the bed, but he resisted, tearing his mouth from hers and drawing deep breaths.

He shook his head. "Enough of this for now." He made her stand on her own two feet. "Do as I say, Lily. Pack that bag. We're leaving here."

Although drugged by his kisses, she knew he meant business, and she whirled about the room, grabbing her hairbrush, her cosmetics, her perfumed powder, her robe and slippers, and throwing them all into the bag. Stuffing them down with the heels of her hands, she then closed the bag. A draft crept over her bare feet, and she gasped.

"I can't go like this. I'll catch my death out there. I must dress."

"No. I like you just as you are."

He removed his cloak in a sweeping motion, and it settled heavily over her shoulders. Dressed all in black, he looked so much as he had that first night that Lily feared this was all a dream that would vanish with dawn's light. Griffon removed her carpet slippers from her travel bag and tossed them to her.

"Put those on," he ordered. "Then we're off. I have a horse outside."

"Griffon, I simply must leave Father a note." She pushed her feet into the warm slippers. "It'll only take a few seconds." She headed for the secretary, but Griffon's hand on her arm brought her up short. "We'll send him a wire tomorrow."

"But he'll worry about me and—"

"Let him worry. It'll do him good." He slipped an arm behind her knees and swept her up into his arms. "We're off."

Lily grabbed handfuls of his shirt, and within seconds he'd carried her outside into the biting rain. She recoiled from the helplessness of her situation.

"Griffon, enough is enough. Let me down. We'll wake my father and you can ask for my hand. We should do this in the proper, civilized manner." She clung to him as he began his descent down the side of the balcony, using the ivy-covered lattice attached to the house as a ladder. "This is romantic, but it's raining buckets out here! Let me down, Griffon. I'm no longer amused."

"I'm not trying to amuse you," he growled, swinging her about as if she were nothing but a sack of coal. "I'm kidnapping you, damn it all. And I'm in no mood to be civilized or proper. The time for that is past."

"I was on my way to you. I only stopped to tell my father of my plans." She sighed with relief when her slippered feet touched the sodden ground.

"I gathered as much. I also sensed your indecision. You still don't know your own heart. You think you can make your father accept you, especially if you turn your back on me. What other things will you sacrifice for your father's inconstant love, Lily?"

"Griffon, you don't understand. It's not that way. I've come to realize that—"

He didn't let her finish. Keeping hold of one of her hands, Griffon swung into the saddle of a prancing horse and pulled Lily up behind him. She adjusted the hood of the cloak and had a moment to wrap her arms about his waist before he shouted the nervous steed into a jolting gallop. Griffon pressed his heels to the horse's sides, and the stallion burst into a breakneck race with its own moon-shadow.

The clatter of hooves against the brick street was deafening in the dark night. The cloak flew out behind her, but Griffon's body heat kept her warm. She buried her wet face between his shoulder blades. Would they ride all the way to Boston? She hoped not, for her body was already complaining about the jarring ride. The rain abated as they reached the edge of town. Clouds overhead thinned to reveal a heaven full of stars. Peeking around Griffon's shoulder, she spotted her travel bag, its handle looped around the saddle horn. Her gaze traveled up to Griffon's handsome profile. Diamond drops sparkled in his dark hair, and rivulets marked his lean cheeks. His earring winked at her.

Happiness curled through her like a bright ribbon. Her sensitive fingertips detected in him elation and iron-ribbed determination. How could she ever have doubted that he and his life were meant for her? Maybe it was habit, she reasoned, this tendency to do whatever would please her father. Her father made her doubt her decisions and caused her to hide from herself. But Griffon wasn't blameless, she reminded herself, sitting forward until her lips brushed his ear.

"You could have just told me you loved me and saved us both a lot of trouble!" she shouted above the pounding of hooves and the rattle of harness.

His response was to veer the horse before a lighted inn. The stallion pranced to a stop, and Griffon helped Lily slip from the saddle before joining her. He tied the horse to the hitching post.

"We're stopping here for the night? I trust you will engage two rooms."

His slashing glance called her every kind of fool. He grasped her hand and pulled her along behind him inside the rustic inn. A rotund woman spun around behind the registration desk and clasped her hands under her chin in a seizure of joy.

"Finally!" She turned and shouted into the other room, "Leopold, they're here! Bring Albert and your Bible!" She motioned frantically. "This way, this way. We'll do it in the parlor."

"Do what?" Lily asked Griffon, stumbling along as they followed the woman. "Griffon, what's going on here?"

"I'm only doing what I should have done back in Van

Buren, instead of letting you sashay out of my life and leave me heartbroken.''

Lily found herself in a cheery parlor. The chubby woman stood beside the fireplace, an expectant expression bathing her face. Lily pulled the cloak tighter around her, knowing her nightdress was soaked and transparent by now. The hood had kept most of her hair dry, but tendrils curled near her face, dripping wet.

"How's this?" the woman asked.

"Perfect, Hanna." Griffon stood before the woman, tall and erect. "Hanna Morgenstern, this is Lily Meeker."

"So happy to make your acquaintance," Hanna said in heavily accented English. She shook Lily's cold, damp hand. "This is all so exciting! Oh, there you two are," she said, addressing the two others who had entered the parlor. "Miss Meeker, this is my husband, Leopold, and my son Albert."

Lily nodded at them, too confused to speak. White-bearded Leopold took his place beside Hanna, and the couple's gangly, cowlicked son stood off to one side. Leopold opened a Bible and smiled.

"Dearly beloved, we are gathered here—"

"Hold on just a minute," Lily interrupted, shifting her gaze frantically from Leopold to Griffon. "Is this man marrying us?"

"Yes, if you'll cease the interruptions." Griffon ran a hand over his wet hair and flung raindrops off the tips of his fingers. His black shirt clung to his wide chest and muscled arms. His black boots were splashed with mud. "Go ahead, Leopold."

"No!" Lily snatched her hand from Griffon's. "You haven't even asked me to marry you! How dare you! This is the most important decision in a woman's life. I won't take it lightly. The kidnapping was one thing, but this . . . this is . . . is . . .''

"Lily, I love you."

Her breath whistled down her throat. "Wh-what?''

His eyes bored into hers, and she felt his love coat her like honey, seep into her pores like sunlight, nestle in her heart like it belonged. Lily drew in a trembling breath, and everything in her world was set right.

"I love you, too," she whispered.

Marry me, Lily. Make me the happiest man on God's green earth by marrying this arrogant Gypsy goat.

The words rang clearly in her mind, and she smiled. *Fortunately for you, I love arrogant Gypsy goats.*

He laughed, and she knew he'd heard her mind and heart speaking to him.

Lily faced the whiskered man holding the Bible. Her eyes filled with happy tears. "Marry us, please."

The ceremony was as simple as truth and as sacred as a blessing. Lily and Griffon vowed their love and devotion, and Griffon slipped a gold band on Lily's finger. Their first kiss as husband and wife sent longing surging through Lily's veins, and she offered no resistance when Griffon carried her upstairs to their room in the inn.

"I like being a robber's bride," she confessed as he set her on her feet and closed the door behind them. The room was small but inviting. Red-orange lilies sat in a crystal vase on the bedside table, filling the air with their delicate perfume. "You've thought of everything, I see."

"So you aren't angry that I snatched you from your father's home?"

"No, but Father will be livid." She giggled and shrugged out of the heavy cloak.

"I know you told him about me."

Lily nodded. "He disapproved."

"What about the rest of your family? Did you tell them you love me?"

"Yes. I even told Uncle Howard and Aunt Nan about my trances. I explained to them that I sensed things. They were very understanding, although they don't grasp the concept of 'tactile memory,' as you called it." She frowned and edged away from his intense, blue gaze.

"You're still a little frightened of yourself."

Lily wandered to the vase of lilies. She stroked a velvety petal. "There is so much about me that I don't understand."

"You will, Lily. I'll be your lantern. I'll shine my light on all the darkness and chase away the shadows."

She turned at his approach and laid her hand along the side of his face, loving him so much it hurt. Her wedding band glinted richly. "I believe you, Griffon. Oh, it's taken so long for me to completely trust you, but I do. With all my heart and soul, I do." A loose piece of puzzle floated into her mind. "Griffon, how did you know I was at my father's home?"

He smiled in answer.

"Oh, you!" She swatted his shoulder playfully, and he took her into his arms. "I'll never be able to keep secrets from you."

"You can turn the tables and read my thoughts." He nuzzled the side of her neck. "You sensed me coming for you in the caverns, remember?"

Lily nodded, recalling how she'd thought he'd called out to her. Only in retrospect had she realized that his speaking had been only in her mind, and that she'd called out to him in the same fashion. His arms tightened possessively.

"What about your father? Can you be happy with me if he never accepts our marriage?"

"I have spent most of my life trying to be someone my father could love, but no more." She shook her head, and her hair spread over her shoulders, some strands still damp from their midnight ride. "When I realized it was you standing on that balcony tonight, I knew such a supreme happiness. Everything was suddenly as clear and bright as the north star. You love me. The real, unadorned, unvarnished, ungilded Lily. Oh, what a relief to be loved by you. What a relief and what a blessing." She lifted her face to his swooping mouth.

His kisses knew no restraint. His stroking hands peeled the nightgown off her shoulders, down her hips and legs. She stood naked to his lambent gaze. Trembling with desire, Lily unbuttoned his damp shirt and discarded it. She stroked his wide shoulders and silky-haired chest. Her mouth loved him, leaving moist circles on his skin until he, too, trembled. He was so many things to her: her mentor, her lover, her champion, her *husband*.

"I'm your bride, Griffon," she whispered between fire-laced kisses. "Now make me your wife."

Griffon plucked the bouquet of lilies from the vase and scattered the flowers over the sheet-draped feather bed. He lifted her and settled her in the center of the bed of flowers, releasing their sweet fragrance. After removing the rest of his clothes, he joined her. His muscled, rangy body was a welcome blanket upon hers.

"Oh, how I love you," she whispered, framing his face in her hands and bringing his lips to hers. She drank in his passion until she was overflowing. "I never dreamed I could love so deeply, so completely. I want your baby inside of me, Griffon."

He raised his head to reveal his surprise, then he laughed and landed a stunning kiss on her smiling lips. "Your skills are improving. You just read my mind."

Griffon's hands and mouth were as soft as petals on Lily's skin. Soon, her budding desire blossomed into passion.

And she burned. Oh, how she burned.

Avon Romances—
the best in exceptional authors and unforgettable novels!

America Loves Lindsey!

The Timeless Romances
of #1 Bestselling Author
Johanna Lindsey

ONCE A PRINCESS   75625-0/$5.95 US/$6.95 Can
From a far off land, a bold and brazen prince came to
America to claim his promised bride. But the spirited vixen
spurned his affections while inflaming his royal blood with
passion's fire.

GENTLE ROGUE   75302-2/$4.95 US/$5.95 Can
On the high seas, the irrepressible rake Captain James Malory
is bested by a high-spirited beauty whose love of freedom and
adventure rivaled his own.

WARRIOR'S WOMAN   75301-4/$4.95 US/$5.95 Can
In the year 2139, Tedra De Arr, a fearless beautiful Amazon
unwittingly flies into the arms of the one man she can never
hope to vanquish: the bronzed barbarian Challen Ly-San-Ter.

SAVAGE THUNDER   75300-6/$4.95 US/$5.95 Can
Feisty, flame-haired aristocrat Jocelyn Fleming's world
collides with that of Colt Thunder, an impossibly handsome
rebel of the American West. Together they ignite an unstoppable firestorm of frontier passion.

DEFY NOT THE HEART 75299-9/$4.50 US/$5.50 Can
To save herself from the marriage being forced upon her,
Reina offered Ranulf, her kidnapper, a bargain: *Become my
husband yourself. In exchange for your protection I will make
you a great lord.*

America Loves Lindsey!

The Timeless Romances
of #1 Bestselling Author

ONCE A PRINCESS
75625-0/$5.95 US/$6.95 Can

From a far off land, a bold and brazen prince came to America to claim his promised bride. But the spirited vixen spurned his affections while inflaming his royal blood with passion's fire.

Be Sure to Read These Other
Timeless Lindsey Romances

SILVER ANGEL	75294-8/$4.95 US/$5.95 Can
TENDER REBEL	75086-4/$4.95 US/$5.95 Can
SECRET FIRE	75087-2/$4.95 US/$5.95 Can
HEARTS AFLAME	89982-5/$4.95 US/$5.95 Can
A HEART SO WILD	75084-8/$4.95 US/$5.95 Can
WHEN LOVE AWAITS	89739-3/$4.95 US/$5.95 Can
LOVE ONLY ONCE	89953-1/$4.95 US/$5.95 Can
TENDER IS THE STORM	89693-1/$4.50 US/$5.50 Can
BRAVE THE WILD WIND	89284-7/$4.95 US/$5.95 Can
A GENTLE FEUDING	87155-6/$4.95 US/$5.95 Can
HEART OF THUNDER	85118-0/$4.95 US/$5.95 Can
SO SPEAKS THE HEART	81471-4/$4.95 US/$5.95 Can
GLORIOUS ANGEL	84947-X/$4.95 US/$5.95 Can
PARADISE WILD	77651-0/$4.95 US/$5.95 Can
FIRES OF WINTER	75747-8/$4.95 US/$5.95 Can
A PIRATE'S LOVE	40048-0/$4.95 US/$5.95 Can
CAPTIVE BRIDE	01697-4/$4.95 US/$5.95 Can
TENDER IS THE STORM	89693-1/$4.95 US/$5.95 Can

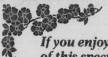

If you enjoyed this book, take advantage of this special offer. Subscribe now and . . .

GET A *FREE* HISTORICAL ROMANCE

── NO OBLIGATION(a $3.95 value) ──

Each month the editors of True Value will select the four best historical romance novels from America's leading publishers. Preview them in your home Free for 10 days. And we'll send you a FREE book as our introductory gift. No obligation. If for any reason you decide not to keep them, just return them and owe nothing. But if you like them you'll pay *just* $3.50 each and save at least $.45 each off the cover price. (Your savings are a minimum of $1.80 a month.) There is no shipping and handling or other hidden charges. There are no minimum number of books to buy and you may cancel at any time.

send in the coupon below